Like a
POWER PLAY

ELLE SPRINKLE

AUTHOR NOTE

There is a cruel expectation set by the world for people with disabilities, particularly in that their worth lies in overcoming them. We see it everywhere. In videos of people scaling mountains in wheelchairs or painting masterpieces with their teeth. And while those stories are beautiful, and full of persistence, and strength, they are not the only stories.

At least, they are not mine.

For all the narratives that insist we remain exactly who we are after becoming disabled, or limited in some way, I've found the truth to be far more complicated. If you have too, you're not alone.

It's the entire reason Darcy Cole exists: To prove that you are worthy, even if you cannot "persist". Even if you had to give up a piece of yourself. Even if you are simply too tired to try.

Disabilities look different one everyone. One person's experience is extremely unlikely to be exactly the same as another's. That's why the version of Rheumatoid Arthritis portrayed in Like a Power Play is the version I know (though some researched tweaks have been made for the sake of plot). The symptoms, the timeline, and the emotional impact may not reflect everyone's experience, but I hope that if you live with RA, some part of this feels familiar. Or at the very least, understood.

At its core, *Like a Power Play* is about two kinds of grief. Darcy must learn to let go of something she loves. Peyton must learn how to hold on to something she was born with, and make peace with the privilege that came with it. What they don't realize is that the pain of the two are relatively the same. Whether you're learning how to keep something or learning how to let it go, there will always be pieces that stay with you, and pieces that don't.

Basically, Peyton's standing on the edge of Vormir, tossing her nepotism-less dream off the cliff to get her soul stone (a pro career she's worked her ass off for, even if her last name played a role in landing it). And Darcy's alongside her, chucking *her* old career into the abyss, so she can wake up in a weird-colored puddle clutching *her* soul stone (a version of hockey she can reclaim).

Yeah, I know, I'm watching too many Marvel movies.

Anyway, as for the hockey itself, I did my absolute best to research and honor the landscape of women's hockey. That being said, there are some things you can really only articulate when you have been a part of the experience, and I, admittedly, have not. So if you're a female hockey player, first of all, hi. You're cool as fuck. Secondly, I sincerely apologize for any inconsistencies, whether intentional for the sake of comprehendible fiction, or accidental due to the endless void of all-nighter research. You can pick which inconsistencies were purposeful and which ones make me look like an absolute buffoon. You've earned it.

I want to acknowledge something I know readers will notice, especially compared to my debut, *Puppy Love*. While I loved the abundance of open-door scenes in that book, this story is completely its own. It has its own journey, characters, and pacing. That said, there are still some open-door scenes here, just fewer in number. Some are going to hate me for that, and listen, I love sapphic sex as much as the next person. But the fact of the matter is:

Not everyone fucks 87 times before falling in love.

Heartbreaking, I know.

Rest assured, my smut lovers, as there will be plenty more overly-descriptive spicy books to come.

Lastly, and most importantly, I want to acknowledge the content warnings in this book. If any of the triggers listed below are known to affect your mental health, please consider choosing a different book or checking in with a trusted friend or therapist before reading. Your well-being matters far more than finishing this story, and there will always be more books waiting for you when you're ready.

This book contains brief mentions of the following: alcohol consumption, weed consumption, animal abandonment, medication, needles, surgery, and blood.

This book contains heavy mentions of the following: chronic pain, chronic illness, flare-ups, and social and romantic expulsion of a disabled individual (not done by the current love interest).

Before I go, I have to give a shoutout to Angela Ackerman and Becca Puglisi. You're probably thinking, "But Elle, isn't that what the acknowledgments section is for?"

I refuse to be governed.

Their collection of writer's thesauruses was absolutely crucial in shaping this book, and in improving my writing overall. This is not a paid promo, I promise. I just honestly don't know how I managed to write *Puppy Love* without the fundamental understandings that I now have.

From the person who finally (kinda, sorta) figured out how to write a halfway decent author's note,

xoxo,

Elle

For those whose bodies forced them to let go of what they loved.

It's still yours. You just might have to learn how to hold it in a different way.

TEAM ROSTER

Paula Cole—Head Coach

Darcy Cole—Student Assistant Coach

Peyton Clarke—Center & Team Captain

Caydence Wright—Center

Harlowe Ayers—Goaltender

Zayda Kamal—Alternate Goaltender

Bailey Cunningham—Defensewoman

Lena Brady—Left Winger

Indigo Browne—Right Winger

Faith Simmons—Right Winger

ONE

Darcy

PEOPLE WITH ANXIETY DISORDERS make the best coffee, and the Grizzly Grind at Greenrock University is proof. It's never too sweet, never too milky, and I'm convinced all the panicking baristas are psychology majors, because their bizarre concoctions of syrups and rich espresso have a way of grounding me rather than revving me up.

Usually.

I used to think coffee turned me into a sledgehammer—blunt, swinging down with reckless force, intent on destruction. Turns out, that's just who I am, and coffee simply gives me the energy to act on it.

And right now, I have more than enough reason to swing.

You know that saying, "Hell hath no fury like a woman scorned"? I'd like to propose an upgrade:

Hell hath no fury like a *daughter* scorned.

And the yellow slip clenched in my gloved hands might as well be stamped with "SCORNED" in bold red letters.

I slam it onto the table in front of my mother, sliding it across to her like a bomb ready to detonate.

"What the hell is this?" I ask, folding my arms, a poor attempt at guarding myself from what I already know is coming. My mother frowns, adjusting her glasses, flipping the paper over to read it. Only, by the time I've made it from the dean's office to this coffee shop, I've read it at least twenty-two times. So, instead of letting her answer, I do what any scorned daughter would do: I cut her off.

"You asked the board to make me a *student assistant coach?*"

Paula Cole has a few titles under her belt: NCAA Coaching Champion, Patty Kazmaier Award Winner, and #1 Mom (courtesy of the mug I gave her in second grade). But her most impressive, most defining achievement of all?

Gold in Meddling.

She leans back in her chair, arms folded over her chest like the sheer presence of her sitting there will somehow convince me this is all for my own good. It's what makes her the best coach on the west side. She's got a talent for making everything she says feel like an undeniable truth. It makes it nearly impossible not to believe her, not to play along. But I'm not playing her damn game. Though, let's be real: when I do, has she *ever* let me win?

She picks up the slip of paper and holds it between us like a peace offering, but even if I wanted to take that olive branch, I'm sure it would give me splinters. Thin, sharp irritants, digging into my skin, festering until I ripped them out with blood-stained tweezers. Worse, I think, would be if they stayed there too long. If my skin grew over them and every time I pressed down, I'd wince, knowing in this exact moment I could've said no but didn't.

She looks at me like she's waiting for me to say more, and I stop myself from rolling my eyes. Because no matter how infuriating my mom can be, I will never love anyone more. Which is the only reason I'm still sitting here, having this conversation, because honestly I'd rather drag my nails down a chalkboard until my teeth shatter than ever, *ever*, step foot near an ice rink again.

"Darcy, you're getting course credit for it," she presses gently. It's how she coaches, too. She's firm but sweet, wearing you down without you even realizing it, until you're completely drained but somehow still smiling. "This could be good for you. Just getting close to the ice again, seeing how it feels. You don't have to get *in* the rink, sweetheart. Just... *observe.* Give a few pointers."

I scoff, and despite the intoxicating cocktail of honey and lavender syrup wafting in the air, nothing is quite sweet enough to counter the bitterness seizing my throat. It rises quickly, fast enough to spill out over my tongue.

"Observing is *worse*."

My eyes fall to the paper again. As much as I hate looking at it, I can't meet my mother's eyes without seeing my own reflected back at me, and somehow, disappointing myself feels worse than letting *her* down. My stomach churns, either from the conversation or the fact that I forgot to ask for almond milk instead of whole milk, and can already feel the clock ticking down to my inevitable sprint to the bathroom.

Unfortunately, my eyes are not the only thing I inherited from my mom. Neither is my lactose intolerance. Because if I'm a sledgehammer, then she's a bulldozer in a fleece-lined windbreaker, and if I don't put up a fight, she'll flatten me.

"You know," she says, her tone deceptively light. "You can't stay away from the ice forever. It's part of you. You're strong, you'll figure it out."

Strong.

I fucking hate that word. I hate that people think a diagnosis comes with armor. That strength is some automatic response to pain.

I'm not strong. I'm just tired.

Bone-deep exhausted from pretending that the emptiness inside of me doesn't expand with each reminder. The sound of skates on ice, the photos my old teammates post like nothing's changed, my jersey hanging in the closet, sleeves peeking out as if it's still waiting for me to slip it on.

The worst part of losing the thing that made you is that the only thing you can do is marinate in its absence.

"Mom, I don't want to be near the ice," I snap, harder than I mean to, as I stand up. I'm pacing now, right in the middle of the coffee shop, knees pulsing and scraping, clutching this steaming cup of laxative that would be burning me if I weren't wearing gloves. I should put it down, stop drinking it altogether, but my fingers refuse to let go. If I don't have something sweet to tame the sour taste in my mouth, I'm going to say something to my mom I can't take back. "You think it's *just* about being near the ice? It's about losing something I thought I'd have forever. Losing my entire *life*. And now you want me to just—*go back*?

Just like that?"

My heart pounds in my chest, each beat another threat to shatter my ribcage, to amplify that sharp, stinging sensation that spreads over my body, twisting, tightening, ready to snap.

I lock eyes with her, and for a moment, the stern coach face melts away. She doesn't look like a D1 trainer anymore. She's just... *Mom*. And that loosens the aching lump in my throat, just a little bit.

She sets the paper down, eyes softening as she leans forward. "I know you're hurting, sweetie. I do. And I'm not asking you to play again. I'm asking you to *be around it*. You're right. It was a huge part of your life. And that's why I think it's important for you to not cut it out."

Fighting back the sudden pinch behind my eyes, the sting of saltiness willing to spill over, I swallow. She's right. She's *always* right, but it doesn't make it any easier to hear. I can't just pretend everything is fine. I can't just step into her world and act like nothing's wrong when the last time I was there, my body betrayed me. Pulled the rug right out from under me so fast, I didn't even realize I'd hit the ground until the pain shot through.

Tears prick my eyes, and my lip starts to quiver as I fall back into my seat.

"Mom, I... I can't," I choke, taking in a shuddered breath. "I'm not ready."

She studies me like she always does. The thing about my mom is, she gets me. And sometimes, that's the problem. When the pain is this raw, this consuming, the last thing you want is for someone to understand, because if they did, it would mean they've felt it too. It's easier to suffer alone than it is to know that the misery is shared by someone you care about. You don't want to be understood. You just want to survive it.

She reaches past the coffee cup in front of me, her fingers grazing mine, and I can't stop myself from melting into it.

"You don't have to go out there, Darcy. I won't make you. But I don't want you to avoid it forever. You're more resilient than you give yourself credit for." She pauses, a teasing smile tugging at the corners of her lips. And I hate that, for a second, the warmth of her hand through my gloves makes me feel like maybe she's right. Maybe I *can* do this.

"I mean, you are my daughter. And what didn't I raise?"

Despite myself, a smile creeps across my face. I roll my eyes and whisper, my voice barely above the hum of the coffee shop, "A wuss."

Our eyes lock, and laughs spill out the two of us in unison, as if we've rehearsed it. For a second, a fleeting second, I feel normal. Just a daughter, with her mom, laughing in a coffee shop. Warmth pools in my chest, and I brush a long lock of red hair from my eyes. But then she lets go of my hand, squeezing it once before she retreats back to her side of the table. And just like that, the warmth fades, and I'm back to the mess of it all. That nauseating, throbbing sensation floods my body, and I have no other choice but to drown in it.

It's not that easy. Nothing ever is.

"I'll think about it," I mutter, but it feels like I've already conceded. Like I have no other choice. She leans back in her chair, not fully satisfied but accepting my answer. She's got her way, as always.

"Okay," she replies quietly, reaching for the paper and folding it neatly. She slides it back across the table, tilted endearingly. We might share the same eyes, the same dietary sensitivities, even the same force. But my mother has one thing I don't: charm. "That's all I ask."

I nod, sharpness still piercing my chest, but I finally manage to force out a weak "Okay."

Mom stands up, the soft rustle of her coat harmonizing with the buzz of the café as she moves. She doesn't say anything else, just gives me a smile I know too well. The one that says she's not giving up, but she's giving me space.

"I love you, Darce," she says, her voice soft and warm, and my heart tightens.

"I love you too," I reply, and before I know it, she's pulling me into a quick hug. It's tight, familiar. My second favorite feeling in the world.

Well, now my first.

She pulls away with a soft kiss on my temple, then heads for the door, leaving me alone with that damn antagonistic yellow piece of paper.

I slump back into my seat with an exaggerated sigh, glancing around the café to assess just how much of a scene I've caused. Most of the students are oblivious, headphones in, heads bobbing to whatever soundtrack they've got going while they study for majors that were probably their first choice. There's a guy in the corner staring at me with a raised eyebrow—I think he's in my biomechanics class? *Great.* Whatever. I don't give a fuck.

I settle deeper into the chair, reaching into my pocket for my phone. But before I can even grab it, I hear a voice I know all too well.

"Well, that was... *dramatic,*" Cleo says, sliding into my mom's chair like she's been waiting for it to open up. She's gripping her phone in one hand, and a Redbull in the other. I glance up, startled, and she shrugs. "What? You didn't think I'd come spy?"

I groan, dropping my head into my hands. "Oh my god, Cleo. You're like a stage mom."

She grins, unphased. "You can't send a text that says, *'My mom signed me up to be a coach. I'm meeting her at GG. SOS. Or just kill me'* and think I'm not gonna show up to witness the chaos."

I roll my eyes, letting out a quiet laugh. I've only known Cleo for two months, but in that time, she's pretty much deemed herself my best friend. I'm not sure why. She's got a dozen friends already, and it's not like I really bring much to the table.

Honestly, I don't think she can help it. She's practically an over-caffeinated hamster, running circles on a wheel that never stops. I'm more of a tortoise, at least these days. It's not like I mind it, though. She's nice enough and always invites me to her social shindigs, though I never show up. The only downside to living with Cleo is her cat.

Socks is a menace, through and through. His sole mission in life? To make mine as miserable as possible. The first night I moved in, I woke up gasping for air.

Turns out, he decided to make a bed out of my face.

Cleo insists it's a sign that he "likes me," but I swear, the little fucker is plotting my demise.

"Well? Rotten Tomatoes rating?" I ask, taking a regretful sip of my latte.

Cleo taps her finger against her lips like she's considering something monumental. "Eighty-eight. Honestly, I almost called in a fake tragedy when you started pacing. It looked like you were about to have a full-on meltdown." She raises a pierced eyebrow, putting on her best serious face. "But then it seemed like you had it under control. Kinda anticlimactic, if you ask me."

I roll my eyes again but can't stop another laugh from escaping. "Oh, well, I'll try to throw in a plot twist next time."

Cleo smirks. "Maybe a surprise musical number? ABBA really sells it for me." She snorts, eyes falling onto the slip on the table, and without another thought, she scoops it up. "I'm *joking*, Darce. You think I'm just here for the drama? I'm here for *you*."

I flash her an earnest look, one that *lyingly* says I don't believe her. The annoying part is, I do believe Cleo. And that messes with me. She cares so much about me, when she doesn't even know me. Not to say I don't care about her. I do. Honestly, besides my mom, she's the closest thing I have to a friend. But that's what's terrifying.

I don't do friends anymore.

I watch her carefully, jaw tight, breath lodged in my chest as she unfolds the paper. Her gray eyes scan the words, dark bushy brows knitting together.

"So, basically, you have to coach for ten hours a week and go to all the games?" She looks up at me, searching for confirmation.

I nod.

"And in return, you get paid *and* a course credit?"

I nod again. The ball of tension in my jaw tightens into something heavier, which sinks into my chest.

While Cleo's head tilts, the rest of her posture seems to straighten. "Sounds like a good deal to me," she answers, shrugging.

"But—" I start, but she cuts me off with a telling look.

"Darcy," she says softly, her gaze flicking to my cup. Her eyes narrow as she spots the "whole milk" label and shakes her head. Without skipping a beat, she swaps her drink with mine. I don't have it in me to explain that energy drinks trigger my flare-ups, so I just stay quiet.

"I get it. Well, no, I don't. But your mom does. And she's right." She meets my eyes, her tone more serious now. "You're never gonna be happy if you try to completely cut hockey out of your life. It's like spiders. You can spray the house till the cows come home, but they'll always find a way back in."

A frown creeps across my face as I process her analogy. "Do we have spiders? Should I call pest control?"

She ignores me, taking a sip from what *was* my latte, and wrinkling her nose. "*Ugh.* Peanut butter? Seriously?" She swaps the drinks back with a grimace. Thankfully. "Honestly, babe, staring at the dusty box of trophies in the living room is making me kind of depressed. Put them on the mantle. Donate them. I don't care. Just *do something*, you know?"

I open my mouth to argue, but the words die on my tongue because Cleo's right. Hockey isn't just a sport to me. It's who I was. Who I still am, even.

No matter how much it hurts to admit.

My stomach twists as I look back at the paper. I want to grab it, tear it into a million pieces, and toss it into Sock's litter box. But where would that leave me?

Still here, studying for a degree I never thought I'd need, working some job I'll never love, and, eventually dying alone, buried under a pile of cats who suffocated me.

Cleo leans across the table, a dimple popping into the side of her lip. "Look, you don't have to throw yourself out there, alright? Just show up once. See how it feels." She gives me a small, encouraging smile.

I know what I *should* do. I know what's right, even though every bone in my body feels like it's about to crumble at the thought of it. Even though my muscles flare in protest, already waging a war against the idea, aching at the sight of that damn slip. Maybe I could do what she's asking: show up for practice, see how it feels.

Get a glimpse at who I used to be.

"I'm not a coach," I mumble, and Cleo deadpans.

"Darcy, you moved in two months ago and negotiated like, twenty house rules. You'd command the sky if it listened."

Something between a sigh and a chuckle slips out of me, and I shake my head. If I'm being completely honest, it's not *only* the coaching that's stressing me out. It's what comes after. I'm bracing for that moment when I have to walk back onto the ice. Because one way or another, I know that moment is coming.

"I'll think about it," I repeat.

TWO

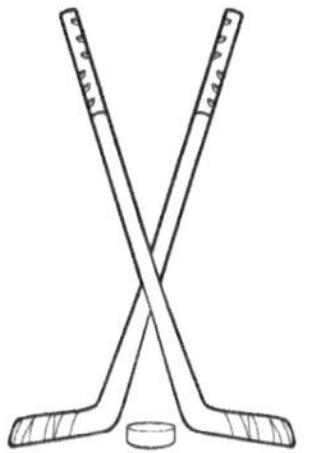

Peyton

MY ANKLES FEEL LIKE someone took their anger out on them with a Razor scooter. It's a deep ache that thrums in sync with my heartbeat, tempting me to stop, but I don't. Stopping is for the weak, and weakness is not a luxury I can afford. Every part of me is begging, *pleading* for a break, but I know better. I know the Sabertooths wouldn't stop. My dad wouldn't either.

So I won't.

Despite the burn in my thighs, and the pulse pounding in my eardrums, I push off the ice and start again. The mid-October air bites at my skin as my blades carve through the rink, weaving around the cones, my stick following the puck like a shadow.

I'd be at the indoor rink if my access card worked at this hour, but it only grants entry during regular school hours, which unfortunately doesn't begin at four a.m. The outdoor rink's not so bad, though. Some think it's haunted, because it's eerie when the sun is still down, but I like it. The overhead lights illuminate nothing but the ice below my feet, making the rest of the university, the rest of the world even, disappear. But even here, alone on the ice, I can't escape my biggest competitor.

Myself.

I crank up the volume, some self-help audiobook blasting in my ears, but no matter how loud I turn it up, my internal voice demands to be heard.

Sharper turn there, she says. So I start again, pushing harder, faster, as though out-skating the voice might make her disappear.

It never works.

The crunch beneath my skates is familiar, each dent and crevice in the ice a testament to my repetitive failures from this morning's solo practice. As I near the goal, my gaze locks onto the right corner of the net—the one the Glacier Giants' starting goalie always seems to neglect. My grip tightens around my stick, fingers sinking into the worn tape as I draw it back to shoot.

But just before my blade makes contact, a loud thud echoes through the rink, and something in my peripheral vision barrels toward me, driven by a vendetta.

I spin around, eyes locked on the rogue puck as it glides across the ice, coming to a stop right in front of my feet.

Shit. Is it possessed? Why is Bailey always right?

My grip on my stick tightens, just in case I have to start fending off spirits, but as my eyes scan the arena, the only thing they land on is a woman, who, despite her pale, freckled cheeks, seems to be very much alive.

She stands by the short gate into the rink, auburn hair loosely tucked in the fold of her black turtleneck sweater. Her lips part, as if calling something to me, but the monotonous voice in my ears swallows it up. Normally, I don't halt a practice for anything. Not the weather, not the fact that the rink is *technically* closed, and certainly not for a girl who was rude enough to toss a puck at me. But when her lips quirk into a smile, one like I've never seen, my stomach flips.

I should know this smile. I should know this *woman.*

Despite its mathematical improbability, I know just about everyone at Greenrock University. Or—know *of.* The ice skaters, the theater stoners, the psychology baristas, the biology gamers, the frat boys who hoard the gym but never seem to actually lift. I make it a point to be at almost every event, to weave into every corner of campus life, so that everyone has at least one person cheering them on.

But this woman? She hasn't fallen into any of those categories. I would've seen her at a game, or a concert, or some random late-night study session. If she'd been there, I'd remember.

I'd remember that smile. Those red strands of hair catching the light as she peeks out from the shadowed stadium seats. I'd remember those freckles, and when she tilts her head, I'm certain I'd have remembered that too.

So, despite my better judgment, I find myself gliding in her direction.

The low hum of the rink floods my ears as I pull the earbuds free, strands of sweat-soaked hair sticking to my cheeks. I drift toward her, the sound of my skates cutting through the ice now oddly magnified.

"What did you say?" I call out, feeling a slight tug at my lips.

The pretty woman leans forward, as if what she's about to say is so substantial, it demands the force of her entire body to hurl it across the ice. "I said," she starts, her voice clear as that bright grin deepens. "You're *overcompensating*."

What the fuck?

Paralyzed by disbelief, my body still drifts toward her, helpless against the slick of the ice. Did she just say what I think she said?

It's not the words that unsettle me. It's the way she says them. The ease in her tone, as if we've shared a thousand inside jokes, as if we've exchanged the same worn-out band tee, as if she's earned the right to say them with that kind of blunt familiarity.

I have no idea who this woman is and yet, she's speaking to me like we're already monumental parts of each other's histories. Normally, I wouldn't mind it, but like I said, I don't usually stop practice for anything. And now I've halted it just to be insulted.

I don't even know how to respond.

So I don't.

Instead, I cross my arms, my posture stiffening. "You threw a *puck* at me?"

She shrugs, and a strand of strawberry hair slips free from the confines of her turtleneck. It tumbles down her chest, a fiery cascade that could set the world alight in its path. "I was trying to get your attention. You know, I don't think you're supposed to be here this early. Most people aren't even awake at this hour."

My gaze flicks to the coffee cup gripped in her hands, streams of steam lifting off the rim. "You're awake," I say pointedly, prying my anchored skates free as I glide toward the boards.

I don't know why I do it. Maybe I just want to look this woman in the eye while I tell her to mind her own damn business.

But that was a mistake. Because when I finally look her in the eyes, words evaporate. The dictionary? A distant memory. Those dark green gems stare back at me, layers of fern and ivy tangled within, a deceptively serene secret garden that could have convinced me this woman is a breath of fresh air, if she hadn't already proved herself to be pollution personified.

Her lips lift again, soft freckled skin stretching, nose glowing red under the fluorescent lights. "I'm an early riser."

"What, so you set a three a.m. alarm to come throw hockey pucks at people?"

"I didn't throw it *at* you," she challenges, thin brows furrowing. A crease forms between them, and the freckle in the center of her forehead vanishes in it. "I threw it *near* you."

Clicking my tongue against the roof of my mouth, I pause just long enough to stop myself from snapping at her, but not quite long enough to lose the attitude entirely. "Right. You know, you could have banged on the fiberglass or something."

She doesn't seem to mind my petulance. In fact, she glides right over it. "How often do you practice like this?"

I pause again, suddenly struck by the thought that maybe I don't recognize her because, *maybe*, she's not a student at all. My heart rams against my ribcage as my gaze draws down her body, searching for any sign that she's got some kind of authority. Maybe a badge, or a notebook with the words *Peyton Clarke violating rink rules again* scrawled across the page. But all I find are baggy sweatpants, black gloves, and eyes like emeralds, glowing in the light as if she's studying me right back.

"Couple times a week," I admit, gaze narrowing skeptically. She nods, the golden ring dangling from her septum glistening. A beat of silence follows, tempting me to put my earbuds back in and get to work, but then she continues, her tone assured.

"You're going to burn yourself out."

My jaw tenses, fingers drumming against my stick.

Who the fuck does this girl think she is?

"Sorry, do you even play?"

The question comes out condescending, but honestly, I couldn't care less. Okay, maybe I feel a *little* bad. But I've been skating since I could walk. Who is this girl to give me unsolicited advice? She's probably never even touched a puck, until she gathered the audacity to throw one at me.

Her posture snaps rigid and she pushes away from the boards, arms crossing defensively. "When I was younger."

Despite my (admittedly) feeble efforts, a dry laugh tumbles from my mouth. "Yeah, okay. No offense," I add, fully aware it's about to be offensive. "But I don't need advice from someone who couldn't even stick with it."

The woman's expression shifts, that freckle on her forehead disappearing again, lips tightening into a line as if they were stitched shut. Her eyes sharpen, pinning mine with a challenge. "Look, I'm just saying, I've seen it before. Overworking yourself like this is only going to do more harm than good."

"And *I'm* just saying, that if you were willing to give it up, you clearly haven't been in my shoes." I take in a steadying breath, a futile attempt at soothing the irritation swelling in my chest. I'm supposed to help Zayda, our alternate goalie, study for a test at five, and I'm running out of time. But this woman isn't on my time, so instead of backing off, she doubles down.

"I get it, you love it." She hitches a shoulder, letting a sigh slip out. "And there's power in that. But you're going to lose that power if you overdo it."

A scoff slips from me, disbelieving and bitter. I'm supposed to, what? Take this *random* woman's advice after she hurled something at me and then followed it with an insult like it was prophetic hockey wisdom?

I should brush it off, turn the other cheek, be the bigger person. My brother can be like this—blunt, nosy, a little too comfortable in his own opinions—I'm used to it. But this? The way she talks to me, like she's my goddamn coach?

Yeah... I don't think so.

"Lose my power?" My brow twitches for a second, and then I burst into antagonizing laughter. My side aches as I clutch it, allowing the cackle to bubble in my chest. I'm being an asshole. I hate being an asshole. But sometimes, I'm not as mature as the "C" on my jersey suggests. I shake my head, managing to force out a weak "I didn't catch your name."

"Darcy," she replies plainly. "You?"

"Peyton." I wet my lips, the cold air rushing over my tongue. "You know, *Darcy,* I've been playing since I was four, so, if I was going to 'lose my power,' as you put it, I think it would've happened by now."

She frowns, briefly, before adjusting her pronounced expression to something daring.

"Let's see it then," she declares, leaning against the gate. My head tilts, searching her face for something that tells me she's joking. But I don't find it. Instead, those taunting green eyes stare me down, and I know I don't *need* to prove myself to this woman, but I want to anyway. Not because she's clearly out of her element, or because I want to put her in her place, but because it's all I've ever done.

Try to prove myself.

"Fine."

I push off the ice, skating back toward the puck she tossed at me with careless precision. Her gaze never leaves me, and in spite of the nervous flutter in my stomach, I flash a sly grin, praying for the rush of victory. I draw my stick back and slam it down, sending the puck hurtling across the rink in a perfect snapshot.

It soars through the air like a prowling bird, descending with speed into the net. An explosive twang echoes across the rink, but then, to my surprise, another one follows. My eyes widen, brows shooting to my hairline as my brain tries to process what just happened. And then I realize—

The puck split in *half.*

One half stays caught in the net, while the other flies through the spaces between, slamming against the boards, punctuating the silence. I glide over, scooping a piece into my palm, then thrusting it into the air, spinning around to face her as I call out, "How's that for power?" with a cocky grin.

Darcy rolls her eyes, but I can tell she's impressed by the cute tug at the corners of her lips. I skate over to her, waving the piece of rubber tauntingly in her face.

"Impressive," she admits, eyes sparkling beneath the rink lights. "But broken pucks won't save you from tendinitis."

"Speaking from personal experience?" I pry.

She doesn't budge. "Nope."

My tongue traces the inside of my cheek, fighting back a grin. "Are you a business major by chance?"

"*No*," she answers, tone flicking hesitantly at the end. "Why?"

I shrug, no longer fighting the smile threatening to show, and letting the full arrogance of it conquer my face. "I just figured, since you like to give unsolicited advice and all—"

A laugh breaks out of her, partially amused, but mostly annoyed. Her shoulders square, but just as her mouth opens to respond, a loud *clank* echoes through the rink—the sound of the surrounding gate unlocking.

"*Shit!*" I whisper, my heart leaping into my throat as a beam of light suddenly slices through the darkness of the stadium seats. I throw a frantic glance at Darcy, waving my hand for her to follow as I shove open the rink gate, and step off the ice. "*Go!*"

Her eyes widen, and without hesitation, she spins around, darting for the fence. Instinctively, I grab her arm, my glove slipping against the soft fabric of her tight black turtleneck. "What are you doing?" I hiss under my breath. "You're going to get caught. Get over here!"

I jerk my head toward the back row of seats in the stands. We're hidden there just in time, crouching down as the footsteps of campus security shuffle along the concrete, the flashlight beam sweeping lazily across the stadium like a spotlight on a show I want no part of. A show that could get my spot as Captain ripped away from me. My breath is shallow, the air too thick, and the close proximity of Darcy only makes it harder to concentrate on my quiet breaths. I shift, slipping off my gloves, pinning them between my armpit. A sharp jab hits my ribs, and I snap my head over to her.

"Ouch," I mutter.

She's not having it, though, whispering through clenched teeth, "You're on my *foot.*"

My eyes dart down. My skates are planted directly on her worn, white, slip-on sneakers. I shuffle to the side, heart racing, hands sweating so intensely that the broken puck gripped in my palm nearly slips. I set it on the ground beside me.

"Sorry," I murmur, and then, silence. The only sound in the stadium is the footsteps of the security guard, and with every beat of my heart against my chest, they seem to get louder. Closer. Darcy's gloved fingers wring around one another nervously, the almost silent scrape of fabric complimenting her breath against the back of my neck, quick and uneven. I glance at her briefly, before locking my gaze back onto the light as I whisper softly, *"Chill out.* We're fine."

Her eyes flick up, brows pressed tightly together as she practically mouths her response. "I *just* transferred. I'm gonna get suspended after a month?" She pauses. "My mom is going to kill me."

So that's why I don't know her.

I roll my eyes. "You're not gonna get suspended. *Relax.* I've done this for three years and never been caught."

She waits an almost comedic beat before responding. "I caught you."

"Well, most people aren't wandering around at four in the morning," I snap back, head tilted slightly in her direction, just enough to get a whiff of her perfume. It's fruity and soft, dark cherry and almond floating in the little space between us, drawing me closer.

"I was *exploring!*" she hisses, too loudly, and the flashlight beam swings toward us. My pulse quickens. I hold my breath. We don't move, not even a twitch, hearts thundering as the footsteps grow louder, sweeping across the paved ground.

Our gazes are locked, holding one another hostage, or maybe that's just how it feels, because Darcy's eyes are a shade of green that I swear holds my breath, and everything else inside me, still. I can feel her heartbeat, pulsing from her shoulder through mine, probably communicating in morse code that she hates me. But just as the footsteps start to rise toward us, a loud, staticky voice breaks the moment.

"We've got some drunk students breaking into the Grizzly Grind, need units over here. Rogers, you got it?"

A high-pitched beep pierces the air, followed by a low murmur, responding from nearby. We don't move. Don't breathe. "I'm on it."

The flashlight swirls one more time, and then, finally, the guard's footsteps descend. We both exhale slowly, listening as he approaches the gate. "That was close," I mutter, still crouched, but Darcy shoots me a death stare.

"I told you we aren't supposed to be here," she whispers sharply, pointed jaw clenched. "But since you want to be fucking Icarus—"

"*Icarus*?" I blink, the warmth of her breath brushing against my cheek. I wipe it on my damp shoulder. "What is that, a disease?"

"Wha—*no!*" Her hands toss up, brows weaving together. "It's the boy who flew too close to the sun. And *you*—"

I can't help the grin tugging at my lips as I swipe at the lock of her red hair that's tickling my nose. "Look up, Kim Possible. Do you see the sun?"

Darcy's expression turns mocking as she peeks cautiously over the top of the stands, eyes shooting wide when she spots the security guard still lingering near the gate.

"Oh my god. Shut. Up. *Shut up!*" she hisses, grabbing my arm and yanking me toward the ground, even though I hadn't even stood up yet.

My lips quiver in amusement, but I manage to bite it back, the pulse of her heart returning against my arm, almost in sync with my own. And only when the clink of the gate finally sounds do we straighten up, slowly.

"Oh my god, you lived!" I mock, pressing my hand to my chest in exaggerated surprise. Darcy's eyes narrow.

"You really are insufferable," she says, the corners of her lips defying her, and I can't help but smile wider.

"Why thank you."

"That's not a compliment."

My posture straightens fully now, and I brush a hand through my sweaty hair, heading for the aisle. "Anything is a compliment if you want it to be."

Her gaze drops to her shoulder, the spot where hers had brushed against mine. There's a dark patch on the fabric, almost wet.

"Is that... your *sweat*?" she asks, wrinkling her nose.

I glance down at the dampness on her shirt and then back to myself. "Appears so."

I begin stepping backwards down the steps, internally cringing for the sake of my skates' blades, grinning as Darcy grimaces in disgust.

"Consider yourself lucky!" I call out, stepping onto the ground level. "That's the sweat of the team captain."

THREE

Darcy

S OME PEOPLE WAKE TO a birdsong. Soft, floaty melodies, drifting through open windows, lashes fluttering with the breeze. Others wake to honking taxis and yelling neighbors, a grease-stained stench assaulting their noses.

Me?

I get the divine privilege of waking to a harmony. A blaring alarm that pairs perfectly with the scream of my joints—the familiar gnawing ache that greets me every morning. It starts in my fingers, stiff and swollen, and spreads up my arms like a wildfire. By the time I sit up, every articulation in my body is begging for a generous layer of WD-40.

I slap my phone to silence it, reaching for the rattling plastic container on my nightstand. The sorted pills fall into my palm, then I swallow them down, letting the cool water numb my throat, and pray that today will be the day relief slowly begins to seep in.

Since I was diagnosed with Early-Onset Rheumatoid Arthritis back in March, I've tried three different medications to help soothe the pain. The first gave me morning sickness so intense, it would give pregnant women nightmares. The second seemed to work adversely, making every nerve in my body burn like the depths of hell, and every muscle so sore I could hardly lift a fork to my mouth. So now, I'm two weeks into a new one, and so far, nothing has happened.

No side effects.

No improvements.

Socks leaps onto the nightstand with a dramatic thud, his claws clacking against the wood as he barrels toward me. I hardly have time to react before he sends my pill organizer and my water bottle tipping to the floor. The little menace quickly follows, tumbling off the table, only to leap back up, this time aiming for my head. I throw my arm up, blocking his landing, forcing him to fall into my lap instead.

"For fuck's sake," I mutter, plopping him onto the covers, but he's relentless, crawling his way back into my lap with innocent eyes. Eventually, I give up, setting him onto the ground and standing up with a grunt of effort, my knees creaking like ancient hinges. I shuffle to the living room, ignoring the ache climbing my back, and find Cleo sitting at the kitchen counter, the morning sun catching the rows of gems on the shells of her olive-toned ears, casting soft colors on the bartop.

"You know," I say, plopping into the barstool beside her. "I'm going to have to lock that damn cat out of my room if he keeps treating me like a helicopter pad."

Cleo lifts a brow but doesn't take her eyes off her phone as she gives me the same response she always does. "You should be honored."

I grunt, reaching for a banana. As I peel it open, my eyes land back onto her, her gaze still unmoving, but an intriguing smile tugs at her lips. I peek at her screen, only to be greeted with a reflection of the sunrise.

Finally, I ask, tone light, but taunting, "Who ya talking to, Cleo?"

Cleo's smile drops instantly, and she shoots me a horrified gaze. Without breaking eye contact, she turns off her phone before sliding it into her lap wordlessly.

"Okay, not suspicious at all." I take a bite of the banana.

Her lips stay pressed together, like she's holding something in, probably because she is. And although Cleo and I still have a lot to learn about one another, I know enough to say that any minute now, she's going to break. She stares at me, jaw tense, lips rolled, until finally—

"I bumped into Will Carter yesterday—like *literally walked into*—it doesn't matter. Anyway, we were outside the linguistics building and we started talking about English majors and now, like, we're meeting up for coffee to talk about it and I—I don't even know what to do!"

She slaps a hand over her mouth like the words will absorb back into it, but my jaw has already fallen to the counter. I pick it back up, just to point out the obvious issue I'm sure she's well aware of.

"But Will's—"

"A football player, I know."

I stare at her, blinking in disbelief, as if doing it slower might make all of this click. "And—"

"And I *loathe* football players. I know."

I take another bite of fruit, the potassium doing nothing to dull the shock that's making my head spin.

Cleo's been flirting with new majors since before I moved in. Not that she's ever formally changed anything. It's more like a revolving door that she steps into, only to get off at the exact same spot every time. Biomed to psychology, then art history, then pre-law, then back to biomed. Each week, it's a new dream, a new identity, but none of them seem to stick.

"Oh my god," she groans, tipping her head into her hands. "What am I gonna do?"

I shrug, failing to bite back the provoking smile tugging at my lips. "Will, apparently."

Cleo shoots me a daggered look, while I chuckle at my own joke. Normally, it's the other way around, and I have to admit, it's fun being on this side of it for once.

"You know it's not like that."

A laugh tumbles out of me as I take another bite. "Do I?"

Her head bobs along for a second, lips pressed in a flat line. But when her gaze darts back to me, there's something pressing in it.

"So, are you going to tell me who *you* snuck out to see this morning? Or are we going to pretend that didn't happen?"

I pause mid-chew, a pit forming in my stomach.

"How did you—"

"Socks."

My gaze flashes to the chunky tuxedo cat, tail swishing as he eyes my banana like it's the last meal on earth. I pull it back, narrowing my eyes. It wouldn't be the first time the little thief snatched food right out of my hands.

"Snitch," I mutter, and Cleo rolls her eyes.

"Oh, that, and the fact that you were brewing coffee at three a.m. You know, I have a very sensitive nose."

A sheepish smile creeps across my face, and I hop off the stool to toss the banana peel in the trash. "Sorry."

Cleo just stares at me, like she's waiting for more. She does that a lot. Sometimes it works. Most of the time, it doesn't. Don't get me wrong, I really like living with Cleo. But just because we're roommates doesn't mean we need to be best friends.

Cleo doesn't agree, of course.

I hate that I like that about her.

"Well?" she presses again, brows raised, dimpled chin jutting out. "Who is it?"

A nervous chuckle slips from the back of my throat. "Nobody."

She blinks.

I blink back.

She blinks again. *"Liar."*

"I'm not ly—"

"So you just left at three a.m. to, what? *Walk around?*"

"Yes," I reply defensively, but Cleo isn't buying it. She spins around on her stool, eyes locking with mine. "You know I've given up on all that relationship shit."

"So, you were alone the whole time?"

Fuck.

"AHA!" She jabs a thick finger in my direction, a mischievous grin spreading

across her face. "You *were* with someone!"

"No! Well, *yes,* but—"

"Who?"

"It's not like that, Cleo. I didn't—" And she's not listening. *Great.*

"Darcy." She levels me with a look, and an irritated huff escapes me.

I know she's not going to let up. Not until I give her a crumb of information to chew on. So, I throw myself onto the couch with all the drama I can muster, pulling a blanket over my burning, freezing toes.

"I didn't sneak out to see anyone," I repeat firmly. She leans forward, perched on the edge of her seat. "But I did bump into the women's hockey captain."

"Peyton Clarke?" Cleo's brows shoot up, silver irises swirling as her plush lips fall open.

I nod, exhaling a steadying breath. It feels like I'm standing in a confessional booth, about to admit my sins. *Forgive me, Father, for I have snuck into the Greenrock University ice rink and argued with a cocky bitch who has a stellar wolf-cut and smells of sweat and lavender.*

Before I can finish, Cleo jumps in again. "Oh, you do *not* want to go there." She laughs warningly.

My brows drop. *"What?* No! I wasn't—"

She doesn't let up. "I mean, she's totally nice and everything, but she's *way* too focused on hockey for anything serious. Especially with her dad."

The cackle that bursts out of me is almost malicious. I shake my head, running my hand through my un-brushed hair, fingers catching on the tangles.

I learned a lot about Peyton Clarke in the short time we spent together. First, she's arrogant as hell. Second, she smells way too good for someone who had just been practicing. And third?

"She is *not* nice."

Cleo purses her lips. "Hate to break it to you, Darce," she says, hopping off her stool. "But you're not exactly the best judge of that."

I frown, even though I know she's right. I haven't been the warmest person since I came back to Seattle, but that's kind of the point. People don't get close to cold people. Well, except for Cleo, apparently.

"Wait... her *dad*?" I ask, the words finally clicking in my brain. Cleo's head tilts in surprise.

"You don't know?" she asks.

I pull the blanket tighter around me, scrunching my toes in an attempt to boost my circulation. "Know what?"

A sly grin breaks across her face. "Does the name *Harrison Clarke* ring a bell?"

My throat goes dry. *Harrison Clarke?* No way. No *fucking* way.

"You're not saying—"

"That *retired* pro right-winger from the Boston Boas is Peyton's dad?" She feigns a wince, the corner of her mouth twitching. "Yeah."

I swallow hard, my head dropping into my hands in frustration. Of *course*. Because the universe clearly has it out for me, I had to go full teacher-mode on the daughter of a *pro*. Makes sense why she acted like she knew everything.

Pinching the bridge of my nose, I exhale slowly, my body sinking further into the couch.

"Nepo-baby or not," I mutter, "she's still a nightmare."

Cleo rolls her eyes, flopping down beside me. "And you're the only one in history who believes that."

I cross my arms defensively. "She called me Kim Possible."

A puzzled smile tugs at Cleo's lips. "That sounds like a compliment to me."

"In this context, it's really not."

"Well, what *is* the context?"

I pause, recounting the scene. Okay... maybe I wasn't the *nicest*. "Well, I threw a puck on the ice while she was practicing. Which, in hindsight, wasn't exactly polite, but—"

"*Darcy!*"

My hands toss up in defense. "Okay, okay, but I was trying to get her attention!"

Cleo scratches her temple thoughtfully, then pats her lap so Socks will jump up and curl into a ball like the two-faced monster he is. Her tone comes out with extreme condescension, but the sweetness of her smile makes it impossible to be offended. "Did you try, I don't know, *talking* to her?"

"Yes," I declare, pointing a finger for emphasis. "But I could hear her earbuds blasting from the boards. Seriously, she's going to lose her hearing."

Cleo ponders this, eyes tracing the ceiling before landing back on me. "Okay, yeah, that's fair actually."

"Thank you."

"But why'd you want to interrupt her practice in the first place?"

Ah, the million-dollar question. I wasn't supposed to be at the rink. I only meant to take a quick peek. Sometimes, if I lie down too long, my joints start to flare, so I decided to stretch my legs, loop around campus, check out the facilities.

But then I saw her. And it was too hard to look away.

Watching her glide across the rink, the puck slicing through the air, it wasn't like watching a clunky hockey practice.

It was like watching a ballet.

Every move was choreographed. Practiced. Even the way her hair swept behind her in fluid waves, how her fierce amber eyes fixed on the goal, seemed rehearsed, perfectly in sync with the rest of her.

But the longer I watched, the more something about it nagged at me.

She wasn't taking breaks.

After every shot, every sharp turn around the cones, she'd just restart, ignoring the pain I know too well. It took everything in me not to throw myself onto the ice. To shout at her to stop. That's why I tossed the puck. I had to say something. Because if she keeps pushing herself like that, she's going to be sidelined for the rest of her life.

I tried to tell her. But she didn't seem to care.

"I was trying to help her," I admit, glancing down at the time on my phone. Class is coming up, but right now, my body feels like it's been run over by a Zamboni. Walking helps, I know, but sometimes, just moving feels like I'm dragging myself through wet concrete. After my lap this morning, I'm not sure how much energy I have left to push through it all today. "She's going to hurt herself."

There's a long pause, like Cleo's letting the words settle, making sure I'm really finished. Then a soft smile pulls at her lips, and she smooths her hand over Socks' back, a low purr rumbling from the cat's chest.

"Well," she says casually, hitching a shoulder. "It's a good thing you're about to be her coach, then."

My stomach pretzels into an iron knot, sinking lower and lower until I'm sure it disappears. How the hell am I supposed to help Peyton when her ego's too inflated to hear anything I say?

"Yeah," I mumble. "Good thing."

O F ALL THE PROFESSORS at Greenrock University, Professor Palit is by far my favorite. My mom, in her usual meddling fashion, arranged accommodations with the Services for Students with Disabilities board the moment we decided I should move back to Seattle. Most professors only agreed because they had no choice.

Professor Palit? He agreed because he's a genuinely good person.

I emailed him this morning, asking if it was okay to attend today's neuroplasticity lecture via video call since I felt like I'd been hit by a truck, and he responded with:

"If you make a snack, turn your camera off. I'll get jealous."

He also assigned us a case study analysis—you win some you lose some—but as I read in depth about John Doe's traumatic brain injury, I try really hard to enjoy it. Which sounds fucked up, now that I think about it, but no sports physical therapist should hate neuroscience. Not if they want to be good at their job.

And seeing as it's pretty much my only option at this point, I *have* to master it.

I pull out my journal, flipping through today's lecture notes when my phone buzzes on the table. I glance over, Mom's photo lighting up the screen. Ecstatic at the excuse to procrastinate homework, toss my laptop to the side, and press the cold device to my ear.

"Hey, Mom. What's up?"

"Hi sweetheart!" My mom coos through the phone like I'm still six. And I don't mind it one bit. "I was just calling to see how your day was." *Three... two... one...* "And to check in about your first day of coaching tomorrow."

Mom was *thrilled* when I said yes to the student assistant coach position, not like I had a choice. I knew this call was coming. I'd already mentally prepared my response last night, while I was sprawled on the couch, bawling with Cleo while watching *Lord of the Rings: Return of the King.* I try to calculate the seconds between the end of her sentence and the beginning of mine, so it can feel natural.

"Oh, I'm good. Just working on some neuroscience homework." I pause, for effect. "Oh, coaching? Yeah. I'm... *super excited.*"

"Yeah?" My mom's voice sounds light, hopeful, and I can't find it in my heart to crush that hope. To remind her that the only reason I'm accepting the position is because I need the credit to graduate. "If they give you any trouble, you'll tell me, right?"

I nod, as if she can see me. "Of course, Mom. Always."

"Alright then." A soft sigh slips through the receiver. "You'll be great, Darce. They're lucky to have you."

"I get it from you."

A bright laugh bursts through the speaker, and even though there's this tightness in my chest, it makes everything else feel a little looser, if only for a second.

"You're such an ass kisser," she teases.

I laugh. "That I get from Dad."

My mom laughs too, but it fades fast. A quiet moment settles between us—one second, two maybe—and then her voice is softer. Hesitant.

"Hey, Darce?"

"Yeah, Mom?"

"I'm—" She stops, like she's debating what she wants to say. When the words finally come, they're not what I expect. I don't think they're what she expected either. "I'm just really glad you're back with me. Even if—"

"I'm glad I'm back with you too," I cut in, swallowing back the dry lump in my throat.

The silence stretches a bit longer, just the hum of the baseboard heater filling the dated apartment. Then, with a soft sigh, Mom shifts gears. "Well, I'll let you get back to work. Your dad's about to drag me on a date," she says, trying to sound upbeat again.

"Okay, have fun." My lips tug into a small smile despite the weight in my chest.

My parents have that disgusting kind of love. The kind where the honeymoon phase never ends. As a kid, I hated it. But now, it's kind of nice. It reminds me that relationships like that actually exist outside of fantasy movies and romance novels.

"We will. Love you, Darce."

"Love you too, Mom."

The line goes quiet, then she hangs up. I toss my phone onto the table, glancing back to my laptop just in time for Socks to hop up on the keyboard.

"*Shit*. Socks!" I groan, snatching him up and plopping him onto the ground. I point my finger at him, like he gives a single fuck about what I have to say. "Don't climb on my stuff!"

Socks meows, probably telling me that he was here first and if I don't like it, I can leave.

I sit back and pull my laptop onto my lap, ready to get back to work, but when I look at it, my assignment's gone. Instead, there's a photo stretching to each corner of the screen. My stomach lurches, and I freeze, staring at it.

It's me. From March, during the WCHA championship. I'm in mid-shot, poised in front of the net with the puck just about to release from my stick. My eyes are locked on the goal, a fierce determination sewn into my face, even though the clock behind me shows only one second left. The arena around me is a blur, but in the background, you can see the look of pure anticipation on my teammates' faces. Some of them are frozen mid-scream, others with hands gripping their sticks like they can already taste the victory.

The shot, the last-second miracle that sent the crowd into a frenzy and the team to the NCAA Women's Ice Hockey Championship. It was the game-winner.

It was also the last time I stepped onto the ice.

So now, looking at the photo, all I feel is heaviness. The weight of the fact that everything I had, everything in reach, is gone, and there is nothing I, nor anyone else, can do to bring it back.

I slam the laptop shut, the force of it startling Socks as the image burns behind my eyes. I bury my face in my hands, something hot simmering deep inside my chest as a teary breath slips out. It's crazy how love magnifies everything. Happiness, anger, grief. It feels ridiculous, grieving something that was never alive, but I guess that's how hockey made me feel.

Alive.

Socks meows from the side, and I groan, lifting my head up to see him hop up onto the couch beside me. He purrs, rubbing his head against me, before setting a single paw onto my leg. I push him away, half-heartedly. "Not now, Socks."

But he doesn't listen, of course. He simply plops down, all thirteen pounds of him curling onto my lap. And something about the warmth of his tiny body, the rhythmic pressure of his kneading, lightens the weight, just a little. I lean back, my body sinking into the pillows of the couch. Maybe I am grieving, or maybe I'm just stuck in the past. I know change is inevitable, but how do you let go of the very thing that made you who you are?

Socks purrs loudly against me, and I hate to admit it, but it's nice. He might be a pest, but I'm suddenly a little more understanding of why Cleo loves him so much. I close my eyes for a moment, breathing, letting the soft kneading of his paws ground me.

I don't know how long I stay like that. Sitting in silence. Reliving the past.

But eventually, the stillness becomes too much. It's just hockey. It's just a game. But it was *my* game, my identity. And now it's gone. There's nothing I can do to get it back.

...is there?

FOUR

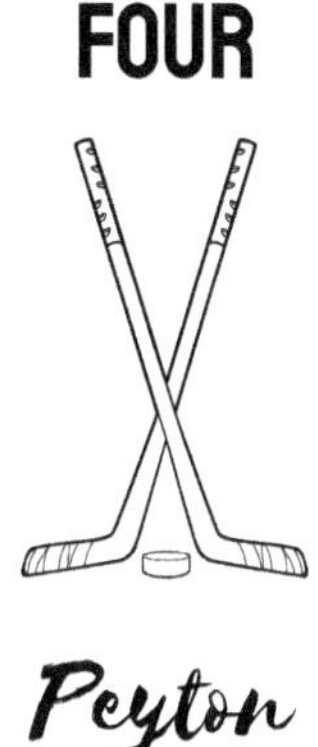

Peyton

FINAL CHAT FR THIS TIME

Goooood morning ladies! Quick reminder that we're starting in the training room with Kaiser at 6.

Also LNHL Countdown: 18ish weeks

What?!

Shittttt I forgot

Yeah so I'm actually coming down with something. Don't think I'm gonna make it.

Same

CAPTAIN CLARKE

Does that "something" happen to be a hangover?

YERSIE

…

Z

Come on, Pey. You know Kaiser is going to eat us alive.

CAPTAIN CLARKE

Best I can do is Monsters and gas station breakfast sandwiches.

HAMMIE

Deal.

CAY

Oooh purple please!

SIMS BUT NOT THE GAME

Blue pls. But not the cobalt blue the light blue.

BRADY

Can you get me a Honey Bun too? I'll send $.

YERSIE

Eating a Honey Bun before lifting is absolutely vile.

BRADY

I'll take no criticism from the woman that puts everything bagel seasoning on her ICE CREAM.

YERSIE

Fair point

Hey, anyone know what this "big announcement" that Coach has is?

Not a clue.

Nope.

I think she mentioned something about administrative changes?

CAPTAIN CLARKE

Look! Little Brownie paid attention! We're raising her so well.

I vaguely remember the admin thing, but I don't really know. Guess we'll find out! I'm running to the gas station. See you all in thirty!

I T'S SEVEN IN THE morning, and I've already peed six times today. Granted, it's better than the rest of the team's hangover dehydration, but the pressure building between my thighs is not the pleasant kind. And if I have to ask Coach Cole to use the restroom in the middle of her lecture, she'll have me skating laps for a week.

"Alright, listen up everyone!" she announces, eyes wandering over us as her thin brows press together. I glance at the rest of my teammates on the ice, and while their skates are laced up and ready to go, *they* most certainly are not.

Harlowe, our primary goalie and my best friend, is practically falling asleep, icy eyes dipping in and out of consciousness, while Bailey, the toughest defense-woman this side of the Columbia, also my best friend, is clutching her stomach like the contents of it are traveling northbound. How they made it through Kaiser this morning is beyond me.

I can only pray my exhaustion looks different from theirs, which seems to be answered because when Coach Cole's eyes fall onto me, she says nothing. Her throat clears, pen tapping against her clipboard, before she continues.

"Before we get going, I've got an announcement. Some of you've only known me for about a month, but for those of you who were at the weekend camp back in July, you already know I don't exactly do things the usual way."

Harlowe's eyes snap open, and she shoots me a quick, concerned glance. We both attended that camp. After a scrimmage Coach Cole called "divided" (whatever that meant) she had us sit in the stands with pens and paper. She instructed us to write a letter to someone we were mad at, someone who'd gotten under our skin.

Yeah, a *letter.* Like the kind you fold and stick in an envelope with a stamp. No filters. No holding back. Once the anger was out, we folded the letters and tucked them between our jill shorts and our pants.

I don't know if it was the psychology behind it, or just the extra weight, but when we got back on the ice, it was like we all understood a new, unspoken language. Caydence knew when I was going to pass the puck, Lena wasn't hoarding it anymore, and Harlowe blocked every single shot the other team made.

It was weird.

When our old coach, Coach Kaiser, thought we weren't working as a team, she'd just scream in our faces until we could all bond over the vein in her forehead. Thankfully, she got demoted to being our strength and conditioning coach after an altercation with a ref, so we only have to deal with her on training days.

But Coach Cole? She's different. That's not to say she's soft, though. When Indie, a sophomore who just joined the team, showed up late on the first day of practice, Coach had her skating suicides until she could explain why. Only, Indie must really hate herself, because she never did. She just skated, back and forth, faster and faster, pushing herself until she was nearly sick.

"...Right now, like me, she's a stranger. But she's got experience, and she's going to be working with us to help develop your skills, both on and off the ice. She might be just what we need to get to the NCAAs. So, treat her with the same respect you'd show me." Harlowe and I exchange worried glances again.

I should've been paying attention.

My heart pounds, and my stomach churns. I blink a couple times, trying to wet my dry eyes, the sharp, throbbing pressure in my bladder screaming for relief. That's what happens when you pound two energy drinks before six a.m. The kicker? I'm still fucking tired.

I should've known better than to go to Will's party last night—stupid move if I'm serious about the PWHL, more specifically the Sabertooths. Then again, with my last name, they'd probably let it slide. To be fair, everyone would've gone whether or not I agreed, and the football team deserved to celebrate their win. So I made an appearance, kept an eye on my team, poured a couple cocktails. And though I never drank one myself, the exhaustion from only three hours of sleep is almost as punishing.

A bead of sweat rolls down my neck, but I don't dare move. I must be making some sort of face, because Coach's brow flicks up, her eyes scanning me with a keen, almost predatory focus.

"Student coaches usually work with the team they've played on, but the board was willing to make an exception. So, I want you all to meet my daughter, Darcy."

Darcy.

When that name leaves her lips, my stomach sinks, the weight of it pressing against my bladder, and I swear to god, if I piss myself right now, the team will never let me live it down. Coach gestures to the side, and in walks Darcy. The Darcy I may or may not have hidden from security guards with at four in the morning yesterday, after a solid three-minute argument with her.

Wait, did she say *daughter?*

Darcy's straight, auburn hair sways with each step, like a ribbon caught in the wind, while her emerald eyes scan the ice. A wave of heat rushes to my cheeks. My body pulses, my heart or my bladder, I have no idea. All I know is that when Darcy's eyes lock onto mine, when her thin, red brows lift in recognition, I'm already halfway off the ice, calling out to Coach like I'm in a position to be on her bad side.

"Sorry, Coach!" I yell out. "I really have to pee!"

I don't dare look back to see her reaction, though I can hear the muffled giggles of my teammates echoing behind me. I have no idea why; there's absolutely nothing funny about this situation. I sprint, as fast as I can manage in these damn skates, off the ice, through the tunnel, and into the locker room.

With frantic hands, I yank open my padded pants, digging my fingers under the layers until I finally feel my skin, and then rip them down to my knees. I barely make it to the toilet before I collapse onto it, the pressure finally releasing in a rush, my heart still hammering in my chest like I'm about to be a dead man.

Which, you know, *I am.* Because if the look in Darcy's eyes isn't enough to kill me, when Coach finds out I'm feuding with her daughter, she'll do the damn job herself. It's clear they're close—if not from the fact that Darcy (despite her total lack of experience) is assistant coach, then from the fact that for the last few weeks since practice has started, Coach Cole has mentioned her daughter at least three times a day.

"Oh, my daughter just moved back from Minnesota."

"Oh, my daughter took that same course."

"Oh, my daughter braids her hair like that too."

Would've been nice if she'd dropped the name at least *once!*

The sink water in the locker room is cold on my hands, making them tremble as I scrub them together, or maybe it's just the nerves surrounding my potential demise. I splash some onto my cheeks, the sharp chill biting into my skin, sending a shiver that ripples through me. Droplets trace the curve of my face before dripping down, leaving behind a faint sting. I stare at myself in the mirror, the reflection slightly distorted by the moisture, my eyes heavy and tired.

What.

The.

Fuck.

A loud creak interrupts my internal spiral, the metal door swinging open, slamming against the wall. My gaze snaps over, landing on a head of flowy red hair, lingering in the doorway. Darcy props the door open with her foot, her thin, gloved fingers gripping a clipboard that matches her mother's, and I wonder now how I didn't see it before.

Maybe it's because Coach's hair is brown, and thin, or maybe because Darcy towers over my 5'4" stance, but the straight narrowness of her nose, the freckles scattered across her cheeks like constellations, it's unmistakable now.

"Coach says you better get your ass back on the ice." Her gaze snaps back to me, and my gut twists, brow twitching like it's got a mind of its own. I swipe at the water on my cheeks, but it doesn't soothe the tingling sensation washing over my skin.

I should learn from my mistakes. Just nod, comply, pretend like we've never met. But there's something about the way she looks at me that makes my blood hot. Maybe it's the superiority in her eyes, or the way she cut me down the other morning. Or maybe it's the fact that she *knew* we'd be seeing each other today—and didn't say a damn word about it.

The words claw their way up my throat, and before I can stop myself, I snap. "Nice of you to mention you're the student coach. Or, y'know, Coach's *daughter.*"

My arms fold across my chest, a wall I know won't do a damn thing to protect me. Darcy's already proven to be a pin, digging under my skin in a way nobody else has ever managed. I can handle assholes. Hell, I can even enjoy the challenge of them. But assholes who act like they're *innocent*? That's something else entirely.

Darcy tilts her head. "You never asked."

"Oh, so I'm just supposed to go around asking everyone about their family ties?"

"*You're* going to talk about family ties?" She scoffs. "You know, if you pulled your inflated head out of your ass for more than a second, you might've realized I actually knew enough to help you."

I can't suppress the sour laugh that tumbles from my lips. "Please. The only thing you've helped me with is confirm my suspicions."

Darcy's brow quirks, and she steps closer. "Which are?"

"That coach's daughters are *entitled brats.*"

Oof, Peyton. Low blow.

Darcy's eyes narrow, and her lips purse like she's savoring the insult she's about to drop. "Says the daughter of the retired *NHL legend.*"

"Hey, I've earned my spot on this team," I shoot back, but the waver in my voice doesn't convince her any more than it convinces me.

The corner of her mouth twitches, and the bubbling pit in my stomach broils into molten lava. "Sure." She shrugs, her expression stiffening into something colder. "But you can lose it just as easily."

With that, she spins on her heel, and the door slams behind her with a harsh *clang.*

Shit.

I follow, my skates scraping against the ice as I shuffle back on. The moment my blades meet the surface, every set of eyes locks onto me, like I've just walked out of the grave. *Fuck.* Am I dead? Did Darcy already finish me off in the locker room and I just don't know it?

I glide toward my teammates, whipping around to get in line, the movement making my stomach tense. Bailey leans in, her arm brushing against mine as she whispers.

"We're caught."

I don't divert my gaze from Coach Cole, but I feel my brow cock.

"What do you mean?" I whisper back, but Coach clears her throat, and Bailey jumps, straightening herself back up.

"Nice of you to join us again, *Captain,*" she chides disapprovingly. "I was just telling these fine players of yours that I have a *zero-tolerance policy* for hangovers at practice."

Fuck. Fuck. Fuck.

Her gaze skirts across my face, like she's waiting for me to confess, but before I have the chance, they narrow onto Indie. Sweet, innocent, never lied a day in her life, Indie.

We are so *fucked.*

"Tell me that you're all exhausted from a late-night study group, Browne."

Indie swallows, like, visibly gulps, the small bump in her throat bobbing as her gaze falls to the ice. Silence is certainly a choice. I'm not sure if it's the right one, but it's the one Indie makes. She glances at the rest of us, a silent question, and in Harlowe's eyes, I can see her begging. But just as Indie's lips part to speak, Coach Cole continues on.

"What you do on your time is your business. But as long as you're a Grizzly, you're on *my* time. I didn't transfer from Glacier just to join a circus." Her gaze flicks back to me, and even though we're relatively the same height, I feel a hell of a lot smaller. "*Bag skates.* Until someone throws up, or I tell you to stop. Whichever comes first."

"Hams, take one for the team," Harlowe whispers, with just the slightest lisp. Bailey shoots her a look, like she wants to kill her but is also considering the proposition. Me?

I just can't seem to take my eyes off Darcy.

She's standing there, long legs leaning against the wall, gaze fixed on the clipboard in front of her. There's a pen gripped between her teeth, her fingers drifting across the page as she reads whatever secrets lie upon it. Coach approaches her, exchanging words I can't quite hear, then pulls something out of her pocket and plops it onto her clipboard. A smile breaks across Darcy's face, a genuine one, and it catches me off guard, something in my chest tightening.

It's weird. I've never had my chest tighten at the sight of someone before. Sure, I've felt a flutter here and there, people notice me, I notice them, it's a game. But this feels different, like hearing nothing but lyrics your whole life until suddenly, one day, there's music behind them. A melody of sound filling the air, the space between us, cellos and trumpets and clari-fucking-nets, reeling me in, wringing me out, until nothing is left to settle in the void in my stomach but flushed intrigue.

Coach pats her on the back, and when Darcy lifts the object off her clipboard, the music comes to a screeching halt. It's a whistle. And when the shiny piece of metal lifts to her lips, I swear to god, she *smirks* at me. *What a little—*

Wheeeep!

The sound cuts through the air, and in an instant, we're off, blades cutting the ice as we start our grueling agenda. The moment I move, my lungs begin burning, my heart starts palpitating, and the wind sucks what little moisture my eyes had been granted. We just started and I can barely hold myself up, every part of me begging for mercy, but I can't stop. Not with Darcy watching. Not with Coach's eyes following our every move. And not with the letter "C" stitched to my chest, a reminder that, whether I like it or not, I'm supposed to be a leader.

Most days, it's validating. Right now? I'd consider trading it for a lemon-lime Gatorade and a solid excuse to lay in bed.

The cold air cuts into my skin, sharp as glass, but it's the only thing keeping me from collapsing. The steady rhythm of my breathing is broken only by the sound of my skates carving through the ice and the thud of my own heartbeat throbbing in my ears. I know I'm not the only one struggling. Everyone else's grunts and gasps mix into the symphony of pain that replaces the one from Darcy's smile, but it doesn't matter. Darcy just keeps blowing that whistle, like she's daring me to fall apart.

But I won't. I can't. I refuse to give her more fuel to add to the fire. So, I push harder, even though every fiber of my being is telling me to stop, to take a break, to throw in the towel and let the ice swallow me whole.

A strange, gurgling noise bubbles up from the pit of Bailey's stomach, and I glance at her, watching as she presses one hand against her abdomen, legs still driving forward in rapid, sprinting motions. She groans but draws her arms back to her side, continuing the exercise.

The whistle blows again, just as my skates reach the center line, and I propel myself into the opposite direction, casting a glance at Darcy. Her eyes are fixed on me, direct and calculating, lips pulled up into a satisfied smirk.

Masochist.

I'm slowing down, I can feel it, and no matter how hard I try, no matter how fast I feel like my legs are moving, exhaustion is setting in. I look back ahead, preparing to make another sharp turn when the merciful sound of that beautiful metal whistle rings longer through the air, and Coach's voice calls out.

"Time!"

I come to a screeching halt, my skates digging into the ice as powder flies behind me. My legs are on fire, my chest violently heaving, and sweat pools in every crevice of my body but at least it's over. The team gathers, panting, trying to take steadying breaths, and Coach's gaze sweeps over us. She shakes her head.

"I hope you've all learned your lesson," she says, assessing us warningly.

I glance at Darcy, expecting something. Maybe a smirk, or a nod, but she's already lost in the details of her clipboard again, scribbling down notes. I can't help but tilt my head, wondering what on that clipboard could be more entertaining than the team wiped out at her instruction.

Coach steps forward, sharp jaw tensing as she claps her hands together. "Now, let's get to the real work."

I'M SHOCKED, HONESTLY, THAT not a single one of us threw up during practice. There was a moment or two when I felt I might, from the sheer exhaustion and caffeinated syrup sloshing in my stomach, but I choked it back, knowing that I don't have the privilege of messing up. At least, not again.

Besides, vomiting rights were best reserved for Bailey. I think it's safe to say our rage room plans have been moved to Saturday.

The feeling lingers as I toss my jersey into my duffel bag, pulling my green Grizzlies hoodie over my head. My sports bra is drenched with sweat, clinging to my skin, but I embrace the body odor and slap on an extra layer of deodorant.

"I need food," Harlowe grumbles, slamming her dry stall shut. Beside her, Bailey lets out a soft but telling groan.

"I think I might vomit if I eat something," she whines. Then her gaze narrows, brows weaving together as she considers it. "I think I also might vomit if I don't?"

I chuckle, smacking my hand against her back. "I'm going to the diner. You guys coming?"

They both nod, Harlowe peeling off her sweat-soaked socks and tossing them into her bag with a wrinkled nose. Her eyes flick up, a taunting smirk tugging at her lips as she stares at someone behind me.

"Nice going, Browne," she teases. "Really stood up for us there."

I whip around, gaze landing on Indie, who is innocently clinging to a towel like it would be a crime to see her naked. Her cheeks flush, and she begins stammering over her words, none of them discernible.

"I—well—um—" She sighs, and I can't help but feel sorry for the kid. She hardly said three words at camp, and it isn't *her* fault that Coach pitted her against us. Honestly, I was shocked to see her at the party last night, but it was quickly cured when she left shortly after exchanging class notes with Will. I flash her a smile before spinning back to Harlowe and putting her in her place.

"Oh, shut it Harlowe. If Coach was interrogating you, you would've rolled like a dog."

Bailey barks twice, and I don't hesitate to jump on her either. "Oh that's funny? Your groaning was probably the reason we got called out in the first place."

"Either that, or your bladder," Harlowe fires back, and everyone, including Indie, breaks into laughter.

"Ha-ha, very funny," I snipe, tossing my sweaty towel at her. She shrieks, gagging as she rips it off, and throws it onto the ground.

"Jesus, Pey! Wash the thing, weekly at *least.*"

I chuckle, but when I catch a whiff of it, I have a visceral reaction.

Tongue-tensing, gag-reflexing, nose-scrunching reaction. A stream of air blows through my puffed cheeks as I lift it up, everyone in the room groaning and pulling their shirts over their noses.

"That's like, a biohazard," Bailey says. Then, she chokes. "Seriously, get it out of here!"

I fish in my pocket, pulling out my keys and tossing them to Harlowe. "Can you get the car warmed up?" She nods, jingling them between her fingers, and I toss my head in Indie's direction. "And take her with you."

"*Me?*"

I spin around, catching her eye. Her finger is pressed to her chest, hazel eyes blinking in innocent surprise. I shrug.

"You hungry?" I ask. She nods. "Then get dressed, *Rose*. We're not reenacting the Titanic."

A smile breaks across Indie's face, cheeks flushing as she scrambles in her locker to gather her clothes. I hold the towel out at arm's distance, like I didn't just use it to absorb my own bodily fluids. All my teammates step aside, creating a path lined with disgusted expressions. Some of them even pinch their noses as I walk past, and I start to wonder how long it's actually been since I've washed it. I step outside, the cool fall air enveloping me as I stroll over to the dumpster.

The satisfying weight of the towel sinks into the trash, but as I turn to head back, I hit something. My head bounces off the warm body, and I stumble back, blinking quickly, trying to steady myself. My lips part to speak, to apologize for not watching where I was going, but when my gaze flicks up, I freeze.

Deep green eyes stare back at me, *down* at me, even, as Darcy pulls her dark red hair over one shoulder.

There it is. That knot in my stomach. God, I feel stupid for how I snapped earlier. Even though she'd been rude, even though she's clearly got some sort of vendetta, it's not like me to escalate things. To be that person. To make it worse.

I blink, my mind scrambling for words. *Any words.* Something that might make this right. Part of it's guilt, truly. But if I'm being completely honest, another part of me is panicking. If Coach finds out what I said, I might as well kiss my Captain label goodbye. Hell, the way she looked at me earlier when she found out we were at that party? I'll be lucky to keep any spot on this team.

But if we don't handle this—if we don't squash this stupid dispute now—I'm as good as gone.

And I can't lose this.

I search those eyes, and I blame the absence of words coming to my mind on the fact that I seem to be getting lost in them. Darcy simply raises a brow, her thin, freckled lips parting.

"Tired?" she questions, her tone baiting. She's clearly looking for a reaction, and I can't help but wonder how our stupid bickering yesterday was enough to constitute her enjoyment of my suffering. I cross my arms, shifting my weight to my right leg, because my left feels like it's going to fall off.

Don't bite, Peyton. *Don't. Bite.*

"No," I lie.

Something flickers in her eyes, but I can't quite pin it. Maybe amusement at my transparent fib, or maybe irritation that her dig didn't land quite like she wanted. Either way, it doesn't matter. Even though what I said in the locker room was the truth, that stupid knot in my stomach refuses to loosen until I apologize. Until I can do my part in wiping the slate clean. I open my mouth to speak, but before I can get a word out, she cuts in again.

"You know, you seemed really serious about hockey the other morning. Practicing really hard."

Was that—did she just... *compliment me?* For a brief moment, I think maybe I'm not completely dead. Maybe, this was all just a misunderstanding. Maybe I got a little sensitive. Maybe—

"Turns out I was wrong. Showing up hungover? This sport isn't a joke, *Captain*. Start leading like it matters."

Then, before I can even process her words, or the antagonistic way she used my position, Darcy plants her heel into the ground and spins around on it, her soft strands of hair brushing against my nose as she moves past me. Her almond-cherry scent lingers just long enough to make me dizzy, and she strolls away, pace unhurried, as if I were just another dumpster she'd walked around. And maybe I am. I don't know if I'm supposed to intimidated or offended, but I do know this:

I'm not letting some failed player, coach's daughter, push me around.

FIVE

Darcy

FINAL CHAT FR THIS TIME

****Bailey Cunningham has added you to the chat****

HAMMIE

Everyone say hi to Darcy! I thought she should be in the chat so she knows the ins & outs :)

CAY

I thought the whole point of this chat was that our coaches weren't in it

Z

don't be an ass, c

DARCY COLE

Sorry, what?

CAPTAIN CLARKE

Oh Jesus. Really Hammie?

HAMMIE

What? It's not like she's our coach coach, she's our assistant coach. Besides, she's practically one of us.

YERSIE

As long as she takes turns buying energy drinks idc.

DARCY COLE

I'm confused. What is this?

BRADY

Unofficial group chat!

DARCY COLE

Like for game announcements and stuff?

I thought I was already in that chat.

HAMMIE

That's the official chat. This one is more for fun.

YERSIE

Like parties.

BRADY

Or venting.

BROWNE

Or helping with homework.

DARCY COLE

Oh.

Thank you, but I'm good.

Darcy Cole has left the chat

"ORANGE OR GREEN?" CLEO'S voice pries me from my thoughts as she holds up two dresses, one in each hand, giving them a little shake. Her eyes flick between them, calculating, as if the trajectory of her entire life hinges on this one decision.

My brows furrow as I study them. "I thought you and Will were just talking about majors," I say, suspicion creeping into my tone.

"We are."

"Then why are you dressing up?"

Cleo's nose wrinkles, her expression shifting in a mix of bewilderment and mock offense. "You don't ever dress up for yourself?"

I pause, considering it. I used to dress up all the time, mostly for the satisfaction of knowing I looked damn good, but in the past few months, my skin's felt like it's been set ablaze.

That part's called Raynaud's. It makes your blood vessels shrink like wool in a hot washer. Sometimes it's because of the climate. Sometimes it's for no reason at all. My skin flushes purple, and it starts burning, itching, like I've been dipped in a swarm of fire ants.

Not all people with RA have Raynaud's. I'm just one of the lucky ones, I guess.

So I've been defaulting to anything that keeps me warm, and doesn't aggravate my tingling skin. Loose sweats, soft turtleneck sweaters. Gloves. Half the time, it's as if I've picked out my outfits with my eyes closed. But when your body feels like a burning pit of itchy, brittle lava, the last thing you care about is what you look like.

"Not for a while," I admit. "Good point."

Cleo studies me earnestly. "Well, you really should. Even just once a week. Confidence is scientifically proven to make you feel better."

I chuckle softly, unable to suppress the small smile that tugs at my lips. She's trying so hard to be a friend, and though I might not be completely ready for that, I'm not going to pretend I don't appreciate it. She waves the dresses again.

I give them both another careful look before responding, "Green." Cleo nods, sliding the rust-colored dress back onto the rod with a satisfied sigh.

"Thanks. Okay, sorry, what were you saying?"

I press the rewind button in my brain, trying to recall whatever thought was about to leave my mouth before we got sidetracked into the depths of fashion and mental health.

What was it again? *Oh, right.*

"She's just so *cocky!*" I exclaim, flinging my hands in the air like I'm measuring the sheer volume of Peyton's arrogance, as if it's a physical thing that can be quantified.

If it were, it'd be Mount Everest. A towering monument of cockiness so high, it'd give you altitude sickness. The Great Wall of China, stretching for miles, so long even binoculars couldn't make you see the end of it. No, scratch that. If Peyton's arrogance could be measured, it'd be a wormhole. A paradox of an ego that sucks everything into it, leaving no room for anything but her self-absorption.

"She's a hockey player" Cleo shrugs, as if the fact explains itself. But it doesn't. I've been around hockey players my entire life. I am—*was* a hockey player. Arrogance isn't a hockey player thing. It's a having-a-pro-dad-and-thinking-that-automatically-makes-you-untouchable thing.

I roll my eyes, letting them drop to the clipboard in front of me. The sound of my pen scribbling over my notes fills the quiet space. "Are you nervous for your *date?*"

Cleo's brows knit disapprovingly. "It's not a *date.* It's just two people grabbing coffee and talking about school."

"Mhm," I hum in response, flashing her an unconvinced look. Cleo pretends not to hear me, turning back into her closet.

"So what are you going to do?" she asks.

I tilt my head. "About…"

A chuckle escapes her as she leans down, rummaging through her shoes desperately like a possum digging through a dumpster. She tosses them aside one by one, clearly frustrated with every single pair.

"About Peyton," she clarifies, her voice carrying the "duh". She holds up two shoes, dark brown flats and beige wedges, and I gesture toward the flats.

"What do you mean, what am I going to do about Peyton?"

Cleo stands up, narrowing her eyes, and for a second, I feel like I'm back on the ice, surrendering to my old coach. "Well, it kinda seems like you two are stuck together. At least until the season's over. Are you planning to keep up this *feud* the entire time?"

I can't stop the eye roll from slipping out, the noise of my scoff escaping me. "It's not a feud. She's just—"

"Wait, wait. Let me guess." Cleo traces the ceiling with her eyes, tapping her chin like she's deep in thought. Then she sticks out her hand, counting off fingers. "Cocky. Careless. Arrogant. Reckless. Bitc—"

"Okay, okay, I get it," I cut in, rolling my eyes again, though this time a small smile curls at the corners of my lips. "Look, I know you're right. But what am I supposed to do? It's not like she's going anywhere. And if I want to graduate on time, I can't either."

Cleo pulls her shirt over her head like we've been doing this our whole lives. I'm used to it, after years in the locker room, but I'm surprised she's so comfortable with me already. Hell, she hadn't even seen me without my gloves until two weeks ago.

"Well, have you tried talking to her? Clearing things up?" she asks, her voice softer as she pulls her pants down next. I glance away. Not because she's not nice to look at—damn, if Will Carter doesn't want Cleo, I could name a hundred people who would—but because I'm not ready to solidify that level of our... *acquaintanceship* yet.

A laugh bursts from me, louder than I expect, and my back tosses against the bed. I stare at the ceiling. "Clear up what? That people would kill for her spot on the team, and she's trivializing it by showing up hungover?"

"I mean... *yeah,*" Cleo says, her voice muffled, as if suppressed by fabric. I can hear the difference when her head pops back through. "Maybe she just needs a reality check."

"Oh, she'll get one," I respond, propping myself up on my elbows. She's dressed now, her black pixie cut softly tousled. The moss-green dress compliments her strong, stocky frame, and the rows of gems lining her ears catch the light in warm, earthy tones. "Either when they cut her for insubordination, or when she pushes herself too hard and ends up injured. Hey—how can someone be so careless, and yet try so hard?"

Cleo tugs the lip of her flats over her heels, then steps out of the closet, pulling the door closed behind her. "I don't know. Her dad's a pro, so maybe it's just how she balances things, you know?" She plops down beside me on the bed, her knees knocking against mine, and continues. "I'm not trying to make excuses, though. I know how important hockey is to you, and—"

"Thanks, Cleo," I cut in softly, though I feel bad interrupting. I'm just not ready to have that conversation. Not with her. Not with anyone.

The only reason she knows about my RA in the first place is because one night she brought home a bottle of Peach Smirnoff and a list of questions concerning my gloves, my box of dusty hockey trophies, and a screenshot of an article about me back in Minnesota. It's the only time she's really asked, and the only time I was drunk enough to give her an answer.

I smile. "You look nice."

Cleo grins, her pretty, high-bridged, statuesque nose scrunching. "I know," she replies simply. "But thank you."

We pause, just staring for a beat, until suddenly, we break into laughter. My rib pops painfully as I clutch my side, and Cleo swipes at the tears pooling in her eyes. Her warm hand clutches my shoulder, and I remember, briefly, the good side of having friends. The late-night talks. The weekend trips. *This.*

My gaze darts back to her, and she's still a giggling mess, her bright smile gleaming in the morning sun. My chest feels like it's vibrating. I want to be for her what she always tries to be for me, just this once.

But I can't.

"I F YOU THINK THIS class is complicated now, just wait until we dive into neurons next week." Professor Palit pauses, a proud grin sweeping over his deep ochre cheeks. "They've got more connections than your ex's DMs."

Half the class groans, while the other half erupts into laughter. Both sounds bounce off the cement walls, amplifying the reaction, which makes Professor Palit's smile grow even wider. He chuckles, punctuating it with a loud "that's all for today, brainiacs!" which is what he likes to call us even though I'm pretty sure I'm the only one who actually likes this class.

I watch everyone file out, backpacks tossed over shoulders, some rolling their eyes at the joke, while others are already begging to swap notes. Switching off my recorder to save my wrists the strain, I scrape my scattered papers off the desk. Professor Palit catches my eye, and flashes me a warm smile.

"How you feeling today, Darcy?" he calls out casually, plopping down into his swivel chair. I shove the loose papers into my notebook, then slide it into my bag.

"Oh, I'm good today," I say, as if I am ever "good". Sure, there are days where my joints don't creak like a door from a horror movie, but usually, it just gets swapped for unexplainable muscle pain. Though, other than my Raynaud's flare, it's manageable today, so I guess I have to be somewhat grateful. Professor Palit nods, eyes fixed on the computer in front of him.

"I'm happy to hear it." He pushes his glasses up the bridge of his hooked nose. "Now get out of here. I have to record myself practicing lectures and it's embarrassing."

I chuckle, sweeping my green messenger bag off my chair, and sling it over my shoulder.

"Bye, Professor!" I wave, and he doesn't look up at me as he waves back.

I climb the steps up to the door, waiting patiently for my turn as the rush of students flows out. Whipping out my phone to kill time, I click on the notification I got from Cleo during class to finally read it.

"I've got it for ya'."

My head snaps up at the peppy voice, and standing in front of me, with her hand propping open the door, is a girl. Dark blunt bangs, brown eyes, and a sweet smile tugging at her chiseled cheeks.

She looks familiar, but I can't quite pin it.

"Thanks," I manage, slipping my phone into my pocket. She pushes the door open further, warm fall sunlight flooding us as we step out into the hall.

"Palit is something else, huh?" she asks, a humored smile twisting on her lips. I nod, stepping to her side so I'm not blocking the doorway.

"He's..." I trail off, flipping through my brain to find the right words. "Honest about who he is."

The girl hitches a shoulder, nodding in agreement. "Totally! Which, to be honest, I like. It's easier for me to be invested in what he's saying when I know it's not just bullshit."

I smile. "Right? Like, how do you expect me to listen when everything that comes out of your mouth sounds scripted." I run a hand through my hair, the soft strands feathering between my fingers, then falling back flat against my head. "My anatomy professor is like that."

Her gaze shoots to mine. "You're Darcy, right?"

Shit. I don't know this girl's name. Am I supposed to know this girl's name?

I give a half-nod. "Yeah. Sorry, do I know you?"

Her grin widens, charmingly so, as she leans against the wall. "I'm Bailey. Cunningham. We talked this morning in the group chat. I'm a defense-woman on the hockey team? Everyone just calls me Hammie, though."

"Right," I respond with a nod, the vague memory of her clutching her stomach yesterday flashing in my mind. Ah, another victim of Peyton's poor leadership. "Sorry. I should've known that."

She shakes her head, swishing a dismissive hand around. "Oh it's fine. There's a lot of us." She pauses. "*Anyway,* I just wanted to introduce myself. And—" She reaches into her back pocket, pulling out a folded piece of paper and handing it to me. "—I wanted to see if you'd be interested in joining my D&D campaign. Cleo and I host it together on Tuesdays."

A valley etches between my brows as I open the flyer, suspicion scrubbing goosebumps down my skin. I study her—her posture, her tone, the way that bubbly grin settles in the groove of her mouth—and something doesn't sit right. I lean back slightly, my fingers drumming against my bag.

"Why?" I ask hesitantly.

She shrugs, way too casual. "You seem cool."

Cool? My gaze narrows, and the hairs on the back of my neck stand up in alarm. Her lips tighten, the smile fading, the nervous tension in her face clear now.

"I'm cool?" I repeat flatly, and she nods. *Bullshit.* "Did Cleo send you to befriend me? Because—"

"*No!* No." She shakes her head, eyes widening as panic creeps into her voice. "Well, she might have mentioned that she was *worried* about you, but—"

"Unbelievable," I mutter, pushing off the wall and whipping around to face her. Poor girl looks terrified, but I already have a meddling mother. I don't need a meddling roommate too.

Bailey tosses her hands up in defense. "Look, I'm sorry. I wasn't trying to be weird or anything. Cleo's just been talking about how worried she is about you, and since you're new and all, I just figured I'd invite you. Just in case."

My teeth scrape against the inside of my cheek as I study her like I've got a polygraph machine built into my DNA. She looks a little less nervous now, the tension in her expression loosening. Maybe she is being honest, but you never really know, do you?

A soft sigh escapes me, and I take a step back, offering her an apologetically distant look. "Thanks for the invite," I say, the words surprisingly genuine as I force a smile that definitely isn't. "But no thanks."

Bailey's expression falters, briefly, but enough for me to catch it, before she's back to that soft, bubbly grin. "No worries. I wanna ask why, but I won't."

"I appreciate that," I say, and I do.

She slips off the wall. "But hey, if you ever want to hang out or exchange notes or whatever, just let me know, Darcy."

A sheepish grin tugs at the corners of my mouth. "I will," I say. "Thanks."

Bailey nods, then starts strolling down the hallway. Before she gets too far, she turns around with a grin.

"Hey Coach?" she calls out. My stomach does something fluttery when she calls me by that title. I catch her eye, and her grin widens. "Welcome to the team!"

"**L**ET'S TRY THAT AGAIN!" my mom's voice cuts through the rink, and instantly, the players on the ice scatter, heading back to the starting positions of the drill. Drill... *Right. Drills.*

I jot that down on my clipboard, before shifting my gaze back to the ice. When the whistle blows, the players spring into motion, a blur of green and white. It's chaotic, non-methodical, but they're much more animated than they were on Wednesday. Watching the team glide across the rink—

I can almost feel it.

Blades carving through the ice, wind slapping my face, that prickling jolt that absorbs into the stiff gloves when puck and stick collide.

I've tried to forget that feeling. Tried to bury it beneath distractions, TV, books, homework, anything that keeps me from thinking about it. But even when it's not dangled right in front of me, I'd never forget it.

I think about it every time I swallow my meds. Every time I reach for a sweater and my fingers brush against the jersey I can't bring myself to throw away. I think about it every time my mom looks at me, or when Cleo tries to pull me out of the house, to get me to feel something normal. But right now, I think about it the most. Watching them play, not even aware of how fleeting this is.

I wonder if any of them know how lucky they are. How many of them lace up their skates and think about how easily this could all be taken from them. It's clear Peyton doesn't. But then, neither did I. Not until it was already gone.

It's hypocritical, really. How easily I took it all for granted. I was no different than them once. But now, here I am, bitterly pretending it doesn't sting. Pretending I wasn't just like Peyton, stupid enough to think it would last forever.

Jealousy is a green-eyed monster, and her name is Darcy Cole.

The whistle blows again, the drill falling apart. My mom shakes her head, shouting out to them.

"You *have* to *see* it *through!*" she says firmly, gesturing with her hands through the movement of the play. She skates over to them, her voice fading as the team pools around her.

I should just let her coach. We've made it nearly to the end of practice without me needing to say anything. Wednesday, I had the excuse of paperwork to keep me busy. I'm not stupid enough to think I'll glide under the radar forever, but I'm going to stay out of it as long as I can.

Everyone looks at me like I shouldn't be here.

They're right. They're just right for the wrong reasons.

I was adamant with my mom that nobody find out about Minnesota. If they find out about Minnesota, they might find out about my RA. And then, I won't be the spoiled coach's daughter anymore, like Peyton said. Instead, I'll be fragile. The pitied ex-player who lost it all. And that's so much worse.

"Darcy, you got anything to add?"

Shit.

I glance up at my mom, only to find over twenty pairs of eyes trained on me. The most intense of them all? Peyton's, naturally. Her golden irises glow even from the stands. Bright, almost jarring. I hate how they burn right through me, like a magnifying glass in the sun. Like any second, ribbons of smoke will lift from my body, and the layers of my already scorching skin will wear away until everyone around me sees who I really am.

I shake my head, but my mom catches my gaze with a warning look, a reminder that she's not just my mother, she's my boss. So, I get up and head toward the bench. A sharp pain flares in my chest, the rhythm of my heart pulsing faster, harder.

A deep breath expands in my lungs, and I square my shoulders. It doesn't matter what they think. I know my stuff. So I lift my chin and say it.

"Cunn—*Hammie* should switch spots with Clarke," I say, surprisingly steady, even after stumbling over Bailey's name. "If Clarke's in the slot, and Hammie's net-front, she can slide over and take a pass from..." I squint at Lena's jersey. "*Brady*. Then Clarke's got a clean one-timer off Hammie's pass."

My mom's mouth twitches in amusement, but she doesn't say anything. Neither does anyone else. They all just stare at me, blinking like I've descended from space.

That is, until someone breaks the silence.

"That's pretty risky, don't you think?"

My eyes snap to Peyton. She's tugging off her helmet, damp hair plastered to her forehead as she shakes it free. Her gaze locks onto mine, waiting. Feeling those eyes bore into me? It makes my heart crawl into my throat.

"Not a risk taker?" I ask, lifting a brow.

If there's anything I know about Peyton, it's that "risky" is her middle name.

Well, actually, according to a Reddit thread speculating about her potential

PWHL debut, it's *Bauer*—which really had me rolling my eyes.

She shrugs. "Just shocked you are." Her eyes flick briefly to my mom, like she'd forgotten she was here, then back to me. She clears her throat. "You're really gonna bank the whole play on whether or not I can hit a one-timer?"

I cross my arms. "Can you?"

She forces a laugh. "Of course I can. I'm just not sure it's the right move. I mean, why swap me with Hammie when her timing's just as good as mine?"

The question catches me off guard. Not because I don't know the answer, but because I figured that Peyton would take any chance to score. To prove to me how good she is. She didn't hesitate the other morning.

But something about the way she's moving today feels different. Rougher. Clunkier. None of the smooth, choreographed precision she had skating alone.

Still, I push the thought aside, put my heart back where it belongs, and answer.

"Because she's a lefty," I point out. "She'll have better control down low."

Bailey grins, clearly impressed by my knowledge, but my eyes snap back to Peyton. She's watching me intently, one dark, sculpted brow arched.

"Okay," she says slowly, nodding like she's humoring me. Like she's still not convinced I know what I'm talking about.

"It's not risky if the flanks are moving like they're supposed to," I explain. "Just because it's a power play doesn't mean we can coast. Right now they're stagnant, but—"

I flip to a blank page on my clipboard, click my pen, and start sketching. The lines come without thinking, a trail of ink gliding across the paper like muscle memory. Like I'm back on the ice, breaking down the play for my team. The tremble in my hand, the waver in my voice, is replaced by arrows and loops, streaking across the page.

"If Brady moves here—" I draw an arrow curling away from the right flank. "—she pulls the PK with her. That creates space *here*." I circle the slot. "And if these two—" I tap the dots to the side. "—are ready for a rebound if you miss, we're covered."

When I glance up, Peyton's amber eyes are locked on me. Not quite skeptical, but not fully convinced either. Her lip quirks. These little crescent-shaped divots settle into each of her rose-washed porcelain cheeks, and it makes my skin hot.

"I don't miss."

I tuck my clipboard against my chest. "Then it should be easy."

Another short, airy laugh slips out of her, and she casts a glance at the team, gauging their reaction. She looks back at me.

"I'm not opposed," she starts, though her tone makes me think otherwise. "It just feels like you're not giving room for anyone to trust their instincts. Instincts are half the game," she adds, explaining it to me like I'm five.

I can feel every set of eyes on me now. The team. My mom. Peyton. I could back off, let her win this round, and see how far that gets her. But that stupid fucking smirk still lingers, like this—*me*—is a game.

So instead, I clear my throat, and step forward. "Sure, but that doesn't work when everyone's got different instincts. You need to be on the same page. You need a plan."

"We *have* a plan," she fires back, and now, that grin drops. "But we're not going to overthink it. Heavy structure like that never works in a game."

Before I can stop it, my inner sledgehammer slips out. "If preparation never works, then maybe you're not actually prepared."

A chorus of "oooohs" ripples through the team like an elementary class when someone gets sent to the principal's office. Guilt floods my stomach as Bailey catches my eye, winking at me.

Then my mom's voice cuts through the sound.

"Okay, alright," she says, all no-nonsense. "Different perspectives. That's good. Clarke—" She turns to face Peyton. "We'll try it Darcy's way a couple times. If it works, it works. If it doesn't, it doesn't."

Something flutters in my stomach, but it sinks just as quickly. I don't know how I'm going to survive the season if every time I speak, I'm having to prove I belong. If I have to justify every word. Then again, I'm not sure I do belong. It feels like I belong to the rink, but it doesn't belong to me anymore.

And I don't know how to cope with that.

Peyton shoots me an annoyed glance, and it's childish, but I feel triumphant. She knows better than to challenge my mom, though. Instead, she takes a steadying breath and flashes a tight smile, channeling that cheaply chirpy voice. "Yes, Coach."

Immediately after, she takes charge. Gliding over to the team, pointing and giving orders, directing everyone into position. It's effortless for her. Like most things when it comes to her career. But there's a moment, a split-second pause.

It's almost unnoticeable. Everyone else is flying around her, getting into position, but for a fleeting second, she hesitates. Her eyes drop, her body stills, and she runs a hand through her dark, layered hair. But before another passes, her gaze snaps to mine. She pulls on her helmet, and pushes off, rubbing her hand across the "C" on her jersey.

I lean back against the bench, gripping the clipboard like it validates my existence.

"Get out of the crease, Bails!" the goalie—I'm pretty sure her name's Harlowe—grunts, shoving her broad frame into Hammie's.

Hammie huffs, scooting forward maybe an inch. "I thought you liked spending time with me, Yersie," she shoots back.

Harlowe—or *Yersie*, apparently—blows her a kiss.

The rest of the team files into position. The whistle blows. They run through the play, and it pans out exactly how I envisioned. A clean sweep. A perfect execution.

The puck glides from stick to stick, the satisfying *clack* as it bounces off Hammie's, right to Peyton's, then slams into the net.

I watch with a grin as the team erupts into high-fives. Yersie hangs her head. And the smallest spark of satisfaction settles in.

I didn't suggest anything monumental. I was just doing my job. But there is something so sweet about being right when it's at Peyton's arrogant expense.

Before I get caught staring too long, I direct my attention back to my clipboard, scrawling in the margins of my notes. The whoosh of skates fills my ears, and my eye catches on Peyton in my periphery. She stops in front of me, her breath slipping out in small, controlled puffs.

She doesn't say anything at first. Just stands there, waiting for me to look up. I know no good can come from it, but I pry my gaze from my clipboard anyway. If arrogance and recklessness weren't oozing from every pore, she'd be… well, *breathtaking.*

Even through the cage attached to her helmet, those amber eyes shine. The way her lips curve, that cocky little smirk, the creases around them deceptively sweet. Sweat gathers at her neck, just beneath her helmet, and I can't help but follow the trail of it, journeying down to her broad shoulders, tracing the curve of her chest.

"You shouldn't smile like that. It's false advertising," she chides.

My gaze snaps up, my expression instantly scowling. *God, she's infuriating.* My lips press into a tight line as I narrow my eyes.

Her smirk only deepens.

"Attagirl." She winks, pushing off and skating away.

Yeah, she *would* be breathtaking. But I'm breathing just fine.

Just. Fine.

SIX

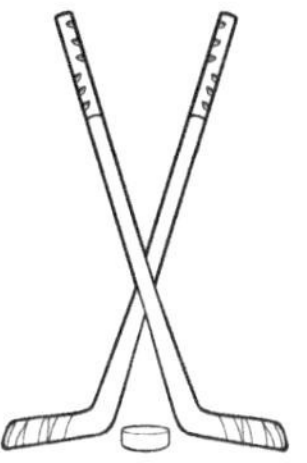

Peyton

I KNOW MOST PEOPLE hate it, but I love living on the third floor. The view is better, a snow-dusted Mount Rainier creeping above the skyline like a Seattle postcard. It's quieter too, mostly because *we're* the noisy neighbors up top, and most thieves aren't motivated enough for heavy cardio, so the likelihood of getting robbed is slim.

It has its downsides, though. When Bailey, Harlowe, and I first moved in, we had to drag this ancient sectional up three flights of stairs, to find out that it didn't fit through the doorway. Thankfully, Bailey had found it on the side of the road, so the loss was mostly time. It gets hot too, in the summer at least, and the window AC unit breeds mold at a rate that would impress rabbits. But the worst part about living on the third floor?

Mr. Bubbles.

Mr. Bubbles is the tawny English Mastiff that we found last winter, tied up outside a bar we tried—and failed—to sneak into. He was young, skinny, trembling in the snow while his human sat inside, sipping cheap beer by the warmth of the bar's heater. We sat with him for at least thirty minutes, trying to comfort him the best we could, and Harlowe even wrapped her coat around him to shield him from the cold. But after another three minutes, we realized we couldn't leave him there. So we slipped the collar over his head and booked it.

I'd say he has a pretty good life now. Ever since he started therapy dog training, the school lets him come to practices—and sometimes games—as our unofficial team companion, which makes our social media manager's life pretty easy. He eats better than we do, wears drool bibs on the daily, and even has an entire wardrobe for different occasions, including pajamas that Bailey swears he likes.

There are only two things Mr. Bubbles can't stand:

1) Green beans

and

2) The sound of footsteps up the stairs

So a couple mornings a week, I have to sneak back in without setting him off. It's a game to him. He knows my routine by heart, even walks me to the door when I leave. But when I come back? The slightest creak of the floor, the softest whisper of a footstep, and he's belting out a symphony of low, husky barks.

The front door cracks open, the old hinges threatening to squeak, but I slip through before they have the chance. A slow exhale tumbles from my lips as the heat of the apartment envelops me, the start of the pink sunrise peering through the window. My weight shifts onto the tips of my toes as I latch the door behind me and step onto the plush carpet, my feet sinking into it like sand.

Listening for the low grumbles of Mr. Bubbles, I pause, but the only sound is the fan from Harlowe's room, buzzing quietly. I take another step. Nothing. Then another. And just as I reach out for the doorknob to my room, a thundering roar cuts through the apartment.

Shit.

"Bubbles!" I hiss, whipping around to look at him. The one-hundred-dred-and-thirty-pound puppy curls his smooshy, drooly lips, and barks once more to spite me. I snap my fingers, pointing at him with a serious look, which was a mistake, because like I said, this is a game, and I've lost it. He billows again, this time sitting at my feet and howling like a tattling toddler.

"*Mister!*" Harlowe calls, her voice dragging a bit on the "s".

Oh fuck.

Her stomping footsteps approach quickly, and I have no time to throw myself into my room before she swings open her door, greeting me with furrowed brows, pouty downturned lips, and flared nostrils.

Like Mr. Bubbles, there are two things that piss Harlowe off:

1) Missing a save on the ice

and

2) Being woken up

And her goalie gear is tucked safely into the trunk of my Outback right now, so when Mr. Bubbles continues his baritone concert right in front of her tired face, I know I'm fucked.

"What the hell, Pey?" she snaps, voice like rough gravel, round cheeks reddening. I force a sheepish grin.

"Sorry. Mr. Bubbles just—"

"Peyton," she cuts in before I can finish, sticking a hand into the air. "You knew he was going to do this. It's four in the morning." Her ocean blue eyes dart up, narrowing onto mine. *"Four. In. The. Morning.* Can't you sneak in practices *before* we all go to bed?"

Mr. Bubbles, without a care in the world, trots over to her, ears perked and tail wagging. She scratches the top of his wrinkled head, allowing a gentle smile to tug at her lips, until she catches sight of me and scowls again.

"The rink is in use until seven." I shrug, still giving her an apologetic look. "And then there's homework, dinner, Mr. Bubbles' walk—"

"What's going on?" My gaze flicks to Bailey, looming in her doorway. The cream-colored nightgown she's wearing makes her look like a Victorian ghost, one hand rubbing at her eyes as she stares at the chaos unfolding.

"Peyton's doing early practices again," Harlowe answers, crossing her arms. Her fine, blonde hair sticks up in every direction, striped sleep shorts hugging her plush hips, and I want to tell my best friend how cute she is, but she'd probably bite my head off right now.

Bailey frowns, casting me a disapproving look. "You were out *again*?"

Here we go.

Bailey and Harlowe have been my best friends, and teammates, since we were four. We all grew up in the same small town, Greenrock Valley, Washington, went to the same schools, and somehow, all made it onto the D1 team for Greenrock University. Fate, talent, or maybe just a severe shortage of women's hockey players, I'm not sure. All I know is that, since we were kids, we've all followed the same path: going pro.

What I think they don't get is that "going pro" is different for me than it is for them. For them, it's a dream. A goal they've worked toward their whole lives, something challenging but no doubt within reach, as long as they keep putting in the work. But for me? For me, it's expected. Of course, the daughter of retired NHL star Harrison Clarke is going to go pro. It's almost a rite of passage.

But here's the thing: I don't want to get into the big leagues because of my dad. I want to make it because I'm good. And judging by the fact that I didn't get drafted this past summer, I'm not there yet.

Hence the early morning practices, and the hyper-persistence audiobooks. Bailey and Harlowe think it's excessive, but they have no idea what it's like to live under this kind of pressure.

"I couldn't sleep." I shrug. My friends exchange a glance, one I'm not particularly keen on, then Harlowe levels me with a satirical look.

"Really?" she asks, head tilting condescendingly. "That's so weird, because *I* was actually sleeping great until—"

"I'm going to make breakfast," Bailey interrupts, swooping past us in a flurry of long alabaster legs, and black box-dyed hair. She glances at us over her shoulder, a silent plea to stop bickering and follow her.

I sigh. "Alright, I'm coming." I look to Harlowe, who's still boasting a displeased expression. We stand there in silent debate, her threatening to whirl around and go back to sleep, and me pleading with her to humor Bailey, so that we can avoid hurting her feelings.

Bailey's pretty sensitive. Not in a "can't take criticism" way, but more of a "automatically assumes the worst" way. She'll never make a spectacle of it. She'll just hold it in with a smile, until suddenly, she's an isolated ball of tears, doubt, and hyperventilation.

Harlowe breaks. "Fine," she grunts. "But you owe me a coffee before practice."

We follow Bailey to the kitchen, hopping up onto the bar stools as she pulls out a hefty tray of eggs. I'd offer to help, but the only mean bone in Bailey's body seems to be activated when someone comes in the kitchen while she's cooking. So instead, I pull out my phone, mindlessly scrolling with one hand, while the other scratches behind Mr. Bubbles' ears.

"Protein pancakes or protein smoothies?" Bailey asks, seamlessly cracking open one egg in each hand and dropping them into the pan. It sizzles as she reaches for another pair, doing the same with them in a practiced technique. On the weekends, Bailey's a line cook at the Puget Diner, a restaurant around the corner from campus. Sometimes when we're bored, Harlowe and I will hang out in the back booth and yell out recipe ideas. If other people are dining, the owner will chew us out, but when it's just us, Gerald always gives us hot cocoa on the house.

"Mmm pancakes please," Harlowe answers, propping her elbow onto the counter and sinking her chin into the crevice of her palm. "With my seasoni—"

"With your seasoning," Bailey cuts in. "Got it Yersie"

There isn't a single food on this planet that Harlowe Ayers doesn't add Everything Bagel seasoning to. Eggs, pancakes, lasagna, cannolis. She even brings a bottle with her on away games. I'm not saying it's a problem, but restaurants across the region have questions.

Those blue eyes fix on me, light lashes flickering as she lets out a reluctant, "Sorry for chewing you out, Pey."

I can't fight the teasing smile tugging at my lips. "And the Queen pardons!" I gasp. She flips her middle finger into the air.

"Fuck off."

Bailey turns to us, holding up a bag of chocolate chips in one hand and dehydrated strawberries in the other. She wriggles them back and forth in a wordless question, brows chasing the movement. I point to the strawberries, and she turns back to the stove.

"Peyton?" Bailey asks, her voice light and curious.

I smile at her. "Bailey?"

"Did you see any ghosts when you were at the rink?"

She blinks at me slowly, her doe-like brown eyes glimmering. When Bailey's not flipping burgers at the diner, defending the forwards with her life, or playing a roleplaying game that takes too much creativity for me to understand, she's researching—in deep detail—how to be medium. And the presumed ghost haunting Greenrock University is her first subject.

I shake my head, flashing her a sorrowed look. "Sorry, Hams. No ghost."

She lets out a soft sigh, turning back to the stove. "I'll have to look for her at practice then."

Harlowe erupts with a booming laugh. "The only ghost you're going to see at practice is Peyton when Darcy gets her hands on her."

I frown, crossing my arms. "Funny."

She shrugs. "I know."

"I still don't understand why you hate each other," Bailey cuts in, the pan sizzling beside her as she flips over a perfectly browned pancake. Harlowe grins.

"Because Peyton's a try-hard," she taunts, and I stick my middle finger up right in front of her nose.

"I don't hate her," I correct. "But she *does* act like she's God's gift to hockey. I mean, she literally said it herself. She only played when she was young. Then she strolls in, guns blazing, whistle blowing like she's some sort of expert?"

Harlowe hums, which is something she does on the rare occasion she chooses to bite her tongue. Surprisingly, Bailey doesn't hesitate to fire back.

"Love you so much, Pey," she begins, and I can already feel the sweet burn coming. "But maybe she *is?* I mean, her mom's a professional coach. You of all people should know how much influence a parent has on their kid. Sounded like she knew what she was talking about to me."

My stomach sinks as the words set in, and I slump back in my seat. Darcy *did* sound like she knew what she was talking about. Maybe she just threw out enough hockey jargon and got lucky. But the play she called... it made sense. Too much sense for someone who gave it up so quickly.

"Yeah, that was some pretty good advice," Harlowe chimes. I shoot her a betrayed look, and she shrugs. "What? You'll always be my number one."

"I know you guys think I'm crazy," I say. "But there's something off about her. And I'm going to figure out what it is."

SEVEN

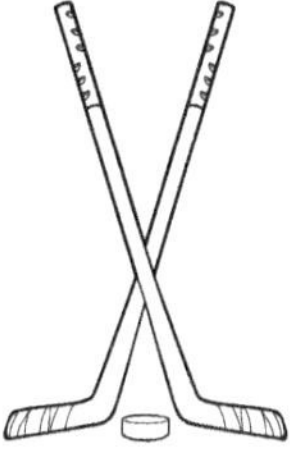

Peyton

FINAL CHAT FR THIS TIME

Tell him I'm still in love with him.

Not happening Hams.

:(

You know, we'd probably get more eyes on us if he showed up to the games this year.

Hammie disliked Cay's message

What? It's true.

Well yeah but you're not supposed to say it.

Yeah dude. Not cool.

All I'm saying is what's the point of nepotism if you won't put it to good use?

Browne has left the chat

You have added Browne to the chat

You have changed Browne's nickname to Rose

T HERE'S NO BETTER AROMA than the smell of an ice rink. It's a faint, almost stale scent, crisp air and sweat and rubber. One of my favorite things about playing hockey is that the ice always smells the same, from the first time I stepped on it at two years old to now, as a college junior.

I'm here early, as usual, stretching my limbs out in the cold while the rest of the team trickles in. My skates chip the ice as I hold myself in a plank position, rolling my hips in slow circles. Good thing I practiced solo this morning, because my body was practically cement from staying posted on the couch over the weekend. Bailey, Harlowe, and I spent both evenings in heated debate over whether indie rock sensation Atticus Amelie is hot, or just tall.

I don't know how the results were inconclusive, seeing as there's an odd number of us, but it happened. I didn't even care about the stupid argument, I was just grateful for the distraction.

But now it's Monday, and everything feels... *off*.

The rink smells different, the air is too thin, and the hype playlist I made, titled *Puckin' Vibe*, seems to have been replaced by... *pop*. I like pop, sure, but usually in the context of my car, when I'm stuck in traffic and pretending to be in a 2000's chick flick. On the ice? I need something invigorating. Something that makes my feet hit the ice like I could shatter it with only my blades.

I want to shake the rink like my dad, not float through it.

I exhale, stretching to the sound of Britney Spears, breath visible against the ice as my mind travels to the entire force behind my need for a distraction. The vexing and masochistic force being Darcy, of course.

We left off on bad terms, *again*. Darcy clearly thinks this is a game you can plot, and she's insufferably confident in that assumption. Granted, I didn't exactly help the case.

But everything, my entire career, depends on how well this team can come together.

Kendall graduating last year left a sizable dent in our defense, and if the new-recruits don't fill it, we'll never get past the final round of the LNHL (Lakeshore Northwest Hockey League) conference championship. Not that we ever have before, but this year, I'm determined to change that. Recruiters from the Sabertooths have been at the LNHL finals two years running, and both times they've drafted straight from the winners.

I want us there. I want a shot. At the NCAA championship. At the Women's Frozen Four. At the Sabertooths.

And there is no way am I going to let some green-eyed, off-the-ice student-coach, who has no clue what it means to bleed for this game, get in my way.

Coach's voice cuts through the air, the rest of the team tumbling onto the ice at her instruction.

"Clarke, lead warm-ups. When I get back, we'll do drills." She casts a trusting glance in my direction, and I pull myself to my feet, nodding. "I have to go take care of something."

"Yes, Coach."

I school my expression into stillness, even as my stomach knots itself. After last week, she pulled me aside and tore into me for letting the team show up hungover. I'd stood there, nodding, taking it, because... well, I deserved it. I am the Captain. It is my responsibility.

The silence that follows stretches through the rink, a quiet so deafening my ears begin to ring, as everyone around me waits. I was voted Captain during training camp, but honestly, I think it's just because everyone sees someone in me that I'm not sure is really there. While skating has been second nature to me for as long as I can remember, leading the team still feels like foreign territory.

My brother Avery once told me that herding dogs are born with the instinct to gather, to guide. But that doesn't mean they know how to do it right away. They have to learn when to run, when to stop, when to turn. Without training, they might just sprint in circles, biting ankles, confused by the very drive that's supposed to define them. I wonder if that's me right now, standing at center ice with my team behind me. Feeling the instinct but not yet knowing what to do with it.

I try to shake it off, to push the uncertainty aside, but as I turn to face my team, my eyes get caught on her, like skates snagged on chipped ice. My body freezes, but it feels like I'm jolting forward, tumbling to the ground, so that my palms meet the ice in a skin-scraping, heart-stuttering slip. Darcy is sitting in the stands, pen tucked behind her ear, completely absorbed in that *damn* clipboard again. Her brow furrows as she draws her arm up to her face, swiping the pen into her hand and scribbling something down, lost in her own world of ink and paper, with no idea that I'm watching.

I can't believe she had the audacity to claim I treat hockey like a joke, when she spends more time staring at that clipboard than she does the ice.

"Uh, Cap?"

My gaze snaps to Indie, who's using her stick like a table, chin propped upon it as her hazel eyes stare out. *Jesus, this kid needs work.* I clear my throat, gloved hands tightening around the faded blend of yellow, blue, and pink tape on my stick, before I smack it to the ground in one, swift clap.

"Alright, team, listen up!" Everything feels like it's shaking: my breath, my voice, my hands. But when I glance down, my stick is steady as ever. So I inhale, let the air fill me up, then exhale slowly, hoping to smooth out the tremor inside me. "Get down. We're gonna stretch."

My teammates drop to the ice without hesitation, then stare at me expectantly. It's a strange thing, being the center of attention. Anywhere else, I don't mind it. Screaming at football games, dancing on tables at parties with Bailey, laughing a little too hard at the theater majors' plays just to make sure they know someone's paying attention.

But here, on the ice?

The rink, usually so full of noise and urgency, feels quiet with the expectation that I know exactly what I'm doing.

But I'm just D1, like the rest of them. I haven't proven to be anything more.

I swallow, the uncertainty curdling in my stomach, and I reach for something in my chest, something that can convince them the "C" clinging to my jersey is where it belongs. The word comes out, but it's softer than I want it to be, reminding me that I'm still trying to convince myself too.

"Lunges," I say, hoping it's enough.

M Y MUSCLES FEEL PLIABLE now, not like the stiff limbs I woke up with, and when Coach strolls back into the arena, the team is prepared. She claps her hands, the short *pop* echoing off the plexiglass.

"Clarke, Browne," Coach says, glancing at Indie and me. Indie swallows hard, and I can see the anxiety building inside of her, brick by brick. "You're together. Cunningham, Simmons, you too. Pioneer two-v-twos, let's go."

Faith Simmons, the first-year right-winger, doesn't hesitate. She pulls her helmet over her French braids, posture snapping straight as she glides to the opposite corner of the ice. Indie, on the other hand, just swallows again.

I give her an assuring nod.

"Helmet on, Rose. Let's do this."

Indie pulls her helmet over her head. I know she's got more in her than she lets on—otherwise, she wouldn't be here. But damn, she's so good at hiding it. Indie crosses the ice, finding her spot opposite Faith.

Bailey elbows me as we make our way to our corners.

"Your ass is grass, Cap," she taunts, smacking the side of her helmet.

I grin. "Yeah. And you have allergies."

"I need some goalies out here!" Coach calls. Zayda skates over to one of the goalposts without missing a beat, but Harlowe's too busy vibing to the music blaring around the rink to hear.

Also, her eyelids are flipped inside out. Two plump pink lines of flesh sitting over river blue gems that have to be as dry as the *Sahara*.

"Whoever picked the music today," she starts, pausing to mime a chef's kiss.

I roll my eyes, but before I can defend *my* playlist, Coach is already on her like a ref on a foul.

"Ayers, get your ass in line!"

Harlowe spins around, cheeks flushed, eyes wide. "Yes, Coach."

She fixes her eyelids and slides over to the other goalpost, getting into position just as Coach draws the whistle to her lips. The whistle blows, Hammie pushes off the ice, and I pass the puck to her. I skate hard, closing in on her as she stickhandles through the neutral zone, trying to break past me. When she passes the blue line, she spins around to attack, but I'm not making it easy. I'm on her like a shadow, granting her no room to shoot.

She takes a quick look for an opening, but I'm blocking her options. When she cuts to the left, I mirror every step ruthlessly, eyes narrowed, powder flying behind us.

I don't mean to take my eyes off the ice. I almost never do. But in my periphery, I see a wave of red in the stands, and just for a second, I glance up.

Darcy's eyes are on me, an intense, emerald stare watching with expectant anticipation, as if she already knows my next move but wants to see it for herself. *Good. She's watching.* I look back to the drill, her gaze burning through the top of my skull as I skate.

Her snide voice echoes in my mind: *This sport isn't a joke, Captain.*

A joke? I'll show her that to me, it's anything but.

The second whistle blows.

"Simmons, Browne!" Coach calls.

We spin around, skating toward the other end of the ice, while Indie and Faith push off, taking the puck from their end and continuing the drill. Indie dodges Faith as she bolts toward the goalpost.

I race to shield her, but Hammie slips in front of me, blocking me so that Faith can wrestle the puck away from Indie. I glance over to my teammate. She's hesitating, handling the puck but hardly making an effort to get around.

Did they recruit the wrong Indigo Browne?

"Rose!" I call out, trying to get her moving. "Get in there!"

With that, she finally perks up, pushing off the ice to whip around Faith. She tries to pass, but it's too soft, too slow. Hammie's all over it. I can see her coming, ready to intercept, and I sprint to get in position. The puck squirts out, and I scoop it up, the wind slapping my face as I glide toward the goal. My stick is heavy in my hands, the worn tape grounding me as I push past.

Each stride I take is measured, each breath sharper, time slowing as my focus narrows to the tiny sliver of space between Harlowe's legs. My eyes lock onto it, heart thudding against my chest. It's the sweet spot. The moment where everything aligns, ready to shoot.

And then, that *fucking* voice.

"Hey, Cap!" Darcy calls from the bench, that irritatingly assured tone rolling off my skin.

I don't stop skating, but the moment is gone, Faith moving in and blocking my shot. I don't look up. I just push my way around her, blazing past only to be closed in on by Hammie.

"Pass it!" Darcy continues, like my lack of response is her encouragement.

My gaze flicks to Indie, who's gripping her stick like she's scared to drop it. "She *just* passed it," I call back, forcing my voice to stay level. "We've hardly attacked."

Coach blows the whistle, a long, sharp tone to punctuate my point.

"Alright, alright, *enough!* Come here, Clarke. Then we'll run it again."

I glide toward Coach, irritation singeing my chest from the inside out. Darcy's climbed down from the stands, posting beside her with that stupid clipboard. She's in that same black turtleneck, the one that hugs her chest and dips at her waist. Bailey calls it the "slutty-villain effect." Like when an anime guy has that perfect little waist, and you just *know* he's pure evil.

Yeah, I'm pretty sure *this* is what she was talking about.

"You're forcing plays instead of reading them. You had an opening for a pass, but you didn't take it. You're not the only player who can score," Darcy shoots.

My jaw tenses, and I fire back before I can think better of it. "So Friday you wanted me to follow the plan, but today you want me to abandon it? I was *going to* shoot."

Darcy raises a challenging brow. "So, your plan was *what?* Barrel in and hope for the best? That was a clear pass."

"It was a clear *goal*," I say, trying my hardest to keep my tone steady. "It's called taking a risk. I thought you liked those."

"It's *called* being reckless. You can't just do what you want with no plan, and call that a risk. You have no calculations, no backup."

I huff a laugh, shaking my head, and whatever self-control I had moments ago has completely disintegrated. "Right. Is that what they taught you in—what was it?—second grade?"

Before Darcy can fire back, Coach cuts in, her tone edged with finality. "She's right, Clarke."

You've *got* to be—

"We didn't even get to—"

Coach Cole sticks her hand in the air, cutting me off, though she's more polite about it than Darcy. "You're more focused on scoring than communicating.

This is a *team* effort."

I swallow, blood rushing to my cheeks, my nose, and the tips of my goddamn ears.

"It's hard to communicate when she—"

"Sorry, I'm talking to the *Captain*, right?"

Heat crawls up the back of my neck as an intense pressure settles in my chest. I've always known the significance of this title, the responsibility it carries. But right now, standing here, it feels even more suffocating. I've already screwed it up. The hungover teammates, the slip of my words. I don't need anyone to remind me that I've let the team down. I'm already living with the bitter taste of failure, choking on it with every breath.

I wonder if my dad ever made a fool of himself as Captain like this. Probably not. That title suited him. The C on his jersey always looked like it belonged there, like it had been carved into him.

Unlike me.

I nod, jaw clenching. "Yes, Coach."

"Then act like it. If Browne is struggling to find her place, it's up to you to guide her. Got it?"

I nod again, the taste of metal flooding my tongue as I gnaw the inside of my cheek raw. She's right, of course. I'm failing. I know it.

Coach sighs, her stance softening just slightly. But it feels like a concession I don't deserve. "Look. I know this is your team as much as it is mine. We have the same goal, alright?"

It's not you I'm worried about.

It's unintentional, against my will, but my gaze flashes to Darcy. I correct it the moment I focus on her stupidly thick red lashes, but Coach clearly catches me, clearing her throat and straightening her posture.

"Darcy knows what she's talking about, Clarke. She's here to help, not step on your toes."

"*Paula.*" A loud sigh tumbles from Darcy's freckled lips, her tongue scraping across them as she dips her head into her hands. "Just—"

Coach looks back to me, waving her hand in a dismissive gesture, bringing her silver whistle to her lips.

"Alright," she says. "Get back to it, Captain."

So I do.

EIGHT

Darcy

"**Y**OU'RE DOING IT AGAIN," my mom's voice hums softly. My eyes flick up, and I quickly tuck my clipboard against my body. I don't want her to see what I've been working on. Not yet.

A frown tugs at the corners of my lips, and I lift my chin to meet her gaze. "Doing what?" Mom props a hand on her hip, narrowing her eyes. I roll mine, exhaling loudly. "You're the one who signed me up for this. Am I supposed to coach or not?"

"You're *supposed* to support the team," she says, her tone warm but firm. The *Paula Cole Specialty.* She slides onto the bench beside me, the soft squeak of the cold plastic harmonizing with the slap of pucks against sticks. I turn my gaze to the rink, letting the blur of bodies and the crisp, artificial chill in the air occupy me.

"Feedback is support," I mutter.

Mom nudges her shoulder into mine. "Darcy, you're a student coach. And as a student coach, criticism needs to be—"

"—softer, I know," I finish for her, sighing dramatically. Our eyes lock, and the words spill out in an irritated, defeated breath. "I'm sorry. She's just *so...*" My jaw clenches, the scrape of my teeth rattling my skull. "*Arrogant.*"

"Oh?" Mom raises her brows, surprised at first, then softens her expression.

I search her face for any sign that she's messing with me, but her eyes meet mine with genuine curiosity. "What? You don't see it?"

She shrugs nonchalantly and glances back toward the ice. I follow her gaze, landing on that *stupid* number 11.

I'd never say it out loud. Even thinking it feels like a betrayal. But Peyton's magnetic. It's still not the way she skated alone that morning, but somehow the rink bends around her just the same, and even the puck seems to follow her lead. Her green jersey lays flush against her body as she glides, hair in a loose bun that sways with every shift. If she wasn't so thoughtless, if she bothered to consider what she stood to lose with those endless solo practices and dumb frat parties, she could easily land a spot on any team she wanted, given she learn how to work as a *unit*. But she doesn't—so she won't.

Mom clicks her tongue thoughtfully. "I see a lot of *you*, actually."

An offended scoff tumbles out of me. "*Really?* You mean the blatant cockiness, or the obvious disregard for the rules?"

"You had that same drive, Darcy," she answers. "Same passion."

"I was more careful," I mumble, eyes fixed on the rink. "I didn't throw away my spot for a stupid party or—"

I catch myself almost exposing Peyton's morning practices. Maybe I should. I mean, if she keeps it up, she's going to hurt herself. Not to mention she's breaking school policy. Still, for some inexplicable reason, I can't bring myself to tattle. So I just snap my jaw shut.

"Maybe," she says. "But you had a coach as a mom. She's got a pro player for a dad. It's different."

"What's that supposed to mean?"

She shrugs. "Sometimes people aren't what they seem."

I frown, trying to make sense of it, but I can't. "Yeah, I don't get it."

Mom chuckles softly, a sound warm and familiar that lightens my chest. Her fingers move toward me, brushing the curve of my cheek as she tucks a stray lock of hair behind my ear. "Remember the first time we flew together? When we boarded that plane to Nashville?"

I groan, already regretting where this is headed. "Mom, please. Not now."

She's undeterred. "You looked like you didn't have a care in the world. You were excited, relaxed. It was like you'd done it a thousand times."

I shift uncomfortably in the hard plastic seat. "I don't remember."

She smiles a little, crossing her arms. "When we landed, I asked you how you felt. Do you remember what you said?"

"No." *Liar.*

"Terrified," she answers. "You told me you were terrified."

"Yeah, well, flying in a hunk of metal 30,000 feet in the air will do that to you," I chide, scanning the rink to avoid her eyes. I know where this is going, but I'm not biting. My mom's a coach, not some philosophical artist, and this isn't the picture she thinks it is. Peyton's not some terrified player weighed down by fear. She's someone with nothing to lose.

Or so she thinks.

"If she was so terrified," I mutter, narrowing my eyes, "she wouldn't be showing up hungover or arguing with the coach."

Mom raises a brow, lips twitching with a knowing smirk. "Oh, so you never argued with your coaches? Interesting. Because I *distinctly remember—*"

I raise my hand, cutting her off. "*Don't. Even.*"

She chuckles. I keep my focus on the rink.

"You two should talk, you know," she suggests casually.

I let out a dry laugh. "Yeah, that doesn't exactly seem to work out too well."

She just smiles, unfazed. "I think once you're on the same page, you might learn a lot from each other."

There's a lot I want to say, but instead, I just nod, keeping my eyes on the ice, watching 11 dance across it. I don't know how I'm supposed to be on the same page as Peyton when we're not even reading the same damn book.

As practice winds down, my mom's words repeat in my mind. The last few drills fizzle out, and I'm left staring at the ice, tracing the blur of Peyton's jersey. She moves across the rink like it's her world. Like nothing exists beyond the boards, and the chipped ice beneath her feet. It doesn't help that I can't look away, can't stop watching how she holds the game in her palm, molding it to her will. I try to ignore it, but it's impossible when she makes it all look so easy.

It's *not* easy. I of all people know that. But she's got this flow about her, something that creeps beneath the violent strides and heavy hand, that makes me wonder if she's always glided through life as if she's floating, or if it's the gift of her father's influence.

I shift in my seat, my grip on the clipboard tight enough to leave scallops on my fingertips. When the whistle blows, signaling the end of practice, I push myself off the bench. No matter how hard I tried to talk myself out of it, I don't want to be stuck in this stupid dispute all season.

Peyton steps off the ice, sweat-soaked hair clinging to her flushed cheeks, strands escaping the messy bun at the nape of her neck. Her bright amber eyes dart toward the ground as she drops onto the bench, muscles rippling under the sleeves of her jersey. There's a sheen to her skin, a bead of sweat slipping down the curve of her temple, catching against the dark lashes framing her eyes. My pace quickens, fumbling a bit as I approach, my pulse ticking up for no reason at all.

"Peyton, can we talk for a sec?" I call out, trying my hardest to sound innocuous.

Tugging at her skate's chartreuse laces, Peyton's head tips back to meet my gaze, hooded eyes squinting.

"Do I have a choice?" Her tone is playful, but that full-lipped grin sewn into her cheeks gives it away. *Mocking.*

"...Yes?" I reply.

She shrugs, glancing away and grabbing her water bottle, squirting a stream of water into her mouth. I shouldn't notice the way her neck tenses as she swallows. In fact, I don't.

"Pass, then."

My expression curdles, stepping in front of her and crossing my arms. This ends *now*. "Okay, I lied. *No.*"

She shrugs the worn strap of her duffel bag over her shoulder, pushing herself to her feet.

"Well, that's deceptive," she says, that cocksure grin deepening. "If this is about the 'no fun' rule, I think I got the message." She lifts a hand to her brow in a mock salute. "Copy that, Kim Possible."

A curt, annoyed chuckle slips out of me as I step closer, shoving my hands in my pockets. My gloves make it a tight squeeze, and I'm pretty sure I'm cutting off circulation to my fingers, but at this point, what's a little more discomfort?

"I—" I start, but she cuts me off. Her brows weave, button nose scrunching to form rosy rays on the bridge. A short, pointed finger jabs against my sternum.

"What is that?" she asks.

I glance down, just a millisecond too late to realize what an idiot I am. Before I can spare myself the embarrassment, her finger draws up, hitting me square on the nose. An arrogant grin breaks over her face, and without another word, she spins and heads toward the locker room.

I want to lose it. Demand an ounce of professionalism. Remind her who's the coach and who's the player. But if I'm going to get on her good side, or at the very least, get off her hit list, I need to keep my focus on resolving this. On making peace.

I take a steadying breath, watching her solid body sway as she marches forward.

"Look, I'm sorry if you felt like I was stepping on your toes back there," I call out. Peyton stops.

Good. This is good.

Her head turns slightly as she casts a glance over her shoulder.

"Oh, it's fine," she chimes sarcastically. "You didn't step on them. You practically cut them off. So..." She shrugs, turning back toward the locker room. "All good."

Before she can take another step, I jog forward. A hot throb pounds in my knees each time the soles of my arthritic loafers hit the concrete, but I don't stop. "Okay, hold on." Peyton begins to walk away, and before I know it, the damp sleeve of her jersey is gripped in my hand. The moment I touch the sweaty fabric, her muscles stiffen. I quickly let go. "I really didn't mean to—"

She spins around, those amber eyes burning.

"And yet, you did," she fires back. Her volume stays the same, but the cutting edge in her tone makes it feel as if she's yelling "You called me out in front of the team, like I didn't know what I was doing. Not the greatest look for a first-year captain, is it? I had a plan."

I need to calm down. Breathe. Keep my eye on the prize: surviving this season without pulling out my hair. But then I see Peyton's jaw tighten, her posture shifting like she's waiting for me to back down. Like she *expects* me to. Part of me thinks I should let it go, for the sake of my sanity. But then what? She'll just keep brushing me off, ignoring my input, making sure no one takes me seriously.

I don't like failing at things. Frankly, I'm a really sore loser. Board games, hockey games, tests—I refuse to fail at this too.

"You think I wanted to embarrass you?" I say instead, cursing myself for being so stubborn. "I'm just trying to do my job. You're the captain, sure, but you're not the only one who knows what's going on out there."

Solid apology, Darcy.

I stare at her, lips pressed in a flat line, but she steps forward anyway, closing the space between us. Close enough that I can feel the heat rolling off her skin, smell the jarring contrast of her sweat and lavender perfume. Close enough that when she exhales, the warm brush of her breath ghosts over my lips, sending a shiver down my spine that I refuse to acknowledge. Our chests press together, and the damp heat of her jersey soaks into my sweater, reminding me of that morning. Of the way we hid, bickering behind the stadium seats. My breath catches, just for a second, but I don't move.

Neither does she

"Yeah?" she murmurs finally, voice lower now. Rougher. "Well, maybe if you paid attention instead of staring at a piece of paper the whole time, you'd know what was actually going on." I can feel the enunciation of each word against my lips. Her mouth curls, and she tilts her head condescendingly. "You think I'm some rookie who needs a lecture from you? From the person who *quit?*"

With that, something inside me sparks, small at first, then blooming into a flame that consumes everything in its path. The fire is ravenous, flames licking at my chest, rising faster, hotter, until it engulfs every mature thought, charring it to dust. My mouth opens, words forming, but before they can escape, before the fire can leave my tongue, she turns around and storms away.

Fine.

I was already done.

Done with her condescending little mouth. Done with her belief that she's untouchable. And done trying to prove myself to someone who can't even see the silver platter their life was handed to them on.

I was totally, completely done.

I'M ALL FOR CHARITY—FOOD banks, animal shelters, hell, I even used to volunteer for a kids' hockey league. But there's a line, and the idea that Cleo thinks I'm pitiful enough to need volunteers for friends? Way, *way* past that line.

"I told you," she says, flipping through the mess of class notes sprawled across the floor. "I didn't recruit Bailey to be your friend."

"No, you just explained in vivid detail how lonely and friendless I am, until she felt so bad she had to take pity on me." I drop down beside her, peering at her notes. My nose wrinkles. "Is that—"

"A diagram of a human liver?" She sighs, eyes meeting mine with a deadpan look. "Yup."

I squint at the sketch, which looks like a cross between a slab of meat and a clogged drain. "And that's—"

"That's an obstructed bile duct," she confirms.

I nod, scratching the back of my head as Cleo slides the paper to the side with a sigh. Socks pads over, stepping on every last corner of her notes before curling up on top of them, the papers crinkling beneath his weight.

"Sorry." She smile sheepishly, flicking her gaze from the cat to me. "I wasn't trying to paint you as some lonely charity case."

I flash her a brief smile. *"Thanks."*

"I've just been worried about you," she continues. "Ever since you moved in, you've barely gone anywhere but class and practice. People need people." She pauses, drawing her gray eyes from my feet to the top of my head. Slowly, on purpose. "Even people who don't *like* people."

I trace the seam of my pants as I listen. I know Cleo's right. I know that isolating yourself, especially after losing something huge, is the worst thing you can do. But once you're comfortable in your own silence, the noise of other people can feel deafening. Threatening, even.

"I go out," I insist, but Cleo just stares at me.

"Going to dinner at your parents' house doesn't count as 'going out'." She curls her fingers into air quotes.

I frown. "I went to—"

"Doctor's appointments don't count either."

I toss my back against the base of the couch and huff. "Well, if you're going to put all these *stipulations* on it," I mumble, and Cleo lets out a soft laugh.

She sits up, grabbing her phone from her pocket and tapping at the screen. The soft clack of her nails fills the air before she holds it out to show me. It's a Halloween party flyer, all orange and purple, with little doggie ghosts decorating the sides.

I eye it for a second before looking up at her. "Yeah, I don't know about that," I say flatly.

Cleo's eyes narrow, expecting me to surrender. I don't.

"See, I'm more of a Christmas person, so—"

"Oh, come on," she groans, tossing her phone onto the floor beside us. "Don't you think it's time you did something? Like..." She eyes me up and down with that same judgmental look Socks gives me when I say the word "no". *"Anything?"*

I sigh again, glancing over at the cat, who's lounging on the notes like a king on a throne. Maybe he's got the right idea. Cats don't need friends. If they don't get along with other cats, people just call them independent and feed them kitty

Chex Mix while they bask in the sun. They don't get dragged to parties or told that they "need other cats."

"Come on. My friends will love you." Cleo grins. "And I'll do the dishes for a week."

She sings the last few words like we ever have dishes to clean, and I can't help but smile, even though I don't want to. Maybe Cleo's right. It would be nice to go somewhere besides my parents' house once a week. It would be nice to actually *have* fun. But I'm not sure if that's even possible anymore. Every memory of being happy, especially with other people, just feels... tainted now.

I chew the inside of my cheek, wrestling with the decision. Cleo slips her hand into mine, her fingers warmer, even through my gloves. She squeezes gently.

"I won't make you," she says, quieter now. "But I think it'd be good for you."

My stomach twists, an ache throbbing at the base of my throat. The voices in my head remind me of what happened last time I had friends—the way it all fell apart. But when I look at Cleo, all I see is her. And, for the first time in a long while, I want to believe it could be different.

I tilt my head against hers, letting my eyes fall shut for a second. "I don't have anything to wear."

NINE

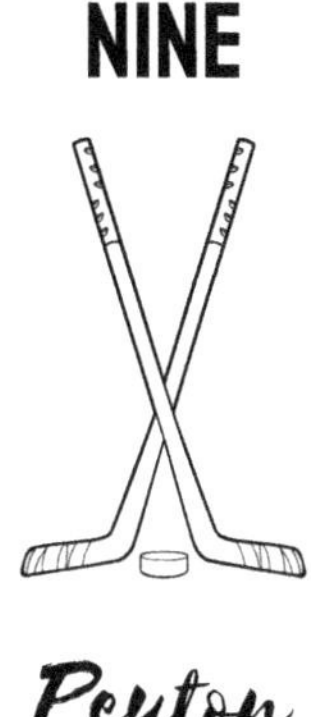

Peyton

FINAL CHAT FR THIS TIME

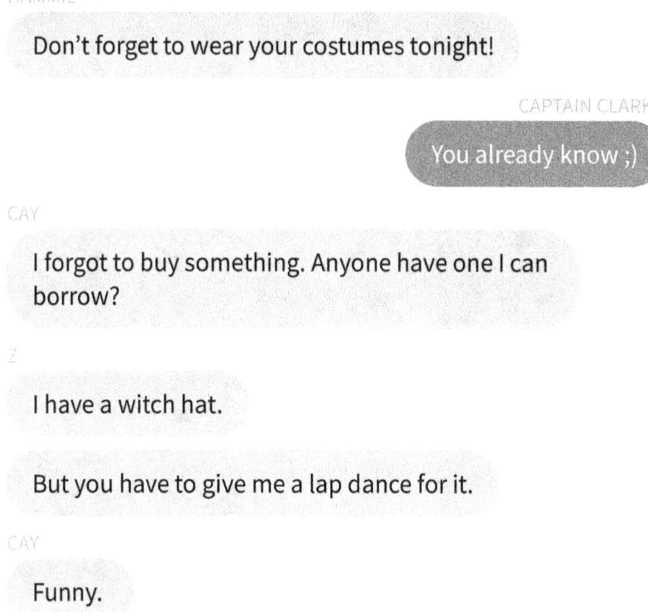

YERSIE

I just want everyone to know that the costume rule was not set by me and I don't actually give a fuck if you wear one or not.

BRADY

Dude. Hammie made it sound like it was life or death.

SIMS BUT NOT THE GAME

I'm not even going.

BRADY

WHAT

SIMS BUT NOT THE GAME

I have homework.

CAPTAIN CLARKE

Yeah, I'm supposed to be going to a fundraiser at the GG in the morning. So… we'll see how that goes.

Z

Lena, let's not pretend you didn't already have all that pink cheetah print in your closet.

BRADY

It's the principle.

HAMMIE

I thought we could all use a little Halloween spirit. Besides, it will be fun seeing everyone dressed up.

CAPTAIN CLARKE

Who's "everyone?"

I DON'T KNOW EXACTLY how this happened, but I'm pretty sure our apartment is violating multiple fire codes. We're lucky this is a student complex, because if our neighbors weren't already here, they'd probably be calling the cops. This was supposed to be a small thing, just a little Halloween-themed get-together for Harlowe's birthday, but that's what I get for leaving Bailey in charge of the invitations.

I weave through the sea of bodies, my Sprite sloshing precariously over the edge of my plastic cup as I spin, duck, and contort my body in ways I didn't even know were possible. The living room is a pressure cooker, jammed to capacity with people from every imaginable corner of the university.

Bodies spill out onto the overloaded balcony, art students leaning over the railing, their voices cutting through the bass-heavy music as they hurl drunken banter down to someone in the parking lot. I pass a group from my econ class taking shots, before squeezing past some guys from the men's hockey team. They all clap me on the back, knuckles rapping against my cardboard turtle shell, whooping and hollering.

"Sick party, Leonardo," one of them says, tipping his cup against mine. I'm pretty sure some of his beer spills into my drink, but I just grin back at him.

"Thanks, Kai."

I scan the crowd, intent on locating my posse. Lena and Z are playing DJ, letting the vodka dictate the playlist. By the television, Caydence is clutching a cup of something that could violate all ten commandments, staring at Will Carter. I spot Bailey—masquerading as Michelangelo—standing on our coffee table, shaking her ass to *The Monster Mash*. Her orange mask slips as her head tips back, a loud, drunken laugh spilling out as she yanks Rowan, one of the baristas at the Grizzly Grind, up from the crowd. That table is one misstep from total collapse, but she looks so happy, I don't want to ruin her fun.

Her round brown eyes lock onto mine, hands waving frantically like two people on a rickety table isn't already a recipe for disaster. I shake my head, shouting over the music: "You break it, you buy it!"

She shrugs and salutes me. I chuckle, roll my eyes, and spin toward the kitchen—or what *used* to be my kitchen. I don't know where the big plastic foldable table came from, but it's eaten up the entire space while Harlowe dominates a 1v3 beer pong match against a group of football players. She looks like she wants to murder them, but judging by the sailor hat she's traded for her red Raphael mask, she's actually flirting.

Which just leaves... Indie. *Shit. Where* is Indie? I scan the room, searching for her. After practice the other day, Coach and I had a heart-to-heart that led to the painfully obvious conclusion that Indie's struggling to find her rhythm, both on the team and off it. She's still figuring out how to balance everything, the pressure of college life and trying to make her mark on the ice. And it's my job as captain to help her.

Which is why she's here in the first place. I figured it would be good for her to get out, spend some time on campus, mingle outside the plexiglass of the rink. And yeah, I know Coach just chewed us out about coming to practice hungover, but we don't have to meet again for two days.

And besides, she didn't say we couldn't party—just that we couldn't drink.

I was supposed to keep a close eye on Indie, to make sure that didn't happen, but I've been too busy making sure nobody puts holes in the walls or bypasses the "do not enter sign" for Bailey's bedroom, where Mr. Bubbles is sleeping peacefully, blissfully unaware of the chaos outside.

"Fuck me," I mutter, stretching my neck to look over the crowd. What if she's drunk? What if she's somewhere getting crushed in this mob? "Indie!" I call, my tone edging toward panic.

And then, finally, I spot her. Pressed against the wall in full Donatello gear, her cardboard shell flattened like roadkill. She watches the party unfolding in front of her, gripping a can of sparkling water.

I nudge my way over, throwing an arm around her shoulder. "Jesus, Rose. I was about to send out a search party. You okay?"

Indie shifts uneasily, chewing on the corner of her lip, eyes darting toward the door like she might bolt. Her fingers twitch at her sides, and she shifts her weight from side to side.

"Are you sure I'm not intruding?" she asks, meeting me with a worried, hazel gaze. I chuckle softly, gesturing to the crowd. It's not like this is an *exclusive* event.

"Indie, half the people here are intruding," I joke. "You are *not* one of them." She laughs softly, tilting her head with a nervous smile.

"Yeah, I thought you said it was just going to be a *few* people."

I study the room. Theater students are in the corner, ranting about a casting disaster. To the left, the campus stoners—including my study buddy Cleo—are passing around what I'm pretty sure are weed-infused chocolates. And on the couch beside us, a couple is having a very emotional, drunken argument. I look back to Indie.

"I thought it was going to be."

She nods, gaze drifting to the scene. Her shoulders are stiff, arms nearly glued to her sides. Then, her brows furrow. "Do Ninja Turtles have butt cheeks?"

I blink. "What?"

She gestures vaguely to her costume. "Like, their shells normally cover their backs, right? So... do they have... *cheeks?*"

A laugh spills out of me. I tilt my head, genuinely considering the question, but I come up blank. "I'm not really sure," I answer. "Why do you ask?"

She extends an arm, sticking her finger out toward Bailey, who has tossed her cardboard shell aside, revealing her green corset, short shorts, and yes—green-painted butt cheeks. The paint was meant for our faces, but Indie was the only one willing to put it on with me. Harlowe refused completely, and Bailey, apparently, only used it to paint her ass.

I watch as Bailey and Rowan take turns pouring shots into each other's mouths. Jesus. I am *spectacularly* failing at my job.

"You know, I'm more concerned about the fact that she doesn't have her shell.

Don't turtles die without them?" a voice asks.

I turn to find Cleo slipping into our bubble of space, draped head-to-toe in green and black spandex. A matching neon barrette clips into her hair—pointless, really, since there's barely enough of it to hold back from her face, but it's Cleo, so it works.

She sweeps into an exaggerated bow. "Leonardo," she greets, then straightens and turns to Indie, mirroring the gesture. "Donatello."

Indie looks at me nervously, and I smile. "Hey, Cleo," I say.

"*Shego*, actually," she clarifies, snapping the tight green suit against her body.

I chuckle, turning to Indie. "Indie, this is Cleo. We study together sometimes. Cleo, this is Indie. One of our new players."

"No shit!" Cleo grins, pulling Indie into a hug without another thought. Indie flashes me a wide-eyed stare, and I grin apologetically. Cleo's the best. Seriously, I would not be making straight Bs without her. Her only requirement for friendship is basic human decency.

We share that sentiment.

"So I'll be seeing you at the games then?"

She lets go, and Indie nods shyly. "Yeah," she manages with an awkward smile. Cleo snaps Indie's purple eye mask against her cheeks.

"Well, I'm super excited to meet you." She taps me on the shoulder, pointing to the beer pong table. My eyes follow her finger just as Harlowe waves me over.

"Come on!" she calls. "I'm bored kicking their asses, they need help."

The football players erupt into murmurs before looking at me and nodding.

"Please?" one of them begs, his drunken eyes drooping. I feel bad for them. Harlowe never loses at beer pong.

I look back to the two beside me. Cleo rolls her eyes, while Indie waves me off. "Go," she says. "I'll be fine."

"Don't worry, Pey. I'll take care of her."

I blink.

"Fine," I relent. "But don't get her high." I point a finger at Harlowe and the guys. "And I'm not drinking."

I DON'T KNOW HOW long we've been playing but based on the graveyard of empty cups in front of us, it's been a while. Harlowe is still undefeated, despite the combined efforts of me and the football players.

"You're actually a menace," I grumble, watching her line up her final shot.

She winks at me. "You knew what you were signing up for."

The plastic ball soars through the air, landing cleanly in our last cup. The guys groan, and I sigh, shaking my head as Harlowe throws her arms up in victory.

"Four and oh, baby!" she crows, pumping her fist.

Ray, one of the football players, nudges me. "Dude, you were supposed to help us."

"I tried," I say, raising my hands in surrender. "Some forces are just unstoppable."

Harlowe smirks. "You boys want a redemption round?"

The guys exchange uncertain looks. I, on the other hand, am already backing away. "You guys have fun. I need a break."

I weave through the crowd, my stomach growling in a hungry demand. Between the heat, the noise, and the scent of cheap beer, I realize two things: one, I'm starving. And two, I need space.

My eyes squeeze shut, fingers gripping the doorknob to my room as I silently hope—no, *pray*—there isn't a couple tangled up on my bed doing the horizontal tango. I push the door open cautiously.

It's clear.

A sigh of relief escapes me as I slip inside, locking the door behind me. I collapse onto the bed, taking a steady breath. Don't get me wrong, I love the chaos. But sometimes, I just need to be alone.

Which is unfortunate, because suddenly, a voice breaks through the silence, loud and slurred and grating. "You're missing your wings, Icarus."

My gaze snaps to the corner, landing on a head of red hair and freckles. Darcy's clearly intoxicated, her lids heavy over those emerald eyes, lips pulled into a slanted smirk. She sinks deeper into my black beanbag in the corner, scanning my room. *My* space. Posters of old punk bands, torn concert tickets, and childhood hockey trophies are scattered in chaotic clusters. It's how I like it, messy, lived in. And I can't help but feel like Darcy is judging it.

The last time we spoke, we nearly tore each other apart. The smart thing to do would be to ignore her, to let her find someone else to entertain her drunken antics. Or just let her pass out in here, and drag her home later. And yet, I stay planted.

I don't know why. Maybe it's because this is the first time in hours I haven't been crushed by bodies. Maybe it's because everywhere I turn, I see my teammates doing things I know I should've stopped. Or maybe it's because I feel bad for getting in her face at practice.

She *was* trying to apologize, and I... I just snapped. I felt like a child again, throwing a fit over one of my brother's meltdowns. I should know better by now. But lately, it feels like no matter what I do, I can't get anything right.

And Darcy pointing it out tipped me over the edge.

"Dude. You're like... *really green*," she drawls.

I exhale sharply through my nose, reluctant but unable to resist meeting her gaze. Her eyes are narrowed, head cocked, and there's this ridiculously cute crease between her red, sculpted brows. I shouldn't find it cute. I shouldn't notice it at all.

A sigh slips out, half annoyance, half amusement, and I turn fully to face her.

"Yeah, I'm a Ninja Turtle, Darcy," I say, pointing to the blue mask tied around my head. "Leonardo?"

Darcy lets out a drunken giggle, strolling over to me as she swats her hand in the air. I don't think I've ever heard her laugh without a degrading undertone. Something intended to poke at me, irritate me. But this is different. It's brief, hiccupped, and despite the way she's slurring, it causes that stupid tightening sensation to return to my chest. I should probably get that checked out. Family history of heart disease, y'know.

"Yeah, yeah, I knew that," she dismisses. "But you're *really* green, you know?"

She leans in, and I don't think she means to, but her palm presses against my chest. I hold my breath, desperate for my heartbeat to return to normal, to be slow. Steady. Unrestrained. But the tightness inside me only deepens, curling around my ribs, spreading like an ache I've never been victim to before. Her scent clings to the air, just as sweet, as tart as I remember. I wonder if she can feel it too, the way my chest constricts, like I'm one breath away from collapsing under the weight of her hand.

"Like, the Hulk green. Wait—no, no, no, no. *Way* better than the Hulk green. You're like..." She pauses, and her thoughts are clearly weighing her down, because her head tilts to the side, and the rest of her follows. Without thinking, I reach out to steady her, my hand landing on her waist. The second my fingers brush her abdomen, her eyes snap up to meet mine.

I almost pull away—I swear I felt a jolt of electricity rush through me—but then she smiles.

It's a different kind of smile. One that makes you *feel* something. One that leaves you breathless. Not smug and triumphant, but like the first time I saw it at practice. Like watching the sun break over snow-capped mountains.

"You're like, Kermit the Frog green," she finally finishes with a grin.

Despite every cell in my brain begging me not to, a low chuckle slips out of me. "That's better than the Hulk?" I ask. Darcy cocks a brow, like the answer is obvious.

"Duh."

I shrug. "I don't know. I was kind of hoping for Gamora green. Or like, sexy M&M green?"

The moment the words leave my mouth, I want to reel them back in. But Darcy's eyes widen, those pretty jade jewels shimmering. "Oh my god," she gasps. "You are *totally* sexy M&M green!"

Blood rushes to the tops of my cheeks, and I'm thankful for the fact they're painted so that she can't see it. I don't know why it happens. It's stupid, and

Darcy's just drunk. But hearing that word slip from her mouth, much less concerning me, creates a chemistry experiment in my stomach. Something hot and bubbling fills up the inside of me, and it needs to be extinguished.

"Did you just... compliment me?"

Darcy shrugs, glancing around the room like she's looking for something. "Depends how much you like M&Ms." Her gaze flicks back to me. "Do you know Cleo? Cleo Mardas? I can't find her anywhere."

I should be relieved. She'll be gone soon, and I can pretend this conversation never happened. I'll see her at the game on Saturday, where she'll tell me how shit I played, and everything will fall back into place. No more odd compliments, no more worrying about my cardiovascular health.

"Umh..." My tongue clicks against the roof of my mouth, torn. I *could* just let her walk away, leave her to find Cleo and forget this whole conversation. But when she tilts her head, and those pretty eyes catch the light, I can't bring myself to do it.

"Not for a while. I think she and Indie went off somewhere."

Darcy's brow twitches, but she doesn't ask any more questions. She just nods, spinning in the opposite direction and strolling toward the door. Which is when I realize that my hands are still on her goddamn waist.

I don't even know why I'm still touching her. But her skin is warm beneath my palms, her thin waist a delicate line I trace without thinking.

For a moment, I decide she can take care of herself. Darcy isn't my problem.

But then she glances over her shoulder and I realize that, bratty coach's daughter or not, I'd be a shitty human if I let her walk away. I sigh, my fingers sinking deeper into her waist to slow her down, then turn her to face me. Another sunny giggle slips out of her, and her gloved hand lands on my shoulder, the weight of it making my throat dry.

What is it with this woman and gloves?

"Did you come here with Cleo?" I ask. She nods, her eyes glimmering.

"She's my roommate."

I flash her an earnest look. "Did you come with anyone else?"

She tilts her head, lips pursing like she's considering something. "I don't even know anyone else."

I want to make some snide comment about how maybe she'd have more friends if she wasn't such an uptight, nosy know-it-all, but as I part my lips to speak, nothing comes out. Instead, I just sigh.

She doesn't move back. She doesn't say anything. She just looks at me, like she's waiting for me to look away, and for some reason, I don't. Making eye contact with someone you can't stand is supposed to make you uncomfortable. Make you irritated, make your skin crawl.

So why is this the calmest I've felt all night?

"Your blade is worn out, by the way," she says suddenly.

I rear back. "What?"

"Your blade." She points to the corner of my room, and I follow her finger to my stick. I almost dismiss it, about to roll my eyes, but then I catch the tape. The familiar blue, yellow, and pink, my pansexual pride tape. It's... new. *Clean.* I look back at Darcy.

"Did you tape my stick?" I ask, brow wrinkling in confusion.

She's busy studying a Green Day poster on my wall. "It was frayed. You know, if you do toe tape instead of a full sock, the puck will glide off faster."

I pause, still absorbing the fact that she *re-taped* my stick. Why would she do that for me? I let go of her waist, more reluctantly than I care to admit, and stroll over, picking it up to inspect it. The tape job is meticulous. Perfect. I've been taping my stick for years, and I get the job done, but this? Every line is perfectly parallel, no creases, no gaps.

"Yeah, I know," I murmur, still examining it. She hesitates.

"Right. Sorry."

"You got this really straight," I say, a little too impressed.

She shrugs. "Took my time."

"Thanks."

I set it back down, and I can't help but wonder how long she's been in here. What else she'd touched.

"Anyway," I shift. "What are you doing in my room?"

She shrugs again, still studying my walls. I hate that. Her judgmental eyes drifting along. "Just hanging out."

And then, out of nowhere, she turns toward the door again. "I'm going on a walk," she announces. My brows draw together, and I glance around. Honestly, I could use some air too, but doing that with Darcy? I'd be manifesting disaster.

"Yeah, I don't think that's a good idea."

She frowns. "Why?"

"Because it's dark and cold, and you're drunk. And besides, you don't have a jac—"

It's just now that I realize, drawing my eyes from the tip of her scuffed black boots to the rim of her turtleneck, exactly what—*who*—Darcy is dressed as. It's pointless. I could super glue every nerve in my face, and still, the smile gripping the corners of my lips would triumph.

I reach out, tugging gently on the rim of her turtleneck with a taunting grin. "Kim Possible," I point out. Her gaze darts to mine, arms tucked tight across her chest. "Was that for me?"

She rolls her eyes. "Don't flatter yourself, Peyton. Cleo wanted to go as Shego, and I already had this in the closet."

I nod, antagonistically. I believe her, but she doesn't need to know that. Her strawberry brows furrow deeper, that cute freckle disappearing as the crease pops back up.

"It's true," she states defensively.

"Sure."

Darcy steps closer, her tart cherry scent a cocktail with her vodka breath. "I wear this shirt all the time—"

"Haven't noticed."

"—and I bought these pants because of the pockets." She turns to the side, gesturing down her leg to what looks like twenty of them. "I can fit all my stuff in these."

I'm about to ask what "stuff" she's referring to when she begins unsnapping every pocket, pulling out the most random items—phone, wallet, house key, a pack of Cheez-Itz, a pill bottle, an actual paperback book, socks, and a—

"Is that the puck I broke?" I ask, peering at the jagged piece of rubber amidst the pile of junk spread out on the bed. Darcy's eyes widen, the proud grin on her face dropping.

"No," she says, quickly reaching for it. But I swipe it up before she gets the chance, holding it up in my fairy lights to get a better look. I flash her a wolfish grin.

"Oh my god, it totally is!" I beam. She scowls, trying to snatch it out of my hand, but I hold it behind my back.

"I must have forgotten it was in there," she says defensively, those strawberry eyebrows furrowing. "You left it on the floor."

I flash her a skeptical look. "You weren't wearing those pants that morning," I point out. Darcy's face flushes a shade of red that's cute but almost concerning.

"*You* shouldn't remember that," she shoots. Then, she frantically snatches it from my hand, shovels the rest of her pile back into her pocket, and spins on her heel, reaching for the doorknob.

She's not wrong. I shouldn't remember that. But instead of sitting on it, I react. "Hold on a second, Ms. Possible." I grab her sleeve—not her waist this time, just her sleeve—and pull her toward me. "Where are you going?"

She doesn't turn back to look at me. She just keeps trudging forward, dragging me behind her like a horse and carriage.

"On a walk," she mutters.

I shake my head, letting her go for just a second, then squeezing my way in front of her, sticking my arms out to block the exit. "You can't just go on a walk by yourself."

Darcy tilts her chin up, eyes gleaming with challenge. "Well?" she asks. "Are you coming then?"

For a moment, I think she's teasing me. But she just stands there, perfectly still, eyes fixed on mine. I glance around, half-expecting some hidden camera to appear, but all I see is an otherwise empty room.

Turning back to her, I try to match her stare. "That's not a good idea."

She rolls her eyes. "You know, with the way you overexert yourself, you're probably right. You'll get a stress fracture or something."

"That's not why."

"Then what is?"

An awkward laugh stumbles out of me. "I don't know, Darcy. You're kind of drunk. And you don't like me, I don't like you—"

"You don't like me?"

I freeze. The words don't hit me right away, but when they do, it's like a skate to the shin. She's staring at me with those expectant eyes, and heat pools over my cheeks. *Fuck.* That was a really asshole thing to say.

"I—umh—" I stammer. A nervous laugh slips out. "I mean... you—*we*—"
Shit.

Darcy's still staring, and my stomach starts to sink, until my eye catches on the slight grin playing at the corner of her mouth.

That little brat. She's totally fucking with me.

"Oh, fuck off, *Coach*," I say, dragging out the title like a taunt. Darcy rolls her eyes, grabbing my wrist.

I'm definitely going to regret this.

But we have to mend fences somehow.

I tug my hoodie off the back of my bedroom door on the way out. It's cold out, and I'm not about to let her go out there in just that little black turtleneck.

"Here," I say, tossing it in her direction. "It's cold."

She catches it, face lighting up like I've handed her the sun. Without hesitation, she pulls it over her head. The hoodie's a little tight, the sleeves a bit too short, and sure, I should probably grab one of Harlowe's instead, but there's something about seeing her in *my* hoodie, my number on her arm, that makes my chest do that unwarranted, unexplainable tightening thing again.

"Thanks," she says casually, tugging the sleeves down.

I nod, clearing my throat. "'Course."

And without another word, we step out into the hall, the door clicking shut behind us.

TEN

Darcy

ISN'T ALCOHOL SUPPOSED TO make you hot? I mean sure, it's October, and yeah, it's raining. But the volume of vodka in my veins should be enough to keep me warm. Still, goosebumps flood my skin as the icy breeze blows past, sweeping my hair away from my face. City lights blur around me, and I can't quite tell where I am right now, but I don't care. I just keep walking, boots thudding against the pavement, dissonant to the rhythm of Peyton's. Her shorter legs move quicker, taking nearly double the steps to keep up with me. She doesn't make a fuss about it, just moves beside me as I force out a breath, the pounding in my chest long eased since we left.

I thought I could handle it—get out, mingle like Cleo suggested. One drink to calm my nerves, another to loosen up. After the third, I realized it wasn't in my prophecy. I wasn't becoming more social. I was just getting sloppy and honestly, a little sad. So I slipped away from Cleo and her friends, telling them I'd be back, only to find myself hyperventilating in a bedroom that, to my surprise, turned out to be Peyton's.

I just needed a moment. A break from it all.

The noise, the bodies. The flashing lights and polite greetings from strangers who clearly couldn't tell I wanted to be left alone. Girls offering shots, guys making their moves, all of it felt like too much. Too loud. Too friendly. I'd known it going in: I wasn't ready for any of it.

I guess I'd hoped that pretending would be enough.

Peyton's face glows in the streetlights, green streaks of color smearing on her cheeks as rain softly rolls down them. She's still wearing that ridiculous blue mask, and I would make fun of her for it if I wasn't so damn hesitant to break the silence we've had for the past fifteen minutes. She hasn't asked why I wanted to leave. I haven't asked why she cared enough to come with me.

And both of us seem to be ignoring the fact that it's happening altogether.

Another breeze hits, creeping beneath my layers. I know it's cold enough to make Peyton shiver, and sure enough, she pulls her arms tighter inside her sleeves, the cardboard shell on her back doing nothing to shield her. She shudders, and I feel this strange pinching in my chest.

It's dumb. She's the one who forgot a jacket. But then, maybe, she was too busy making sure I had one to think about herself.

Huh. Peyton Clarke actually put someone else first. Well, that's a shocker.

I spend the next few minutes debating asking her if she'd like to turn around. Or, at the very least, if she wants her sweatshirt back. Not that I mind wearing it. It's a little short, a little tight around the armpits, sure, but I like the way it smells. Like lavender and the faintest hint of salt. I'm blaming the enjoyment of that on my blood alcohol content.

The soothing patter of the rain picks up, and she weaves in front of me, guiding me underneath an overhang to avoid the drops. Just as we step under, a loud melody springs from her back pocket, causing her to come to a sudden halt. I nearly ram into her, tipping back as I dig my heels into the ground to avoid a collision. She spins to face me, but reaches for her phone first, brows furrowing as the blue light from the screen illuminates her whiskey-colored eyes. After declining the call, her gaze catches mine, but that valley stays etched between her brows.

"Why'd you come to our party?"

Peyton's tone is soft. Nothing lies beneath it but pure, innocent confusion, those glowing amber eyes smoothing into something gentler. Something warm enough to wash my goosebumps away. I steady myself against the brick wall.

"To be fair," I hiccup, "Cleo withheld that information from me."

Peyton forces a smile, letting out a soft "Oh" before spinning back around, and taking a few more steps. The moment I begin to follow, she stops again.

"Would you have come if she didn't?" she asks. I'm hardly polite when I'm sober, so being intoxicated, I don't even pretend to consider it.

"Probably not."

She nods again, then keeps walking. The shell bounces against her back as she moves, and a soft sigh slips from her throat.

"I'm sorry." The words spill out of her, but her feet don't slow down. Mine nearly stop in their tracks, but I force them to keep moving. "For being a dick at practice the other day. And... the days before. I know it's your job to give me feedback, and I just got—I got insecure. I don't think I've ever had someone tell me I was doing something wrong before."

Fuck. We're doing this now? Couldn't she have brought it up on Saturday? Or at the next practice? Or... *never?*

I don't respond right away. Part of me is still processing what she said, while the other half of my brain is trying to figure out if it's some kind of trap. And no, I don't have a clear idea of how this trap would work, but if I weren't drunk, I'd see the pattern.

I'm sure of it.

I take a deep breath, short clips of that conversation flashing through my mind. How angry she looked. How I made it worse. How I could feel her breath against my lips, warm and frustrated.

Heat spills across my body, a pulse growing between my thighs, and I force words, any words, to come out of my mouth, so she doesn't spin around and see the unwarranted burn in my cheeks.

"It's all good," I say quickly, nearly stumbling behind her.

"No it's no—"

"Really, I get it. I probably could have gone about it in a better way myself."

Peyton laughs softly, and I can't see her face, but her shoulders seem to loosen a bit. "Yeah..."

A heavy gust blows past us, and she shivers, the dark strands of hair on her arms prickling. I take a steadying breath, then finally force myself to ask.

"You okay?"

Peyton spins around to face me, walking backwards. The wind catches her hair, sending loose brunette waves tumbling in front of her face. A grin tugs at her lips as she tilts her head.

"Never better, why?" she calls out, her voice battling the breeze.

I put a hand on my hip, looking at her skeptically.

"Peyton, you're freezing."

She looks down at her arms, then meets my eyes again, shrugging. "I don't mind the cold."

There's something about the way she says it, a slight hitch in her shoulder, the little divot in the side of her cheeks, that makes me want to catch up with her, instead of insisting on turning back. Like if Peyton Clarke doesn't mind the cold, maybe braving it with her wouldn't be so bad.

I've definitely had too much to drink.

Her back straightens, eyes glowing as an excited gasp escapes her. "Hey, do you want to go see the Ferris wheel?"

I raise an eyebrow, pulling back in surprise. I'm not shocked by her spontaneity. Peyton's made it clear she does what she wants, when she wants. What's surprising is that she's asking *me* to be part of it.

"The Ferris wheel?"

She nods, stepping into the purple glow of the streetlights. Just as she leans forward to press the crossing button, her eyes catch mine. And I don't know if it's the stress or the alcohol, but I swear:

Rain has never complimented someone so perfectly.

Watching the drops trace paths down her green-streaked skin, pooling in the edges of her lips, the damp strands of hair clinging to her cheeks, and those golden eyes drinking in the indigo glow of the lights above, the air in my lungs freezes.

And I realize that maybe Peyton *is* breathtaking, even in spite of her arrogance.

"I've never been," she continues, rocking back and forth on her heels.

I straighten up, prying myself from my drunken Peyton-induced daze, feeling my brows wrinkle. "Wait, you've lived in Seattle since freshman year, and you've *never* been on the Ferris wheel?"

Her head shakes, lips pressing in a disappointed pout.

I throw my hands up dramatically. "That's, like, freshman 101. You know, visit campus, check out all the local sights. I—" I cut myself off, the words dangerously close to spilling about Minnesota. I swallow them back, praying the alcohol hasn't loosened my tongue too much. It tends to have that effect on me. "I mean, every transplant has to go see the Ferris wheel. Pike Place, the Space Needle..."

Peyton just shrugs, hugging herself tighter. "I've been busy, I guess."

Her fingers fidget in her sleeves, eyes falling to the cement. And suddenly, my tongue loosens just a little too much. "Busy with what?" I ask, stepping into the rain. "Practicing till your knees give out?"

It's meant to be a jab—light, playful. Our usual back-and-forth. But instead of firing back like I expect, instead of giving me one of her usual sarcastic comebacks, Peyton just... *shrinks.*

I don't know why it surprises me. She's smaller than me, I guess, but I've never really noticed it before. Not until I put on her hoodie, but even then, she always seemed bigger than me. Like she took up the space around her whether she was supposed to or not.

But now, with her eyes averted and her shoulders recoiled, she suddenly seems so small.

And I hate myself for it, because I know exactly what it feels like. The pull to disappear, to fade into the background so nobody notices when I'm not okay. The way my body has taken up less and less room since everything started, and how I've tried to make myself as invisible as possible.

But Peyton, she doesn't seem like she should be the same. She's always been the one who stands tall. Too tall, for someone of her stature. She doesn't hide.

Or so I thought.

My lips part, likely a sad attempt at a tipsy apology, but before I can, Peyton cuts in.

"Does it matter?" Her voice is steady, not soft, but not harsh either. She just asks the question. And suddenly, I'm caught in this tangled mess of irony, each thread twisting and tugging, threatening to snap.

The fact that I spent my entire life training cautiously, just to lose it all to an illness.

That I stood by every single person on my team when they needed it, but when it was my turn, nobody showed up.

That I dreamed of escaping the constant Seattle rain, only to end up out here, walking through it with a woman I can barely stand on a Thursday night.

A hollow laugh slips out before I can stop it. I shake my head.

"Nothing matters," I answer. It's the kind of thing I would've said back in middle school, the angsty, melodramatic version of myself. But it *does* feel true. Everything I've worked for, everything I've sacrificed—it's all gone now. So why did it matter?

And if Peyton wants to push herself until her career burns out early? That doesn't matter either.

Peyton stands beside me, squinting into the rain as it picks up. We should turn around, head back to the party, so she doesn't catch a cold. But she doesn't even seem to notice. She's focused, set on whatever thought is running through her mind, and for a second, I wonder if she even heard me.

Finally, she glances up, her arm looping through mine. Without a word, she tugs me across the street.

I let her.

Our boots splash through the pooling puddles, raindrops pummeling our skin, but somehow, Peyton's arm still feels warm against mine. It singes the fabric, igniting my nerves and stinging my skin against the contrast of the frigid air.

The ground tilts beneath my feet and I struggle to find my balance, the world around me swaying as my rigid, uncoordinated legs fight to keep up. We hop back onto the sidewalk, bodies moving fast, my heart even faster. I try to slow the palpitations, but then her arm tightens against mine, pulling me closer.

My heels dig into the ground. It takes a sharp pull for Peyton to notice I'm not moving anymore. She stumbles, caught off guard, and falls back into me. Confusion pools in her eyes as she catches herself, turning to face me.

"Where are we going?" I shout over the rain.

Peyton uses the sleeve of her shirt to wipe droplets from her face, the green paint trailing down her neck, nearly gone now. Above us, a neon sign flickers, a glowing cherry red bleeding into her dark lashes as she blinks.

It makes her look dreamlike. Sultry and velvety. I can't help but wonder what she might look like under every hue of light.

"You're in the depressing stage of drunkness," she explains, and a small smile edges at her lips. "Which means it's time for food."

ELEVEN

Darcy

T HE PUGET DINER IS a hole-in-the-wall, mom and pop, delightfully disgusting establishment. The booths are practically begging for retirement, with threadbare upholstery that's seen better days. And by "better days," I mean whatever day in ancient history the fabric didn't have holes big enough to give you a clear view of the yellowed foam cushions beneath.

Despite it being completely empty when we walked in, not a single table is free of crumbs. There's a thick layer of grime on the floor, and you could hear the bottom of our shoes sticking to the tiles with every step we took before collapsing into the booth. It's no wonder I haven't heard of it until now. My mom's pretty big on health code violations.

I squint at the laminated menu, a thick layer of dried, unidentifiable residue sticking to it. "What the hell is a—" I pause, trying to decipher the letters through the grime. "A Grilled Cheesus?"

Across the table, Peyton's eyes light up as a smile breaks across her face. "Oh! That's one of Bailey's creations." She reaches behind her head and pulls off her mask, revealing a little indentation on the bridge of her nose where it's been pressed for too long. For some bizarre reason, I feel this overwhelming urge to smooth it out with my finger. I ignore it. "It's a grilled cheese with six different types of cheese, paprika, breakfast sausage, green onions, garlic butter, and crushed X-tra Cheddar Goldfish," she says, counting off her fingers. "Oh, and it's dipped in gravy."

My stomach grumbles at the mention of food, followed by an involuntary protest to the sickening combination. "That sounds disgusting," I say, raising an eyebrow. But the low gurgle from my gut betrays me, a sobering reminder that I'm starving, and have just enough alcohol left in my body to convince me that grease is a current necessity. "I'll have it."

Peyton grins. She strides up to the counter to place our order, returning shortly after with two steaming mugs of hot chocolate, each crowned with a mountain of whipped cream spilling over the sides. I can't help but raise an eyebrow as she slides one of them over to me.

"I know, I know. Athletes and their diets," she says, blowing gently on the rim before taking a sip, leaving behind a fluffy whipped cream mustache.

I take my mug, slightly skeptical about the cleanliness of it, but I'm not one to pass up chocolate. "Actually," I start, taking a cautious sip, only to scorch the tip of my tongue. "I was going to say that hot cocoa should always be fifty-percent whipped cream."

Peyton's grin widens as her brows shoot up in approval. "Exactly!" she exclaims, slapping the table with a little too much enthusiasm. From the counter, an older man glares at us. "Sorry, Gerald!" Peyton calls with a half-hearted wave. He just grunts and buries himself deeper in his newspaper.

"Wait, you said Bailey invented the—what was it called again? Cheesus Christ?"

"The Grilled Cheesus," she corrects, giving her cocoa another casual blow. "And technically it was a group effort, but yes. Bailey's the grill cook here on weekends."

I blink. "Huh. Didn't know that."

Peyton shrugs. "Didn't expect you to," she says nonchalantly, her eyes catching mine. She doesn't mean anything by it, I know that. If she wanted to poke at me, she'd just do it.

But still, it stings a little.

Why *would* anyone expect me to know anything about them? I'm not exactly winning any team bonding awards. I've never really made the effort to get to know anyone off the ice. Not anyone here, at least. But as much as I complain about this job, there's a part of me that wants to be good at it. And knowing the little details—the stuff that makes them *them*—matters more than I care to admit.

I shift in my seat, the worn booth groaning beneath me, a sharp spring digging unceremoniously into my hip. The silence between us stretches, the soft buzz of the overhead lights, and the occasional page flip of Gerald's newspaper the only sounds. We sip our cocoa, the warmth spreading down my esophagus, expanding through my chest, but even that can't chase away the uneasiness settled in my stomach.

Finally, the plates arrive.

Gerald sets them down with a grunt, and I stare at the monstrosity of the so-called Grilled Cheesus in front of me, its greasy steam rising to my nostrils. The other dish—a weird amalgamation of breakfast and appetizers—sits in front of Peyton, a heart attack on a plate.

"Thanks Gerald." Peyton smiles. Gerald cocks a bushy gray brow at her.

"How's Bailey feelin'?" he asks. Peyton pulls some napkins out of the dispenser beside her as she answers.

"Oh, she's good. Having fun at the party that's for sure!"

A frown conquers Gerald's already-less-than-friendly expression. "Party?" he asks gruffly, folding his arms. "She told me she was sick. Jasmine called out, I was hoping she'd cover."

A red hue washes over Peyton's cheeks, her honeycomb eyes widening. Then she clicks her tongue once against the roof of her mouth. "Oh! Oh." She chuckles nervously, and I tip my head into my hands. "She is. *Super* sick actually. You know—" She feigns a gag, and Gerald and I exchange a glance at her theatrics. "Practically on her deathbed."

Gerald isn't amused. "You just said she was at a party."

"She is! It's a uh—like a *Get Well* party. You know, tea, naps, Nyquil. All the rage these days."

"Mhm," Gerald mumbles before strolling away. Peyton lets out a relieved breath, her body relaxing.

"Do you think he bought it?" she whispers, and it takes me a moment to realize she's serious.

I blink. "The Nyquil party?"

She nods.

"No."

Her expression drops, and a heavy sigh tumbles out of her as she picks up her fork. It clinks against the plate, and I finally muster a meager "Thanks" before adding a slightly stronger "For walking with me."

Peyton glances up from her plate, a lazy smirk tugging at her lips as she shovels a forkful of the grotesque food into her mouth. "Anything for Disney sensation, teenage spy Kim Possible," she mocks.

I flip her off.

My gaze falls to the sandwich in front of me, and I hate to admit it, but it looks good. *Really* good. I pick it up, slowly dipping the corner of the garlic-buttered toast in the cup of country gravy, letting the thick sauce absorb into the bread. Then, I pause, staring at the mess. Peyton's watching me with an amused look.

"It's not going to kill you." She rolls her eyes.

"It might," I gesture to the diner.

Her gaze drops to my hands, a valley forming between her brows as she studies me. "Aren't you going to take off your gloves?" she asks, that little indent on her button nose deepening.

I look down at the black pleather, the grease already seeping through my fingertips. I shake my head. "Nope."

Her frown deepens, and she points a finger toward the stains already starting to settle into the gloves. "But you're getting them all greasy."

"I leave them on while I eat," I lie. Obviously, that's completely unhygienic. I never, *ever* eat with my gloves on. But it's better than watching her reaction when she sees my bent, swollen, discolored fingers. It's easier than explaining why they look the way they do. My stomach twists, my throat constricting, and I grip the sandwich tighter, the toasted edges crunching beneath my fingers. "It's a texture thing."

She doesn't say anything. Her eyes just dart silently between my hands and my face skeptically. But after a moment, she just turns back to her food, letting it go.

I take the first bite of the sandwich.

Dammit. It's delicious.

The cheese is rich, the sausage tender, and maybe it's the alcohol talking, but this gravy is so creamy I could chug it. My stomach growls in approval, and for a moment, all my self-control slips away. I let out a strange sound, tilting my head back as I take another bite.

Then another.

Then another.

Peyton just watches, completely entertained, and honestly, I don't even care. She can stare all she wants.

While I demolish my food, Peyton finally begins digging into hers. Turns out, when she's not talking, she's almost tolerable. But the longer I sit here the more confused I become. Each passing minute clarifies the last remnants of the alcohol's haze, and with that, the doubts begin to claw at me.

Why am I sitting here, alone with Peyton Clarke?

Why is *she* sitting here with me?

I swallow a hefty bite, glancing up to find her still staring.

"Why did you come with me?" I ask.

Peyton pauses mid-bite, her eyes narrowing thoughtfully. She studies me, her fork resting halfway to her mouth. Then, with a half-smile, she shrugs. "I'll answer your question," she says, her voice teetering on the edge of teasing. "If you'll answer one of mine."

There are a thousand questions Peyton could ask, and none of them are ones I'd want to answer. My stomach gurgles. "Depends on what you want to know."

Her eyes fall to my gloves, and I immediately regret entertaining the idea. There is no way in hell I am telling Peyton, of all people, about my diagnosis. The woman already thinks I'm some uneducated coach's daughter. The last thing I need is for her to think I'm weak on top of it.

I take a breath, preparing myself to shut the conversation down, but just as

I'm ready to revoke the offer entirely, Peyton finally speaks.

"Why do you still have that broken puck?"

Everything in my body freezes, and it feels like there's a rock in my throat. I should be relieved, right? I mean, at least she didn't ask about my "younger" hockey career, or my gloves, or why on Earth I'm a student coach. But somehow, this feels worse. Mainly because I'm not really sure I have a proper answer.

It's just a puck. A broken piece of rubber that's not even usable anymore. But then again, maybe that's exactly why I slipped it into my pocket. Why I've been carrying it around. It's something that once had purpose. The game couldn't play without it. And now it's just discarded. Replaced with a new one.

But it's not just a puck. It's proof of Peyton's endless hours. It's time, and effort, and passion, and pain. It deserves to be recognized for what it was, not just for what it's lost.

Obviously, I can't say that out loud. Peyton would think I'm insane, and not that I care about her opinion, but it would be a lot easier to get her to respect mine if she believes I'm sound of mind. So I lie.

"I collect junk." I shrug. "Make collages with them in my free time."

Peyton arches a sculpted brow, an intrigued smile tugging at her lips. "Oh! You're one of those people," she says, and I get offended even though I'm not.

"What do you mean *one of those people*?"

She waves her hands, rectifying. "No, no. Not like that, just, *y'know*. One of those people who upcycle trash. It's awesome, actually. Bailey went through a phase like that, but we had to cut her off when she started bringing in soggy cardboard from the dumpster."

I force a shallow laugh, a pit sinking in my stomach. I don't know why I feel guilty for lying. It's not like Peyton cares any more about my life than I do hers. Still, from a coaching perspective, it was a mistake. Trust is crucial in my job, and clearly, we don't have it.

"Got it," I say, nodding. Peyton brushes her hands together, shaking off crumbs, then keeps talking through a mouthful of food.

"I walked with you," she starts, eyes fixed on me. Sometimes, when she looks at me, it makes me uneasy. Not for any particular reason, other than the fact that

I don't like being stared at. Most people make eye contact for a few seconds, then look away. Peyton stares until I forget how long it's been since I blinked.

The view's nice, I'll give her that. There's something about the dark, almost bronze flecks swirling around her irises like autumn leaves drifting in the wind. Still that doesn't make it any less intimidating.

No. She doesn't *intimidate* me. She just... distracts me. Bothers me, even.

"I walked with you because even though we don't get along—"

"You don't like me," I interrupt, quoting her from earlier. The corners of her lips curl, and she shoots me a defensive look.

"That's not—"

"Your words." I shrug.

She rolls her eyes and ignores me. "You're a pretty woman who is tipsy, this is Seattle, and I have basic morals."

I almost laugh, but it catches in my throat. At the end of the day, hockey players will be hockey players. I cock a brow, ripping a page from Peyton's book, and reading it right back at her. *"Pretty?"*

If she's flushing the way I'm pretending not to, she's hiding it well. She leans forward, breath grazing my lips as a smug smirk tugs at hers.

"It's a fact, not a compliment. Don't let it get to your head."

A flutter stirs in my stomach, that pulse striking between my thighs. At first, it's almost pleasant, something warm spreading through me, and I wonder if it's from the heat of her breath, or how dangerously close this feels to flirting. But we don't flirt. And this isn't real. And suddenly, that flutter shifts, transforming into something more unnerving. Bubbling. The warmth evaporates, replaced by a sharp pain piercing my abdomen.

No. It's not her words or her breath. It's not *her* at all. My face goes cold, blood draining from my cheeks.

Peyton notices before I can mask it, brow creasing with concern. "Are you okay?" she asks.

I nod vigorously, slipping out of the booth with haste. "Yup!" I manage through a wince, clutching my stomach. "I just remembered I'm lactose intolerant."

TWELVE

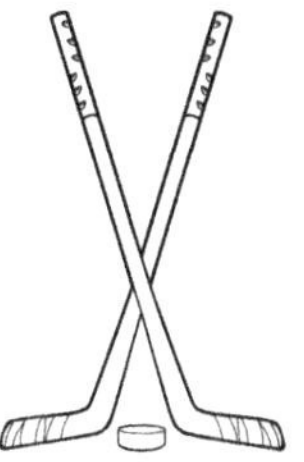

Peyton

Hey Peanut! How are you feeling?

MY HIP COLLIDES WITH the wooden door, slamming my dry stall shut as I stare at the screen. Across the visitor's locker room, Bailey is braiding Indie's hair, while Harlowe jogs around, shaking people's shoulders and riling everybody up.

"You ready to kick some Glacier ass?" she calls, jumping side to side, throwing fake punches. Caydence rolls her eyes, turning back to the mirror to finish tying back a straight brown ponytail so tight one movement could make the strands snap. That's probably why she's always in a mood. Tension headaches.

"I think the real question is, are you going to let Clay Matthews get past you like they did last year?"

Harlowe's smile immediately drops, and she stops jumping. "That's a low blow, Cay."

Caydence shrugs. "Just a question."

My phone dings again, and I glance down at the screen.

Remember to stay calm. Trust yourself. You will be amazing.

I take a deep breath, my fingers tracing the edge of my phone, like the cool feel of the metal will soothe me. It doesn't. That same, panicked tingle still creeps up my spine.

Another ping.

DADDIO

> You're not just wearing a jersey, Peyton. You've got the Clarke name on your back. Show them what that means.

The words slip under my skin like an infection. Illusive. Insidious. They're meant to be a cure, an encouragement to abandon the doubt that pools in my stomach. Instead, the waterline begins to rise. It tickles the bottom of my lungs, wearing down the layers of cells until a hole begins to form.

And then, they flood.

The first time this happened, I was seven. Like today, it was the first game of the season, and I was ecstatic. Not because I wanted to win or because my dad had just taught me a new move that I was dying to show off. No, I was over the moon because it was *fun*. Playing with my friends, taking shots, watching Harlowe block the other team. There wasn't a single thing that I loved more than being on the ice with my friends.

But as we warmed up, I realized, for the first time, how many eyes were on me. In the beginning, it was exhilarating. I was a kid, so I was flattered that all these people cared to watch me. Until I heard what they were saying.

"You know that's Harrison Clarke's kid?" one of them asked. Another looked surprised.

"Really?"

"You think she'll be as good as him?"

They shrugged. "It won't make a difference. She's already got the name. Doesn't need the talent."

I wasn't stupid. I knew my dad was a legend in the hockey world. While other kids watched *Blues Clues* or *Mickey Mouse*, I was glued to reruns of Boston Boas games. Watching my dad on the ice, weaving through players, making impossible shots, it was surreal. Before that day, I thought he was nothing short of incredible. After? All I could think about was how, even if I ever reached his level, all anyone would ever see in me was him.

The realization anchored in my bones, and for the first time in my very short life, they began to feel brittle, as if a single step could crack them in half. The rink around me blurred, while my heart thrummed so violently I couldn't hear anything else. And then, the pressure began. It started the same as it does now—low in my stomach, until it spilled over into my lungs, filling them with water, drowning me in the cold, hard truth.

No matter what I do, I will always be "Harrison Clarke's daughter."

It wasn't that I didn't love my dad. I did. I *do*. But until that moment, I'd believed I could carve my own path. I didn't understand that the whistle had blown before I even had the chance to step on the ice.

Tears welled in my eyes, and as the air in my lungs grew heavier, my breaths turned staggered. My coach noticed when my body began to tremble, yanking me out of the rink. I didn't get to play that day.

And now? That same suffocating weight is swelling again.

But I don't have the luxury of youth to crumble under it anymore. I don't have the option to just sit this one out. If I'm going to drown, I'll do it with the blade of my skates carving my name into the rink beneath me.

"You okay?"

My heart stops, gaze snapping up. First, I see a pale freckled chin. I have to tilt my head back slightly to fully catch Darcy's ivy eyes.

It takes me a second to register she's speaking to me, and an even longer moment to realize that she's being friendly. Or, it appears she's trying. After she blew up the Puget Diner bathroom on Thursday and I called her an Uber, I figured that was the last I'd hear from her drunken bittersweet alter ego. She'd go back to being the unapproachable, annoying thorn in my side, and I'd keep getting defensive over whatever advice she had for me.

But instead, she's standing here, looking at me with that same gleam in her eye. A subtle tug etches into the corners of her lips, and all I can manage is a nod. She presses on.

"Who ya talking to? Boyfriend?"

I slide my phone into my bra, hoping my dad's words don't absorb into my chest, don't spread through my bloodstream and taint the way I play. He means well, I know that. But every time I'm reminded of the name on my back, my jersey feels tighter.

Darcy's brow cocks as her gaze drops to my chest. And for a split second, I'm terrified she'll see right through me. Like her eyes could peel back my skin and reveal the wild thud of my heart, the flood of my lungs, the nerves twisting inside me, forming little knots along their fibers.

But then her eyes meet mine again, and I remind myself that one drunken conversation doesn't mean she knows me. Coach probably sent her over here anyway. Just a way of smoothing things over, to get some of the weight off my shoulders before the game.

I decide to test this theory. See if she's really going to keep up this new act or if she'll drop it just as quickly as she dropped the game. I lean in ever so slightly, forcing the anxiety down and tacking on a sly smile. "Jealous?" I ask.

Unsurprisingly, Darcy immediately closes the space between us, rolling her eyes. "In your dreams, Clarke. I'm just making conversation."

Phew. Same old Darcy.

I tilt my head, narrowing my gaze just enough to make her shift uncomfortably. It's a bit of a power move, sure, but it's also satisfying, seeing her wriggle under my stare. If my dad taught me anything, it's that when someone pushes you, you push them right back. "Every night." I wink. "How's your stomach, by the way?"

"Fine." She huffs, looking around the room, then back to me. "How's the team?"

"Good," I answer without a thought. But then I glance around, studying them all for a moment. I swallow, lowering my voice. "Well, *mostly*. It doesn't look like it, but Indie's lowkey freaking out, and I'm a little nervous about Faith's focus. She's been going through a breakup, and is *not* handling it well."

Darcy's head tilts curiously. "How do you know that?"

I shrug. "It's my job to know. They're my people." My gaze snaps to hers, and for a moment, everything else fades. The locker room, my dad's texts, the pulse in my ears. A soft smile tugs at her lips as I continue, "Nothing means more to me than them."

Darcy opens her mouth to respond, but before she can, a sharp clap echoes through the locker room, making her jump back like she's been shocked by a live wire. It's almost comical how far she pulls away, as if being seen within a five-foot radius of me could ruin her entire life. Coach Cole stands in the doorway, steadily scanning the room.

"Alright, team! Let's get out there and kick some ass!" her voice booms. The team erupts into excited murmurs, moving toward the door. I open my stall, shoving my phone inside and start jogging in place, trying to shake off the nerves. The movement is less about warming up and more about trying to stir up some adrenaline, like if I move fast enough, the butterflies in my stomach will hit their heads and black out.

But just as I start toward the door, something catches my sleeve. I take another step, but still, there's resistance. I glance over my shoulder.

Darcy's fingers are wrapped around the fabric of my jersey, pulling me just enough to halt my movement. I frown, spinning to face her.

"Can I... help you?" I ask hesitantly. Those freckled lips part, snap shut, then part again, chasing a verbal breakaway. I cock a brow, waiting, until finally—

"I just—" She clears her throat, straightening her posture. "I just wanted to tell you that you've got this," she says, finally letting go of me. "You're one of the best centers in the conference, this *division*, even, and I can tell how much this team means to you, and—well I just wanted to say that..." She pauses, taking a deep breath.

What?

I study her, trying to sort through the mess of her sentence. I can't tell if she's being sincere or if this is just another passive-aggressive jab wrapped in a pretty, red-headed bow. I look at the door. Coach Cole stands there, arms folded, eyes glued to us. When I catch her gaze, she doesn't even blink. She just stares at me like she's waiting for something.

Right. Sent by her mother.

I turn back to Darcy, the corners of my mouth twitching as I prop a hand on my hip. "This is really hard for you, huh?"

She pauses. "Yeah." After a beat, those emerald eyes widen. "Not because I don't believe it—"

"I know, I know," I cut her off, grabbing my helmet from the bench. I toss a smile over my shoulder as I move toward the door. "Thanks, Coach."

My stomach flutters when she smiles back. "Go get 'em, Cap."

THIRTEEN

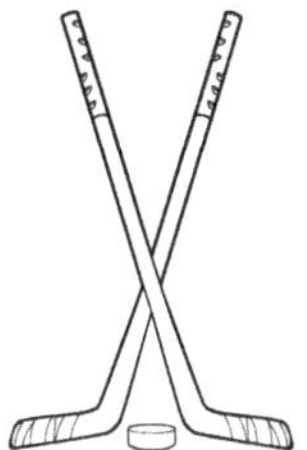

Peyton

WHOEVER THE DJ IS at Glacier University really needs to rethink their career. Instead of getting pumped up to kick off the season, Hozier has me deeply considering disappearing into the wilderness and living off fish and acorns. Honestly, fish and acorns don't sound half bad right now.

But rather than escaping through the trees, my skates slice over the ice as I warm up beside my team.

"Who's that?" Indie asks. I follow her hazel stare across the rink, landing on Clay Matthews, the starting center for the Glacier Giants. They glide around, shoulders square, short silver hair catching the light. They're on the smaller side, smaller than me, even, but they move so solidly you'd never really notice. Something curdles in my stomach, too hot, too cold, all at once when I catch their eye.

"That's Clay Matthews," I answer, stretching.

"You've never heard of them?" Bailey questions. Indie looks at me anxiously, then back to Bailey, shaking her head.

"They're a sophomore. Last season, they got hat-tricks in three games, *and* made All-Conference," Bailey explains. "Right next to Pey, of course."

I turn my attention back to Clay, studying them carefully. There's a predatory gleam in their eyes—hot, fiery. It rattles me, sure, but it also stirs something under my skin.

The only way to prove you belong somewhere is to fight for the space you take up. And I plan to take up every inch of it.

Indie, though, she's not so sure. I catch the audible gulp, the hitch in her chest. The sweat pooling at her temples catches the light, and I can almost feel the electric thrum of her nerves buzzing beneath her skin. For a second, I start to feed off that rush, slipping back into the panic. I wonder if she'd believe me if I told her we were in the same boat. If I told her I was the one driving it. But she doesn't need to know that I share her insecurities. She needs to know she can count on me.

So I shake it off, take a calming breath, and push it down like I've done too many times to count.

"Hey, Rose," I say casually, like we're striking up a conversation at a coffee shop.

"Hey, Cap," she sighs. She's trying to be peppy, but she's not quite making it.

"Look at me." Her eyes flick up tentatively. When they meet mine, I let a small, easy smile conquer my face. "You got family here?"

Her gaze drops, chin dipping low. She shakes her head quickly.

"Good. Me neither. Means we don't have to worry about anyone watching us, huh?" My voice stays light, trying to float above the doubt weighing her down.

She gestures toward the overstuffed stadium. "Seems like a lot of people are watching," she says softly.

"What do you think they see?"

She chews on the inside of her cheek, a nervous habit I know all too well. "A rookie."

I smile, a little more than I mean to. *"Exactly."*

Uncertainty pools in her eyes, taking root, preparing to infest her whole body. I continue before she has the chance to let it.

"But that's good," I add quickly. "That's exactly what we want them to think. Let them underestimate you. When they least expect it, *that's* when you unleash hell. Got it?"

She nods sharply, her posture loosening a bit. Her smile is still nervous, but it's there, and I'll take it.

"Got it."

When the whistle blows, I slip into position for the faceoff. The puck drops between Clay and I, and everything suddenly feels heavier: the stick in my hands, the skates on my feet, the weight of my dad's eyes through the television screen. I can almost hear him in my head, repeating those words.

You've got the Clarke name on your back.

Clay's fast. Faster than I remembered. For a second, their stick catches the puck, and my stomach drops. But before they can get away, I lunge, a loud *crack* echoing through the air as my stick collides with theirs. The second my blade touches the puck, I swipe it, pushing off, every muscle driving me toward the goal.

I weave through a sea of sleek black jerseys: a flash of green to my left, Lena, and to my right, Indie. Lena's eyes catch mine, a silent signal for me to pass, but when I look ahead at the goal, the top right corner is free, just as I had practiced. As I close in, the noise of the crowd swells, and all I can think about is the journalists in the stands, waiting to see which headline they'll run:

Harrison Clarke's Legacy Lives On

or

Even NHL Blood Can't Touch Men's Stats

Either way, I'll never be enough. My successes will always be owed to my dad, and my failures will always serve as proof that not even nepotism can make women's sports worth watching. Still, I know he's there—hands clasped behind his head, eyes glued to the flatscreen. Waiting for me to prove them wrong.

I have to do this. I have to score. *For him.*

I slip past one defender, then another. As I wind up to shoot, everything slows. My labored breath clouds in the cold air, synchronizing with the violent thud of my heart. Behind me, bodies, but it's like they're paralyzed. Frozen in time. Or maybe I am.

With a quick shift of my shoulders, the lift of my left foot, the puck connects with my blade. A buzzing tremor climbs the shaft, slipping through the thick gloves, flooding my hands with a numb, electrifying tingle. The puck arcs in the air, the Giants' goalie lunging a millisecond too late. The net ripples as the rubber disc sinks in, and the blast of the whistle breaks the haze, everything stirring back to life.

The roar of the crowd, the glowing orange **1** on our side of the scoreboard, Lena slapping the back of my helmet as my teammates swarm me, passing me around like a trophy. It should feel like a victory.

But as I skate toward the bench, catching my breath, the truth settles back in. The outcome's still the same. I'll never have my own name.

Coach fist-bumps me as I hurl myself over the boards, but I don't get a chance to acknowledge Darcy—or the slight downturn of her lips—before Bailey climbs in behind me and yanks me onto the bench.

"Nice shot, Pey!" She grins, her porcelain cheeks burning red.

I pant, adjusting my cage. "Thanks, Hammie."

I glance back at Darcy. She's staring straight ahead, eyes fixed on the game. My gaze shifts between the play unfolding and the intensity in her expression, the two in perfect sync, like she's the one controlling it. Cause and effect, conductor and symphony, stick and puck. But disapproval still clings to her lips. I know what she's thinking. That I should've passed to Lena.

And she's right.

I should have.

But sometimes, I find myself chasing the proof. Putting myself above the people who count on me, because I need to be the one to silence the doubt. The funny part is, it never works. Every time I choose to put my image first, that voice inside me gets louder.

I'm a selfish captain. I don't know why they gave me this role.

When Caydence scores and the glowing 1 flips to 2, I jump back on the ice, those words replaying in my head.

I'm a selfish captain.

I'm a selfish captain.

I'm a selfish captain.

As I glide up to the faceoff circle, Clay's eyes catch mine. And this time, I'm not rattled. *I'm frozen.* The whistle blows, and before I can react, they swipe the puck and dart to the side, slipping past me like I'm stagnant. I snap out of it quickly, desperate to steal it back, but I'm not fast enough.

Clay moves like me, like they've been doing this their whole life, like nothing in the world matters more. They weave through the mess of skates and sticks, slipping in and out of players with precision, sending Indie, intentionally or not, tumbling to the ice. I try to close the gap, but each time I push, they're already one step ahead.

As Clay flies toward the net, Bailey and Lena rush in, but it's already too late. Clay winds up for a shot just as I'm closing the gap, their stick coming down with a calculated swing. Harlowe drops low to block it, her body crashing to the ice, and all I can do is stare as the net gives way, the puck sinking into it with a *thwack.*

The whistle sounds, a familiar shrill pitch that rattles my skull. My stomach drops, but I don't get to dwell in the feeling.

Instead, I'm interrupted by a loud *clang* echoing through the rink, my attention darting to Harlowe. Her cheeks are flushed, eyes burning furiously as she slams her stick against the goal. The ref, Carlos, blows his whistle, shooting her a warning. She bites back a curse, forcing out a quick, reluctant apology.

Our eyes lock, and I see it building, all her fury simmering beneath the surface. Harlowe has a way of collecting her anger, like a river that slowly fills with rain. Unless she's woken up early, she's pretty good at containing it. But when she steps on the ice, when she misses a save, when the game slips through her fingers? The floodgates open. All that pent-up frustration surges out, and in those moments, it's up to me to stop the rush before it drowns her.

Clay shouts something at her—I miss what—but they're gone before I reach her. My hands land on her shoulders, steadying, and the front of my helmet gently taps hers.

"You good?" I ask, still gasping for air.

"Fuckin' Caydence got in my head," she mutters frustratedly.

I give her helmet a firm pat, stepping back to give her space. "Matthews had to get past all of us before they got to you. *Fuck Caydence.* She could never do what you do."

Harlowe exhales slowly, rolling her neck to shake off the tension. She meets my gaze and nods, her shoulders relaxing a little. "Thanks, Pey."

The first period is a blur after that, shifts on and off the ice, the Giants capitalizing on a power play after Caydence's tripping call, Lena responding with her own goal right after.

Mid-way through the second the score's 2-3. I take my place at the faceoff circle, and this time I don't hesitate. My skates dig in, eyes locked on the loose puck. Clay catches my gaze just as they wrestle it from my grasp, lips pulled into an arrogant grin. They're pushing me, making me work for it, making me prove myself.

And I'm going to make them regret it.

I drive forward, closing in as Indie and Lena flank beside me. Clay's eyes stay locked on the rink ahead, but I know we're both thinking the same thing: One slip, one inch, a fraction of a second too slow or too fast, and the puck is mine.

Then I see it; Clay stumbles, just slightly. I pounce, scooping the puck and flying toward center ice. But the Giants are closing in fast.

I glance at Indie, who's wide-eyed, shaking her head. Lena's boxed in, no passing lane there either.

It's now or never.

My eyes lock on the right corner of the net, tracking the angle. I swing just as Clay does. The puck cuts wide, slamming into the boards with a heavy thud.

There's not a second to drop my head before the whistle cuts through the rink, the ref signaling icing. My body moves on instinct, but my gaze drifts to the stands. Darcy's eyes are fixed on me, and for a split second, the rest of the world fades away. It's like we're two spotlights in the dark. I forget about my dad, Coach Cole, Clay, the ref, the crowd.

I just see her.

I shouldn't care. I shouldn't *need* her approval. But the way she looked at me in the locker room, how she said she believed in me like she meant it? For once, I don't want to prove Darcy wrong. I want to prove her right.

Swallowing the ache in my throat, I skate toward the faceoff circle near our goal. I screwed up. Clay got that first goal because of me, and now they're about to drop the puck inches from our net for the same reason.

I don't deserve to be here.

I get into position, the puck drops, but before I can even lunge for it, a jarring honk echoes in the arena, signaling the end of the second period. Frustration burns in my chest as I coast toward the bench, then down the tunnel, skates clacking on the rubber mat.

Ahead of me, the team strides excitedly toward the locker room, their voices echoing in the tunnel while they ride the high of the lead. But behind me, Harlowe and Indie shuffle in quiet self-reflection.

I don't want to talk. I want to be pissed. I want to wallow—*boil*—in my own anger at myself. I want to replay that miss over and over again until I figure out exactly what my dad would have done instead. But I know they need me. So I slow my pace until I'm beside them.

"How you feelin' Yersie?" I ask, heat swarming my sweat-slicked skin as we stray further from the ice. Harlowe grunts, tugging off her helmet, which is as much of a response as I'm going to get.

I look to Indie. She's adjusting the pads under her jersey, gaze drifting some place far away. I nudge her with my elbow.

"You okay, Rose?"

She lets out a sigh and gives a small, tight nod. Just like earlier, it fails to convince us both.

"You're doing everything you can out there, okay?" I say. "That last play was all on me. Not you."

She shakes her head faintly. "I should've been there for you to pass to."

I reach over and press a hand to her shoulder. "You tried."

It's the simplest statement. And it's the truth. Sometimes, all you can do is try. I don't know why I feel like I'm exempt from it. Like because of where I come from—*who* I come from—I'm not awarded the same grace. I know I'm privileged. Lucky. But sometimes I wonder if things would be easier if I wasn't. Everyone else gets to fail and learn. But when I fail, I just prove the media right.

And let my father down.

I don't realize I've stopped walking until I glance back up and see Indie and Harlowe disappear into the locker room. I take one breath, then another, trying to summon the version of myself I know Coach wants to see. The version who's proud, who believes her own words. The version I'm unsure exists. As my left foot inches forward, my skates like cinder blocks bound to my feet, a sea of red pools in my periphery.

Darcy must have been behind us this whole time, and now, she's standing right beside me. She doesn't speak. She just stands there. And before I can stop myself, the words tumble out.

"If you're going to berate me and tell me I shouldn't have taken that shot, I'm already aware," I mutter.

Those emerald eyes trace me from blade to brow. And for some absurd reason, all I can focus on is how the stance between us has shifted. Most people wouldn't notice. Especially not when spiraling about their career failures. But from this angle, the extra boost of my skates, our mouths nearly align.

"Actually, I was going to tell you good job," she replies.

My gaze from her lips to her eyes, and I frown. "What, no pointers? No tips all of a sudden?"

She tosses her sleek, red hair over one shoulder and shrugs. "I think you did what you could in the moment. And when you get back out there, you're going to put them in their place."

An ache throbs in the base of my throat, dry and hard, and I squirt a stream of water into my mouth in a futile attempt to cure it. "You know, you don't have to be nice to me just because we're at a game. It's not like your mom is watching or anything."

The corners of her lips turn up. "Who said I was being nice?"

Is it weird that this is making me feel better? Her biting remarks? Her annoying advice? I trace the chewed dent on the inside of my cheek with my tongue, smoothing out the beginnings of a simper.

She continues, "But I do have one pointer. If you want to hear it, that is."

If you asked me a few days ago if I wanted to hear anything Darcy had to say,

I wouldn't even have wasted my time with a response. But now, as she asks, my gaze flicks to my stick, studying the now-worn tape hugging the blade. I wanted to be mad that she touched my stuff. That she touched my lucky stick, of all things. But it was so surprisingly perfect that I couldn't. And the thought that Darcy might know more than I originally believed—that she's the only one in my entire career who's cared enough to challenge me, to go head-to-head instead of assuming I'd get by on my own—makes the satisfaction of ignoring her advice start to fade.

My brow twitches, a bead of sweat tickling my skin. "What is it?" I ask.

She leans in, that deep cherry scent sanctifying me, voice dropping low.

"You're telegraphing your moves. Like Clay does."

I blink. "Telegraphing?"

She nods, tucking her clipboard against her chest and straightening up. "Yeah. You tend to look at where you're passing before you make the move. Your head dips a little while you try to decide. It's a small thing, but it's enough to give away what you're about to do. Clay does the same thing."

I stare at her, lips dropping open in surprise. "And you noticed that?"

She shrugs. "I've *been* noticing it." A bright, kinetic gleam pools in her eyes. "You're better than that. Pay attention, to you *and* to Clay."

A wave of something I can't quite name—relief, admiration maybe—washes over me, and I look at her intently, nodding.

"Alright."

Darcy's brows lift in surprise. "Alright?" she questions.

I nod once more. "Alright."

I HATE TO ADMIT it, but Darcy's right.

I can't unsee it now—the slight dip of Clay's head before they pass, before they shoot. I'm not sure how I missed it before, but now that I know, swiping the puck from them is like taking candy from a baby.

And I'm not the only one back in my groove. After our regroup, and my surprisingly sincere speech in the locker room, everyone's firing on all cylinders.

Especially Indie.

She's got the puck now, and she's a blur, pushing forward with strong strides. Something tells me that if anxiety wasn't eating away at her, she'd be faster than Clay and I combined. I can tell she's nervous, feeling the Giants on her trail, but Bailey's right behind her, blocking their advances. The whir of the crowd amplifies as she gets closer.

This could be our chance to put another one on the board.

But just as she glides toward the crease, #10 materializes. With one swift motion, they swipe the puck away from Indie, sending her stumbling to the ground again.

I should turn around, follow them, and regain control. But something stops me, tugging at my chest, pulling me back.

That letter "C."

Indie's sprawled on the ice, her breath heavy and frustrated, gloves slipping as she struggles to pull herself back up. Her helmet's askew, a tendril of hair falling loose, and when our eyes meet, I see the hint of tears threatening to spill.

I slide over to her, offering my hand.

Her eyes shoot up, surprised, and for a moment, her body tenses, like she's about to push me away. As if accepting help would make things worse. I know that feeling. But she takes my hand anyway, fingers locking tightly around mine. I pull her to her feet, patting her shoulder just as the crowd erupts into a deafening roar.

The Giants scored another point.

By the time I even register it, the score's already on the board.

3-4. Even though we're still up by one, my stomach sinks. But it's fleeting, because somewhere behind me, I hear a voice.

"I don't know if you know this, but you're supposed to block it," Clay sneers, a cocky grin spreading across their face as they hover in front of the net. Harlowe's eyes narrow, and something smoldering sparks in her gaze.

Oh shit.

"What the fuck did you just say to me?" she growls loudly. Her body tenses, the heat in her cheeks spreading down her neck.

Clay doesn't back down. The space between them shrinks until they're nearly mask to mask. The sound of my pulse is heavy in my ears as I move toward them, trying to break it up.

But I'm too late.

A shove from Clay, their hands pressing into Harlowe's chest, and she's on them in an instant. Tossing her stick to the side, her fists come up—first one, then the other—landing hard against Clay's shoulders, their helmet, anywhere she can get a hit.

Gloves hit the ice in a clatter, lost in the chaos that follows. I watch in a daze as Harlowe's fury is unleashed in merciless strikes. But Clay's no victim. They shove her back, throwing a punch that catches her square in the chest. She stumbles, but she doesn't stop; she's right back on them, fists flying.

Everything around me blurs. I should step in. I should break this up. But I'm frozen, watching as a fight begins to spill across the ice. Sticks, helmets, gloves, limbs.

And then something in my peripheral grabs me. My eyes dart across the rink, catching on #10. Her gaze is locked on Indie, who's standing to the side, staring in horror. It's intentional, aggressive, and I don't know what comes over me, but they'll have to carry me out on a stretcher before anyone lays a goddamn hand on that girl.

I slam my skates into the ice, pushing off harder than I thought possible. My heart is pounding, legs burning as I fight for every inch of space between me and #10. I don't even brace myself as I crash into them with all my weight, the impact knocking the wind out of both of us.

We tumble to the ground, gloves and helmets slipping off, the cold ice sinking into my jersey. I barely have time to process the feeling before I glance over my shoulder.

Darcy's eyes are locked on me, and in that split second, the world slows to a suffocating crawl. I feel it, the jagged edge of glass tearing into my chest. Her expression is frozen, a perfect, disheartening compound of anger and disbelief, like she's waiting for some impossible shift in the universe. A rewind.

I never knew fire to be green until I look into her eyes and see the flame.

It hits me then, what I've just done.

She believed in me. She *trusted* me. Finally began to understand what this means to me. Thought that I was all in. That I was serious.

And in one swift motion, I lit the match that burned her.

I try to move toward her, slipping as I pull myself up, lips parting to call out. When suddenly, a blur of black and white—then a sharp *crack* sears through my jaw.

FOURTEEN

Darcy

WHEN I WAS TEN, I went for a bike ride with some of the neighboring kids. My mom told me to be back in thirty minutes, but after a few laps around the block, the new neighbor girl, Brenna, invited me over for lemonade and the new NHL 12 PlayStation game. I didn't own NHL 12 (I only had NHL 09 on the computer) so the lure of playing a newer version was too much to resist. I was so giddy about another female hockey player moving to my block that I didn't think to check with my mom first. I just left my bike leaning against the back fence and darted into Brenna's house like I had all the time in the world.

We spent hours playing, listening to "Mony Mony" by Billy Idol through the television speakers. She brawled with Tim Thomas and won. I played against the Tampa Bay Lightning and lost. I had never had so much fun with someone off the ice.

When the first wail of sirens pierced the walls of her house, my stomach instantly dropped.

I'd never told my mom where I was.

My heart pounded as I looked out the window, red and blue lights lighting up the neighborhood. I knew they were there for me. And even though I felt like I was going to vomit, I had no choice but to own up.

I waved to Brenna, grabbed my bike, and made my way to the closest car. The cops escorted me back to my parents.

I'll never forget the way my dad clung to me when I arrived. His breath was ragged, face swollen and red from crying. I was struggling to breathe with how tight his trembling arms had squeezed me. It was like if he let go, I'd disappear again.

But my mom?

She didn't say a word.

She just kissed my forehead with her cold, pale lips, then turned and walked to her room, shutting the door softly behind her. There was something painful in that moment. Worse than being yelled at, or grounded. It was the one and only time I ever saw my mom so upset that words ceased to exist.

Until now.

The crowd's roar tunnels through the arena, rattling up the bench and vibrating in my legs. On the ice, refs and linesmen swarm the tangle of bodies—blowing whistles, yanking at limbs, peeling players off each other.

But my mom says nothing. Her eyes sweep the bench, a silent warning that somehow triumphs the sound of the arena.

Me? All I want to do is scream.

It's no secret that fighting's against the rules in women's hockey. Unheard of? Not exactly. But when your *captain* joins in instead of stopping it, it's more than just a bad look.

It's a message.

That we're undisciplined. That we're emotional. That we're everything critics say women's hockey is. And it doesn't just hurt the team. It drags the whole league down with it.

The penalties are one thing. But the headlines? The soundbites? The ammo it gives people already convinced we're not worth watching? *That's* what sticks.

Maybe it cuts deeper because I'd give anything to still be out there. To play. To have one more chance at this life, and calm the storm. But instead I'm watching our so-called leader lose control in front of thousands. Charging at opponents and knocking them to the ice.

I can't tear my eyes from the chaos as the pile of bodies finally starts to separate. Players scatter, gliding back to their respective benches.

But I just stare at one player in particular.

Peyton glides toward the penalty box, helmet in one hand, gloves tucked beneath her arm, blood pooling in her bruised jaw. Lena follows, frustrated, and behind her, Bailey—stuck serving Harlowe's penalty since goalies can't—looks just as pissed.

I rise to my feet, my gloved hands stinging against the frigid air as the blood inside me heats to a boil. My mom's hand clamps down on my arm.

She doesn't say anything, just shakes her head once.

I'm burning from the inside out. But I sit anyway.

The ref approaches the boards, raising his arm.

"Number 72, green—two minutes for roughing," he says, nasally tone clipped. "Number 40, green—two minutes for roughing. Penalty will be served by number 9. Number 11—"

At the sound of that number, my eyes can't help but flick back to Peyton. She slams into the box, collapsing onto the silver bench. My jaw is so tight that my back teeth scrape together, sending a nauseating chill down my spine.

"—green—five-minute major for fighting."

Shit.

"Numbers 10, and 23, black—two minutes for roughing."

Clearly they didn't see that punch.

"Number 87, black—five-minute major for fighting, game misconduct."

"Holy shit," Caydence whispers. "Clay just got ejected."

But I don't care about Clay Matthews, or their ejection from the game. I care about Peyton.

I can't believe I fell for it. Her hollow rhetoric about the team and what it means to her. She locked eyes with me as she shoved 10 to the ground—an impertinent reminder that no matter how much I wish she was different, Peyton is nothing more than a reckless, privileged player.

A five-minute penalty. That's the rest of the game.

She should be spending it on the ice, driving this home, racking up her stats. Instead, she's stuck behind glass, watching uselessly as the rest of the game unfolds.

We hold the lead, likely due to Matthews being out.

We kill the penalty. The buzzer sounds. The crowd roars.

But I don't feel like celebrating.

IN THE HALLWAY OUTSIDE the locker room, the fluorescent lights flicker, an eerily spasmodic beam that raises the tiny hairs on the back of my neck. Everyone's already packed up and headed for the bus, leaving me alone in the vacant stadium. Since Glacier's only twenty minutes from the apartment, and we already did post-game cleanup, I asked Cleo to come get me.

Riding a bus packed with sweaty hockey players and my angry mother is the last thing I want right now. Besides, Cleo and I have plans to try this new Mediterranean restaurant.

An itching, burning sensation sparks suddenly in my hands. It starts off slight, but within seconds, the scorching, prickling fire spreads. I glance up and down the hall. Empty.

I peel off a glove. My skin is red, splotchy, fingers swelling from the damp heat. Quickly, I push into the locker room, heading for the sink. The hinges creak as the heavy metal door closes behind me, the potent scent of sweat and metal flooding my nostrils.

But I stop in my tracks.

Standing in front of the mirror, adjusting the straps of her forest green sports bra, is Peyton. Her face is flushed, skin still damp, and there's a swollen cut near her bottom lip, oozing. She doesn't even look at me. She just keeps staring at her reflection, pulling her hair into a high messy bun, a bead of blood trickling down her chin. Dark, sweaty tendrils fall around her face, framing her amber eyes and clenched jaw.

She either doesn't notice me, or she simply wants to act like I don't exist. I wish I had that type of control right now. Things would be easier if I could pretend Peyton doesn't exist. If I could act like her selfishness, her recklessness, has no effect on me.

It shouldn't.

Like I said the other night, I shouldn't care if Peyton wants to work herself into an early-ending career. I shouldn't care if she takes her privilege for granted. If she drags the team down with her. If she drags the sport down too. Caring won't give me my career back. It won't give me my body back.

I should walk out of here, let Cleo feed me hummus while she explains cumulonimbus clouds and her new fixation on meteorology. Being in any close proximity with Peyton right now is possibly the worst idea anyone could have. But the longer I look at her, the more I see the 11 flashing on the ice, just before she shoved #10. All of it, the anger, the envy, boils inside me, and before I can stop myself, the words are already spilling out in a bitter laugh.

"You know, you really had me fooled," I spit, stepping behind her. Those amber eyes catch mine in the reflection, and she doesn't turn around, but she doesn't look away either. "For a second there, I really thought you meant all that bullshit about the team and how much this means to you."

Her gaze narrows, brows weaving together as her hands fall into clenched fists at her sides.

"I already heard it from Coach. I'm going to hear it from the media. I don't need to hear it from you."

I try to take a soothing breath, but it's no use. It's as shaky and shallow as the one before it. As shaky and shallow as the one that follows.

"See, I think you do," I shoot back. "Because clearly, none of it's getting through. You don't act like a captain. You don't lead. You don't sacrifice. You don't even want to pass during a game. Since I got here, all I've seen is you breaking rules, turning a blind eye while the team gets drunk with practice the next day, and doing what's best for *you*. People would kill to be in your spot,

Peyton. And you act like it's your birthright."

She jerks around, chest rising and falling in quick, uneven breaths. Her posture stiffens, and even though she's a good five inches shorter than me, I suddenly feel like I'm shrinking. She steps toward me. I take a step back.

"You think I don't know that?" she snaps, her voice rising with each word. "You think every time I step on the ice, I don't look around and wonder if I'd even be there if it weren't for the name glued to my back? That every time I make a decision, I'm not questioning if it's the right one?"

"No, actually," I answer, jaw ticking. "I don't. I don't see any proof that you think about *anything* before you do it. Not unless you know it's going to put you in the spotlight."

A humorless laugh slips from her lips, and she shakes her head, those molten amber eyes locking with mine as she takes another step.

"Why do you think I'm on the ice at four a.m. *every morning?* What, you think somehow that'll prove that I'm better than everyone? When nobody is around to watch me?" She shakes her head. "I'm not trying to prove I'm better, Darcy. I'm trying to prove I'm enough. That I've *earned* this."

My mind flashes back to practice, to the way she traced that C on her jersey like it was foreign. To the word "insecure" that she dropped in the rain the other night. To that morning, when we met, how many times she restarted her drills, that disappointed furrow in her brow each time she messed up.

"You're the captain. You're one of the most highly regarded centers in the *region*. You're the child of a professional athlete. You have it all, why do you need to *deserve* it?"

Tears well in her eyes, chest heaving with shaky breaths, but she doesn't look away. I should leave. I know I should. But I only manage a single step back, before my spine presses against a cold metal locker.

She steps forward, so close that her breath ghosts over my lips.

"You don't know a damn thing about what it's like to live up to everyone's expectations," she starts, her voice low but steady. "To have this shadow hanging over you because you're 'Harrison Clarke's daughter'. Not 'Peyton Clarke', not 'rising star', just 'Harrison Clarke's daughter'."

Her voice cracks, just barely, and she swipes at the water pooling in her eyes.

"You think I don't *know* that I'm privileged? You think I need you to tell me that? That *privilege* consumes every inch of my mind, every second of every day. I can't get away from it."

My heart pounds mercilessly, each beat rapping against my ribs. My breath staggers, rising and falling in sync with Peyton's. It's strange how often that happens. How time and time again, our bodies seem to remember each other, responding in tandem. With each shallow, unsteady inhale, my chest brushes hers. And when I glance down, I'm suddenly reminded of the fact that she isn't wearing a shirt. Her soft, creamy skin grazes against my windbreaker.

A pulse sparks in my core, and I force my eyes from the valley in her chest, meeting her gaze. There's a fire in her eyes, yes, but despite that, I can't look past the tears. It tugs at my chest, at my lungs, at my heart. I swallow hard, fighting the sudden and unwanted urge to close the little space between us. To wipe those tears. To steady her breath.

"You're right," I say, my voice softer now, betraying me. "I don't know what it's like. I don't know what you've had to do or haven't had to do to get here." I rake a hand through my hair, sighing in frustration. "But that fight earlier? It could've cost us the game, Peyton. We could be looking at fines, suspensions. We could get banned from the NCAA championship! For some of these girls, this is their only shot. You're the captain. You're supposed to stop fights, not jump into them."

I see the shift in her eyes before she says anything. The fire inside them doesn't die, but it softens. Like embers fading in a cold wind. Her plush lips fall open, but she takes a calming breath before she gets the words out.

"I know," she whispers. "I was just trying to protect Indie."

It's so soft I almost miss it. But it lands in the pit of my stomach, a drop in a puddle, sending a ripple through my body.

Protect Indie? Protect her from what?

For a second, I wonder if there was something I didn't see. Something I missed. And suddenly every instinct I've tried to bury claws its way to the surface. My fingers lift to her chin, curling just beneath it, gently tilting her face up to mine. Forcing her to look at me. To see me. To hear me.

My glove grazes the split on her jaw, and she flinches—not away, but into the touch. Honeyed eyes lock on mine, and suddenly, everything I've been trying to hold together feels like it's unraveling.

I should just tell her. Explain why I care so much. Let the truth detonate because it's going to implode anyway.

"*Peyton*—" I start, but it catches in my throat. I want to say something, *anything*, but the words won't budge. The anger is still simmering. The guilt too. But something else is taking hold, latching on, planting roots.

She grips the front of my jacket, fingers clutching the fabric desperately. And I know—*I know* I should step back. Create space. Remind myself of the reality of the situation.

She's my player.

I'm her coach.

She just got in a fight on the ice. She's impulsive. Reckless. The one who doesn't seem to care about consequences.

And I'm the one who aches to be in her place. The one who would trade anything to feel what she feels to the point where I hate her.

Or to the point where I try to.

But her lips brush mine, and my heart stutters so violently I'd lose my balance if I weren't pinned against a locker. Everything inside me goes up in flames, starting in my chest, spilling downward, an insistent flaring ache only cured briefly by the contracting of my thighs. My gaze flicks from her eyes, to her full, round lips, watching her tongue slip across them. I want to touch them.

I want to touch all of her.

I lean in, tracing my finger up the side of her jaw and—

BANG!

Peyton jerks back, falling into the sink, body going rigid. My eyes snap to the door just as it slams shut behind Indie. My pulse batters my ears.

Did she see me? Did she see *us?*

A breath catches in my throat.

There was nothing to see. Just a trick of proximity. Bad timing.

So why am I still on fire?

Indie doesn't look at us. I don't even think she notices we're here until Peyton calls her name, and her head snaps up.

"Rose?"

Her hazel eyes dart between us before her mouth pulls into a tight, forced smile. It's an expression so brittle it could shatter with a breeze.

"Hey, Cap," she manages, her voice hoarse. She shifts her eyes to me and forces another smile, just as broken as the first. "Hey, Coach."

Peyton and I exchange a concerned look, but she doesn't hesitate another second before stepping toward her.

"What are you still doing here? Didn't the bus leave already?"

Indie nods, averting her gaze. "Yeah. I was just going to catch city transit."

Peyton pats the bench, collapsing onto it in unison with Indie. Watching them, watching *her* know exactly what to do, almost stings as much as watching her on the ice. I don't know Indie well. I don't know exactly how to be there for her in the way she needs. And the sudden realization that I haven't been doing my job either plagues me.

Swallowing the dry ache in my throat, I cast Peyton one last, useless glance. But her gaze stays fixed on Indie, like I'm already gone. Wordlessly, I step into the hallway, the florescent light washing over me. I smooth out the wrinkles on my jacket where her hands used to be, and I pray, to whoever might be listening, that Peyton will pretend this never happened. Like I plan to.

This job was never going to work. It's like trying to mix oil and water. We're always going to clash. I keep getting pulled in, invested in something I'll never have—what she has, what I lost. And if I let her keep dragging me into this, let her make me care, I'll never move on.

And *god*, I really need to move on.

FIFTEEN

Darcy

"**F**UCK!" I LIFT MY foot, cool air rushing to my skin as my sandal slips off, revealing a sore patch of heel where they've been glued to me for far too long. Squatting down, I yank the damn pine needle from the small hole it's made in my compression socks. "Fucking trees," I mutter, scowling at the offending plant.

I don't mind nature in small doses. Mostly when it's framed on a calendar or viewed through the safety of a car window. But trekking through it? Mountain climbing? Walking through a forest that looks like it was designed specifically to test my patience?

Not exactly my idea of fun.

My skin starts itching the second I step out, my eyes swell at the mere existence of the breeze, and this sounds childish, but I fucking *hate* dirt. I can't stand it. The gritty, powdery texture it leaves on my skin, the way it clings to my socks and stains my gloves.

No thanks.

"You good?" Bailey's voice breaks through my irritated thoughts. She's walking beside me, a giant mastiff—*Mr. Bubbles*—lumbering along at her side, drool spilling from his mouth and staining his custom green Greenrock University bandana. Bailey's brows are furrowed, her brown eyes flashing with genuine concern.

Despite my confusion over the fact that she's even talking to me at all, I force a smile and lower my foot back down.

"Yeah. Just a pine needle."

Bailey scrunches her nose, eyes darting to the towering trees surrounding us like something out of a horror movie. "They're the worst kind of tree," she mutters, still eyeing the pines. "Seriously, why do trees need *needles?*"

"I'm pretty sure the scientific answer is water retention, but I'm going to stick with 'to make us miserable'."

Bailey nos. "Yeah, that tracks."

The team floods into the main cabin of Pineview Resort, and Bailey and I exchange a look which I read as:

What in the fresh hell is this?

I'd been hoping the retreat would be at a hotel, maybe somewhere in the city. Somewhere with air conditioning, Wi-Fi. At the very least, I was hoping for a place not half a mile deep in the woods. Actually, I was hoping to skip the retreat altogether after I tried to resign. But my academic adviser made it clear I'd have no chance of getting the credit elsewhere, and the look on my mom's face when I told her? Yeah, I was better off suffering in the wilderness.

It's been a week since the fight on the ice, and neither my mom nor I have been in the best of moods. She recovered from the silent treatment quickly. I'll never forget the wide-eyed terror on Indie's face when my mom stomped across the locker room that first practice back, yelling about what an embarrassment they all were. Poor kid looked like she was about to shit herself.

"I hope I get you for my room assignment," Bailey whispers, surveying the mounted animal heads on the wall like they might come to life. "If I get stuck with Harlowe or Peyton, the only time I'll see the hot tub is from the top of a cliff." She shudders at the thought, visibly recoiling.

"Wait, room assignments?" I frown. Bailey looks at me earnestly, patting Mr. Bubbles on the head.

"Two to a room. Didn't you hear Coach say that on the bus?"

The entire bus ride, Peyton had been sitting in front of me, turning around every few seconds like she was trying to get my attention. I avoided her gaze like the plague. Since that night in the locker room, we've hardly spoken.

Or, I guess, *I've* hardly spoken.

Part of me is still pissed—fuming, really—that she'd been so reckless. Another part of me feels this annoying, inconvenient pity. And of course, there's the… *yeah*. We don't need to talk about that.

So no, I wasn't paying attention to my mom on the bus. I was too busy convincing myself that avoiding Peyton was the right thing to do.

"I kinda zoned out," I mutter, and Bailey shoots me a proud gleam.

"Look at you, *Coach*," she teases, jutting her elbow into my side. "Doing something rebellious for once. Good for you."

I roll my eyes, but a smile tugs at the corners of my lips. "Is that *good?*"

Bailey grins wider, her pale cheeks glowing under the orange light. "I'm a firm believer that rules are meant to be broken," she says with a wink. "Though, I *might* spend a little too much time with Peyton."

My lips purse into a telling line.

Mom claps her hands together, cutting off the murmurs of conversation. The crease in her brow—the one that's been there since that fight on the ice—still hasn't budged. I can't help but wonder if it's become a permanent feature on her face.

"Listen up!" she commands, her tone domineering. "I'll be calling out room assignments. No bitching, no moaning, no swapping."

Harlowe raises her hand, grinning like a villain. My mom doesn't even look up from her clipboard.

"*What*, Ayers?"

Harlowe clears her throat. "Is moaning allowed if I'm fuc—"

"Don't. Say. It." My mom's voice is ice-cold, and Harlowe shrinks back dramatically, but not before winking at me.

I glance at Bailey, startled. "Did she just—"

"She does that to everyone," Bailey says, waving a hand dismissively. "Ignore her. She acts like a top, but—" she lowers her voice to a whisper, "she really isn't."

Harlowe glares at Bailey, who just shrugs, unfazed. My mom continues, refusing to acknowledge the stupidity of the conversation.

"Because this is a *team* retreat, and you all want to *fight* like a team—" She pauses dramatically, the corner of her mouth twitching, reveling in her own cleverness. "I've paired you all *strategically,* with people I think you need to spend more time with. This person will be your buddy the entire weekend. Where they go, you go, until I say otherwise."

Oh. She's not pairing them with who they want to room with. She's playing some twisted matchmaker game to fuel her own agenda.

I can't say it's a terrible strategy. Tension has been building in the team since the Glacier game. Caydence and Harlowe can't stop butting heads, Lena is mad at Bailey for tripping her by accident.

I'm lucky. At least the coach is my mom, so I get to room with her and avoid the chaos.

"Ayers, Jones," my mom calls, tossing her head at Harlowe and Caydence. "Room 206. Cunningham, Brady—"

"Dammit," Bailey mutters, low enough that only I catch it.

"Room 207. Clarke, Cole—" I freeze, looking at Peyton, whose eyes snap to mine like she's been electrocuted. Mom clears her throat. "*Darcy* Cole, Room 208."

Every drop of blood in my face evacuates. My pulse is pounding so loudly I can barely hear my mom continuing to call names.

She *didn't.*

She *wouldn't.*

My mind races, replaying every word, every *touch* from Peyton and I's last conversation. The way her gaze cut through me like daggers, how her eyes welled with tears, how her breath felt so close to mine, how her hand gripped my jacket.

Peyton and I haven't even been able to tolerate each other during practice. How the hell are we supposed to survive a weekend sharing a *room?*

My breath catches in my throat, and I force myself to swallow it down, trying to ignore the rising panic in my chest. Peyton's gaze stays glued to mine, and for a split second, I see the same disbelief mirrored in her eyes. This *has* to be a joke.

A *bad* one.

My mom *does* have a dark sense of humor.

But she just keeps calling out names. I'm barely hearing any of it, plotting a way out. There's no way we can survive this. She has to know that, right?

When she finishes broadcasting assignments, and the team begins to spill out of the lobby, I march right up to her, nostrils flaring.

"You're joking, right? I'm staying with you?" I manage to keep my voice steady, but inside, I'm anything but calm.

She looks at me like I'm any other team member. "No, Darcy. I'm not joking."

I open my mouth to argue, my brain scrambling for something to convince her to change her mind. But she cuts me off before I can speak.

"Clearly, there's a rift here. You two have the weekend to fix it, or you'll lose your job, and she'll lose her title" she says.

I pull back, brows furrowing, heart sinking. "But if I lose my job, I won't graduate on time."

Her gaze settles on me, softening just slightly. "I'm sorry, sweetheart. But this has gone on long enough."

Heat floods my chest as I stare at her in disbelief. She pats my shoulder with a quiet finality, then strolls away.

I just stand there. Contemplating.

I could do it. Plenty of people don't have college degrees. My dad never graduated, and he turned out to be a great... stay-at-home father.

Oh god. I do *not* want to be a mom.

No, no, I could do something else. Plumbers make good money... though I have a strong sensitivity to human fluids. Okay, scratch that. A realtor? What do I care about houses? I'll never afford one. A mechanic? A pilot?

My gaze flicks to Peyton. She's watching me with an indecipherable expression. Something in her eyes sends a hot jolt through my body, and I hate it.

I hate that when I look at her, every memory of me in Minnesota floods back.

No matter how badly I want to quit, I can't. It's like trying to stop my heart from beating. Trying to stop my lungs from breathing. Quitting is foreign to me. I've never been able to do it. Not until the doctors told me I had to, and even then, I fought. Persistence is woven into my DNA—so fundamental that to erase it would take rewiring my entire brain.

I could walk away from the ice. Hell, I could run. But I'd just keep running in circles, always ending up right back where I started. It's why I'm still here. Why I still have that damn clipboard.

I snatch my bag off the floor, and without another word, storm off toward Cabin 208, cursing myself. My stupid DNA.

SIXTEEN

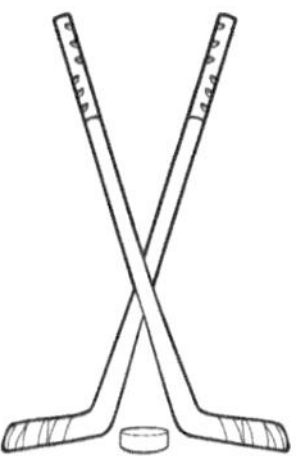

Peyton

S HE'S *DROOLING.*

Full, open-mouthed, loud-snoring, drooling. I can't help but grin cautiously as I watch Darcy's chest rise and fall in a rhythm, her silky black sleep mask snug over her eyes.

God, she really is a diva.

I slip my finger into the back of my worn sneakers, lifting the heel to slide my foot in. I'm not sure why I can't bring myself to untie them. It's just one of those things. The soft November sunlight filters through the small cabin windows, illuminating Darcy's fiery hair.

It's stunning. *She's* stunning. Even with the puddle of drool pooling on her pillow, and the nearly perpetual frown creasing her lip.

I shift to my other foot, wriggling my toes to maneuver into the shoe. But my finger slips, sending the sneaker tumbling to the floor with a *thud*. I freeze, holding my breath as Darcy shifts under the covers.

I probably *should* wake her up, given that we're all supposed to be meeting at the rink soon, but I have a feeling Darcy shares Harlowe's hatred for mornings. And if that's the case, I do *not* want to set her off.

She lets out a soft, indiscernible mumble, and I quickly drop down.

My hand blindly pats the floor, searching for the lost shoe, trying my best not to wake her up—but failing miserably at resisting the urge to keep my eyes glued to her. They drift down the thin slope of her nose, tracing the constellation of freckles scattered across her skin, then journey down her pale arms, pausing at those damn gloves. I swear, she has a pair in every color.

But I'm more interested in how the hell she sleeps in them. And more importantly, *why?*

I'd ask her, but she hasn't said a single word to me since the night of the fight. Not at practice. Not even last night when we filtered into the cabin and I asked which bed she wanted.

She responded by dragging one of them all the way to the opposite wall from mine. Then spent the rest of the night staring at that clipboard, ignoring me.

Look, at first, I understood. She needed space to cool off; I did too. I shouldn't have jumped into that fight, and she shouldn't have stormed in on me, acting like she knew my life story. I gave it a few days, wallowed in Coach's lectures, letting it all breathe. But when a couple practices passed, and Darcy still hadn't talked to me, *looked* at me, it all began to feel excessive.

I didn't join in to piss her off. I didn't even think of her when I stepped in to stop #10 from swinging at Indie. I was just trying to protect my rookie. But she's acting like it was a personal affront. A vendetta.

And that's eating me alive.

It doesn't make sense. Darcy and I haven't gotten along a single day since we've met. Not sober, at least. So why I suddenly care that she disappears right after practice, why it's causing this incurable sinking sensation in my stomach, is a mystery. A confusing, irritating, pointless mystery.

I make my way toward the rink, my duffel bag dragging me down with every step. The weight pulls me to the side, and I let it, because my brain is too busy dissecting our last conversation to have strength for anything else. The fresh, pine-scented air fills my lungs, and normally, I'd be reveling in it. But all I can think about is that night.

About her, pressed against the locker, brushing her lips against mine

When the rink comes into view, I can't help but smile. This is perfect. No stands. No florescent lights. No rows of judging eyes. Just the team, the ice, and miles of trees.

"You look like shit."

I glance up at Harlowe, her ocean eyes still crusted with sleep, short blonde bob sticking out in every direction. I fling my bag onto the bench beside her, the wood groaning under the impact.

"I just love hearing your sweet voice in the mornings," I retort, flopping down and pulling out my skates. I catch her eye, really noticing how exhausted she looks. Prying off my shoes, I add, "What happened to you?"

She lets out a telling sigh, eyes rolling to the sky, and I swear, for a second, they get stuck. "Caydence is a total *priss*," she starts, bending down to tie her skates. "She has to sleep with one of those stupid sound machines. Guess what she puts on?"

I glance across the rink at Caydence, that painfully high ponytail swaying behind her. "Uhh... white noise?"

"*Nature sounds*. Which, y'know, would be fine, if we weren't already *surrounded by it*. The noises kept overlapping with the actual sounds outside the cabin, and—"

Blood rushes to her cheeks, and she blows out a frustrated breath. Caydence isn't the only thing bothering her. After last week's fight, Coach Cole and Coach Pike—the Glacier Giants' coach—came up with a joint punishment for Harlowe and Clay. Starting next week, they'll be volunteering together at the local youth league. Three hours a week, *until summer*.

When she found out, Harlowe spent four hours in the gym, pounding the heavy bag until her knuckles were shredded.

She shakes her head, calming herself down. "So what about you? How was bedtime with *Yours Truly?*"

"Oh it was great," I answer sarcastically. "First, she dragged her bed the furthest possible distance from mine. Which turned out to be an act of mercy, because she snores like a—"

A sharp whistle rings through the air, and every head turns to look at Coach. She's... *strangely peppy* for someone who threatened to revoke my title yesterday when I tried to reason with her about the rooming arrangements.

In some strange, fucked up way, being reminded that my position is at stake was validating.

Coach presses her glasses up the bridge of her nose, a charmingly bright smile sewn into her cheeks. "Alright, ladies, let's do some warm-ups!" she calls, gesturing us onto the ice. Her eyes scan us with a glimmer that terrifies me. She has something up her sleeve. I just don't know what yet. I stroll over to the rink, but just before I can step on, Coach sticks her arm out, blocking my path.

"Clarke, where's Darce?" She raises an inquisitive brow. Mine drop in confusion.

"I don't know. Still in bed, I guess." I shrug, turning back to the rink, but Coach's arm doesn't budge.

Fuck. Me.

I turn back to her, a sheepish grin stretching across my face. "Yes?" I ask coyly.

Coach just stares at me, unamused. I sigh. "Okay, I *was* going to wake her up, but she looks like an angry morning person and—"

She cuts me off with a raised hand. "Where you go, she goes, Clarke."

I pause, gnawing on the inside of my cheek. I have two choices here:

1) Piss Coach off

or

2) Piss Darcy off

Either way, I'm poking the bear. It's just Black versus Grizzly.

"Coach, if you saw the way she was looking at me—"

"I know exactly how my daughter can be, Peyton."

I nod apologetically, and her eyes flick up, peering over my head. I spin around.

Damn.

You know in those rom-coms when the protagonist's alarm goes off, and they roll out of bed looking effortlessly perfect? Their hair is styled, they wipe their eyes, and *boom*—they're ready to take on the day and make a seven-course breakfast with $80 worth of fruit?

Yeah, Darcy is definitely *not* that protagonist.

Her red hair is an absolute mess, sticking out at angles that feel gravitationally impossible. There's an annoyed crease on the bridge of her nose, dark circles under her eyes, and she's still wearing her pajamas—fluffy pants patterned with dragons and scrolls, though at least she's tugged on a hoodie. And, of course, she's clutching that stupid clipboard.

"I'll be back," Coach says, but I don't pry my gaze away. "Stay here."

Unlike the one Darcy had borrowed from me, this hoodie hangs loose. Her gloves—pink now—swim in the sleeves, and my brows furrow when my gaze draws up her arm to her shoulder.

#40

What the hell?

I blink, spinning toward Harlowe, who's already pissing Caydence off based on the glare in her unsettling bright eyes.

"Darcy stole your hoodie," I tattle, tossing a thumb over my shoulder. Harlowe quirks a brow, glancing at Darcy, then back to me. She waves a dismissive hand.

"Nah, I lent it to her last night. She was shivering at dinner."

I don't realize my jaw is clenched until my teeth slip, sending a grating scrape through my skull, vibrating through every bone in my body. The corners of my lips turn down, and I cross my arms.

"What'd you do that for?"

Harlowe's eyes draw up from my feet to the top of my head. "Because she was cold and I have two mothers who taught me chivalry?"

I shake my head, looking back at Darcy. She's in some heated argument with Coach, and I can't make out all the words but I think I hear "phone died" and "that arrogant bitch" somewhere in the mix. My eyes catch on that number again.

Stupid number. It doesn't even look right on her. I mean, Darcy doesn't have a number but if she did, it *definitely* wouldn't be forty. And the way the sleeves consume her hands, I mean, really, how does she plan to get anything done? Half my wardrobe is baggy clothes, but even *I* know when you're working, you need something that fits right. A little tight, even. Something where the sleeves won't get in the way.

Red strands flow as Darcy feathers a hand through her hair, letting out what appears to be a frustrated breath. She nods at whatever Coach says, then they both begin walking toward me.

I quickly avert my eyes, suddenly very interested in... *this cool leaf on the ground in front of me.* I bend down to pick it up, studying it for the sole purpose of looking busy.

It actually *is* a cool leaf. It's got these orange lines, bleeding into the—

"Clarke, take those off," Coach calls out, tossing her eyes toward my feet. My head tips down to look at my skates, then back up to meet her gaze. I'm about to ask why, when she flashes me a look that tells me my life would be a hell of a lot easier if I just listened. So I collapse onto the bench and untie them.

"We're doing some trust exercises," she explains, flipping through her clipboard to look for something. Whatever it is, she doesn't seem to find it, because she just drops it back down to her side. "Given certain circumstances, you two will be doing a different exercise, here in the stands."

My gaze flashes to Darcy, who quickly looks away from me, absolutely swimming in that damn sweatshirt. She didn't need to borrow Harlowe's. I'd have given her mine, if she'd asked. But of course, that would require conversation, which seems to be off the table.

"What's the circumstance?" I ask, looking back to Coach. I'm about to follow it with a snarky remark questioning if Darcy can even *balance* in a pair of skates anymore, but Coach flashes me another look, and I decide against it. "Never mind. What's the exercise?"

"T HEN TWO—NO—*THREE* PEOPLE ARE by the blue line, one of them is like...closer—" I drone, gesturing my hand around in a circle, as if that helps my absolutely useless explanation, "—and then the other two are kinda by the face-off spots." I raise a finger, pointing it down. Then mirror it with the other, punctuating it with a "doop".

Darcy just stares at me, like she's praying I'm done. And thank Jesus, I am.

This is a completely pointless exercise, and she isn't making it any more productive. I don't see what audibly describing game strategies has to do with trust, but whatever flipped psychology this is supposed to do, isn't working. You see, in order to give feedback on the descriptions of the drills like Coach instructed us to, you have to actually *talk*, and Darcy's hardly budged.

Frankly, it's rude. When it's her turn, I actually give her solid critique. Though to be honest, she's a hell of a lot better at explaining it than me. When it's my turn?

She calls out the name of the strategy, pretends to listen, and then just *nods*.

Just bobs that pretty freckled face and keeps her mouth closed. It's maddening. And I loathe to admit it, I really, *really* do, but I miss when she wouldn't shut up. When she kept calling out unsolicited advice, kept telling me what to do.

I crave it, even.

I crave her attention like skates crave the ice. I crave the razor-sharp edge in her voice when she warned me about something I was already acutely aware of. I crave that triumphant smirk curling at the corners of her lips when I'm finally forced to heed her.

It's absurd.

But her suggestions weren't just bossy commands anymore. They made me feel like what I did on the ice mattered. Like the moves I made were significant enough to command her attention.

I'm used to the spotlight, accustomed to the weight of eyes on me. But there was something different about having someone who cared enough to tell me when I was wrong. Someone who didn't just pat me on the back or offer empty praise, but who challenged me to be more. Someone who tossed my name aside like it was insignificant, and dug beneath my surface, demanding I become better.

Throughout my life, my coaches have always told me how great I was. How I'm just like my dad.

I'd love to be like my dad.

But more than that, I'd love to be better.

I want someone to look at me and see more than just a daughter. To see untapped potential and not assume I'm already at the top simply because he was.

Darcy did that.

And yeah, I know, I pushed her away and ignored her, and argued with her, but I realize now, how I looked forward to it. The truth is, I'd take the attitude, the pompousness, those cocky little smirks, *anything,* if only she would look at me.

It's like I'm stuck, stranded in the sin bin, waiting on a timer that might never end.

"Do you have any feedback?" I ask. Darcy just shrugs.

"Not really."

"Oh, come on," I roll my eyes, scooting an inch closer. She scoots two inches back. "That was awful. My communication sucks; you've said it yourself. Come on." I beckon with my hands. "Give it to me."

But she doesn't. She just gives me another barely-there shrug.

Quiet settles between us, only broken by the soft melodies of birds scattered in the trees, and the cut of blades on the ice. We sit there in silence, and she stares out at the rink, like she's somewhere else.

But I watch her. I watch the way her shoulders rise and fall with each breath, I watch the way her jaw tightens as she clutches that damn clipboard like it's the only thing in the world that matters.

Her gaze flicks to mine, before darting away.

"You're staring at me," she says flatly.

"I am," I respond.

"Why?"

Because I like looking at you.

The uninvited words teeter on the tip of my tongue, and I bite down in shock, a metallic taste flooding my mouth. With a wince, I quickly manage to blurt out something else

"You've been avoiding me."

Her brows furrow defensively. "No," she says, but the word is thin. A long, defeated sound spills out of her. "*Yes.*"

"Why?"

She hesitates, her freckled lips falling open, then closing again. When she finally does speak, it's almost a whisper. "I don't know."

I know I shouldn't press. I shouldn't push her. But when something eats away at you for so long, it leaves you starving for answers. I chew on the inside of my cheek, the small bite of pain grounding me. "It kinda seems like you do know."

Her eyes snap to mine, and I should feel bad for upsetting her. But all I can think about is how that glaze over her eyes evaporates. It's replaced by a flickering flame, but I like the smell of smoke. "Peyton, I can't do this right now."

She pushes herself to her feet, but before I can think about it, my hand is on her sleeve, *Harlowe's* sleeve, stopping her.

"What?" I can't stop myself now. The words spill out pathetically. "Suddenly you don't have anything to say to me? You tear me apart every day, pick through everything I do, and then when nothing's left, you just act like I don't exist anymore?"

Her gaze narrows, arm ripping away from my grasp. "*Now* you want feedback?" She snaps. "You spent *weeks* ignoring every word I said. *Weeks* acting like I didn't know a damn thing. And now, when I finally give up, when I stop wasting my time on someone who won't listen, you suddenly care?"

All the air in my lungs vanishes. "Yes," I admit. "I suddenly care."

Darcy shakes her head, her eyes darting away from me, lips curling into a dry laugh. "Look, Peyton, I don't have the energy for this." She waves a hand between us. "Whatever *this* is. You need validation? Fine. You can get that from anyone else. Are you really so self-absorbed that you need it from me too?"

Something strikes against my chest, like a match on hot concrete, and as much as I want to let it burn, I extinguish it with a deep breath.

"I hate it," I admit, brushing a hand through my hair. My gaze falls to the dirt ground below. "I hate that everyone acts like I've peaked. Not because I'm great, but because my dad is. I *hate* that. I need *this.*" A desperate breath slips from my lips, my gaze catching hers as I gesture between us. "I need *you.* I need you to tell me when I'm wrong, to push me. I need the back-and-forth. I need someone who doesn't just praise me when I haven't earned it. I need someone who makes me *better.*"

A red hue tints her cheeks, spilling out from under those freckles. Her hands begin to tremble, clipboard rattling against her side. "I can't do that anymore."

I shake my head. "Why?" I hate how desperate I sound. How desperate I *feel.* "What is it? Is this about the fight? Because I thought we settled th—"

"It's not just the fight."

"Then what is it?"

"I—" She falters, voice cracking. "Look, it's complicated, okay?"

And suddenly, I'm back in the locker room. Back where she watched me fall apart. Where she wiped the tears from my face. Where her lips ghosted over mine.

Why is it that I want to do the exact same thing right now?

"Is this about what happened in the locker room?" I ask. "About us—"

Her eyes widen, and she cuts me off harshly. "Are you insane?" Her gaze flicks to the rink, looking to see if anyone is watching, then back to me. "Whatever happened, whatever *almost* happened, didn't. It *didn't* happen."

"So it is about that," I say coolly, though a sharp feeling prods at my chest. Darcy shakes her head.

"It's about everything! It's about you, it's about B—"

"*What the hell* is going on over here?" Coach asks, leaning against the edge of the rink. Her thin brows are knitted together, lips twisted into a disapproving frown.

Darcy and I both take an instinctive jump back, like guilty children caught in the act. Darcy tucks a loose strand of fiery hair behind her ear, clutching her clipboard so tightly, it might snap in half.

"Nothing," she mumbles, but Coach isn't buying it. Her finger shoots out toward the cabins, the sharp line of her brows drawn tight.

"Darcy," she says. "Go to the cabin. I'll deal with you later."

Darcy's brows furrow, defiance pooling in her eyes. "But we weren't—"

"I said *go.*"

Without another word, Darcy storms off, her red hair a streak of fire in the breeze. I watch her go, then turn my gaze toward Coach. I silently pray for a quick and painless demise—but knowing her, it'll be drawn out—stabbing, strangling, death by bag skates.

But it doesn't come. Instead, Coach exhales a heavy sigh, pinching the inner corners of her eyes like she's fighting off a headache.

"Why is it," she says slowly, each word deliberate, "that every time I see you two together, you're at each other's throats?"

I glance at the ground, then the sky. Then I spot a distant tree. Then back to the ground, rocking nervously on my heels.

Where did my leaf go?

"Sorry, Coach," I mutter. She shakes her head again, then lets out another breath.

"Grab your skates, Clarke." I swallow, reaching for my skates. But then, a soft smile tugs at her lips. "Looks like you could use some ice time."

DARCY REFUSED TO LEAVE the cabin to eat dinner with me, so I sat beside Coach in the resort cafeteria and we bonded over her daughter's snoring. Afterwards, pretty much everyone headed back to their cabins. It's only a few of us left around the fire—Bailey, Indie, Harlowe, Caydence, and me. Well, and Mr. Bubbles, who is thoroughly enjoying baking by the flame, drooling in the dirt. My eyes burn as the smoke curls into them, but I keep feeding the fire anyway, Harlowe poking at it with a wet stick.

"We totally should've brought s'mores stuff," Bailey pouts, shifting uncomfortably on a log. Her brows furrow deeper. "And a seat cushion."

Harlowe lets out a soft chuckle, and Indie just stares at the flames, not saying a word. Darcy hasn't been the only one damn near silent since the game. Ever since that fight on the ice, every bit of progress I've made with Indie has backslid.

I know she blames herself, for losing the puck, for hesitating when she fell. She started to vent to me about it later that night on the drive home, but hasn't mentioned it since. I need to talk to her more, but between practice, classes, and trying to get Darcy to stop avoiding me, I haven't had the time. So I make a mental note to bring it up tomorrow.

"Guys." Caydence's shocked voice cuts in. Startled, we all turn, watching her eyes widen as she stares at her phone. "*No fucking way.*"

"What?" Bailey asks, leaning forward on her log. Caydence hands her the phone, and Bailey hesitates for a moment before reading. As her brown eyes scan the screen, Harlowe and I exchange an intrigued glance. Bailey's lips part in shock, and she hands the phone back without a word.

Harlowe frowns. "Care to share with the class?"

Caydence glances at Bailey, who shakes her head vigorously, as if telling her to stay quiet. But Caydence just smirks, her eyes sparking mischievously as she clears her throat. And before anyone can ask another question, she begins reading aloud, mocking the tone of a reporter.

"'The women's hockey team at Minnesota State have *big* plans. All except for one college junior, Darcy Cole, 21, who has—'"

"What are you doing?" I cut in. A sudden heat prickles across my skin, and the goosebumps tell me it's not from the fire. Caydence's lips twitch, but she keeps reading.

"'—abruptly dropped the team after three years of service, including landing the winning goal for the WCHA tournament just two weeks ago. A source close to Cole confirms in an exclusive interview: 'This is a high-pressure sport. Some people can handle it, some can't. I guess Darcy just couldn't anymore,' says Brenna Porter, starting left-winger and long-time teammate of Cole.'"

My chest tightens, heart hammering against my ribcage. This is bullshit. It *has* to be. Darcy would've told me if she played for Minnesota. She would've rubbed it in my face. Used it against me.

"'According to Porter,'" Caydence continues, "'Cole was recruited to the Portland Porcupines, set to begin training in a few months—'"

"Caydence, stop. This is private—"

"'There are currently no details as to what led this rising star to burnout,'" she cuts me off, pressing on.

I freeze.

I hate that I freeze. I hate that I didn't immediately make Caydence shut up. I hate that I listened to every word she said like it was my business, and I hate more that I care. A sharp pain pierces my chest. *Why didn't Darcy tell me?*

But then, why would she?

She's made her disdain for me clear. But wouldn't that be all the more reason? She could've used her experience against me. The Portland Porcupines? *The PWHL?* That's every hockey player's *dream.*

And it was in the palm of her hand.

"This isn't yours to share, Caydence," I warn, but she just shrugs, flipping to the next line. I stand up.

"Stop," I say, my frustration palpable. Caydence rolls her eyes.

"There's a picture!" She gasps, leaning in to show us the screen.

And god, why do I look?

I don't owe Darcy anything. This is public record. It's not like we're doing anything illegal. Still, it feels wrong. I *know* it's wrong. If Darcy didn't tell me, if she didn't flaunt it in my face, there's a damn good reason.

Despite my typically unwavering northeast moral compass, my eyes betray me, flicking toward the screen.

The photo is of Darcy, her ivy eyes narrowed, her grip on her stick tight The timer in the background reads one second left on the clock.

I read the caption below it.

***Darcy Cole, 21, starting center for the Minnesota Maver-
icks, scoring the winning goal for the WCHA tournament
and sending her team to the Women's Frozen Four.***

I blink, reading it again. *Starting center?*

What the hell?

"Here I was thinking she was just the Coach's daughter," Caydence chirps, and I want to yank her ponytail and hear every strand of hair snap off her pin-sized head.

"Put it away, Caydence," I demand.

She looks up at me, one eyebrow raised. "What? Touched a nerve? You know, I saw you two walking downtown a few we—"

Before I can snap, Indie speaks up, her voice soft but warning. "Guys?" She points behind us. I turn, my heart dissolving into the acidic pit of my stomach.

There, standing in the flickering firelight, is Darcy. Her eyes glisten with unshed tears, face pale against the warmth of the flames.

Shit.

I jump to my feet, turning to her. *"Darcy, I—"*

But she just turns and walks away, fast, her back to me. I whip around to Caydence, nostrils flaring.

"You're such a fucking *dick* sometimes," I snap. She feigns innocence, her eyes wide with fake surprise. I don't care. I turn on my heel, rushing after Darcy.

SEVENTEEN

Darcy

I CAN'T BREATHE.

I *actually* can't breathe.

Tears stream down my face as I try, but my sinuses are clogged, a wall inside my body. No way in. No way out. My lips part, only for my breath to stall halfway down my throat, caught in a vise. I run, as fast as I can, back to the cabin, but I don't even know if I'm running in the right direction.

I'm such an idiot. I knew this would happen.

I should've just told everyone—told them everything. At least then, when they stared at me, when their eyes carved through my fragile bones, I could've held onto a shred of dignity. A scrap of control. Control over who knows. Over *what* they know.

I slam my palm against the rough bark of a tree, a desperate attempt to ground myself, but the world still spins—a blur of green and shadows. Closing my eyes, I try to coax my breath into something steadier.

Then a voice calls out behind me.

"Darcy!" Peyton's voice cuts through the air, the sound of her footsteps heavy against the ground. "Darcy, wait!"

I push off the tree, moving forward, trying to wipe away the tears, but it's useless. It's like trying to dam a river with a twig. The tears keep falling, each one replacing the last in an endless, unstoppable stream. I hear Peyton getting closer. I feel her body behind me.

"Darcy," she calls again, firmer, and this time, I snap.

I whirl around, not bothering to hide the puffiness in my eyes, the salt streaking down my face.

"Just *don't*, Peyton," I choke, turning away again and walking faster. But she's right on my heels, her fingers brushing my shoulder.

"Darcy, that was messed up. Caydence shouldn't have—"

"No, she shouldn't have," I cut in, voice breaking as I storm toward the first cabin I see. I wipe my blurry eyes and make out the number. *206.*

"Are you okay?" Her voice is soft. Almost worried. I don't look at her.

"Don't pretend you care."

I sniff, wiping the snot dripping from my nose. It's humiliating. All of it. The diagnosis, the article, the tears. I feel like a moth trapped in a jar, wings frantically beating against the glass, desperate to escape. But with every movement, I only draw more attention to myself.

"I'm not pretending."

Peyton's tone is steady, firm—not harsh, not loud—just matter-of-fact, like she's stating something irrefutable. Something you could fact-check.

I wish I could. I wish I could run every word anyone says through some system that would tell me if it's real. If there are motives hidden beneath the surface. If she's going to sell me out to some *ESPN* reporter behind my back.

208.

"Why didn't you tell me you played for Minnesota?" Peyton presses. My feet quicken, my breath catching in my chest. God, my head feels like it's going to explode. I climb the steps to the cabin faster, Peyton trailing right behind me.

"Because then you'd ask me why I don't anymore."

My hand hovers over the doorknob as she asks, "Do you not want me to?"

I twist the knob. "Wouldn't you ask anyway?" Then I slip inside and let the door lock shut behind me.

The second my back hits the hard, twin mattress, the tears spill harder. My temples throb like they're being jackhammered, my skin burns, and my bones are grinding together like rusted metal scraping metal. I clutch the pillow beside me, wrapping it around my chest as if the worn tweed can hold me together. A puff of dust bursts out as I squeeze, causing me to choke.

For a fleeting moment, a brief, stupid moment, I think maybe I could escape this.

They know I quit Minnesota. They know I let go of my place on the Portland team. But they don't know *why*. They don't know about the pill divider crammed into my bag, full of the little things that are supposed to make this all bearable. They don't know about my fingers, bent and discolored, hidden beneath my gloves. They don't know about the days when getting out of bed feels like being hit with a bat. Over and over. When it feels like fire's been set to every inch of my body, and all I want is for it to burn me all the way down to the bone so I don't have to feel it anymore.

I could lie. I could say I chose a different path. I could say I got tired of hockey. That I was bored.

But even as the thought flits across my mind, I know it's pointless. The second the lie would slip from my lips, they'd know. Hell, I can't even sell it to myself.

But that doesn't mean they get the truth. I refuse to be looked at like I'm broken.

My lungs constrict painfully. I stare at the log-paneled ceiling, watching a spider crawl across it, slow and steady, like the ache creeping up my bones. A soft knock raps on the door, Peyton's voice filtering through the wood.

"Darcy," she calls, quieter than before. I don't think I've ever heard her voice so gentle, not even when it cracked in the locker room, tears streaming down her face. I clutch the pillow tighter. "Will you please let me in?"

"Go away." I sniff, the words catching in my throat.

There's a hollow feeling in my chest, like something has been ripped out from deep inside, leaving an empty space. Peyton has a nice voice. It's low and smooth, like black marble, the polished cool of it scrubbing goosebumps down my body. It's a shame that every time I hear it, that hole in my chest seems to expand. "Just... go away."

Peyton calls again, louder this time. "I'm not going anywhere," she says. "You can take as long as you need, but just so you know—I'm sweaty, and covered in soot. The longer I sit out here, the worse it's gonna smell when I finally come in."

She's trying to be funny. I hate that the urge to laugh almost gets the better of me. "I just want to be alone."

Peyton pauses. I hear some shuffling on the other side, then a heavy thud. My head tilts curiously, but I don't say anything. Finally, she asks, "Can we be alone together?"

I sniff, shaking my head at her ridiculousness. God, she's stubborn. I mutter, just loud enough for her to hear, "I'm still not letting you in."

More shuffling.

"Okay."

I DON'T KNOW HOW long I'm there, staring at the ceiling until my eyes dry up, the hole in my chest swallowing me up.

I must have drifted off, because when I blink awake, the sun has finished setting, and the cabin is dark. My body aches as I sit up, stretching, and immediately I'm hit with a pounding headache, a reminder that I cried out every ounce of water in my body. I reach for my water bottle on the nightstand.

Empty.

Getting up with a groan, I slip my slides on and grab my phone for a flashlight so I can head to the water station. I reach for the doorknob, unlocking it and pulling it open.

It's so dark, I nearly trip over Peyton when I step out. She's sitting cross-legged directly in front of the door. Her gaze snaps up the instant I open it.

"Hey," she says softly, a smile pulling at the edges of her lips as she jumps to her feet. I stare at her, disoriented.

"Have you…" I trail off. "How long have you been sitting out here?"

She shrugs, all nonchalant. "I don't know, I don't have my phone." Her eyes flick upward, like she's doing some quick mental math. "I think you stopped talking to me about an hour ago?"

I blink, my head tipping to the left. "You waited out here for an hour?"

She smiles. "I would've waited all night."

My stomach flips. Not the usual tightness, not the mild flutter of nerves. No, it *soars*, tumbling over itself, spiraling until I'm afraid it might never find its way back down. I glance down at her arms, pulled up into her sleeves to shield her from the cold, just like the night of the party. Guilt tugs at my chest. I left her out here to freeze to death.

"Is the fire still going?" I ask. She nods, which only feeds my confusion. "Why didn't you go sit by the fire? Stay warm?"

She swallows, her cheek sucking in between her back teeth the way she always does. I don't know why I like it when she does that. "I wanted to be alone with you." She pauses, then her eyes widen. "Alone *together*. Wait—"

A soft laugh slips out of me, but it sends a sharp ache through my skull. I wince. Her gaze drops to my water bottle, then back to me.

"Going to the water station?" she asks. I nod, the movement a struggle. She hesitates before asking again, "Can I come with you?"

Her eyes lock onto mine, those bronze flecks swirling in them, her pupils dilating as she studies me. It's no wonder Peyton is the way she is. With those eyes, I don't know if anyone has ever been able to tell her no.

I sigh, tossing my head in a painful jolt for her to join me. A smile breaks across her face, those cute little creases framing the edges of her lips. I pull the cabin door closed behind me with a *click*, and Peyton waits for me to step down the stairs first. She doesn't say a word as she follows behind me, she just trails along, bobbing her head like a lost puppy

When we reach the water pump, I find myself staring at the metal handle, raising an apprehensive brow. Peyton reaches out first, grabbing it confidently before holding her hand out, silently asking for my water bottle.

"I can pump my own water, Peyton." I frown, reaching for the handle. She lets go immediately, raising her hands in mock surrender.

"Whatever you say, Ms. Possible."

A grin tugs at the corner of my lips despite myself, and I quickly let my hair fall over my cheek to hide it. Unscrewing the cap of my water bottle, I hold it beneath the faucet and start to pump. My wrists cramp, but I try not to show it. "Keep calling me that, and I'll keep calling you Icarus."

She shoots me a disapproving look. "See, that's not fair. *Everyone* likes Kim Possible. She's every ten-year-old's crush. Icarus sounds like the disease Bailey's fish died from."

A laugh bursts out of me and I quickly bite my lips to stifle it. It's no use. It spills out again, louder this time.

"That's *ick*," I clarify, and she just nods in agreement.

"Exactly."

My eyes catch her jaw. The cut from the fight is still there, still swollen and bruised, but what makes my stomach curdle is the strange, unsettling goo seeping out of it. Shining the flashlight on it, my brows weave as I get a nauseating look.

"*Oh my god*," I mutter, voice dropping as I examine it. It looks... *alive*. Like it's breathing, but not in a fresh, healing way. More like something crawled under her skin and is living there.

Peyton pulls back defensively, her hand flying to cover the cut. "*Hey*," she snaps. "Leave it alone."

My brow flicks up, but then the sound of spilling water catches my attention. "*Shit,*" I mutter, stopping the pump mid-motion. I glance back at her, but she's still covering it.

"Is that what you've *been* doing?" I ask. "Leaving it alone?"

She tucks her free arm over her chest. "Bailey cleaned it."

"When?"

"When it happened."

Shaking my head, I exhale a long, frustrated sigh. I turn toward the cabin, and she follows behind, silently. "We need to clean that up," I say, nose wrinkling as the image of it flashes in my mind again. "There's a first aid kit inside."

I hear a huff behind me, but she doesn't argue. By the time we step back into the cabin, my water bottle is nearly empty again. The moment we're inside, I'm already on the hunt for that white metal box. I pull it out from beneath the bed, patting the mattress beside me for Peyton to sit. She eyes me with suspicion but eventually collapses onto the mattress with a defeated sigh.

Rummaging through the dusty contents, I toss aside bandages and antiseptic until I find the alcohol wipes, gauze, and medical tape. I spread everything out on the shoefly quilt, and Peyton's honeycomb eyes widen, her thick lashes snapping to her brows in alarm.

"Woah, woah." She holds up her hands, shaking her head in a frantic, almost comical motion. "It needs to breathe."

"Oh, it's breathing alright," I mutter, tearing open the alcohol wipe. "If it breathes any longer, some politician is gonna try to give it rights."

Peyton rolls her eyes, eyeing the wipe like it might bite her. She scoots back on the bed. "Ha-ha," she deadpans, but it's clear she's anything but calm. I hold the wipe up, and she visibly gulps.

"What?" I ask, eyebrow quirked.

She stares at the towelette, then throws her hands up like she's about to launch into a lecture. Her eyes are wide, and she scoots back even farther until her back's pressed against the wall. Her chest starts to rise and fall in quick, shallow breaths.

I grin.

"Are you... *scared* of an alcohol wipe?" I tease.

Instantly, she scowls. "No," she snaps, but her body betrays her. "I just don't enjoy the anticipation of the sting."

I stare at her, unable to hide the smirk tugging at my lips. "Peyton, you're a hockey player."

"So?"

"So, even if you don't usually get into fights, you get beat up all the time. I mean, you took that punch like it was nothing."

I see something flicker in her eyes—satisfaction, maybe even pride—before she doubles down. "Yeah, that's different," she attests. "I can take a punch."

"But you can't take an alcohol wipe?"

"I *can*." She crosses her arms over her chest, her defiance still palpable despite the slight tremor in her voice. I lean in with the wipe, and she panics. "Just do it fast, okay?"

"Oh, my *drama*," I groan, pressing the wipe to her skin without another word. She flinches, her face scrunching in discomfort.

"*Dammit, Darcy*," she mutters, but after the initial contact, the tension in her body fades, and she slowly relaxes into the bed. I carefully drag the wipe over her cut, holding my breath as it oozes beneath the pressure.

"I think what you meant to say," I start, grabbing another wipe, "is 'thank you, Darcy.'"

Her eyes catch mine, and she tilts her head. "*Thank you,*" she says with exaggerated sweetness. Then, after a beat, "That sounded sarcastic, but I meant it."

I chuckle, tossing the used wipes aside, and press the gauze gently to her cheek, taping it in place. "I know."

A beat of silence stretches through the cabin, and then another. Finally, just when I'm about to break it, to avoid what I know is coming, Peyton beats me to it.

"Are you feeling any better?" she asks. The base of my throat begins to ache.

"I don't really know the answer to that," I say honestly.

The corner of her lip twitches upward, just enough for me to catch it. "I get that."

And that's it. She doesn't push. She doesn't try to drag it out anymore. She just sits there against the bed, back pressed to the wall, chewing on her cheek. So why it all suddenly slips out of me?

I don't have an answer.

"I didn't want to quit."

I catch her eye, but am quickly overwhelmed. My heart pounds even heavier than before, and I glance away, waiting. For her to press, to ask the questions I know are coming. But she doesn't. She just breathes, quiet, steady. And for some reason, that makes it easier for me to breathe too.

"The first time I noticed the pain was freshman year," I begin. "It wasn't constant. Just aches, here and there. Sometimes, my hands stung, but that was normal for me. I didn't really think much of it." Suddenly, my knees feel weak, so I drop onto the bed next to her, avoiding her gaze. "I thought it was just the intensity of it all, you know? Going from high school sports to D1, I figured some soreness was to be expected."

Peyton watches me, listening intently. I almost wish she would talk. Maybe if she would open that big mouth of hers, it would remind me of what a bad idea this is. Remind me of what happened last time I trusted someone. Of why Peyton's the last person I should try again with. But for once in her goddamn life, Peyton Clarke shuts up.

I didn't know she could do that.

"Sophomore year, it got worse. I noticed my finger was kind of bent? Thought I fucked it up on the ice or something." I shake my head, mentally cursing myself. "I went to the doctor for muscle pain, but they said it was hormones and to eat better and exercise more. I mean, they *literally* told a D1 athlete to exercise more. By junior year, I was pretty miserable. I knew something was wrong, but I didn't want to tell anyone. I was so close to landing a spot on a pro roster..." My voice catches, and I try to laugh again, but it just comes out as a dry, humorless sound.

"So I just worked through it. The grinding joints, the weight loss, the fatigue. If I'd pushed when the doctors downplayed it, maybe I could've kept playing. But now my knees are toast, and my hands..."

I trail off, and Peyton's gaze drops to the bedspread, her fingers tracing absent patterns on the quilt. I can see her debating whether or not she should ask. When her eyes meet mine, I try to soften my gaze so she knows she can.

It must've worked.

"What is it?" she asks softly.

"Early-onset Rheumatoid Arthritis."

Her head kinda tips to the side, and I have to fight back a small smile. Her dark brows knit together. "I don't... I don't know what that is," she admits.

I pause, considering how to best explain it. How to show her, without peeling off my gloves. Without letting her see my swollen ankles. After a second, it clicks.

I hop off the bed and rummage through my bag until I find my pill organizer. Opening tonight's compartment, I pour the five pills into my palm.

Her eyes go wide as she watches, studying them silently.

I point at the pills one by one, ignoring the uneasiness gnawing at my stomach. "These two prevent joint damage. RA basically tells your body to attack the lining of your joints. So, if you don't treat it—"

"Then it can damage them," she cuts in.

I nod. "Yeah. And even fuse them together."

Her eyes widen, and I move to the next pill. "This one's a DMARD—"

"A *what?*"

I chuckle. I never thought I'd laugh when talking about this. I've yelled, I've cried, and I've gone silent. But I've never laughed. "A disease-modifying antirheumatic drug. It does the same thing... I think? Honestly, I kinda zone out at my appointments. Don't really trust the doctors anymore."

Peyton flashes me an earnest glance, but I keep going, my voice steady. I don't understand it. Even just thinking about it sometimes causes a flare in my chest, forces my eyes to well. So how can I suddenly let it all spill out, no Smirnoff, no tears? It doesn't make sense. Peyton being easy to talk to doesn't make sense. "And these two are for the pain."

She nods, her throat visibly working as she swallows. "Does it—sorry, you don't have to answer that actually," she says quickly, shaking her head.

I shrug. We've gotten this far. "I've already told you pretty much everything," I say. "In short at least. Ask away."

Her eyes snap back to mine, searching me. A soft worry pools in the golden flecks, and that, that right there, is what I was afraid of.

"I was just gonna ask... like, *where* it hurts."

A heavy sigh slips from me before I can stop it. I grab my water bottle, twisting the cap open.

"Everywhere," I reply quietly, and I tilt my head back, swallowing the pills with a few large gulps. I wipe my lips, nodding again. "Everywhere."

"Oh." She pauses. "And you can't play anymore? Like, at all?"

I want to lie. But the last time I lied to Peyton, I didn't enjoy it. "I *can*," I admit, and I have to force the rest of it out. "But leisurely. And after I had to quit... I just can't bring myself to do it."

"That's why you get so upset about me practicing so much," she realizes softly. I nod.

"I lost hockey over something I couldn't control. I couldn't imagine losing it over something I could."

"Why didn't you tell me?" she asks. "That morning in the rink, when you threw the puck? You could've shut me up so fast." She says the last words with a half-laugh, but it fades quickly.

I prop my back against the wall beside her. "*That's* why," I say, pointing to her. She tilts her head. "If I had told you, you'd have shut up. Not because I had experience, but because you'd feel bad that I lost it."

Her head snaps toward me, a defensive look knitting her brows together. "That's not true," she testifies. "If I'd known you had a spot on the Portland Porcupines, whatever you said next wouldn't matter."

I force a smile. "I love that you think that's true."

"It *is* true."

I shake my head. "That's not what the look in your eyes says."

She blinks rapidly, like she's trying to flush the pity from her gaze. "What look?"

"The 'I'm scared to break you' look."

"That's not—"

"It is," I cut in softly. "It's how everyone looks at me when they find out."

Going silent, her arms tuck tightly across her chest. She sits there for a moment, pondering. Finally, she speaks. "I'm not scared to break you."

"Sure."

She rolls her eyes, jumping off the bed with an energetic bounce. "C'mon," she encourages, jogging in place. "I'll prove it."

My brows furrow as I watch her move around the room. She reaches for my phone, and before I can grab it, she's already got it in her hands. "Hey, that's mine!" I shoot, trying to snatch it back, but she grins and pulls it further away.

"Then get up, *Coach*," she teases. "Show me you can take it."

I cock a brow. "Take *what*, exactly?"

She rolls her eyes before grabbing me by both wrists and pulling me to my feet. I stand reluctantly, crossing my arms, trying to figure out where this is going. She flips the phone toward me, silently prompting me to enter my password.

I don't know why I comply.

She taps through my phone. I shift impatiently. "What are we doing, Peyton?"

Suddenly, music blasts through the speaker. Loudly. Very, *very* loudly. I lurch forward, grabbing it from her hands and slamming the pause button. She frowns.

"There's a noise curfew," I say pointedly. "What are you doing? Throwing a rave?"

She grins, that mischievous glint back in her eyes. "Okay, firstly, 'Oh, Pretty Woman' is *not* rave music—" She reaches for the phone again, but I pull it away. "Secondly, these walls are sturdy. I bet they can't even hear it outside."

I shake my head, unimpressed. "*No.* I don't want to get a knock at the door for blasting music past curfew."

She rolls her eyes and strolls over to her bag, rifling through it until she pulls out a pair of wired earbuds. She holds them out to me, muttering under her breath. "Such a stickler." I take them, plugging them into my phone. Then I stare at it, confused.

"Wait, why are we playing music?"

She grins widely. "Because we're gonna have a dance party."

I stare at her, waiting for her to laugh. She doesn't.

"You're kidding, right?" I ask.

"Nope." She pops the "p".

"Why?"

"Because," she replies, pressing one earbud into her own ear. "Apparently, I need to prove that I'm not scared to break you. And besides, you need to dance it out."

I blink at her skeptically. "*Dance it out?*"

She shrugs like this all makes perfect sense. "Yeah. You know—" She does a little shimmy. "Shake out all of *that.*" She gestures to me broadly.

"Yeah, I'm good," I reply, holding my phone out to her. She doesn't take it. "I'm not a dancer."

"Well, *duh.*" She rolls her eyes. "That's the point."

"That makes no sense."

She smiles, and without warning, she leans in and tucks a lock of hair behind my ear. My breath hitches as her fingers graze the skin of my neck, and I freeze. She presses the second earbud into my ear, glances at my screen, and presses play. The music floods in, and the percussion picks up with a steady beat.

Peyton starts to bounce around, her movements restrained by the length of the cord. I stare at her with an annoyed expression.

"I can't believe you're playing oldies," I say, unmoving.

She frowns, mid-bounce, her messy brown hair flying around. "What's wrong with that?"

"Nothing," I say quickly. "Nothing at all. Just—" I pause, watching her dance with reckless abandon. "It's a lot different than your bedroom posters or practice playlist."

Her gaze narrows. "*Oh my god,* I *knew* it was you," she accuses, but she doesn't stop moving. She looks completely ridiculous, bouncing around, but the grin on her face is infectious. "*You* changed my playlist."

I shrug sheepishly. "Sorry. It was kinda intense. I think it made Indie nervous."

Peyton chuckles and grabs my hand, swinging it back and forth. Her palm is warm against my glove, small but sturdy. She grips me tight, like she's not scared to hurt me.

"Come on," she urges, those crescents sinking around her grin. My stomach does flips again. Why is my stomach doing flips? "Bailey and I do it all the time. It'll make you feel better."

I stare at her, but she doesn't give me much of a choice when she grabs my other hand, cocooning my phone between our palms. She jumps up and down, pulling me with her, and despite myself, my knees start bouncing in rhythm to the beat, as Ray Orbison belts out the lyrics. Peyton's head bobs, her body moving close to avoid tripping on the wire.

At first, I try to resist. I don't want to do this, don't want to embarrass myself more than I already have. But the more I watch Peyton jump around, the more my feet start to tap, the muscles in my legs loosening just a bit.

Next comes my shoulders, the tension in them slipping, and then my hips. The rhythm is simple but catchy, drawing me in against my will. I start to sway with it. Peyton grins like she's won, her hair bouncing with every movement.

She tugs me closer.

I'm not dancing. Not really. It's more like needing to scratch your back when your nail polish is still wet. My hands move around, lagging behind the music, feet shifting. Not perfect, but the way Peyton's cheesing at me, you'd think it was.

Her amber eyes glimmer in the dim light of the cabin, her voice rising loud and off-key as she sings along. I can't help but laugh. She's awful. But the way she throws herself into it, I think she knows. And for some reason, I don't even care about the noise curfew anymore. She can squawk the lyrics as loud as she wants, and I'll listen to every word.

"You sound like a dying cat." I chuckle.

She grins. "So?"

The wire from the earbud pulls tight, nearly tugging free from our ears. She steps in to adjust the slack, releasing my hand. For some stupid reason, my heart drops. That is, until her palms settle low on my waist, looping around my hips.

She moves with the rhythm, swaying closer, breath warm against my skin. Her eyes flick up to my lips, and for a moment, everything stops.

She's still singing, and I'm still listening, but the air in my lungs freezes, and my heart skips. I wonder if she can feel the static. If her heart is pressing against the walls of her chest, searching for the beat of mine.

As the last "pretty woman" rolls off her tongue, we stand there breathless, faces inches apart. Neither of us moves. Neither of us speaks. Peyton's still holding my waist, her breath still ghosting over my mouth.

Just like the locker room.

And just when I think I can't take it anymore, when my mind is screaming at me to act, to do something, to close the space, she breaks the silence.

"You know, I have articles written about me too," she says softly. My gaze stays trained on those plush, soft lips.

"I'm willing to bet those paint you in a better light than mine," I breathe.

A smile flickers across her face. "Sometimes." She nods. Then her eyes tip up to meet mine, pupils swallowing the golden hue of her irises. "Sometimes not."

I fall silent, just studying her. The slope of her button nose, the shade of her eyes. I fear that for someone who can't stand her, I know a little too much about her every perfect detail.

My heart thuds mercilessly. Hopefully. "What do you do?" I ask, but it comes out as a whisper. "I mean, to help with it."

That little crease sinks into her cheek, and cold air rushes to my lips as she takes a step back. "This."

EIGHTEEN

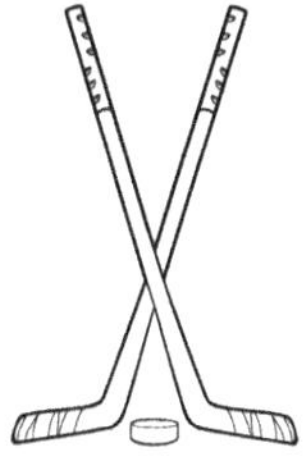

Peyton

FINAL CHAT FR THIS TIME

BRADY

Just through everyone should know the cafeteria has KOLACHES this morning

SIMS BUT NOT THE GAME

Huh?

YERSIE

wtf is a kolache

HAMMIE

???

BRADY

We ate them last year at camp in Texas? You don't remember?

YERSIE

Not in the slightest.

BRADY

I'm wounded.

CAPTAIN CLARKE

Kolache sounds like a made up word.

CAY

All words are made up.

ROSE

A kolache is a Czech pastry, but really common in Texas because Czech people immigrated there in the 1800's. And, also, y'know, Americans love stealing ideas. Sometimes it has sweet filling but in TX it's usually sausage.

CAPTAIN CLARKE

Isn't that just pigs in a blanket?

ROSE

In TX? Essentially.

BRADY

It is NOT pigs in a blanket

Z

photo attachment

looks like pigs in a blanket

BRADY

I swear it's different. You just haven't tried it yet. And the one I had was completely surrounded by the puff pastry, not just half-ass wrapped like that.

"**Y**OU KNOW, JUST BECAUSE I told you, doesn't mean we're friends," Darcy says, eyeing me skeptically.

I shovel a spoonful of scrambled eggs into my mouth. "God I hope not." I grin. Darcy's frown deepens. "But like Coach said, where I go, you go."

"Not on a hike," she argues. "And why are you using a spoon?"

My gaze drops to the metal utensil, and I look back up at her, quirking a brow. "Because a spoon is a completely normal thing to eat eggs with?" Darcy's eyes lock with mine, and she shakes her head slowly. I take another bite, flashing a cocky grin. "What, do they only serve eggs with pitchforks in hell?"

She rolls her eyes, but the corners of her lips twitch against her will. I'll take it. Hell, even just her sitting beside me this morning is a goddamn miracle.

"You're obnoxious," she chides. Then she picks up her fork and makes eye contact as she stabs it into a piece of cantaloupe. "And I am *not* going on that hike."

I catch a flurry of orange—the color of her gloves this morning—as she brings her fork to her mouth. My stomach tightens.

"Are you... feeling okay today?" I ask, lowering my voice. Darcy's eyes flit around the cafeteria, then back to me. She leans in just barely.

"I'm fine, I just hate hiking," she answers pointedly. "Can't we do something else?"

"Like what?" I ask. She shrugs.

"I'm in the middle of a *very* angsty billionaire romance novel that I've been dying to finish so—"

"You read?" My brows shoot up, and the moment the words tumble out, I realize what a stupid question it is. Not just for the question itself, but for the fact that a paperback book was among the many belongings in her pocketed pants. But before I get the chance to correct it, Darcy retorts.

"If you need me to teach you, all you have to do is ask."

I roll my eyes, forcing an intentionally fake laugh. "Funny," I pause. "You know, I didn't take you for the romance type."

Her eyes narrow just a little as she lowers her fork. That damn smirk creeps onto her face, making my chest tighten in a way I refuse to acknowledge. "What? Cold-hearted bitches don't get a happily-ever-after?"

My grin widens. "I guess you'll let me know."

She huffs a brief laugh before looking back to her plate, and when her breath brushes against my cheek, I think of last night.

I'm the person who usually notices things. The one who questions. The one who pries. Not just out of curiosity, though I'll admit, my nosiness has led to some pretty entertaining moments. But mainly out of habit. My brother was never the best at talking about things. He might be three years older than me, but I've always been the one to initiate those conversations. Even when he's the one in the wrong, I always have to push first. A little nudge here, a pressing question there, until he finally gives me a glimpse. He's one of the smartest people I know, but getting him to open up is like trying to get Bubbles to eat green beans.

Darcy's the same, though she definitely has her own way of prying back. I can imagine how hard it must have been for her to open up last night. And as much as I want to sit and dissect every word, every past conversation, to figure out how I could have known earlier, I know that's not what she wants. She just wants to be seen as herself. Not as someone with, what was it called?

Rigamarole Arthritis?

Whatever.

The point is, she doesn't want people to treat her differently because of it. I saw the disappointment in her eyes when she told me, like I'd reacted exactly how she thought I would. I hate that I did that, but I can't change the past. All I can do now is make sure that from here on out, I treat Darcy exactly the same as I always have.

Which suddenly propels me into the realization that I've been *way* too nice letting her bail on this.

I cock a brow, resting a hand on my hip. "We leave in ten minutes."

Darcy scowls. "No thanks."

"Oops, sorry," I say, feigning an innocent tone. "Did I make it sound like you had a choice?"

Her scowl deepens. "Who are you to say I don't?"

I hesitate just long enough to fabricate a white lie. "Your mom said we have to."

If I squint my eyes and tilt my head a little bit, I could argue that I read between Coach Cole's lines of saying we have to stick together, and didn't completely pull this out of my ass.

But Darcy doesn't need to know that. She groans loudly, clearly irritated, and sinks into her seat.

After breakfast, we head back to the cabin to get ready. Well, I was already ready, but Darcy needed to change out of her pajamas. Of course, the cabin is only one room, so I'm stuck on the doorstep again until she's finished getting dressed.

What a shame.

"It's only three miles, which kind of sucks, but there's supposed to be hammocks at the top," I call out through the screened door.

Her silence drags on for a few beats before responding. "Sounds like hell."

"And the view is supposed to be amazing," I continue, ignoring her pessimism. She comes back, tenfold.

"Not really my thing."

"Plus, Mr. Bubbles always gets the zoomies when we hike, and it's really fun to watch his jowls jiggle."

As if she's appeared out of thin air, Darcy's voice sounds right behind me. "Okay, that's cute."

I spin around fast, taking in the sight of her. She's wearing an army green jacket, a matching beanie snug over her now neatly brushed hair, heather gray gloves, and gray joggers that hang off her long legs, a row of pockets bulging at the sides. The sight etches a coy smile in the groove of my lips.

"What'd you pack this time?" I gesture at the pockets. She rolls her eyes, probably a calculated plan in hopes I don't catch the fact that she's smiling while she does it. A failed plan.

"Some snacks, pain meds, water, first aid stuff for your cut, and duct tape."

I frown, confused. "Duct tape? For what?"

She grins. "Just in case you don't shut up."

I clasp a hand over my heart, feigning a wince.

She laughs, shaking her head. I like the little rays that form around her eyes when she does that.

I reach for the doorknob, but just before I turn it, a hand presses to my shoulder. I glance back, meeting her gaze.

"You're not gonna tell anyone, right?" she asks. Those emerald eyes are wide, looking down at me worriedly. I'm almost offended that she feels the need to ask me. But then again, we haven't exactly been on the best of terms.

I pause for a second, then let a coy smile etch into my lips. "Tell anyone what?"

A pink tint flushes Darcy's cheeks as a smile breaks across her face, and I turn back to the door, pulling it open.

M Y BEDROOM IS NEXT to Harlowe's, and still, I have never heard so much moaning in my *life.*

Half of the twenty-two-player team is grumbling as we hike up the trail, but Bailey is the main culprit, letting out a series of long, dramatic sighs every time the flat ground turns into an uphill. It appears I'm not the only one who dragged their "buddy" along. Even Mr. Bubbles is getting fed up with the noise, trotting ahead to sniff the jerky in Coach's pocket. She swats him away at first, but when he presses his wet nose to her side again, I watch as she rips a piece of jerky in half and tosses it to him.

"For someone who can spend hours on the ice without a complaint," Harlowe starts, digging her spiked shoes into the dirt. I like hiking, but I can admit Harlowe takes it to a whole other level. I enjoy it casually—wandering the woods, getting lost, listening to the animals. At my own pace, you know? But Harlowe treats it like a second sport. She wears ridiculous shoes, packs enough snacks to survive a week of isolation, and sports those damn spikes even though there's no ice anywhere. "You're *really* whiny about hiking."

Bailey scowls, trudging along the path in tight jeans, a velvety pink sweatshirt, and brand-new white sneakers. If I were her, I wouldn't be thrilled either.

"Don't pretend hockey is the same as *this.*" She gestures to the path like it's personally offended her. Then she looks over her shoulder, calling out, "Right, Darcy?"

I glance back, catching Darcy's confused stare. Her brows furrow, and she tilts her head. "Huh?"

"Isn't hiking *completely* incomparable to hockey?"

I nudge Bailey's ribcage with my elbow, and she winces, whipping around with a scowl. "What the hell?"

I shake my head, giving her a disapproving look. "Don't do that."

She rubs her rib dramatically. "Do what?"

"*Don't* bring it up," I mutter, shooting her a serious look. Bailey pauses, then shrugs ingenuously.

"I didn't mean it like *that,*" she says, shoving her hands into her jacket pockets. "We were just talking the other day about how we *despise* nature."

I glance back at Darcy. A hint of a smile tugs at her freckled lips, and she gives me a subtle nod.

"Oh," I reply.

When we've made it to the top, we gaze out at the endless rows of trees and snow-capped mountains. The midday sun bathes the forest below, golden rays streaking through the forest. It's absolutely beautiful.

So beautiful, in fact, that nothing should spoil it. But then Caydence steps right in front of me, and I'm instantly proven wrong. She glances over her shoulder, eyeing me up and down judgingly, before turning back to the view.

"You figure out why yet?" she asks smugly.

I shoot her an annoyed look. "Why what?"

She rolls her eyes with exaggerated flair, letting out a huff as she turns fully to face me. "Why little miss coach's daughter over there dropped her spot on a pro league." She juts her chin toward Darcy, who's lazily curled up in a hammock, her long hair catching in the breeze as she scribbles on her clipboard.

I watch her, for just a beat too long, before looking back to Caydence. "Why do you give a shit?"

Caydence quirks an eyebrow, her lips curving into an amused challenge. "Don't you? I figured *you* of all people would be digging for answers." Her gaze drifts from my scuffed sneakers up to my eyes, and it nearly makes me shudder. "Or maybe you're too busy digging for *other things.*"

My brows drop, nose scrunching in confusion. "What's that supposed to mean?"

She shrugs all innocently, and I might not be the sharpest blade on the ice, but I'm smart enough not to fall for it. "Nothing. Just, I've noticed the way you two look at each other. And I saw your arm hooked in hers the night of—"

I cut her off before she can say more, taking a step forward and lowering my voice so that nobody overhears. "You have no idea what you're talking about, Cay," I shoot, my patience thinning. "I see what you're doing here. And it's not going to work. If you're too blind to see that Darcy and I can hardly stand each other, then—"

Caydence tilts her head, that condescending expression creeping across her face. "You two sure talk a lot for people who can't stand each other."

"She's the student coach; I'm the team captain. We don't really have a choice." I start to turn away, but then stop, spinning back around to get the last word. "And for the record? I can't stand *you*, and yet here we are."

Then, I storm off.

Mean? Probably. Immature? Definitely. Regret it? Not for a second.

As captain, I'm supposed to carry myself with a certain level of maturity. I set an example for the rest of the team. But I also have a responsibility to keep my players in check, and Caydence has a way of skating the line just to see how far she can push it.

The idea that something's going on between Darcy and me? Laughable. I mean sure, whatever happened—or as she so delicately pointed out, *didn't happen*—in the locker room was confusing. And yeah, I was maybe slightly tempted to kiss her last night when she looked down at me with those dangerous emerald eyes. But just yesterday morning, I was genuinely worried she'd kill me. And okay, now that I know she was almost in the PWHL, her advice might actually carry some credibility, but that doesn't change the fact that she still drives me absolutely insane.

She's still the same bossy, annoying Darcy. Only now, she has more reason to be.

I pass Indie, gently patting Mr. Bubbles on the head, then Harlowe, who's picking pine needles and leaves out of Bailey's hair. I frown as I walk by, stopping to call out, "What the hell happened to you guys?"

Bailey scowls, shooting a look at Harlowe that's sharp as knives, then back at me. I direct my question toward Harlowe instead.

"What the hell did you do?" I ask, folding my arms over my chest like a parent. Harlowe presses her lips together in a tight, sheepish line.

"Nothing."

Bailey's eyes narrow, and she spins to face her. "*Bullshit!* You—"

I don't stick around for the drama. They might be my monkeys, but right now, I'm *not* in the mood to run the circus. Instead, I turn and head toward Darcy. I've left her alone for most of this hike. Time to annoy her a little.

"Whatcha doin'?" I ask, watching that little crease form at the center of her brows. It's my favorite thing about bothering Darcy—how that crease deepens every time. Sure, I love the pouty lips and her sarcastic comebacks, but that divot, the freckle that vanishes into it?

God, it's hypnotic.

Darcy doesn't even look up. She just keeps writing, adjusting her clipboard slightly to catch the light.

"What does it look like, Icarus?" she drawls, not breaking her focus.

I trace the inside of my cheek with my tongue, fighting the grin creeping up on me. When she calls me that damn nickname, everything gets foggy. I hate how that word sounds, I really do, but the way she says it... Yeah, it's starting to stick.

"What are you always doing with this thing?" I ask, reaching for the clipboard. She quickly pulls it away, tucking it against her chest as always.

"I fail to see how that concerns you," she replies, shooting me a narrowed look.

My expression twists into a mock, and I stick a finger up in the air, bobbing my head around as I repeat the sentence in a grating, high-pitched voice. "I fAiL tO sEe hOw tHaT cOnCeR—"

A dull pain radiates in my arm as she smacks the clipboard against it teasingly. "Oh, shut up."

She's trying to fight it, those coral lips threatening to smile. She rolls her eyes, the motion exaggerated like she's *so over me*, and then lifts her clipboard back up, positioning herself to the side to block my view.

"I'm gonna get a hold of that thing one way or another," I say, crossing my arms. "I mean, seriously. What could be on there that is so confidential? What, a hit list? Nuclear launch codes?"

Darcy's gaze flicks to mine, then back down to the page.

I continue. "If it's a hit list, am I at least at the top?"

"If it was," she says, not breaking her focus. "You would be."

I grin triumphantly, which seems to catch her eye, because her gaze breaks away and she looks at me, confused.

"You want to be at the top of my hit list?"

I shrug. "It means you thought about me."

"I don't even—" She shakes her head, sticking a hand up. "You know not all attention is good attention, right?"

"Depends on who you get it from." My gaze narrows, fixing onto her chest. I frown, pointing at it. "*Ew*. What the hell?"

Darcy's red brows drop, and just as her head tips down to look at the imaginary spot on her shirt, I swipe the clipboard from her grasp. Her grip around it tightens, but the plastic slips through her gloves like butter, and she lets out a frustrated grunt of effort.

"I *cannot* believe you fell for that again." I laugh, taking a hefty step back. Darcy's brows furrow, and she lunges forward, but the hammock begins to tilt, sucking her back down. I look at the clipboard.

Jeesh. It's a mess.

"You know, I thought you were all organized and shit, but..." I flip through the pages, studying the nearly indecipherable scribbles. "This is kind of a wreck."

"Yeah, I know," she shoots, finally prying herself from the hammock. I keep stepping back, sticks cracking beneath my feet as I analyze the pages. She storms toward me, and *whew* she looks angry.

"Give it back, Peyton," she says, sticking her hand out. I nod, hitching a shoulder as I read.

"I will, I will, just give me a minute." My eyes finally catch a legible paragraph.

Shorter periods with more breaks. Drills shouldn't change too much. Specialized skates and medical alert bracelets monitored by coaches/ medical staff. Less contact a—

"Hey, I was reading that!" I frown as Darcy rips the clipboard out of my hand. She holds it over her head, which is totally cheating if you ask me.

"It's not done yet," she snaps, spinning back toward the hammock.

Shit.

I speed after her. "No, it's great," I say, but my voice doesn't sound very convincing. Mostly because I'm not entirely sure what I read. But I'm sure it was good, whatever it is.

She rolls her eyes, dropping backwards into the hammock. "You don't even know what it is."

I pause, letting out a sheepish laugh. "Okay, no, not exactly, but I would like to."

She stares up at me, and as much as I like the fact that she towers over me, I'm enjoying this view of her. Her eyes narrow suspiciously. "Why?"

Always the "why" with this woman.

"Because it sounded interesting and it's clearly important to you," I answer honestly. She looks pissed. In my defense, I really did think it was going to be practice notes and drill strategies. I thought she was just being stubborn.

She looks up at me, jaw tight, emerald eyes simmering. But then they drop, and she lets out a sigh. Her eyes flit around the trees. Everyone else is busy talking or complaining. She looks back at me.

"It's... I had this idea," she says, her voice low. "You know how they have disabled hockey programs? For wheelchair users and amputees and stuff?"

I nod, stepping closer to hear her better. She continues.

"Well, I got to thinking, right when I took this job, about how I could get back on the ice." She pauses. It's a long pause, and for a moment, I don't know if she's going to finish. But then, she does. "What it would take for someone who deals with the same symptoms as me to keep playing. And I came up with an idea. Autoimmune Hockey."

Her eyes lock with mine, and I think this is the part where I'm supposed to say something, but no words come out. She lets out a diminishing laugh.

"Yeah, it's dumb, I know," she starts, but I reach out and grab her hand.

"It's not," I say quickly, and she looks at me like she's trying to figure out if I'm messing with her. I'm not, of course. I don't fully understand what Autoimmune Hockey means, but just the idea of her being passionate about the game enough to plan an entire league is impressive.

It makes my heart flip.

"Tell me more."

She hesitates at first, but after a moment, her gaze catches on her clipboard. She smiles, briefly, then continues. "We'd make the periods shorter," she explains. "Fifteen minutes instead of twenty. Less contact—" Her eyes catch mine, and I flash a sheepish grin. "To avoid serious injuries. Specialized equipment, vital monitors..." She trails off.

And I just grin like an idiot.

"You've really thought a lot about this," I say, surprised for some reason. I shouldn't be. Darcy thinks a lot about everything. It's what drives me crazy about her. But it's also something I admire.

She nods. "Yeah. It'll probably never happen but—"

"Don't manifest failure." I frown. Her eyes roll, then fall back onto the clipboard. She begins dissecting it, and I decide to let her.

"Alright," I say, pushing off the tree. "I'll leave you alone."

"Finally," she mutters, but there's an almost imperceptible smile tugging at the corner of her lips. Something about it makes my heart skip. I take a step back, and then another, watching as she falls back into it.

I like the way she tilts them to get the right lighting. I like the way her free hand gently pushes off the tree to keep the hammock rocking. I like the way she grins as she reads whatever words lie upon the page.

I take another step, then, just before I turn away, I throw one last comment over my shoulder.

"Would it be a bad time to mention your mom *didn't* tell me you had to come on this hike?"

Darcy's face shifts, her lips parting in betrayal. Her green eyes narrow as I keep walking, turning my back to her.

"Peyton Clarke, I can't fucking stand you!"

I grin. "Darcy Cole," I quip. "I think I can live with that."

NINETEEN

Darcy

Y LEGS ARE ABOUT to fall off, and when they do, Peyton Clarke will be listed as the cause of death.

I haven't worked out this much since March, and it's definitely showing.

My thighs feel like they've been run over by a truck, a thousand tiny knives prod at the tendons in my ankles, and every time I shift in bed, my hip gives a loud, sharp *pop.*

It would've been nice to know I didn't *need* to go on the hike earlier. But then again, if I knew, I probably wouldn't have gone. And even though hiking isn't my usual scene—especially since being diagnosed—I'm still a little proud of myself. Because damn it, I did the thing. Even if my legs are now plotting their revenge.

I can only imagine how much worse they'd feel if Peyton hadn't let me borrow her foam roller when we got back.

I roll uncomfortably, fingers tightening around the worn edges of my book. A soft laugh escapes me as I remember Peyton's comment from earlier—how I didn't seem like the "romance type."

Honestly, it couldn't be farther from the truth. I was always the girl who *lived* for Valentine's Day parties at school. The one who went to homecoming with my friends, secretly hoping my crush would ask me to dance (she didn't). I blame my parents for turning me into a hopeless romantic.

What they have is *completely* unrealistic.

Which is why I'd rather devour Aria Petrov forcing a Windy City billionaire onto his knees, than try to date in real life. Well... partially why.

Thankfully, my mom let us all break away from our "buddies" for the rest of the last day of the retreat. Which was fine by me because Peyton was starting to get back on my nerves. Every time I'd pick this damn book up, she'd open her mouth about my Autoimmune Hockey League. She wouldn't stop asking questions until I threatened to sleep outside. Last I saw, she was off with Lena and Harlowe, lumbering through the woods.

With the flip of my page, the cabin door swings wide open. Peyton stumbles inside, her amber eyes wide as saucers.

"You've gotta come with me," she blurts before I can even get a word in.

I blink up at her. "What's going on?"

"Just grab your coat," she orders, turning back toward the door.

Every hair on my body stands, my heart climbing into my throat. I sit up quickly, my body aching in protest while my mind runs laps around it. "What? Peyton, what's going on?"

She glances over her shoulder, and I've never seen such an urgent look in her eye. "Just trust me. You need to see something."

Her earnestness is enough to make me move. I swing my legs off the bed, shoving my feet into my slides as I grab my baby blue jacket from the back of the door and throw it on. I follow her out of the cabin and into the crisp night air. The chill baptizes me, but it doesn't seem to bother Peyton as she leads the way across the grounds. Her pace is hurried, and I try to ignore the soreness in my legs as I match it.

"Peyton, seriously, what's going on?" I ask, pulling my earmuffs from my pocket and tugging them on.

She keeps her gaze straight ahead, her footsteps never faltering. "You'll see when we get there."

My pulse thrums in my ears, the heavy thud rattling my sternum, and I don't really know that I want to find out what this is, but at this point, I don't have a choice. So I keep moving. If Peyton is acting this frantically, it must be important.

The path opens up, and suddenly the rink is in front of me. The ice is so white it almost hurts to look at, bathed in the cold light from the overhead lamps, the quiet hum of the refrigeration system buzzing in the night.

Peyton strides ahead purposefully, her silhouette cutting against the shimmering rink. As my feet slow, my eyes sweep the empty ice. It's untouched. There's nothing. No commotion, no team member collapsed or clutching a knee, no late-night emergency that would make sense of why I'm here. No scuffling feet, no shouting, just a perfect stretch of ice waiting for something to break it. My chest heaves as I look around, spinning in every direction, so sure, so confident that I am missing something.

My eyes fall anxiously onto Peyton, searching for answers, and that's when I see it.

The two pairs of skates, the two sticks, resting neatly on the bench beside her.

A searing flush rushes to my cheeks, my heart thundering hard enough to drown out the buzzing overhead. My stomach is concrete, sinking to the bottom of my body, crumbling when it hits the cold hard ground as I realize exactly what's going on.

She set me up.

I storm toward her, cheeks burning against the biting chill.

"You *lied* to me," I snap.

Peyton raises her hands in defense, the whites of her eyes growing. "Wait, wait, woah," she counters, but her calmness only fans the flames flickering inside me. "I didn't *lie* to you."

I grab one of the sticks, the cool of the fiberglass seeping through my gloves as I shove it angrily into her chest. "Then what is this?" An ache claws at the chords in my throat, and I do everything I can to steady them, though my words still tumble out jagged. "You said it was urgent."

Peyton runs a hand through her hair, forcing a guilty smile. "To be fair, that's subjective," she says, but I'm done being placated.

My eyes narrow and I take another step forward. "So when I try to give you advice, I'm 'nosy,' but when you do it, it's 'urgent'?" I toss the stick back down on the bench with a clatter. "You don't know what you're doing, so just *stay out of it*, Peyton."

I turn away, the raw ache in my throat swelling, threatening to suffocate me. I shouldn't have said anything. I should have let her keep believing I was a quitter, that I had truly moved on from all of this. I should have allowed everything to unravel as it was, slipping from this situation, from this job, to live the rest of my miserable life that I had mapped out for myself since March.

I feel foolish.

Fucking stupid, actually, for not anticipating this. For not *seeing* Peyton's stubborn, relentless nature, and recognizing that I would be nothing more than a project, a way for her to prove something to herself, to inflate her own fragile ego.

Tears well in my eyes, but I swipe them away quickly, my breath trembling as I force myself to step forward. But before I can take another, Peyton's voice cuts through behind me.

"I've seen your stats."

I freeze.

Every ounce of air in my lungs deserts me, my heart sinking to the vacant spot where my stomach used to lay. My teeth scrape together, rattling my skull when my jaw tenses. She had no right to look at my records. No fucking right.

"I don't want to talk about this, Peyton," I mutter instead, trying to stay calm. This is what she wants. To piss me off. To push me.

I can't see her, but from the sound of her voice, from the soft crunch of fallen leaves beneath her feet, I can tell she's taken a step closer. "You're not just good. You're better than every single person on this team, including me."

Tears roll down my cheeks again—fucking traitors—and despite every instinct in my body telling me to walk away, to knock on my mom's cabin, to fall apart in her arms like I've done so many times this year, I turn around. My arms cross tightly, as if that will do anything to shield me from the prying arrogance of Peyton Clarke.

"*Was,*" I say, looking her straight in the eye as tears pour from mine. "I *was.*"

Peyton steps closer, and the hairs on my arms rise, a shiver skittering down my spine. My breath hitches, ragged and weak, but I force myself to meet her gaze.

"See, I knew you were going to say that," she says, and I can hear the smug certainty in her voice. She thinks she knows me. Thinks she's figured me out. "And I think that's part of your problem. You—"

"Oh my god!" My hands tremble as I pinch the bridge of my nose, a humorless laugh slipping out. "Are *you* seriously going to try and tell me what *my* problem is?" I shake my head, blinking back the wetness in my eyes. "Just because I told you doesn't mean you get it. It doesn't mean you know me. You can't *fix* me, Peyton."

She stops. Like for once, for one goddamn second in her privileged life, she's considering that she might not know everything. But of course, it doesn't last. Her voice softens, but it doesn't lose its tenacity.

"I know." She hesitates, chewing on the inside of her cheek. "I can't make this better. I can't fix what you're dealing with, and it kills me. I know it's the last thing you want to hear, but you deserve to know. And it doesn't kill me because I think you're fragile." Her gaze steadies, pressing but not daring. "It's because you're *not.* You're stubborn, and resilient, and because of that, the fact that you've given up... I know this is unimaginably shitty. It's fucking unfair. And I can't change it. I can't make it go away."

She steps closer, her subtle lavender scent encircling me. That throbbing ache tugs at my throat again, but this time, I fight it back. Peyton's hand reaches out, and I should pull away, but my body doesn't even flinch when her fingers intertwine with mine.

"I can't give you your career back. I can't take away your pain. But I would never forgive myself if I didn't try. If I didn't do everything I could to make this easier for you. Even just a little."

Her hand squeezes mine, and every nerve in that arm sparks hot. Her golden eyes look up, soft and round, and I almost believe her. That Peyton just cares. That she's only doing what she thinks is right.

But when has trust ever played out in my favor?

"Look," I force the words out, my voice finally steady. "I appreciate the sentiment, okay? But I don't need this. And frankly, I don't want it. I'm twenty-fucking-two, and I've got a double knee replacement scheduled for next year. Alright? So just *please*, let me be done." I exhale shakily. "I have to be done."

A chill surges over my gloved fingertips as Peyton releases my hand. She steps back, lowering herself onto the bench as she pulls on her skates quietly.

"Okay," she says gently. "I'll leave you alone."

I give a sharp, half-appreciative nod, then begin to turn away, torn between crawling into my bed or seeking refuge in my mother's. But then, under the breath that I have gotten a little too familiar with, Peyton mutters:

"Wuss."

My body locks, frozen in place. A rush of blood courses through me, pooling in the tops of my cheeks. Before I can even think, before I can remind myself that a reaction is exactly what she wants, I'm spinning around, jaw clenched, teeth grinding as the words leave my mouth in a tight rasp. "What did you just say?"

Peyton shrugs, tightening the laces on her skates before straightening her posture.

"Nothing."

Heat expands over my body, crawling down my neck, and I take a step toward her, narrowing my gaze. "No, you called me a wuss."

"I didn't call you a wuss."

"You did."

A creak pierces the air as she opens the gate to the rink, glancing at me with a grin. "Must've been the wind."

My lips drop open to speak, to cuss her out, to yell, or scream, but for once tonight, my body actually decides to listen to my brain, and instead, I simply roll my eyes and turn around.

Not fucking worth it, Darcy.

I take a step, then another. But then—she *meows.*

Yeah. She fucking meows.

I whip back around. "What the hell are you trying to say, Peyton?"

"I have no idea what you're talking about." She puts on an innocent act, tilting her head like a puppy.

"Fuck this," I mutter, spinning on my heel, ready to walk away. But as I start to move, she feigns a cough behind me, choking out the words:

"Scaredy cat."

That's. It.

I storm toward her, shaking with rage, and jab my finger into her chest. "You know what? You're really fucking immature, Peyton."

She grins, pushing off the ice and calling back over her shoulder. "I'd rather be immature than be a wuss."

"I am not a fucking wuss!" I shout, but she's already halfway across the ice, cupping her ear, that smug grin widening.

"What was that?" she calls out tauntingly, her voice echoing off the boards. "I couldn't hear you!"

"I said I'm not a fucking wuss!"

Peyton gestures toward me with a mocking smile as she glides to the center line. She drops the puck in front of her. "Says the woman scared of a sheet of ice."

Then she winds up and sends the puck flying straight into the goal. She spins to look at me, propping a gloved hand on her hip. "You know what I think?"

I roll my eyes. "You don't."

She ignores me. "I think you're just scared that you're going to be rusty, and I'm going to be better than you."

A bitter laugh rises in my chest, tumbling out. Peyton casually glides past, the puck dangling from her fingers like a toy she's trying to get me to chase.

God, she's such a child.

"You're the one who *just* said *I* was better than *you*," I fire back.

"And you clarified that was past tense." She shrugs. "As of now…"

I shouldn't let it get to me. I shouldn't rise to her taunting. But I'm too far gone. The moment she meows again, something inside me snaps.

I grab the laces on the extra pair of skates, my fingers trembling angrily as I pull them loose. Slipping my foot in, I can feel they're a little big, but I tug the waxed laces tight anyway, the tension of them digging into the swollen skin around my ankle.

When I grab the stick, it feels heavier than I remember. Even through my gloves, it's cold against my palm as my fingers tighten around it, digging into the worn tape. I stand up, blades teetering as I step toward the rink.

I close my eyes and draw in a deep breath, the chill nipping at my lungs. It's a metallic, stale scent, a mingling of sweat and ice that used to belong to me, but now I only experience it from the sidelines. It's different, being on it. I let the air sink to the bottom of my lungs, as if the cold can freeze all the uncertainty gnawing at me.

My heart pounds against my ribs erratically, and I reach out, fingers brushing the wall to steady myself. Then, with a sharp inhale, I step onto the ice.

The moment my blades cut into the rink, everything feels wrong. My knees are shaking, my—

My *everything* is shaking.

I grip the edge like my life depends on it, and if you pulled my gloves off right now, the contrast of my knuckles against the purple hue of my skin would be concerning. I shift my weight, but the ice betrays me. My left skate slips, and I scramble to catch myself, the thud of my knee hitting the boards as I pull myself back to my feet.

"Careful there," Peyton calls out. I glance up, watching her skate with ease, a smirk dancing on her face. My jaw tightens.

"Fuck off," I mumble, trying to focus on staying steady.

She was right. I'm rusty—worse than I thought I'd be. It's not *her* fault, but it still feels like it is. If she hadn't pushed me to get back on the ice, I wouldn't even know how much I've fallen behind.

Peyton circles me, closing the distance with that same teasing grin. She moves fluidly, like the rink itself is listening to her commands. I used to move like that. Now, every push feels harder than the last. My breath comes out in frustrated bursts.

"Come on, Darcy, that's all you got?" she taunts. "I thought you were supposed to be a pro."

"Peyton," I shoot through clenched teeth. "I am going to *kick your ass*."

Peyton's grin stretches wider, which should be impossible. "There we go," she cheers, pointing at me. "C'mon, give me more."

I push off the ice again, this time letting my fingers simply hover against the edge. I want to tell her to shut up, to stop making this harder. To stop wasting my energy on her cocky remarks. But when my eyes lock on hers, she's looking at me like nothing in the world matters more than this.

"What's your *least* favorite thing about me?" she continues, gliding slowly beside me. My legs keep moving, picking up pace.

"I hate how you act like you know everything," I say without thinking. Immediately, my stomach twists guiltily, but when I look at her, she's still grinning. She nods her head.

"What else?"

My legs move faster, as my mind races, trying to remember every single time this woman has pissed me off. "I hate that you got into a fight on the ice."

"Good. Keep going."

My hands hover a foot from the edge, fingers aching to keep my balance, knees slowly beginning to settle as I make a hesitant turn around the rink. A cold breath fills my lungs, the chill cutting through me as my mind skates laps, swirling with every frustrated thought.

"I hate that you're good at your position because I *really* didn't want you to be." The words spill out. "I hate that stupid poster in your bedroom with the cats on it." My pace picks up.

"I hate that Cleo adores you because it makes it *really* hard to hate you." Faster still.

"And I hate that in the cabin, when you made me dance with you—" My gaze locks with hers, and suddenly I'm in the center of the rink, the ice gleaming beneath me like a vast, white sea. "I hate that you didn't kiss me."

The moment the words slip from my mouth, Peyton flicks her stick, sending the puck hurtling in my direction. It comes at me like a bullet, too fast for my mind to catch up, but my body kicks into autopilot.

Instinctively, I turn, my wrists driving forward, and the puck slams into the blade of my stick with a satisfying *clack*. It ricochets, flying toward Peyton, but I don't hear anything except the pounding pulse in my ears. It vibrates through every inch of me, shaking my chest, rattling my ribcage, thumping in my fingertips, racing down my legs.

Peyton catches the puck with ease, halting it with the practiced tap of her stick, her grin widening as those damn smile lines crease her cheeks.

"Darcy."

I raise an eyebrow, frustration still bubbling in my chest. "*What?*"

Peyton leans her weight onto her stick, looking at me with stars in her eyes. "You're playing hockey."

My tongue presses against the inside of my cheek as a smile tugs at my lips, despite myself. It shouldn't be there. There's no reason for it. And yet—

"You know I hate you, right?"

Peyton's eyes shimmer, as she lets out a casual, "I know."

We stare at each other for a minute, saying nothing, but eyes saying everything.

Peyton's are saying:

I win.

While mine are responding with:

You're a massive dick. Also, thanks.

She punctuates the conversation with a smile, then pushes backwards, tapping her stick against the ice.

"Come on," she calls out. *"Kick my ass."*

I shake my head with a laugh, propping a hand on my hip. "I think that's enough for one night," I say. Peyton's eyes catch mine, and just when it looks like she's about to give in, I lunge forward and swipe the puck from her possession.

I wish I could see the look on her face as I barrel toward the goal, but my back is turned to her as she calls out behind me. "Cheater!"

A grin breaks across my face as the wind funnels though my ears, my hair flying behind me in an auburn wave. My pulse is fast, but my knees are steady, in spite of the burn creeping up my body. My gaze narrows onto the net, and I can hear Peyton's skates scraping the ice just behind me. Before she can reach me, I wind back, and shoot.

The puck soars into the goal like it has so many times before, and still, I don't believe it as I watch the net give way. Peyton flies past me, scooping it up with a grin.

"You totally tricked me!" She pants, broad shoulders heaving. I smirk, folding my arms.

"And you lied to me, so now we're even."

Peyton glides in a circle around me. "I told you," she says, spinning the other direction. "I didn't lie."

Then she pushes off the ice with everything she's got and planes toward the opposite end. My feet move after her, albeit clumsily due to the ill-fitting form of these skates. I wonder, for a second, who these even belong to, and pray it's not Faith because she's got a nasty case of athlete's foot.

"Come on," Peyton teases, skating backward. "Catch me if you can!"

The cold air stings my cheeks as I chase after her, my heart thudding against my ribcage, thighs practically melting off my body. God, it burns so bad. But then, it burns so good. It's this odd blend of RA aches and second-day soreness. Something harsh yet satisfying. Punishing yet rewarding. Bitter yet sweet. The gap between us shrinks, and I know I'll pay for this tomorrow, but right now, I don't give a damn.

I just want to play.

I'm almost there, close enough to reach out, just inches from the back of her green jacket. I push forward, tilting my stick in an attempt to gain control of the puck, but then—

BAM!

Peyton plummets to the ice. It happens so fast I almost miss it. She crashes down with a dramatic thud, arms flailing as she tries to catch herself, but it's too late. My knees rattle as I dig my skates into the ice, the cold powder spraying out from under them as I bring myself to a halt.

"Shit!" I call out, moving back over to her. "Are you okay?"

Peyton's face down on the ice, her body shaking against the ground.

Fuck.

I lean over her, hand grazing the back of her jacket. "Peyton, are you okay?"

I ask again, heart racing.

A sound comes out of her, and I don't realize that it's a laugh until she flips onto her back, and I see the smile stretched across her face. That cut near her lip is fresh again, though this time it's not oozing. She continues chuckling, body shaking mirthfully as she stares up at me.

"That hurt." She giggles. I roll my eyes, offering her a hand.

"Sounded like it," I respond, releasing a shaky breath as subtly as I know how. I don't need Peyton walking around thinking I care.

She eyes my hand, squinting at me, then grabs my arm with a surprising amount of strength. I shift my weight onto my heels, bracing myself to pull her up, but suddenly, I'm flying forward, tumbling on top of her with a soft thud.

She lets out another laugh, and I want to be mad, but before I can decide it's the route I want to take, I'm laughing with her. Her hand still grips my wrist, and she looks up at me with a triumphant grin.

"Did that hurt?" she asks.

"Yes. And just so you know, when I can't walk tomorrow, I'm blaming you."

Peyton's breath, warm and ragged, ghosts across my lips. Her amber eyes are like sunlight shining up at me, heating my skin everywhere they look. My eyes, first, then my lips; they trail down my neck, pausing on my chest. My breath hitches.

"I'll give you a massage," she says, her free hand tracing an X over her heart. "Scout's honor."

I try to push myself up, palms slipping on the ice, but a gentle pressure holds me down. Her hand rests on the small of my back. Every instinct screams at me to break free, to regain control. But my muscles refuse to obey.

She brushes a stray strand of hair behind my earmuffs, the touch sending an ironically warm shiver down my spine. I'm sure I look ridiculous right now, hovering over her, headband slipping sideways, but she just smiles at me.

"Do you still want me to kiss you?" Peyton murmurs. My hand cups the side of her face in a silent admission.

It's been months since I've touched someone like this. Since I've kissed anyone. Eight to be exact. And if anyone else were asking, I'd say no. I'd make up an excuse—say I have mono, or cold sores, or just inhaled a family-sized bag of Doritos. Anything that would put this possibility to an end.

But none of that comes out.

And for some, demented reason, I can't think of anything I'd want to do more than kiss Peyton Clarke right here on the ice.

"Just do it, Clarke."

She doesn't wait another beat. No hesitation, no delicate tap-in. This isn't some polite peck. This is a sudden death overtime kind of kiss. A full-on declaration of unequivocal intent.

Her mouth crashes against mine, and whatever air I believed I was holding onto slips right through me. The ice beneath might as well be a tropical beach, because the frost is gone, melted away by the scorching, delirious heat of her body.

This isn't just a game anymore. This is a high-stakes, breathless showdown. A winner-takes-all kind of exchange. Every argument, every witty barb, *this* is the culmination. This is sudden death, and like I said before, I don't like to lose.

TWENTY

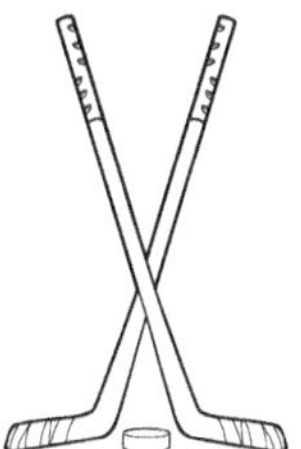

Peyton

I'M NOT MUCH OF a reader. Ever since I could walk, hockey's been pretty much the only thing on my mind. But last year, Bailey loved a book so much that she practically begged Harlowe and me to read it. Harlowe flat-out refused, but I forced myself through it. It wasn't bad, really. It just wasn't easy to focus when I kept thinking about all the time I could've spent practicing. But it made Bailey happy, so I powered through.

I don't remember the title or even the plot, honestly. All I remember is that there were two people who hated each other... and then they kissed. Why am I bringing this up? Because it was *bullshit*. After that kiss, they fell to the ground, all desperately, turning into some messy, hot, wet bundle of... well, *smut*. Basically.

They had sex, is what I'm getting at.

Want to know what actually happens?

"I—umh—" I stutter as Darcy pulls herself off me, helping me to my feet. Her freckled cheeks are flushed, lips still glistening in the pale light. The back of my head tingles where her fingers had gripped my hair, my lips still throbbing with the heat of her kiss. A kiss that was mine, until she stole it. Until she turned it into hers. We both just stand there, blinking at each other awkwardly.

It's not that it was a bad kiss.

In fact, it was everything I hoped it wouldn't be.

I hoped it would be one of those awkward "whoops" moments you laugh about later. I hoped it would convince me that the weird tightening in my chest didn't mean what I thought it did. That the flutter in my stomach was just a result of too much caffeine and sugar, and not because I actually wanted to kiss her. That I wanted her to kiss me back.

Motherfucker.

"Sorry," Darcy says, looking at me awkwardly. I've messed this up. I don't know how, but I've messed it up. I've kissed a lot of people. Hell, I kissed Kai like four weeks ago. It's always been fun. Easy. People say I'm good at it. But with Darcy? The beat's been thrown off.

The moment my lips touched hers, I knew I was done for. It didn't feel easy. It felt like the most terrifying thing I've ever done. It felt like a challenge, one I'm not quite sure I won. And it felt... good. *Too good.* And now, I have no fucking clue what to do.

I shake my head, heart pounding in my chest. "What? Why are you sorry?"

Darcy shrugs, making her way off the ice. "I don't know." She hitches a shoulder. "You just seem... *upset.* So I guess—"

"Upset?" I frown, staggering behind her. When Darcy first stepped back on the ice, she looked like a baby deer learning to walk for the first time. Now, guess who's Bambi? "I'm not upset. I just... didn't expect that."

Darcy plops onto the bench, quickly untying her skates. Or, Harlowe's skates. She'll never know they were gone. Her eyes flick to meet mine, a confused "v" etched in her brow. "You're the one who asked."

I shrug sheepishly, bending down to untie my own skates because sitting next to her right now feels like the wrong move. If I sit next to her, I might want to kiss her again.

Who am I kidding? I want to kiss her again anyway.

"Yeah, I know," I say hesitantly. *What the hell is wrong with me?* Darcy quirks a brow as she watches me fumble with my laces.

"Did I do something wrong?"

"What? *No!*" I take off my beanie, running a hand through my hair. Why is

it wet? "You didn't do anything wrong. You did it right. *Very* right. I'm just—"
I suck in another breath. "I'm just feeling overheated. Are you overheated?"

Darcy blinks at me, then holds up a gloved hand. "Well given that it's thirty-nine degrees and my circulation system is about as effective as a plastic spork—"

"Right." I force an awkward smile. Darcy eyes me skeptically, then pushes herself off the bench.

"Okay..." She trails off, then begins walking. "I'm gonna head back to the cabin now."

I nod, way too enthusiastically, then dial it back as I finally pry off my skates. "Okay! Yeah. Sounds good." I pause, internally kicking myself. "I'm gonna head back to mine too, so..."

Darcy turns to face me.

"Peyton," she says, folding her arms over her chest. When my eyes catch those emerald jewels, I swear I let out a squeak.

"Hmm?"

"We're sharing a cabin."

The realization hits me just as quickly as the cold pavement hits my feet. I reach for my shoes, not caring that the back of my sneakers cave in as I shove my feet on top of them. A nervous laugh escapes me.

"I knew that," I say, even though clearly in the heat of the moment, I had forgotten. "I was just joking."

Darcy stares at me with an unconvinced expression. "Okay. Well, if you want, I can go to my mom's cabin. She won't—"

"Pshhh." I wave a dismissive hand, heat creeping into my cheeks as I try to remember how normal people stand. "That's really not necessary. The more the merrier!"

The more the merrier?

What the fuck?

Darcy's lips press together, but the corners of them sink in a little, almost like she's holding back a smile.

Of course she is, that masochist. This is probably her dream come true, watching me crumble into a flustered, anxious wreck. This has never happened to me before. The only time I have ever felt as stressed as this is before my games, and even that is easier because it's only one feeling. One sensation. This is like—a collage of everything good and everything bad in the world.

"Alright, then I'll walk with you." She offers.

Of course she will.

I don't bother to fix my shoes. I just swoop my skates and stick into my hands, and shuffle over to her like my legs are bound with wire. She studies me but doesn't say anything as we make our way back to the cabin.

This is karma. I can't even pity myself, because this is exactly what I deserve after what I pulled. I thought I was being helpful. Hell, up until we kissed, I was confident that I was successful. And while that may be true, so is this:

I kissed Darcy Cole.

And I liked it.

Darcy hops up the steps first, dropping her skates and stick on the porch. I set mine beside them, putting my gloves down too, as my heart hammers in my chest. She steps through the front door, and this is ridiculous, I should really calm down, but instead I snatch my water bottle off the ledge.

"I'm just gonna fill this up," I say, gesturing to it. Darcy gives me an amused nod, tugging off her earmuffs.

"Alright."

"Okay."

We stand there for a moment, just staring at each other, until finally, I turn, ready to bolt down the steps. But before I can make another move, something grabs my wrist. Darcy's fingers tighten around me and before I can even process what's happening, I'm spun back into her chest.

And then, her lips crash into mine.

For a second—just a fleeting second—my body freezes. But then, her hand slides to the back of my neck and she pulls me in. And suddenly, I'm in the book.

I'm the melting, shirt-grabbing, desperately panting love interest, and Darcy is shoving the door open behind her, still kissing me as she stumbles backward toward the bed.

The mature thing—the *captainly* thing—to do would be to stop.

But I think we've already established that maturity isn't always my strong suit. And besides, I could be the most professional person on the planet, and still, nothing could convince me this isn't worth it.

Darcy's lips are warm and soft and they taste of strawberry chapstick. Her tongue slips against mine, and her fingers tighten in my hair. A quiet moan escapes me, a restrained plea for her to pull me down, to inversely replicate the tumble on the ice. Instead, she shifts, the edge of the mattress pressing against my legs, and deepens the kiss. My body tips backward, my fingers clinging to her jacket as the hard mattress meets my spine.

It's dark in the cabin, but the pale moonlight beams through the small window above, illuminating just a stripe of Darcy's freckled cheeks. She straddles me, still fully clothed, still kissing me like I'm the air she breathes.

And here I am, still loving it.

"Is this okay?" she asks breathily, her lips brushing the sweet spot behind my ear. The softest moan escapes my lips, and I'm already a puddle.

"More than okay."

One hand stays tangled in my hair, anchoring me to the pillow, while the other slips beneath my shirt, Darcy's cool gloves tracing the curve of my ribs. A jolt of pure electricity shoots through me, and I don't know if it's a threat or a promise. I have little to no proof that Darcy Cole wants me alive. Maybe this was her plan all along. Maybe that's why she kissed me on the ice like she was pouring every last watt of energy into it. Like she was trying to cause a surge, an explosion, so she could show up to our next practice without my questioning interruptions.

Maybe she was right.

Maybe I am Icarus.

And she's the sun.

And oh, fuck—I'm going to *burn to death.*

My pulse quickens, traveling though my body, thrumming in my ears, and thudding between my thighs. If I had any survival instincts, I'd be pulling out from under her. Running out the door. Screaming for my life because I just made Darcy Cole step onto the ice, and now she's on top of me.

But if this is natural selection, the pale moonlight of her body, the breeze of her breath, the sweet almond cherry scent as her thigh finds the space between mine and presses?

Mother Nature, do your worst.

"Take these off," I say, tugging at the hem of her gloves as her fingertips toy with the band of my sports bra. Darcy just keeps kissing me, her tongue wandering up the curve of my jaw, and I shudder underneath her before pulling at them again. This time, her hand draws back.

Then her lips.

Then her body.

My brows pinch in concern, and I sit up slightly, trying to meet her eye, though it's kind of hard in the dark.

"Are you okay?" I ask, breath staggered.

Darcy doesn't respond immediately, which makes me all the more convinced that she's about to snap my neck. My heart pounds, breath hitching as she leans back.

Fuck.

Is she getting a weapon?

"Darcy, I—"

"I want to take my gloves off," she says softly. I can't see her, just the silhouette of her body straddling mine. The familiar details I'm so used to staring at—her freckles, that golden ring on her nose, those emerald eyes, all fade in the dark. But it doesn't matter. I could spend years studying the fundamental shape of her.

"Then take them off," I murmur, raising my hand to trace the dip in her cheek, hoping to imprint it on my mind. I'm not a total idiot. I know this is the first *and* last time I will ever touch Darcy. Whether that be due to the realities of her disdain for me, my lack of time for anything beyond this, or the fact that I'm still not entirely convinced she isn't trying to kill me. And if I never get to touch her again, I need to remember *exactly* what she felt like.

Darcy leans forward, her chest brushing against mine as she kisses me.

"I don't want you to see me."

I frown. "It's dark."

I can't see her, but I can physically feel her rolling her eyes. "Figure that out on your own, did ya?"

A slight chuckle slips out of me. Darcy continues.

"Look, it's dark, but it's not dark enough. And I don't want you to see..." she trails off.

My fingers trace down her cheek to her mouth. My thumb brushes over her bottom lip, and I lift my gaze toward the place where I can almost make out the shape of her eyes.

"Darcy, I think you're the prettiest demon I have ever laid eyes on."

She shakes her head against my hand. "If you saw what my hands and ankles look like, you wouldn't say that."

My stomach twists at the thought of Darcy being insecure about herself. About her disease. "I'm not well educated on what Rhinoceros Articulitis *looks* like—"

"Rheumatoid Arthritis."

"—but unless you've grown like, an alligator tail or—"

She laughs, playfully smacking me. "Shut up."

I don't, of course.

"Actually, I take that back. Godzilla was my queer awakening."

"...Isn't Godzilla a boy?"

I shake my head against the pillow. "Actually, in the original films, Godzilla's nonbinary. It wasn't until they did the English dub that they began to use he/him pronou—"

Her lips cut me off, warm, soft. When she pulls back, a sharp breath blows across my lips as she laughs. "Anyone ever tell you your pillow talk is panty-melting?"

I grin. "Only all the time."

Darcy smiles against my neck, then pulls back, leveling herself. "I still don't want you to look at me," she says.

I pause. This is an out. The part of the horror movie where you're screaming at the blonde girl to run upstairs while she has the chance. Where the ship is going down, and there's one lifeboat left.

But instead of blowing the whistle, instead of stumbling up the stairs, that hot pulse sparks in my clit again. It pools between my thighs, warm and wet, and I tighten at the ache.

"Where's your eye mask thing?" I ask.

Darcy hesitates before answering. "On the nightstand."

"Put it on me."

I hear her breath hitch. "I don't want to make you—"

"Darcy," I say, firmer this time. *"Put it on me."*

Darcy obeys, lifting my head to tug the mask around my face. Her silhouette disappears. *Everything* disappears. But the sound of her breath in the pitch black? My pussy tenses. Slick. Hot. *Really* hot.

"Damn," I say, fidgeting with the silk fabric as it slips down my face. I lift my head up to tuck the slack of the strap underneath me, so that Darcy can't claim I'm peeking, no matter how badly I want to. "What's your head size? Wrecking ball?"

The moment it leaves my mouth, I regret it. What if big heads are a symptom of RA?

But Darcy just laughs. "Fuck you," she says, but I can hear the smile in her voice.

"Seriously, Darcy. What are you doing coaching a hockey team when you've got buildings t—"

Her lips press to mine firmly. She doesn't pull back to let me finish my sentence, or to stutter as I'd try. She just keeps kissing me, her tongue slipping between my teeth, chest pressing against mine in a rhythmic wave. And it isn't until her hand slips back under my shirt that I realize:

She finally took her gloves off.

It's just a hand. Skin and bones. But the feeling of her bare fingertips against my body sends goosebumps down my arms. Sends a needy moan tumbling from my lips. The pads of her fingers dip under the band of my bra again, tracing slowly from left to right, and her thigh presses, relieving the wet ache of my clit.

A breath hitches in my chest, and shit, how am I already soaked?

"Fuck," I mutter. Darcy does it again.

"Can I take it off?" she asks, tugging at it.

I used to have dignity, right? Like, I cared what people thought, about me, about my career. But now, with Darcy pressed against me, her thigh grinding, her hands on my skin, her breath asking if she can take my bra off? Dignity's dead.

All I want is her.

"You can do whatever you want."

And that's all Darcy needs to hear. Quickly, breathily, she pulls my shirt over my head. The mask begins to slip, but I'm not about to fuck this up by letting it, by betraying her trust. So I press it tight, maneuvering around the gaps as the clothes begin to fly off. Cold air rushes to my skin as she undresses me, but the heat of her against me is enough to wash it away.

"This is never happening again," she says directly, as her fingers tug at the waistband of my pants. I lift my hips just enough for her to wriggle them down my body, taking my underwear along with them. The insides of my thighs streak with my arousal, and she tosses them both aside.

"Figure that one out on your own, did ya?" I parrot.

Darcy's hands cup either side of my thighs as she slips her face between them. "I can't wait to shut you up, Peyton," she murmurs against my skin, scrubbing goosebumps down my legs. My hips buck involuntarily, which makes the next words to leave my mouth pointless.

"You'll have to do a lot more than that," I say, but it's pretty much a moan. Darcy doesn't respond. She simply smiles against me, causing my already quickened pulse to spike even faster.

Her breath brushes my swollen clit, and as my legs dangle over her shoulders, I realize, at some point, Darcy has stripped. Completely. Her breasts graze my thighs, her lips hover over my throbbing heat. The knowledge that I'm blindfolded, that she's naked for *herself*, ignites a desperate heat within me.

A gasp escapes me as her tongue flicks out, a hot, wet stroke that sends a jolt through my pussy. My fingers dig into the sheets, as the slick heat of her mouth traces circles around my clit. I moan.

"Fuck, Darcy."

"I'm working on it," she murmurs against my slick folds, amusement clear in her tone. I try to respond, to give her some witty remark like usual, but all that comes out is a strained whimper.

"Cat got your tongue?" she teases.

Before I can respond, her tongue plunges deeper, a hot, insistent probe that makes my hips buck. I feel the cut of her teeth, a delicious sharpness against my swollen clit, and my grip on the dusty, one-hundred-and-fifty thread count sheets tightens. The sound of her soft, wet lapping fills the room, and god, I wish I could watch her pretty face as she drags her tongue from my dripping entrance to the throbbing tip of my clit.

"God," I breathe. Her head keeps moving in a methodical rhythm, side to side, and with every brush against that spot, my body tenses.

"So fucking wet," she whispers, her voice a low growl against my cunt. I whimper as she takes one finger and swipes it up my slick center. That pressure, the feeling of her hand between my thighs, vanishes for a moment. I inhale sharply, heart pounding in my ears.

And then I hear it.

The quiet, deliberate suck of her mouth, the soft moan that rumbles in her throat. Not on me. On her finger. I listen, hips bucking helplessly, as Darcy savors every drop of my arousal.

Holy fuck.

I've had sex. A lot of sex. A lot of good, casual sex. But never in my life has someone *licked me off their fingers.* And never in my life did I think I'd enjoy listening to Darcy do that very thing.

"Mmm..." she moans.

Fuuuuuuuuuuck.

My chest heaves, coldness settling where her warmth used to be. "Please," I groan desperately, releasing the sheets to find her body. "I need you."

My palms land on her shoulders, then travel down until I reach her chest. The calloused pads of my fingers graze over her taut nipples, and I wonder what color they are. Pink, or peachy? Pale, or bright? I want to take off this blindfold. I want to devour every curve of her body with my eyes, memorize every freckle, fall in love with every color.

"Darcy," I moan impatiently, body jolting desperately. Finally, her fingers dip back into me, slow, tentative, at first. Two fingertips tease my entrance, and an unbridled moan slips out, louder than before.

"Be quiet," Darcy shoots. "Someone is going to hear you."

My teeth sink into my lower lip as I try to bite back the next one, but when those fingers dive deeper into me, when they curl against the walls inside my body, the next one slips out before I knew it was coming. I feel Darcy's body move against mine, her bare tits dragging up my skin. Her hand stays firmly in place, but now, even in the darkness of the blindfold, I know her face is only inches from mine.

"Are you going to be quiet, or do I need to make you?"

I shake my head, letting out a weak and breathy, "I'm going to be quiet."

I'm a fucking liar. A desperate liar, by the way, because never in my life have I been turned on by a threat. Not until now. And even with the nervous pound of my heart, part of me wants to find out if Darcy's the type to follow through on her promises. Her fingers continue pumping, in and out, the sound stretching to fill every corner of the room as I whimper as silently as I can manage against her lips, arching my back in desperation.

She sucks my earlobe between the cut of her teeth as her hand continues thrusting. Her breath brushes against the shell of my ear as she whispers, *"Do you like that, Pretty Girl?"*

"Oh fuck!"

Shit.

Darcy stops. Her hand. Her breath. I swear, even the pulse between us stops too. I suck in a shaky breath.

"Sorry," I say quickly, body still writhing, desperate for friction. My hips roll against her hand, doing all the work, because if that's what it takes to come undone, then god, I'll fucking do it. Anything, anything at all to cure the ache thrumming between my thighs. Anything to be wrecked by her hands the same way time wrecks plans.

Relentlessly.

Darcy lets out an annoyed sigh, but before I can apologize, beg her to continue because—shit, I have no dignity left so what the hell?—a warm flesh presses to my mouth. It's smooth and supple. Warm.

"If you're that loud again, we're going to have to stop," she says, and my tongue begins tracing her nipple, sucking gently. She moans. "Do you want to stop?"

My mouth parts with her skin only to respond. "No," I breathe. "No, please don't stop."

"Then control yourself," she orders, pressing her supple tit back into my mouth, the taste of her warm and sweet, slightly salty from our time on the ice. My hips continue their needy rhythm against her hand, the slick heat between my thighs making the glide effortless. I can feel the subtle shift of her fingers, the way they press and stroke, and the knowledge that she's controlling this, that she's holding back, sends a wave of frustrated heat through me.

"Darcy," I murmur against her chest I want her to push me over the edge, to wring me dry, but she holds back, teasing, tormenting. Her fingers slide deeper, stretching me, filling me, and I gasp against her skin.

I am excruciatingly desperate.

"I like watching you like this," she whispers. Then she picks up speed. "Needy. Begging." Each stroke is calculated, each brush against my clit with her thumb an intentional tease. Pressure builds in my gut, a tight, throbbing ache that spreads through my entire body. "Listening, for once, like a good *fucking* girl."

Holy fuck.

I press my mouth harder against her breast, silencing the whimpers that threaten to escape. My teeth sink into her skin, and she winces slightly, but she doesn't slow down. I feel the pulse of her heart against my lips. It's just as fast as my own. Her fingers continue. Hot, wet thrusts, and something inside of me starts to unravel as my body jolts and grinds. The tips of her fingers curl against that sensitive spot inside me. Over and over.

"Shit! I'm gonna—" I plead, my voice muffled against her. My body clenches, a desperate, involuntary spasm, and that loosening thread inside me snaps.

"Don't stop," she commands.

A silent cry rips through me, the sound trapped in my throat. My body shudders, convulsing around her fingers, and the throbbing ache in my clit finally bursts. I can feel her fingers, still moving, still stroking, pushing me further, deeper into the white bliss. I cling to her body as the sensation rolls through me, every muscle in my body tightening and loosening at the same damn time.

When the world slowly returns to focus, Darcy's fingers ease, and I'm left gripping her body in a sweating, panting heap. Her breast slips from my mouth as she pulls back, and I let go of her, trailing my pulsing fingertips down her body.

She quickly pulls them away, and my stomach sinks.

"Let me return the favor," I murmur, still panting, tracing her jaw.

I feel her head shake against mine, then, the flat sheet sliding out from under me. When Darcy pulls the eye mask off, it's like I have night vision in contrast to the dark silk I had on before. I can see better now, and I think Darcy's aware, because she's fully cocooned, hands included, in the sheet.

"It's not an exchange," she says, collapsing beside me on the bed. The moonlight sweeps over her briefly as she falls back, and it's like it exists to illuminate her. Our eyes lock for a moment, and then she smiles softly. "Don't take it like that," she says. "I'm just more of a giver sometimes. Helps me feel less insecure." Then her brow quirks. "Didn't take you for a pillow princess though. Huh."

An offended scoffs slips out of me, and I grab the pillow from under my head, and smack her with it lightly. "If you fucking tell anyone—"

She laughs, then settles back into the bed. "Please. You think I want anyone to know I fucked the team captain?"

"Better than the spawn of Satan."

"Hey that's mean." She grins. "I prefer the devil herself."

TWENTY ONE

Darcy

*E*VERYTHING IS RED.

I flick my eyes to the left, then to the right, eyelids still squeezed shut.

Yup. Still red.

Wait—shit. Why is it red?

My eyes snap open, a harsh beam of golden sunlight pouring through the cabin windows. I blink rapidly, stars sparking behind my eyelids. Normally, I'd have my sleep mask on, but—I glance around, spotting it on the floor.

Right.

My legs wriggle, an attempt to peel myself out of bed, but something's weighing me down. I look over. Peyton is naked, pressed against the wall, half of her sprawled across me, the other half twisted into a position that looks like scoliosis. Even as she's relaxed, her muscles ripple beneath her skin, the curves of her pale back carved and defined. She lets out a low groan, burying her head deeper into my chest.

What time is it?

I grab my phone off the nightstand, pressing the cool metal button. Nothing happens. I press it again.

Dammit.

Careful not to disturb her, I slip out from under Peyton and maneuver toward the other nightstand. The cold November air creeps up my pants, the chill nipping at my ankles as I cross the room. I reach for her phone, fingers brushing against the device, and this time, the screen flickers to life.

2 missed calls.

1 message from someone named Avery.

10:45.

Hm. Not bad. Setting the phone down and scanning the room, my eyes land on my bag, half-open, clothes spilling out. I stroll over, rifling through it. The zipper's caught on a sleeve, and I tug it free with a quick flick. Then I dig through the mess, pulling out a soft pair of sweatpants, then reach deeper, grabbing my—

Wait. 10:45?

"Shit!"

Peyton groans from the bed, draping an arm over her eyes. "What?" she grumbles.

My knees drop to the creaky hardwood, a throbbing ache zinging through them as I frantically pack. "The bus leaves in fifteen minutes!"

Peyton's entire body jerks upright, her tired eyes shooting open. The blanket shifts with her movement, slipping off her body and pooling into her lap. In the warmth of the daylight, her pale skin glows with a red undertone, the ample soft swells on her chest perked in the cool air. While I quickly threw on clothes the moment we finished last night, Peyton doesn't make any move to cover herself as she scrambles out of bed.

Not that she should.

Every inch of that body is a dream. Even if Peyton is a nightmare.

She strolls over to her side of the room—yeah, *that* worked—body swaying with each step. Beams of light catch her skin, illuminating the subtle curve of her ass, and I quickly glance away.

Definitely, *definitely* shouldn't be looking at that.

I tug on my gloves, snatching up anything and everything scattered on the floor and shoving it into my bag.

"How the hell is it almost eleven?" she asks, peering at her phone screen with a wrinkled brow. Her hip pops to the side as she shifts her weight, the curve of the bone peeking from beneath her skin, and—

Look away, Darcy. Look away.

"Because we stayed up way later than we should have," I answer, averting my gaze. I sit on my bag to compress the contents inside, zipping it closed. When I sling it over my shoulder and spin around, Peyton hasn't moved an inch. She's still standing there, buck-ass-naked, bush out, ridiculously sexy, tapping on her phone. She looks up, lips curling into a teasing grin.

"I'm pretty sure *you're* the one who kept *me* up," she says, raising an eyebrow. "Not that I'm complaining."

I roll my eyes, spotting a t-shirt balled up on her bed. I grab it and toss it at her. She catches it without even looking up.

"Will you get dressed? We're on a schedule here," I shoot, as though the action wasn't ludicrously attractive.

Peyton grins, shaking out the tee and slipping her arms through the sleeves. As she lifts them to pull it over her head, I get a direct view of her chest again.

Damn.

It's supple, soft, the pink buds of her nipples hard in the cold morning air. I like the way her skin stretches as she reaches up, and the way it folds when she tugs the shirt back down.

"We still have ten minutes. Want to get another one out before we leave?"

My eyes flick up, catching onto hers. She's got this ridiculous grin on her face, and I can't fully tell if she's joking or not, but it doesn't matter.

"No," I say pointedly, ignoring the pulse that sparks between my thighs. "We have to leave. And this—" I gesture between us. "Can never—"

"Never happen again, I know." She rolls her eyes, tugging on a pair of black briefs. They hug her hips perfectly, the muscle in her toned stomach disappearing past the waistband. She adds in a mumble, "Should only count as once if I haven't gotten dressed yet."

I cross my arms. "Would you ever put on clothes if that were the case?"

Peyton's grin widens. "Nah."

"Exactly."

Turning toward the door, my fingers curl around the worn brass knob. I pause, glancing back at her. She really does look beautiful, gray, baggy tee half-tucked into her briefs, her legs smooth and warm in the sunlight. Brown shaggy hair sticks out, dark lashes resting against her cheeks as she stares down at her phone. I clear my throat.

"I know we already talked about this, but... please don't tell anyone."

She looks up, golden eyes glimmering with amusement. "Are you kidding?" she says, a teasing smile forming. "I'm keeping you all to myself."

Heat rushes to my face, and I quickly step into the fall air, hoping it'll cool me down.

Ten minutes later, we're all on the bus. Well, everyone except Peyton.

"Darce, where's Clarke?" my mom asks, staring at the clipboard in her hand as I climb the steps. I hold my breath, scared that if she looks at me, she'll know what we did. What *I* did. My heart batters in my chest, crawling up my throat, and she looks up, frowning. "Darce?"

"I don't know," I answer quickly, hitching a shoulder. Then I wince as I take another step, hamstrings pulled tight.

I catch her eye, and her head tilts in concern. "You okay, sweetheart?"

I swear I feel a bead of sweat drip down my temple. "Flare up." I nod, forcing a smile.

It's true. Between the hike, skating, and.... *that*, every limb on my body feels like it's ablaze. And since I didn't want to risk Peyton seeing anything by following up on her promise of a massage, I had to take an extra painkiller when I was getting ready in the bathroom.

My mom pats my back gently. "Alright. Let me know if I can do anything, okay?"

"Okay."

I push through the rows of seats. Harlowe's already passed back out, drooling on Bailey's shoulder while Mr. Bubbles slobbers in her lap. Behind them, Zayda and Lena huddle, watching what appears to be Love Island. On the right, Indie's sitting alone, while Faith and Caydence talk about a PWHL game they watched at the cafeteria last night. Caydence's eyes lock with mine as I walk past, and my jaw ticks.

I get it.

I understand being curious. I can see how, as the coach's daughter who doesn't play, me coming in and offering advice could be frustrating. I don't like that she looked me up, but I kind of expected it to happen eventually. What really pissed me off was that she shared it with everyone, reading it aloud like it was a joke. I wonder how funny she'd find it if she knew what really happened.

I slip into the window seat of the very last row on the left side, plopping down onto the neon eighties patterned fabric. Instead of packing my bag underneath the bus like most, I keep mine with me. Not only so that I have my meds just in case, but also so that I can set it in the seat beside me, in the event anyone—more specifically Peyton—tries to sit beside me.

I'm still trying to process it all. How she got me on the ice. Why I said I wanted her to kiss me. Why I meant it.

The portable charger in my hand vibrates when my phone chimes, and I glance at the screen.

ROOMIE

oh my god you're finally coming home ****crying emo-ji****

A soft laugh slips out of me as I type.

ME

I've been gone for three nights.

ROOMIE

i know. it's been terrible.

socks keeps meowing at your door. i think he thinks i locked you in there.

ME

Think he's jealous you're gonna get the kill first?

ROOMIE

oh stop it. socks is no murderer.

shit.

ME

What?

ROOMIE

he just knocked your picture frame off the counter

I laugh.

ROOMIE

anyway, i have news!

So do I...

ME

Finally realized your refusal of football players is essentially pointless because anyone regardless of career or hobby can be a pile of shit so you should probably just give Will a chance?

ROOMIE

first of all

i suddenly can't read

and secondly

i'm going to be an acupuncturist!!!

I blink, re-reading the message. *Okay, that's definitely a new one.*

ME

Why acupuncture?

ROOMIE

well i've already taken all of these biology classes so it wouldn't be a big jump

ME

Makes sense enough. How long have you been interested in it?

ROOMIE

huh?

ME

In acupuncture?

ROOMIE

who said i was interested in it?

ME

…

I mean, you said you were going to be an acupuncturist so I just assumed.

ROOMIE

yeah i know. i haven't decided yet.

ME

If you're going to do it?

ROOMIE

if i'm interested in it

ME

You haven't decided if you're interested in it yet?

ROOMIE

yup

I wonder what it's like to live in Cleo's brain. Sometimes it's hard for me to understand how we get along, because we couldn't be more different. I'm decisive. I know what I want, and I plan how to get there. Cleo's a pogo stick, bouncing in every direction, hoping she lands somewhere she likes.

I don't think I do things the right way. And I don't think Cleo does things the wrong way. I think we just both do things our way, and maybe that's why it works.

When I first moved in, I made a point to keep my distance. Just roommates, nothing more. I even went as far as writing my name on all my groceries for the first two weeks to make it clear. I didn't touch her food; she didn't touch mine. My door stayed shut, keeping both her and Socks out. I turned down every movie night she suggested, not budging an inch.

Then one day, I went to make a smoothie. I grabbed my labeled container of yogurt out of the fridge. Plain vanilla, dairy-free, locally made. The only problem? I was supposed to be out of yogurt. So I asked Cleo about it, and she casually mentioned that she'd gone grocery shopping and noticed the empty container in the trash. So, she just grabbed me a new one.

I was surprised, but it was sweet. So I thanked her, then asked for her Venmo to pay her back.

"Nope," she said, waving me off. "I don't take money from friends."

That's when I looked at her and asked, "Are we friends?"

She shrugged. "Yes, I decided so yesterday."

And that, as it turned out, was the only decision I've ever seen her actually stick with.

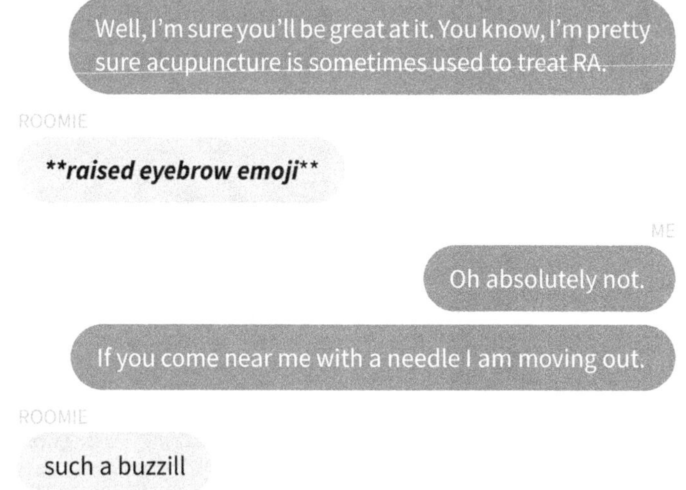

A burst of roaring cheers cuts through the air, and my eyes snap up, locking onto Peyton. She strolls up the steps of the bus, still in that baggy tee, but now boasting a pair of black sweats and worn slippers. She tosses her hair over her shoulder in mock flattery.

"Great timing, Clarke," my mom says flatly, glancing at her watch. "Only one minute till takeoff."

A sheepish smile breaks across Peyton's face, and she runs a hand through her unkempt hair. "Sorry Coach," she says, then her eyes flick to mine. "I had a long night. Didn't sleep much."

I don't glance away. Instead, I adjust my bag on the seat next to me in hopes she'll understand the hint. She understands it, alright. But she sure as hell doesn't take it. Looking me square in the eye, she strolls past the rows, skipping Harlowe, and Indie, bypassing all the open seats, and walks right up to me.

"Is this seat taken?" she asks with a smirk.

I stare at her in disbelief, looking at the bag beside me, then back to her.

"What does it look like?"

Her hand reaches for the handle of my backpack, and that damn smirk deepens. "Like it's about to be."

Immediately, I reach out to grab it. But Peyton's hold is firm, and she tugs it from my grasp. "What are you doing?" I snap, keeping my tone hushed. Peyton sets my bag down on the seat across the aisle, then starts plopping down beside me. I shove my body over to block her, but she pushes back.

"Sitting by you," she says, using her hip to nudge me out of the way.

I push back. "Absolutely the fuck not."

She pushes again. "Yes, I am."

"No, you aren't."

We're in a back-and-forth now, Peyton half-collapsing on my shoulder, and me trying to scoot her out of the way. I lower my voice. "If you sit here, it's gonna look—"

"Nobody's even paying attention," she cuts in, using her weight to shove me over. I try to fight back, but my muscles are slowly giving in. I glance up.

Every eye on the bus is locked on us.

I freeze just long enough for Peyton to wriggle into the seat. She huffs, and a stray lock of her soft brown hair puffs up before settling back against her cheek.

"Sorry!" she calls out, grinning. "My foot got stuck."

Everyone glances around, before turning back to their seats.

"I am going to kill you," I mutter, catching my mom's eye. She quirks an eyebrow but just turns back to the front and flops into her seat.

Peyton leans in, a minty scent brushing against my cheek.

"Only if you can be my last meal," she says with a smirk.

I elbow her. "Knock it off."

"Oh, relax. Nobody heard that."

I shoot her a look, and she raises her hands in mock surrender. "Okay, okay, I'll stop." Her hand slips into her pocket, pulls out her phone, and she starts unwinding her earbuds. I watch her for a moment, waiting. Finally, she looks back up at me.

"What?" she asks innocently.

I frown, eyeing the empty rows of seats. "Why are you sitting here?"

"Oh, there's a reason for that," she says, holding up a finger. I wait. She doesn't continue. I sigh and raise a pressing eyebrow.

"Well?"

Suddenly, she snaps her fingers as if remembering something important.

"Right!" Her knees nudge mine as she turns fully toward me. "So, I had an idea."

I lean back, crossing my arms, and biting back a smile. "Oh? This should be good. It's not often you have one of those."

Her eyes narrow, studying me for a moment before responding, "I'm going to take that as a compliment."

"How?"

She shrugs. "I'll figure it out later." She pulls out her phone, taps at it for a moment, and then looks back up at me, amber eyes glowing. "Anyway, I was thinking about your AIHL—"

"The Australian Ice Hockey League?"

"Your Autoimmune Hockey League."

I groan, my head rolling back against the seat as the bus lurches into motion. "I told you to let this go."

She doesn't budge. In fact, she scoots in a little closer. "I know, I know. But hear me out."

I turn to face her fully, cutting her off. "Peyton, this was a joke. A side project. Something to keep me busy. It's not going to happen. I don't have the resources."

Sunbeams illuminate her eyes, shades of gold and bronze melting into a swirling pool as she stares up at me. Those full lips pull into an electric grin, and she beams.

"What if you did?"

I can feel it, the deep valley forming between my brows. My lips press into a confused line. "Yeah, okay. Not to be a complete cynic, but... *how* exactly would that happen?"

"You know how scouts from the Sabertooths always recruit from the final round of the LNHL championship?"

I nod slowly, still confused. The Sabertooths are one of the top teams in the PWHL. They also happen to be the direct rivals of the Portland Porcupines, the team I was signed to before I got diagnosed. Having their eyes on you is a big deal. Especially for a team who hasn't won the LNHL finals in years—a team still chasing its first shot at the Women's Frozen Four.

Peyton continues. "I want them to pick me in the draft this year. But they only take the best." She pauses and her eyes flick down. "The best of the best."

I wait, expecting her to elaborate, but she doesn't, so I ask, "What does that have to do with me? Or my *imaginary* league?"

Her eyes lock onto mine. "I want you to help me prepare. Just in case we win the finals. Come to my early practices, give me tips. *Help me.* And in exchange, I'll bring your league idea to my dad. He's got connections—lots of them. Even if it starts small, I think it could grow into something huge."

A laugh bursts out of me before I can stop it. It's loud, really loud, and I quickly clamp my mouth shut, shaking my head.

"Funny," I say, tossing my eyes to the worn metal roof.

She frowns. "What is?"

"You." I gesture to her. "That was a good one."

Peyton's frown deepens, and she scoots in closer. "I'm being serious, Darcy," she says, brows drawn tight. "Look, I know you know what you're doing. I didn't want to see it before, but I see it now, and I'm sorry." She sighs. "I was an insecure asshole. And I should have just listened to you in the first place, but... I didn't. But I will now. *I promise,* I will."

My stomach tightens, brows dropping in confusion. Is she actually asking for my help? After all of this back and forth, arguing and fighting, and ignoring my advice?

"Are you... saying that you were wrong?"

I know I shouldn't let it, but my lips pull a little as Peyton responds. She clears her throat, straightening her posture.

"Yes," she admits, almost professionally. "I was wrong. And it's humiliating enough, so stop smiling—"

The corners of my lips drop, which makes me realize that the smile I thought was suppressing had broken through. She finishes. "But I need to get out of my head. To do whatever it takes to get to the Sabertooths. And you're the only one who can help me."

When her eyes fixate on her lap, I know she's telling the truth. I don't think Peyton could look me in the eye when asking for my help. She's too arrogant.

Too cocky.

I flash her a skeptical glance. "Why don't you ask your dad?"

Her throat bobs as she swallows, and an awkward laugh tumbles out. "Contrary to popular belief," she starts, running a hand across the back of her head. "My dad's more of a cheerleader than a teacher. And your mom is fantastic, but I'm not the only one on the team that needs her help. Besides, if she finds out I'm still breaking into the rink most mornings, she'll kick my ass."

I chuckle. "That, she will."

I don't say anything else. I'm not sure what to say. This whole thing feels like a disaster waiting to happen, and frankly, I'm not in the mood to clean up the mess.

My mind drifts back to the retreat, when we were in the stands, doing that stupid exercise. How she told me, begged me really, to keep giving her advice because I was the only one who cared enough to tell her she could be better. It surprises me that her dad, of all people, isn't doing the same. Hell, professional athlete parents are infamous for being overbearing and having high expectations. If I were Peyton, I'd be stoked to have such a mellow father. But I guess I can see the dilemma.

Still, it doesn't make this a good idea.

"You don't have to answer right away," she says, plugging an earbud into her ear. "Just think about it?"

I nod, chewing on my lower lip. She offers me the other earbud, and I know I shouldn't take it.

But I do.

The raw thrum of Swedish heavy metal punches through my ears. I flinch at the sudden blast, but after a moment, I let myself sink into the beat. I laugh silently to myself, unsurprised at how random Peyton's taste in music is. The bus rumbles beneath us on the road, and we just sit there for the rest of the ride, silently listening to music.

I JOLT AWAKE TO a screech, the bus rolling to a steady stop. My head snaps up, then to the side, Peyton smirking when her eyes catch mine.

"Morning, Sunshine," she teases, then her gaze flicks to her shoulder. There's a wet spot on her tee, and—

Oh fuck. Did I drool on her?

I swipe at the corners of my mouth. *Yup. Wet. Awesome.*

She continues, "What'd you dream about? Me, by chance?"

I shoot her a warning glare, and her tongue traces the inside of her cheek as she stands up, casting me one last glance before heading down the aisle. I wait until nearly everyone, including her, is off the bus before grabbing my bag and making my way to the front. My mom's eyes catch mine, but she doesn't say anything until we step off.

"Can I give you a ride?" she asks, jiggling her keys in her hand. "I don't think you should walk that far if you're having a flare up."

I don't process her words immediately. No, my eyes are too busy scanning the parking lot. I don't know what for, but when they catch on Peyton's, a soft smile tugs at her lips, and she gives me a little wave. Not a smirk, or a grin. A smile. I just return with a sharp nod, then look back to mom, fully processing what she just said.

"Huh? Oh, yeah." I pull my bag over my shoulder. "Yeah, that would be nice."

We stroll over to her car, the leather seats cool beneath me as she starts the engine. It's not until I buckle that I feel her eyes burning into me. My head snaps to look at her, and she quickly looks away.

"Why are you looking at me like that?" I ask.

She shrugs. "Am I not allowed to look at the beautiful daughter I created? I birthed you, you know."

"Mother." I say it like a warning.

Finally, her eyes part from the road, just a glance. "I was just wondering what the verdict is. If I'm going to be reaching out to find a new assistant coach."

I hesitate for a moment before answering. "No, we're... good now," I say, and I'm mostly convinced it's true. Sure, she still drives me absolutely insane, but now that she recognizes I'm not completely clueless, things seem to be on an up.

And up.

And up.

And—*fuck.* I need to stop thinking about last night.

"You know that was some real Coach shit you pulled with the cabins," I say, crossing my arms.

An amused chuckle slips from her mouth, and she flicks on the windshield wipers as the rain starts to patter lightly against the glass. "I know." She pauses for a moment. "You know, Peyton told me what you did."

Shit.

Shit.

Shit.

"Umh..." My heart leaps into my throat, pounding so hard I swear she can hear it. What the hell? "She did?"

She nods. *Fuck. Fuck, fuck, fuck.*

"Are you mad? Because I already talked to her and—"

"Mad?" My mom's eyes flick to mine. "Why would I be mad?"

"I—" I start, but nothing comes out. Oh my god. I knew this was going to happen. And now, I'm going to lose my job, which means I'll lose my credit, which means I'll have to take out extra loans to finish college, and then I'll be drowning in student debt, and—

"Darcy, I've been trying to get you back on the ice for months."

Her smile widens, and she flashes me a proud glance. My lungs collapse, pushing out every ounce of air in my body until I'm sure my sternum touches my spine.

"You're... talking about the rink," I clarify slowly, and my mom nods.

"What else would I be talking about?"

Relief floods every inch of my body, and I tip my head forward, pinching the inner corners of my eyes.

"Nothing. Nothing." I pause, the muscles in my body melting. "Just the rink."

The repetitive click of the turn signal fills the car, touching each atom in between us.

"So?" she asks. "How did it feel?"

I'm so relieved that she wasn't talking about me fucking the team captain that I barely process her words. I just answer instinctually, whatever pops into my brain first. "Great," I say, looking out the window. She continues.

"Yeah? That's good to hear. Because, you know, I've been thinking, and I think it would be good for you to get on the ice during practice sometimes. You know, show them instead of just telling."

I nod, shrugging. "Yeah sure, of course mom."

But the moment I say it, I know I'm going to regret this.

TWENTY TWO

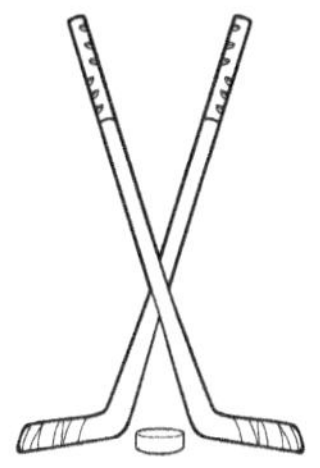

Peyton

LNHL Countdown: 15 weeks

Is anyone coming with me to the chess tournament tomorrow?

Also: Prepare for The Hunt.

HAMMIE

Lena Z and I were gonna go

Wait, already????

YERSIE

Fuck yeah

Z

Wtfff I thought you said you picked a good spot last time

BRADY

> We did! Kai is a cheater, I swear.

ROSE

> Prepare for the *what?*

"IT'S GOTTA BE AROUND here somewhere!" Bailey shouts from halfway across the stadium. Her head disappears into the rows of seats like a leprechaun hunting for a pot of gold. Only, the pot of gold is an eight-year-old mouthguard case. It's an old, dirty time capsule, still containing the overused mouthguard of Lachlan Hunt.

Lachlan Hunt, now the starting left-winger and team captain for the Boston Boas, is *the* guy. The one who's, according to *ESPN Magazine*, "The best thing to happen to the Boas since Harrison Clarke."

It's disgusting, covered in who-knows-what, but it's part of this ridiculous ongoing shtick we have with the men's team since Hunt left for the NHL.

The game is simple: One team hides the case somewhere so well that not even the cleaners can find it, and the other team has to track it down. Last year, they hid it in an electrical panel in the floor, and we didn't find it until six weeks ago, right as the season started. Caydence, Harlowe, and I hid it by the penalty box after that, and this morning, Kai sent a group message letting us know the case has been re-hidden once again.

"Maybe you should ask the ghost," Harlowe calls from seven rows back. Then her nose wrinkles. "Wait! I think I smell it!"

We're all combing through the stands, Mister included, looking for the damn thing. I drop to my knees, peeking under the seats when I hear a voice above me.

"What's going on?"

I try to sit up, but the back of my skull slams into the bottom of the stadium seat. Clutching my head with a wince, I squint up at Darcy.

She laughs.

"Shit, are you okay?" she asks, still giggling.

I want to scowl. To point out how, once again, she's reveling in my discomfort, but the sound is so bright, so unexpected, all I can do is grin. I wasn't sure when the next time I'd hear that laugh would be. Especially after what happened.

The heat of her breath, the taste of her lips, the low growl in her voice... It's all I can think about.

I shake myself out of it and straighten my spine. "I'm good." I stand up, pulling my hair into a bun—because practice is about to start, and definitely not because I'm now sweating.

Darcy nods, still scanning the arena as my twenty teammates rummage through the stands. She looks back at me, brow quirking in a wordless question.

"They're on the Hunt Hunt," I explain, tugging the hair band tighter until I feel a strand of hair snap free from my scalp.

Ouch.

"The what?" Darcy's brows furrow, the freckle between them vanishing. A soft chuckle slips out as I watch confusion pool in those evergreen eyes.

Yeah, pretending nothing happened? Not possible. All I can think about right now is the idea of making those eyes roll back for me.

"The Hunt Hunt," I repeat. "Us and the guys hide Lachlan Hunt's old mouthguard in the stands, and then we take turns finding it." I pause, waiting for the confused wrinkle on her forehead to smooth out.

It doesn't.

"Wait, you guys are looking for a *mouthguard?* For someone who was drafted to the NHL like... what... seven years ago?"

"Eight."

Darcy shakes her head, the wrinkle deepening as more rays appear across her nose. "That's disgusting."

I shrug nonchalantly. "Yeah."

Her eyes catch mine. I want to tell her how good she looks in that outfit—a blue-striped turtleneck, tapered jeans, and these dark blue gloves that I hate because they're covering her hands. Darcy's usually in some form of sweatpants, and don't get me wrong, she pulls them off well, but it's also nice to see her a little dressed up. She looks more confident. Glowing, even. But before I get the chance to compliment her, she spins around and starts heading down the stairs.

"Alright, let's start warm-ups!" she calls. A collective groan ripples through the team.

"Give me three more minutes!" Harlowe begs, sniffing the air like a bloodhound. I laugh, and Darcy just shakes her head.

"Sorry, we've got a schedule to keep."

Harlowe flashes me an annoyed look, and I just shrug, jogging down the stairs toward the ice.

The entire time we warm up, Darcy is staring. Not at me, though. She's staring at that clipboard. At her project. I swear, her eyes don't leave the page once. I don't even think she blinks. It's like she's superhuman.

Which would make sense, because no normal person should look this good under fluorescent stadium lights.

Her long red hair tumbles down her chest, freckled lips moving in a mesmerizing motion as she chews the edge of her pen while she thinks. Her—

Shit.

She's looking at me.

I'm pretty sure the expected thing to do when you're caught staring at a pretty girl is to look away. But why the hell would I deprive myself of the little quirk at the corner of her mouth when her eyes catch mine?

She looks back down at her pages, cheeks flushing as she forces her expression to harden.

Yeah, I don't think she's going to be able to pretend either.

"Alright team!" Coach claps her hands, the sound bouncing off the chipped plexiglass boards. "Let's get into some drills!"

THE BEAD OF SWEAT dripping down my face tickles my cheek, my chest heaving hard as I step off the ice. Practice ended nearly an hour ago, but the ice skating team has a competition at Glacier today, so there was a gap between our practice and the guys'.

Kai fist-bumps me as the men's team funnels in, and I tap my earbuds to bring the loud ringtone in my ears to a halt.

"Hello?" I say through the mic.

"Hey Peanut!" My dad's cheery voice fills my ears, and I can't help but smile. We're pretty close, Dad and I, but neither of us really care to talk over the phone often. Mostly because I'm busy, and he likes to think about things before he says them out loud. Avery and I are more like our mom in that way. We say whatever comes to mind. *Most of the time.* "How was practice?"

I wipe the sweat off my face with my sleeve. "It was good."

"Good, good." He pauses for a beat, then another. "Not overworking yourself I hope."

"Huh? No." I shake my head even though he can't see me. "How's Ayve and Mom?"

"They're good. We're all good. Avery's excited for you to come for Christmas."

"He didn't say that," I reply pointedly, like I know it for a fact. Which I do, because Avery's candidness doesn't exactly reflect his affection toward people.

Don't get me wrong, he's super sweet, if you can look past him pointing out a giant zit on your forehead, or the persistent, antagonizing smirk tugging at his lips. I think I have that too, I'm just more bubbly so I can play it off. Still, when you really get to know him, you'll realize he'd do anything for you.

Avery hates the rink. He can't stand the cold, the smell of the rubber, or the hum of the refrigeration system. To this day, he refuses to go to any games or practices. But there was this one time, when I was seven, that he had no choice but to show up. My mom and him had just come from a doctor's appointment, and she wanted to drop off lunch for my dad and me.

Avery was up in the stands, sulking, when I slammed into the boards. He didn't even think twice. He was on the ice before anyone could blink, wearing nothing on his feet but worn Clifford sneakers. Of course, he slipped and banged his head before he could even reach me and ended up with a concussion instead.

But he tried. He tried to get to me before anyone else could. And that's been his way ever since.

My dad pauses, considering. "No, he didn't. But I know he is. He came by with Pumpkin yesterday and asked what day you'd be here."

"That makes me feel honored, actually."

A laugh escapes him. "It should." Another pause. "How are you feeling about the con tournament? Think you guys have a chance this year?"

My cheek goes raw between my back teeth as I gnaw mercilessly, all the muscles in my body stiffening. Heaviness creeps into the center of my abdomen, digging its way into my stomach, and dragging it down, down, down.

How am I feeling about the LNHLs?

Like I'm going to vomit.

"Yeah," I say, pausing to buy time.

My dad was recruited to the NHL four days after his eighteenth birthday. I'm twenty-one.

Granted I know it's different as a woman. The NHL is never going to seek me out in a draft, and the PWHL was founded when I turned nineteen. Logistically, I could never mimic the pace of my dad's career. And I don't want to. But when I see articles flying around about *Harrison Clarke's Legacy,* I get stressed.

What if this is as far as I make it?

The thought claws at the back of my mind, sinking its nails deeper and deeper until it climbs its way to the front. Part of me wants to pretend I'm okay with that. A small league, just enjoying the game, no pressure. But the other part, the part that's been silently screaming at me for years, knows that it would prove what I've feared all along.

That I'm only here because of my dad.

If the Sabertooths see something in me, if they decide I'm worth it, maybe, just maybe, I'll feel like I've actually earned this.

I force myself to take a deep breath, trying to keep the panic at bay.

"Yeah, it's, um… I really think this is the year!" I try to sound upbeat, but my voice shakes, and my heart pounds against my chest like it's trying to escape. I swallow hard, willing the anxiety back down into my stomach. Willing the water out of my lungs.

My dad shifts on the other end of the phone, his voice soft but steady. "Good. I'd love to make it out to the tournament, but—" I brace myself. "I know it would be better for you if I didn't."

My throat tightens, and I blink hard, trying to fight the sting in my eyes. "I know, Dad. I'm sorry. I promise, when I'm in the pros, you can come to every game you want."

I can hear the small, knowing chuckle in his voice. "Okay, Peanut." He pauses, his tone softening. "You know I'm proud of you, right?"

I feel it then, the ache in my chest. The water rising, the curdling of my stomach. I swallow repetitively hoping the saliva will push it down. "Yeah," I whisper. "Yeah, I know, Dad."

"Okay, good. Because…" He falters, taking his time to choose his words. "Even if things don't go the way you want, you're still a rockstar. And I have no doubt that you'll make it to the pros if it's what you choose. But just—just know that. Okay?"

The tears come without warning, burning my eyes, but I swipe them away as quickly as I can. "Okay, Dad." My voice cracks, and I quickly clear my throat, hoping he doesn't hear how unsure I am right now. How inadequate. How small. "Hey. I've—I've got to get to class, but I'll talk to you soon, okay?"

I slip my phone into my pocket, trying to make out the combination on my locker through my blurry tears.

"Okay," he says. "Love you, Peanut."

I sniff. "Love you too, Dad."

Three monotonous beeps signal the end of the call, just as I pry my locker open. I pull out my earbud, sucking in a shaky breath as my eyes, then my lungs, begin to overflow.

"Peyton?"

I spin around. My pulse should spike when my eyes land on Darcy. When they journey down that flowy head of red hair, and dart to each freckle scattered on her cheeks. But it doesn't.

Instead, it steadies.

Slower.

And slower.

Until I think it may stop.

She's standing across the locker room, brows weaved in concern, hands gripping a stack of little paper cards. Quickly, I swipe at my cheeks, sucking in a shaky breath.

"Hey," I say coolly. Or, I try at least, but let's be honest, I'm not fooling anyone. Especially not her. She takes a step closer to me, head tilting to the side. "What are you doing here? Practice ended forever ago."

Her gaze snaps to the cards in her hand, and she waves them in a gesture. "Compliment cards," she explains. "I figured I better do some damage control after reigning terror the past few weeks."

A soft chuckle slips out of me, and I wipe another tear. I know Darcy sees it. I watch her pupils trace it down my cheek just before it absorbs into my sleeve. But she doesn't say anything. And I'm grateful for that.

"I don't think you've been reigning terror," I say, my voice stuffy from crying. Darcy deadpans, and I let out another laugh. "Okay, maybe a little bit, but only toward the people who deserve it. You were good today. Great, actually."

And she was.

I hadn't seen Darcy so engaged at a practice before. Then again, maybe she's been paying more attention than I realized. She wasn't just giving corrections today. She was actually encouraging people. Indie's face lit up when Darcy complimented her stickhandling. And Harlowe practically glowed when she called her a "brick wall", which would be a really solid insult if she wasn't a goalie.

She even gave me a nod for my slapshot, which, honestly, was about the only thing I nailed today. I was too far in my head to get anything else right.

A soft smile tugs at her lips, and she tosses one leg over the bench, collapsing down on it. I don't know if it's an invitation, but I sit on the one across from her anyway.

"So..." She trails off. My gaze flicks around the room. To the ceiling. The floors. The showers. Anywhere but her eyes.

"So..."

"...Are you okay?"

I nod, probably more than is necessary, forcing out a stiff, awkward laugh. "Yeah, no, I'm good. I'm..." I rake a hand through my sweat-drenched hair, exhaling a heavy breath. I don't know why I say what I do next. Maybe it's because she trusted me with the truth at the resort. Maybe it's what happened before we left. Or maybe it's something else entirely. Either way, it slips out before I can stop it.

"When you were at Minnesota did you—did you ever feel like you were playing for someone else?"

Her eyes catch mine, and she shakes her head. My stomach sinks lower, and I simply nod in response.

"Do you feel like that?" she asks softly. "Like you're playing for someone else?"

"No," I answer quickly, but it feels like a lie. And for some inexplicable reason, lying to Darcy doesn't feel like an option. So I elaborate. "Well, not entirely. Don't get me wrong, I love hockey. I mean..." I chuckle nervously, sucking the inside of my cheek between my teeth. "There is nothing else in the world that I love more. But sometimes... It's a lot of pressure. To be a certain kind of player."

Darcy's eyes stay locked on me. She doesn't usually stare. I've noticed that, after a moment, her gaze tends to drop, like she's trying to avoid being seen too clearly. She probably thinks if she doesn't hold someone's attention for too long, they won't notice the things she'd rather keep hidden.

But there's a flaw in that logic.

Because from the moment I first saw her, I haven't wanted to look at anything else.

"Because of your dad?" she asks hesitantly.

I nod.

We just sit there for a moment, the silence stretching between us. But it doesn't feel like it's pulling us apart. In fact, though we haven't moved, it feels like the space between us has shrunk. After a beat, she lets out a soft, "Huh."

I glance up. "What?"

"Oh, nothing," she says, shaking her head. "It's just weird."

My brows furrow, and I tilt my head. "What is?"

She smiles. "I want you to keep talking."

Against my will, the corners of my lips slowly draw up, and when our eyes lock, a smile breaks across her face too. I clear my throat, taking a steadying, preparing breath.

"I was four when my dad quit the NHL," I begin, and Darcy shifts forward in her seat, looking at me attentively. I take another breath. "My brother had been struggling for a few years by then, but when he finally got diagnosed with autism, my dad decided it was time to focus on us. You know, be there for us, and help my mom."

I pause, watching Darcy's expression drop, and I shake my head before she gets the wrong idea.

"Don't feel bad or anything, trust me. Avery is—" I laugh, running a hand through my hair. "He's fucking fine. He's doing better than I am, that's for sure. But one of his sensory things is that he really hates the cold. My dad tried for years to get him on the ice, and it just never worked out. He liked lacrosse for some reason? My mom played it in college, so I guess it makes sense, but... it broke my dad's heart. I knew he wanted a kid to follow in his footsteps, so... I did.

"And I wanted to, not just for him, but for me. I loved watching the reruns of his games on the television. I loved admiring all his trophies in the living room.

I loved hockey the moment I stepped on the ice. But sometimes I feel like, if I don't make it as big as my dad did, if my career doesn't skyrocket to that same degree…" I trail off.

"You'll be letting him down," Darcy finishes. I nod.

"Yeah."

When I look up, those ivy eyes are locked on me. The corners of Darcy's lips curl subtly, and she gives me a gentle nod.

"That makes sense," she says, then leans forward, eyes intent. "But it's not your responsibility to let your dad live through you."

"I know," I lie. I take a moment to breathe. Then another. "Do you think if I got recruited to the Sabertooths, it would be because I'm a Clarke?"

Darcy's the only person I would ever ask, because she's the only one that I know will tell me the truth. She sits up, studying me carefully. Finally, after a moment, she answers.

"I think the name gives you a head start," she admits, and my stomach begins to curdle. My lungs begin to drown. There's nothing more I want than to play for the Sabertooths, because that's where every prodigy goes. But I only want to play for them if I deserve it. She continues. "But without the stats to back it up, it would just be another name."

"Do you think I have them?" I ask. "The stats?"

Darcy's eyes meet mine, and a teasing smile tugs at her lips. "Is Peyton Clarke asking me if I think she's good enough to play for the Sabertooths?"

"Yes."

She shifts a little. I don't know if I'm truly ready to hear her answer. But I know I want to be. Her throat bobs as she swallows, and she levels me with an honest gaze.

"Objectively," she starts. "Your stats are great."

I nod, sensing the omission. "And subjectively?"

A brief smile flickers across her face, then falters. "*Subjectively*, your stats are great. But I think you focus too much on them. You spend so much energy trying to prove that you deserve to be here, instead of just *being* here." My throat tightens, but I nod, a silent beg for her to continue. To give me what I've needed all my life:

The truth.

"You don't have to score the most points or do the most tricks or play the roughest to deserve a spot on the team. You just need to play as part of it."

I swallow once. Twice. The ache in my throat doesn't go away, but for some strange reason, I don't want it to. It's like what Darcy said hurt, but it was a kind of pain that I needed. Like popping a joint back into place.

"Thanks," I say, pushing off the bench. I slip my bag over my shoulder, and when I look up, she's right in front of me. I can smell her perfume. Feel her heat. Her hand stretches out, and I glance down at the little orange card. I look back up at her.

"I'll do it," she says. "I'll help you, if you help me."

A smile breaks across my face, and I take the card. "Thank you," I say again. Darcy just nods, turning toward the door. Before she steps through, she spins back to face me.

"But if you cross me, Icarus," she says, her brows lifting as she points a finger. "I will end you."

I don't tell Darcy that being killed by her would be my life's greatest honor. Instead, I raise my hand to my brow, saluting. "Copy that, Kimmy."

She rolls her eyes. It's not until she walks out the door that I look down at the card in my hand. My fingertips graze the sharp edge of the cardstock as my eyes scan the message scrawled across it.

Icarus

Your dedication, though obnoxious at times, is unmatched. I envy you, not just because you get to play the game, but for the way you play it. I'm sorry for how things started. Thank you for reminding me of what I love, and how I can be better.

Kim Possible

TWENTY THREE

Darcy

ICARUS

Do you need a lift to the rink?

ME

I'll walk.

ICARUS

Oh, come on. Let me drive you. I'm a very good driver.

ME

Somehow I believe you.

Walking is good to stretch my body after sleeping. But I'll meet you there soon.

ICARUS

I'm adding you back to the group chat btw.

ME

What

FINAL CHAT FR THIS TIME

Captain Clarke has added you to the chat

DARCY COLE

Seriously?

Darcy Cole has left the chat

Captain Clarke has added Darcy Cole to the chat

DARCY COLE

Why are you like this?

And why is your name Captain Clarke?

CAPTAIN CLARKE

You can customize nicknames in the chat.

DARCY COLE

And you nicknamed yourself Captain Clarke?

CAPTAIN CLARKE

Don't be ridiculous. Bailey did it.

Wait, what was I before?

DARCY COLE

...

CAPTAIN CLARKE

You did not put me in your phone as a disease

DARCY COLE

I told you, it's not a disease.

CAPTAIN CLARKE

That's it.

Captain Clarke has changed your nickname to Kim Possible

KIM POSSIBLE

You did not.

CAPTAIN CLARKE

Indeed I did.

> Aw, hi Darcy. Glad to see you finally joined the chat. ****heart emoji****

> Now can y'all shut the fuck up it's 4am.

D IFFERENT. WORD CLASS: ADJECTIVE. Definition: Not the same as another. Origin: My mother.

At least she acts like she invented the word. It's what she says when she's about to do something nobody else is going to like. I know from personal experience.

Anytime my mother said our day was going to be "different" as a kid, we always ended up at the doctor, dentist, or scrubbing the bathroom floor. So when she announces to the team that today we are going to do something "different", every muscle in my body goes stiff. From the looks of it, the team is also well-rehearsed on her antics. Indie's eyes grow wide, and Harlowe's gaze flits around the rink, assessing. It's only Bailey who seems stoked, a bright grin stretching across her face.

"Today, I want to see how well the trust-building retreat worked," she continues, slipping her hand into her pocket. My eyes stay glued to that hand. She's got something up her sleeve. But what? I don't yet know. "Get in two lines, standing across from the person you roomed with."

A flurry of green and white jerseys moves across the ice, getting into formation. I simply watch from the bench, keeping my eyes trained on Peyton. She slips into line, glancing around as if I'd be on the ice. When she finally spots me on the bench, she grins, gesturing for me to come.

I shake my head, but she just keeps waving enthusiastically. Fighting back a smile that I resent for existing, I flick my gaze to my mom, who is... frowning at me?

I tilt my head, shrugging. "What?"

She skates over to me, propping a hand on her hip. "Did I *imagine* that you went to the retreat?" she asks.

My brows draw together, and my eyes scan the rink, confused. "No?" I pause, just long enough to realize what she's suggesting. Immediately, I shake my head. "Absolutely not," I start, but my mom quickly cuts in.

"Get your ass in the rink, Darce," she orders, crossing her arms now. I just keep shaking my head, like maybe if I do it fast enough, it'll fall off and I could avoid this whole thing.

But my mom doesn't budge.

"I only went on the ice once, for like, twenty minutes, and—"

"—And if you can do with Clarke—" She tosses her head toward Peyton, who is staring at me with a crooked grin, "—you can do it with the rest of the team."

A short, stressed scoff slips out of me. "I don't even have skates—"

"Under you," Mom interrupts, pointing under the bench.

Immediately, my expression drops. My hand digs underneath the seat, and I pull out a worn pair of skates.

My worn pair of skates.

"I got the blades sharpened, and new laces, so you should be all set."

I just stare at them. My eyes trace the scuffed toe, up to the worn tongue. They're falling apart. Need to be replaced. In some depressing form of poetry, they retired when I did. And yet, my mom held onto them.

When my eyes meet hers, she's trying not to look soft. She's failing miserably, but she's trying.

My heart stutters as I glance around. The only person who is looking at me is Peyton. Or maybe, when her eyes are on me, they're simply the only ones that I feel.

I swallow, letting out a steadying breath. Then I untie the new waxed laces and slip off my shoes.

When I step back onto the ice, I expect my knees to shake like they did at Pineview. But they don't. Instead, I glide right over to Peyton, positioning myself in line across from her, gripping a stick that my mom handed to me. As I pass by Caydence, I hear her mutter something under her breath, but I ignore it.

"Well, well, well. Look who decided to join us." Peyton smirks.

I roll my eyes, glancing over at my mom who still has her hand in her pocket. *What is she planning?*

"Did this morning not count?" I ask, still looking away. She taps her stick against the ice, clearly trying to get me to look at her, but I don't. Looking at Peyton is distracting, and I cannot be distracted the first time I'm on the ice in front of everyone.

Especially if I want to keep up the illusion that I'm completely fine.

"No, because we didn't even get on the ice," she says, almost in a whine. Before I can catch myself, my eyes flick to hers. I quickly glance away, but it's too late. She juts out her full bottom lip, and I suddenly remember how it felt between my teeth.

I swallow. "Yeah, and your muscles are going to thank me later."

This morning was the first "session" I had with Peyton. Instead of warming up and hopping directly on the ice like she usually does, we spent about thirty minutes stretching, then another twenty talking about how much she misses her brother. By the time the ice skating team showed up for practice, Peyton hadn't even stepped into the rink. She was irritated.

I was successful.

The less time Peyton spends on the ice alone, the less time she'll spend self-sabotaging in her head.

Peyton's lips part to respond, but a loud clap cuts in before she gets the chance. Everyone's eyes snap to my mom, who finally pulls that hand out of her pocket and holds it in the air. I squint, focusing on the sleek strip of black fabric dangling from her grip.

"We're going to play a game," she says, her tone upbeat. "One person blind-folded. The other, guiding. This is about communication, intuition, and trust. Everything this team needs to win the LNHLs."

A few chuckles float through the rink, but it's the sound of Bailey's voice that breaks through the noise. "Oh, Harlowe, you know all about those," she teases, flashing her a taunting grin.

Harlowe just doubles it. "Yeah, and I can give you a lesson later if you'd like."

"All talk, no action Yersie," Bailey fires back.

But I can't focus on their back-and-forth. My stomach's already doing flips, unease creeping up my spine. Out of all the exercises, all the things my mom could have chosen, why, *why* did it have to be blindfolds?

As my mom starts handing out the strips of fabric, my eyes drift to Peyton. My cheeks are scalding, flushed with heat, and I'm pretty sure hers are, too, though for a very different reason. With that smirk plastered on her face, I'm sure her muscles are burning.

"Stop smiling," I command, dragging a hand through my hair. I exhale a steadying breath, but when I look back up, Peyton's still grinning. "It's not funny."

Her tongue pokes at the inside of her cheek. "It's a little funny."

"It's not."

She's still fucking smiling. "Okay. It's not."

"Let's try to be *civil*," my mom's voice cuts in as she holds out a blindfold. My gaze drops to her hand, but my body doesn't budge. Peyton doesn't hesitate to grab it.

"You got it, Coach," she chimes. My mom nods, moving toward the edge of the rink.

"I'll take it first," Peyton says. I watch as she pulls the blindfold over her eyes, fingers fumbling with it behind her head like she can't figure out the damn thing. She mutters under her breath, trying to get it right, but the fabric keeps slipping.

I look away, grateful that her eyes are covered because it means she can't see the flush in my cheeks, or the outline of my heart, pounding against my chest. And as she's standing there, her jersey loose without the padding underneath, the silky black fabric tugged over her eyes, all I can think about is that night. Especially as she curses softly under her breath.

I remember how she whimpered my name. The way my tongue slid between the slick folds of her pussy. How her hands felt in my hair, gripping it tightly in desperation. I shouldn't be thinking about it. I shouldn't find myself enjoying the sight of her, all flustered and clumsy again.

But I do.

"Want some help?" I offer, forcing my tone to be cool. Peyton's lips curl into a pouty frown, like she's preparing to tell me off, so I decide to step in before she gets the chance. My gloved fingers graze against hers as she hands over the fabric, and I glide behind her, gently pulling it over her eyes. My heart pounds heavier, and I swear, when the blindfold presses to her cheeks, her breath hitches.

That soft lavender scent fills the air as my hands move behind her head to tie the knot. The pulse in my body travels to my throat, and I swallow hard in an attempt to drown it.

"Remind you of anything?" Peyton murmurs under her breath. Mine catches, which I know was her goal, so I mentally kick myself for helping her reach it. I don't grace her with a response. I just pull the blindfold tighter, making another tense knot.

When she thanks me, I realize that I haven't let go. I quickly drop my hands back to my side, pulling my stick from the hold between my thighs and gliding back into place across from her on the ice.

The crack of sticks against pucks echoes through the rink, and I glance around, watching the rest of the team beginning to play. I suck in a slow breath, letting the cold air sink to the very bottom of my lungs, and feeling them expand, my chest rising and rising, until finally, it collapses again.

"Alright, I'll guide you," I say, trying to keep my tone even. But there's a slight waver in my voice when my eyes fix on her again. "Just... follow my voice, okay?"

She nods, and her back straightens as she adjusts her stance.

"Ready?" I ask.

She flashes me a cocksure grin. "Always."

I hit the puck toward her, calling out "left" as it glides toward the side. She stretches, her stick swinging just a second too late. The puck slips past her, clinking against the boards.

"Shit," Peyton mutters frustratedly. I skate over the puck, scooping it up, and getting back in line. Even with the blindfold, I can tell she's embarrassed. A warm flush peeks from beneath the fabric, her jaw tight.

"Let's try again," I say, and she nods.

I push another pass to her, letting her know it's a direct path, and this time, she's too quick. Her stick swings before the puck reaches her, and it slides into the boards with another dull thud.

"Come on," she mutters to herself, her voice a little sharper this time. It's clear that as patient as she can be with others, Peyton has no patience left for herself. I clear my throat, reminding myself of our agreement.

"Think before you move," I say. "Listen for the hit, but don't react until you know where the puck is at."

Peyton groans, frustration clear in the way she slaps her stick on the ice. Her shoulders are tense, her posture tighter. "Is everyone else missing?" she asks. I glance at the team, Caydence and Harlowe are passing the puck like dinner rolls, while Indie and Faith fumble a bit, but still catch some. A frown begins to creep across my face; I don't enjoy being bad at things either, but if I tell Peyton that everyone else is making it work, she'll just spiral more.

So I hold back a sigh, biting down on my own frustration and turn back to her.

"Don't worry about them," I say, my tone softer this time. "Just trust me, okay?"

"Remember, communication!" my mom calls, the reminder echoing across the rink. "Trust each other. That's what this is about."

Trust.

It's a two-way street. One I haven't driven down since Minnesota. That is, until Peyton.

Her free hand moves in a wave as she inhales steadily, lips pursed and practiced.

"You okay?" I ask, and I mean it. She scratches her cheek, letting out one last breath.

"Yeah, it's just harder than it looks. I don't like that you can see everything I'm doing, and I can't see you."

I nod silently.

If it were me, starting out with the blindfold on, having to trust Peyton to make passes I could catch, I don't think I'd be doing much better. I've been watching her on the ice for a month now, but I've only played with her once, leisurely. I don't know all the ways she moves. How she tends to aim. But I do know that sometimes, I wish people could step into my shoes. So I do the same for her.

"I'm closing my eyes," I announce, fingers tightening around the foreign stick.

Peyton's voice spills out in a panic. "What? No, that's a terrible idea. How are we going to—"

"Peyton." I say her name slowly, softly. Like I'm savoring it. It melts in my mouth and leaves an aftertaste that makes me crave another bite. "Don't worry about what everyone else is doing. Block it out." I sigh, adjusting my stance as I stare at the back of my eyelids. "Nothing else matters. Just me and you, alone together."

She goes silent. All I hear is the sound of the other players, back and forth. Another heavy sigh slips from her lips, and I take a moment to do the same.

"Okay," she says finally. "Alone together."

The familiarity of technique flicks from my shoulder, down to my stick. The puck barrels toward her, this time with more intention, and to my surprise, I hear a click. Not against the wall of the rink. This is lighter, louder, and when my eyes flutter open, the puck flies right past me.

"I hit it!" she exclaims, and her excitement is infectious. A smile breaks across my face, and I quickly skate to retrieve the puck. When we get back in line, we start again.

I hit it toward her, with more confidence this time, and close my eyes, listening to the ice beneath our skates, the subtle shift of her body as she positions herself. Her stick moves, and then the sharp *clack* of it hitting the puck echoes in the rink. This time, it's clean, and the sound is clearer.

I can't stop the smile that pulls at my lips as the sound of the puck against the ice grows nearer. I'm ready. This time, I strike it back with the same energy, trying to match the rhythm we're suddenly finding.

But when I swing my stick, my timing is just off enough that the puck veers wide, sliding past Peyton with a *whoosh*. The mistake is small, but in the silence that follows, my heart races, hoping she doesn't hear the tinge of disappointment in my own breath.

But Peyton just laughs softly, the sound warm and light. "That was close," she chuckles, then pauses. "Are your eyes still closed?"

"Yes," I answer, then they flutter open. "Again?"

She nods. And when that crooked smile breaks across her face, I feel warm.

When we start again, we both move a bit more deliberately, like we're learning how to dance without stepping on each other's toes.

"Good work, girls," my mom calls from across the rink, and I expect it to startle whatever communication, whatever trust is flowing between Peyton and I, but it doesn't.

TWENTY FOUR

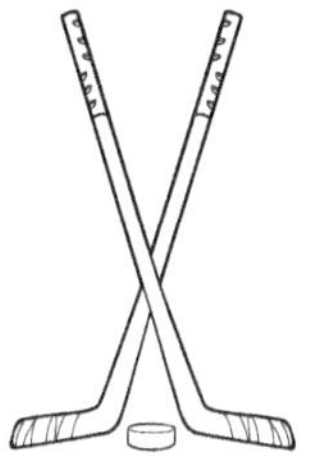

Peyton

"This is Avery. Don't leave a message. I won't listen. Just text me."

A loud beep blares in my ear. I start talking, because no good little sister ever follows instructions from her brother, and even though Avery hates voicemails, I know he always listens to mine.

"Hey, Ayve, it's me," I say, pulling my baggy Nirvana tee over my head. Damp strands of hair cling to my neck as I tug it the rest of the way down, the scent of my lavender shampoo losing its battle against the ripe scent of sweaty skates and freshly used shin guards. The team funnels happily out of the locker room, dragging their sore feet, excessively exhausted from training with Kaiser. Harlowe waves dramatically, off to butt heads with Clay Matthews in front of a bunch of six year olds.

"Just checking in to see how you're doing. Dad says Pumpkin is still alive, which is...honestly...kind of...*alarming*. Anyway, haven't heard from you in a while. Text me. Love—"

A sharp *ding* cuts me off. I pull the phone back, checking the screen.

Caydence Wright sent you a message.

I press the phone back to my ear. "Love you, dickwad," I finish, then hang up and glance around the room.

Most of the locker room's cleared out now; just Darcy, flipping through her post-practice notes, and Indie, swapping her beat-up black laces for new dark green ones for Wednesday's game in Salem. She changes her laces before every game. Hockey superstition, I guess. I roll the cool gel deodorant across my armpits and collapse onto the bench, tapping the notification.

CAY

> *Saw this article. Thought you might want to know what people are saying.*

There's a link attached. A link I *know* by now I shouldn't click on.

I know what Caydence is doing. What she's *been* doing. She was pissed when I got Captain over her, especially since she's a senior. It's why she's had an extra long stick up her ass this season. I know she's angry. I know her weird fixation on Darcy's past is probably just another angle in her long-game revenge plan for me. She's trying to hurt me.

Freshman year taught me exactly what happens when you read something about yourself that hasn't been vetted by someone who gives a damn. And Caydence definitely doesn't.

But because I'm in the business of self-sabotage (as Darcy so kindly pointed out during one of our early practices) I click on it anyway.

A bold black headline fills the screen:

Is Hockey Royalty Losing the Crown? Daughter of NHL Hall-of-Famer Harrison Clarke Misses Again

A thousand pebbles drop into my stomach, one at a time at first, then all at once. They weigh me down, getting heavier and heavier until I'm sure my gut's resting flat against the cold concrete floor.

That should be enough to stop me from reading any further.

But like I said, I'm in the business of self-sabotage.

And actually, I own the damn company. So I keep reading.

In what's starting to feel like a familiar pattern, GU Women's Hockey Captain Peyton Clarke came up empty in Saturday night's third period, sailing a clean look wide during a tied game against Pacific West College.

I pause, swallowing, but the dry lump forming in the base of my throat sticks. *At least they used my name this time*, I think.

Though Clarke has worn the "C," in every game this season, it's unclear to some whether she's earned it with merit, or whether her father, Boston Boas Legend Harrison Clarke, has done the heavy lifting. While there's no denying she's inherited raw talent, finishing seems to be a consistent struggle for the 21-year-old center.

A scoff slips out of me, and I gnaw on the inside of my cheek, unable to pry my tired eyes from the screen. I scored twice in that game—one being a Michigan (do you know how hard that is?)—but of course, they only focused on the *one shot* I didn't make.

There's no winning. Even when I give it everything—no reckless moves, no game-losing mistakes—they still find something to tear apart.

A hot, damp feeling swells in my lungs, like I'm breathing in mist, and I start to cough and choke as I keep reading.

Her father built a career on finishing. She's built hers, so far, on not. Meanwhile, Kai Robinson—son of Carolina Cougars legend Wes Robinson—has had no trouble finding the back of the net for the men's GU team. Robinson is set to join the NHL after this season, ending his NCAA career with a bang!

Which raises the controversial question: does legendary

talent transfer the same way when it's passed down to daughters?

That feeling in my throat tightens, a series of wet coughs slip out, and I can't tell if my eyes are watering from choking or from the article.

I'm blaming the choking.

"Cheese and crackers! Cap!" Indie barrels across the room. "You alright?"

I nod, trying not to laugh at Indie's substitutes for cuss words, which only makes me choke more. I start to actually get scared I'm going to suffocate, so I motion weakly for my water bottle. She spins in place, scanning for it. She doesn't find it, I realize, when I start drinking and the water tastes suspiciously clean.

Definitely not mine.

"Shit! Are you okay?" Darcy's soft voice breaks through the haze, a blur of a red entering my vision. Still half-choking, I nod, tipping my head back and letting the pristine water scrape down the tightness in my throat.

It takes half the bottle, and a couple embarrassing hacking sounds to clear the constriction, but finally, I start to breathe.

"I'm fine," I rasp, my throat raw, chest sore. I hand the green squeezy bottle back to Indie, wiping my wet eyes on my shoulders.

"Thanks, Rose," I manage. She shoots me a concerned smile. "Also, your water tastes like it's been blessed by a thousand non-pedophilic priests."

Her grin deepens. "I scrub it out every day."

Suddenly, I wonder when the last time *I* scrubbed my water bottle was. Too long.

Much too long.

"Are you okay?" she asks again, tilting her head to the side.

I nod. "Get out of here," I say. "Hammie's waiting for you in the car to go grab some food."

Her feathered brows furrow. "You're not coming?"

I shake my head. "I've got some homework to catch up on."

After Indie says goodbye, dragging her duffel bag behind her, Darcy collapses onto the bench beside me, looking at me like I've just sucked out her soul.

"What was that about?" she asks, and though she's trying to hide it, I can hear the worry in her voice. Despite the sinking feeling in my chest, and my stomach, and just about everywhere else in my body, I force a smile.

"You were worried," I say with a shit-eating grin.

Darcy rolls her pretty ivy eyes. "Was not," she replies defensively. "It would just look bad if you died next to me."

"Indie was a witness," I point out. "She'd never lie on the stand."

Darcy smiles, but it's only halfway there. "Something's bothering you," she says.

Not asks. *Says.* Like it's a fact. Which it is, but she shouldn't know that. I clear my throat, shifting on the hard bench, suddenly wishing Indie were still here to baptize my esophagus with her priest-approved water.

"No," I lie, because without holy water in my mouth, I'm fully capable of lying through my teeth. It'd be useless anyway. Darcy is the self-appointed—and *me*-appointed—Antichrist. Holy water or not, she sees right through it.

"What's that?" She gestures to my phone, which is still clenched in my hand, screen lit up, that article front and center. I could turn it off. Slide it into my lap. Pretend it's nothing.

But then I think about practice the other day. How she stepped into my shoes like they fit. How she laced them up without hesitating, even though they were muddy from my perpetual fear of being watched and judged which is all my life has ever been. And I remember hers too. The ones I borrowed when the article about her was shared. We didn't talk about it much, but I walked in them anyway. Blisters and all.

At this point, we're basically sharing athlete's foot.

So I let out a resigned sigh and hand her the phone.

I've never seen that freckle on her forehead disappear so fast. It's like it got sucked into the vacuum of space the second her eyes hit the screen. And for not the first time since I met Darcy Cole, I'm reminded of the existence of green flames.

Her gaze flicks back to me, face growing red. "This is *misogynistic bullshit!*" she explodes, flinging her arm out angrily which makes me briefly concerned for the safety of my cell phone. "You *know* this is bullshit, right?"

I nod slowly, taking the phone from her gorilla-gripped gloves. "Yeah," I say. "I know."

And I do.

I know it's bullshit.

But for some reason, knowing doesn't help as much as you'd think.

And judging by the fact that Darcy's now pacing, cheeks flushed, freckled nostrils flaring, I'd say she feels the same.

"I don't even know how stupid shit like that gets published! Like, hockey is *plenty* interesting without stupid *fucking*—"

"Darcy, it's fi—"

"No!" she barks. "No, it's *not 'fine'!* Because they take *perfectly* good players, players who say nothing wrong, *do* nothing wrong, and always have to—they always have to—"

She snorts.

Like a pig.

An angry pig.

And it's adorable.

"...Criticize them?" I offer.

"Criticize them!" she finishes.

I roll my lips inward to bite back a smile as Darcy collapses back onto the bench. A slight hiss escapes her, which I now know means her knees are bothering her, but I don't dare point it out. A piece of hair falls from her long red dutch braid, and she blows the strand out of her eyes with an irritated huff.

"Peyton," she says, her eyes locking with mine. Feathers stir in my stomach when she says my name, tickling me from the inside. "You played *amazing* that night. You were fast, and vigilant, and—" She sighs, her voice softening. "Sometimes, I can tell you're trying to play like your dad."

My heart sinks.

"But that night—that night was the first time I've seen you play even a little bit as yourself. You were tough, and fast, but you flowed. You were incredible out there."

My teeth find the inside of my cheek, and chew. "Not according to Lexi Norwester," I reply, trying to sound unbothered. She shakes her head.

"Lexi Norwester writes whatever gets her clicks. Whatever makes her money. You know that."

I try to laugh, but it's just a sad exhale. "I guess as long as she's writing about me, she'll always be making money. Everyone loves reading about me failing."

Her green gloves find my hands and squeeze. "Not everyone."

A dry ache forms in the base of my throat.

"It's just like—" I shake my head. "I give *everything* to this sport. Every ounce of time. Like, an *embarrassing* amount of time." A nervous feeling tugs at my stomach. "I get maybe five hours of sleep a night. I don't watch TV. I don't date." A sad laugh slips out. "I've spent so much time chasing the pros, I've *never* even been in a relationship."

At that, Darcy pulls back, her brows shooting up. *"Huh?"*

I shrug, heat washing over my cheeks. "I've hooked up, I've gone on dates, but I've never actually *dated* someone."

She stares at me in disbelief. "You're kidding," she says, like that would be a fun thing to kid about.

"I swear." I raise a hand, mock-solemn. "Hope to die, or whatever. Zero official relationships."

Darcy's eyes narrow. "But you're so—"

She cuts herself off.

Which, of course, only makes me want to know what came next even more.

"I don't have time," I explain. "Which, I *know*, sounds like an excuse, but it's really not. Every minute I'm not practicing, I'm convincing myself I should be. Like if I don't earn every second on the ice, I'm stealing it from someone else. Especially with my dad..."

My voice falters slightly, and I clear my throat. "And if I'm not doing either of the two, I'm at some other event, showing up for everyone else, because it breaks my heart to think that anyone feels that way too. That they don't think they deserve what they've earned. So... I go. To the parties, and the art shows and the study groups. Because if I can't be on the ice, then I need to be somewhere that matters."

Darcy studies me silently. I can see the neurons in her brain sparking behind her eyes, like the information I'm so chaotically dumping on her is something worth thinking about. My heart thunders in my chest, heat spilling across my body in embarrassment. And just as I'm about to apologize, the slightest tug pulls at the corners of her lips.

"That's..." She trails off, like the words on her tongue are painful to admit. "Really sweet, actually."

My eyes fixate on a crack in the concrete floor, and I hitch an awkward shoulder.

"Self-serving purposes," I deflect. Darcy's elbow digs into my ribcage, and it's pathetic, but I'll take any touch from her.

"Shut it," she mutters, somewhat endearingly.

In the quiet of the locker room, her padded fingers tap lightly against the bench, the sound echoing softly off the green walls. After a long beat, she reaches down, unbuttoning a massive pocket on the side of her pants.

"Grabbing your Cheez-Itz?" I tease softly.

She rolls her eyes, her hand disappearing into the pocket, then pulling out what might be the largest book I've ever seen. Like, truly absurd. It's huge, with red painted edges and some strange language script on the sides.

My jaw drops.

"What the hell is that?! *The dictionary?*"

A laugh slips from Darcy's mouth, and when she drops the book onto the bench, it lands with a thud that rattles our seat like an earthquake.

"Lord of the Rings omnibus," she explains, adjusting her position with another flash of discomfort. "Full series. Special edition."

"Of course it is," I mutter, studying the beast. I think it's the same one Hammie has on her shelf. "You and Bailey would get along really well."

A nervous laugh slips from her mouth, and she glances up. "Why?"

I shrug. "You just would. You've got the same kind of hobbies. I'm honestly surprised she and Cleo haven't recruited you into their little dragon cult already."

A laugh bursts out of Darcy. "You mean their Dungeons and Dragons campaign?"

"Yeah, that thing." I wave it off. "You should totally do it."

A quiet, awkward sound escapes her, and she looks away again, arms crossing tight over her chest.

"They asked," she explains, the words coming slower now. "But I said no."

I raise a brow. "Why? Not into board games?"

"It's not a board game," she replies, then meets my eyes again. "And I don't know. Just... seems like a lot."

I study her. Her fingers dig into her biceps, her eyes skimming the room to avoid my gaze. The corner of my mouth twists, just slightly.

"You don't like people, huh?"

Her gaze snaps to mine defensively.

"That's not true," she snaps. "I just don't trust them."

I don't mind the cutting edge in her voice. In fact, I've grown to like it.

Greenrock Valley is full of coyotes. Completely overrun. When I was little, we used to strap a spiked vest onto our dog before letting her outside to keep her safe. It was the first time I realized sharp things aren't always meant to hurt. Sometimes, they're meant to protect.

I think Darcy's like that.

"Is that because of what happened in Minnesota?" I ask wearily.

Her body tenses, but she doesn't pull away from me. Instead, she exhales, then slips her fingers between the pages of the book and flips it open.

There, wedged between two pages, is a photograph.

It's slightly dusty, worn around the edges. She pulls it out and hands it to me.

I lift the hem of my shirt, using it to clear away the dust.

It's her, in a purple and yellow Minnesota State jersey, hair damp with sweat. You can tell she'd just played hard. And something about that causes a low heat to spread through my chest. Seeing her on the ice lately, I've been feeling that a lot.

She's gripping her stick, bag slung beside her, and her jersey number—get this—is *11*.

I don't even need to point it out. The flutter in my stomach is enough of a reward.

My eyes journey through the photo, looking at all the little details. I squint, fixing my gaze on her hands, where glittering pink polish shines back at me.

"You wear nail polish?" I ask curiously. I imagine that little flash of pink trailing down my bare skin, cupping my jaw, slipping inside of me. I had never considered painted nails a possibility when that was happening, but now, suddenly, it's all I can think about.

"Not anymore," she answers. "No point, really."

She reaches over, slipping her hand beneath the photo and folding it out, making me realize I'd been staring at only half of it.

Now, someone's standing beside Darcy, wearing matching gear, and a matching smile.

"Who's that?" I ask, studying the girl with violet hair.

Darcy sighs.

"Do you remember that article?" she asks, her voice surprisingly steady.

I tap my chin theatrically, pretending to think. "Hmm..."

"The one where my teammate sold me out to *ESPN*—"

"Ohhh yeah," I nod. "*That one.*"

She glares. "Hilarious. Anyway..."

She sucks in a breath. A really deep, lung-filling breath, then exhales it.

"Brenna and I... We grew up together. She was a year ahead, but the moment she moved to Seattle, we did everything together. School, hockey, all of it. And I—" Her voice wavers. "I had the biggest crush on her. Like *embarrassingly* massive. But we were best friends, so I kept it quiet. Until we both got into Minnesota. I thought, maybe this was it. Maybe things were lining up."

I try to ignore the strange feeling in my stomach, the twinge of jealousy for someone I've never met, and instead focus on her words. Still, my gut churns.

"And it was good, for a while," she continues. "We dated through junior year. But then I started getting worse. My body, I mean. I could barely handle practice, let alone parties or nights out. I kept asking her to stay home. Movie nights, board games, anything low-key. Anything to give my body a break. She wanted the opposite. I didn't know how to explain that I felt like I was falling apart."

She pauses, eyes falling to her hands.

"*I tried.* I told her I was tired, that everything hurt. And at first, she acted like she got it. But when things didn't get better after a while… I don't know. I think she just got tired of me. When I finally got diagnosed, I was honest about everything. But by then, it was too late. She'd already decided she was done.

"I can't say I blame her. Being around someone like me, someone who cancels plans and is always in pain… It's exhausting. I know. But it still hurt. Afterwards, I wanted to go public in my own way. I thought maybe I could help someone else by sharing what I went through. But before I could, she told the media. When I confronted her, she said it was to 'protect me' from having to talk about it, but really, it was about her. She wanted to beat me to it. Control the narrative. She didn't even *ask*."

My eyes sting, unhelpfully. I swipe at them before she can notice.

"She knew I'd lost Portland," she continues with a sigh. "I think part of her hoped the spot would go to her, but it didn't. And that pissed her off even more."

"Why would she do that to you?" I ask, sounding angier than I had meant to.

Darcy shakes her head. "I think she felt betrayed. Like I shut her out. And maybe I *did*. But it wasn't because I didn't love her. It was because I didn't know how to bring her into it. Into… *this*." She gestures to her entire body. "And nobody else on the team understood either. They all just felt like I gave up. So, when everything went down…" She huffs a sad laugh. "Well, let's just say that I was on the first flight out of there. So you not dating? You're not really missing out."

There's a scalding, heavy feeling in my stomach, like all the pebbles have melted into molten rock. I want Darcy to know that not everyone is like that. That good friends, like Harlowe and Bailey and sweet little Indie, would never pull a stunt like that. But Darcy seems fixed on her decision to be alone.

And I can't say that I blame her.

"Did she ever get drafted?" I ask, and I don't know if it's morally corrupt, but I silently pray that she didn't. That she's out there, miserable without Darcy in her life, because that's what she deserves.

Darcy shakes her head. "No," she says. And god, I'm evil. She continues. "But...she's a ref now."

Not exactly a win, but not exactly a lose either.

I swallow. "For what?"

Her eyes catch mine. *"This."* Tears begin to well, and she quickly blinks them away. "She's reffing the Hornets game next week in Spokane. I just found out this morning."

My stomach drops.

I don't know what to say to that, so I let the silence settle between us, and hope that feels like it did when we were here the other week, pulling us closer instead of pushing us apart.

"I hope you don't feel like you gave up," I say finally.

Darcy's throat bobs as she swallows, but she doesn't say anything, so I press on.

"I think," I add slowly, recounting my own experiences. "Sometimes people take things personally when they don't understand them. Humans like to be knowledgeable. Nobody likes feeling dumb. So instead of admitting they don't get it, they just... get *mean.*"

Her green eyes meet mine, and she tilts her head. "That's... surprisingly insightful for someone who eats eggs with a spoon."

I grin. "I contain multitudes." Then my smile falters. "You said Brenna didn't get it. That you were falling apart, and she just left."

Darcy nods, but doesn't look at me.

"Well," I continue. "Just because she didn't know how to love you through it doesn't mean no one else can."

The silence that follows isn't heavy. It's soft, like there's a blanket thrown over the two of us, blocking out the chaos of our lives.

"Also, just for the record?" I add, just in case I was too subtle before. "If I were your girlfriend, I would've taken a hockey stick to anyone who tried to sell you out to *ESPN*."

A breathy laugh escapes her, and I scoot just an inch closer, so that her thighs melts into mine.

"Good to know," she says.

And she doesn't move away. Not even a little.

TWENTY FIVE

Darcy

I MISS THE GRIZZLY Grind.

I miss the little string lights tangled across the ceiling, twinkling like homemade constellations. I miss the community bulletin board layered in out-of-date flyers, their pull-tabs long vanished into pockets and wallets and lint traps of laundromat dryers. I miss the slow jazz trickling from the gramophone in the corner, and the chipped bookshelves stuffed with used textbooks and copies of *Wuthering Heights.*

But mostly, I miss the coffee.

When I first moved to Minnesota, I told myself the only thing I'd ever miss about Seattle was my parents. But now, standing in a hotel hallway in Salem, Oregon, clutching a *repulsive* cup of Keurig sadness, I realize how I might've underestimated how many pieces of it are worth missing. And that, maybe, calling Seattle "home" again isn't the worst thing in the world.

I shift the hot cup from hand to hand, letting the warmth of it absorb into my gloves. This coffee is too bitter, this hallway too beige, and I am much too awake for someone who isn't being paid for this.

Though, I suppose pitching my nonsensical concept of autoimmune hockey to someone who might actually make it real is a pretty solid form of payment in itself.

I check my phone.

3:44AM.

This is criminal. Actually criminal. I should be dreaming about The Walter Cup or better coffee or kissing someone I shouldn't. Not standing outside Peyton's hotel room. But a deal's a deal. And as I found out yesterday morning, before the win against the Copper Coast Cobras, Peyton's early morning practices do not stop. Not even in Salem, Oregon.

She's exhausting.

And unfortunately, I might be into it.

Not a minute later, Peyton's door swings open. Despite her usual sleek black early-morning practice clothes, and the heart-attack inducing bubblegum energy drink gripped in her hands, she looks beat. Her dark hair hangs limp and oily, the bags under her eyes purple puffs, and her eyelids look like they've forgotten how to be eyelids.

"Morning," she yawns, arms stretching out as her duffel bag slips down her shoulder. I blink.

"Morning," I echo hesitantly. My eyes scan her body, brow quirking in concern. "You sure you're up for this?"

She hoists the bag back over her shoulder and steps into the hallway, the door clicking shut behind her.

"Yes, why?"

"You just look…" I trail off, scrunching my nose as the smell hits. It's equally familiar and disgusting; the rotten funk of sweaty gear and worn-out skates. There's no lavender to balance it out this time. Just pure, unfiltered hockey stench. "*Tired.* Hey, umh—did you *shower* after the game last night?"

Peyton shakes her head. "No." She pauses, catching my recoiled expression. "Is it that bad?"

I think for a moment how to gently say she smells like fermented jill shorts marinated in dumpster juice and sea brine and decide to go with: "Yes."

She lifts her arm, sniffs her pit, and reacts with an indifference only a lifelong athlete could manage. Her mouth opens, probably to argue that it's "not that bad", but I pluck the keycard from her fingers, swipe it, and push the door back open.

Peyton sighs, but shuffles in without a fight.

Seven minutes later, the door swings open again. Her skin is dewy, hair damp and detangled, and the stench is replaced by that soft, powdery lavender.

"Better?" she asks.

I nod and hand her the sad paper cup of lobby coffee I retrieved while she showered. She pounds the last ounce of her energy drink, tosses the can into the trash, and accepts it with a grateful nod.

"Better," I say, then point to her duffel. "You won't be needing that, though."

Peyton's brows pinch. "What do you mean?"

I shrug. "I mean you don't need it."

Her warm golden eyes, now slightly more awake, study me like she's waiting for the punchline.

I don't give her one.

"Right. Okay," she says slowly. "So, I don't know how *cold-hearted bitches* practice hockey—"

I grin.

"—but I, *personally*, need gear. Like... skates. And a stick. Maybe a puck, even. High maintenance, I know." Her tone is teasing, but there's a hint of suspicion mixed in.

I cross my arms. "Do you want my help or not?"

Her mouth opens. Closes. Then opens again. She sighs. "Fine," she mumbles, dropping the bag with a thud. She steps into the hallway, closing the door behind her.

The metal bench at the bus stop is like ice against my body, but I stay seated. Standing feels worse—like hugging a metal pole while someone beats it with a hammer. The four-hour bus ride two days ago left my joints stiff and aching. Too much stillness is what kicked off this mini flare-up. Ironically, stillness is now all I can manage.

Peyton glances sideways. "Where are we going?"

She pulls the hood of her GU sweater over her head—the same one she let me borrow at Harlowe's Halloween-Birthday party. The one that was too snug in the armpits. The one that smelled like her.

"You'll see," I say, squinting at the oncoming headlights trying to guess if they're bus headlights or just regular headlights.

Peyton huffs. "You know, this wasn't part of the deal."

She takes another sip of her putrid "hazelnut" latte that really tastes more like charred dirt. She grimaces at the flavor. The headlights draw closer, then the front of the bus breaks into view. I press both palms—pastel green today to match my pants (thanks to Cleo's fashion tips, and yes, dressing nicer does boost my confidence)—against the bench, forcing myself up with a wince.

"If you're going to keep questioning my methods, we can—"

"No! No," she cuts in quickly, eyes wide. "It's just—the bus home leaves at eight, and if this takes a while, I won't have time to get on the ice."

The bus screeches to a stop in front of us, brakes hissing. She climbs on behind me. I fish a handful of change from my pocket, feed it into the machine, and grab our tickets.

The bus lurches into motion before we're even sat down. I stumble and catch myself on the back of a dusty but occupied seat. The middle aged man in it spins around and glares at me like I've stolen his firstborn child. Peyton nudges me forward, and I see her flip him off out of the corner of my eye.

I'm grateful she's behind me so she doesn't catch the way I smile.

"That's kind of the point," I say, settling in. She flashes me an unamused look. "By the way, how did you manage to get into the rink yesterday morning?"

Peyton grins wolfishly. "You'd be amazed at what the promise of a Harrison Clarke autograph can buy you."

I chew my lip. "Right. Dad perks."

She nods.

As we ride through the city, our bodies swaying with the rumble of the bus, stop after stop rolls by in a dark, tranquil blur. We're sharing Peyton's earbuds again, the wire dangling in the gap between us. Her playlist is the most chaotic masterpiece I've ever heard—starting with the All American Rejects, then shifting to Beyoncé, then 50 Cent, The Carpenters, and Gigi Perez.

The strangest part is that it's not at all jarring. Somehow it works, like different pictures cut into the same puzzle.

After five or six tracks, she turns to me.

"We don't have to listen to this," she says, holding her phone out. "You can play whatever you want."

I shake my head. "I like it," I say.

I don't think I really understood the phrase *her eyes lit up* until I see it happen to Peyton. She doesn't smile. In fact, nothing about her expression really moves. But something in her eyes shifts, and it's like staring at the goddamn sun.

"You do?" she asks. "Really?"

"Yeah," I say. "It kind of feels like the score to a low-budget indie movie. But like...the best movie you've ever seen."

That's when she smiles. A real goofy one. It's one she hasn't shown me before. One I feel privileged to see.

There's something I love about people that you only get to experience when you spend real time with them. Something about watching them be themselves, completely unaware of the way their lips pull, how their hands move. How they talk faster when it's about something they love, and their voice gets louder.

And if you tell them, it'll make them embarrassed. So instead, you just watch and listen, praying that no one points it out—so that the next time it happens, they're not covering their mouth, or lowering their voice. Not shrinking themselves. Not watering down who they are for the convenience of everyone else.

I don't want the watered-down version of Peyton.

I want her in concentrate.

So we spend the last twenty minutes of the bus ride listening to the playlist, making up scene after scene of our imaginary movie.

Gertie, the main character, is sent to live with her emotionally stunted grandparents after her mom dies (*Back to the Old House*, The Smiths). Her dad's off somewhere in Europe pitching wildly impractical inventions to anyone who'll listen. On the train ride to her grandparents' house, the train is raided by land pirates (*Stand and Deliver*, Adam & The Ants) who kidnap her—not just because of the ransom money, but also because she's just *so* beautiful, with her doll-like face and aggressively choppy bangs.

Only, her dad never actually sells any of his inventions. So the ransom never comes.

Instead, she starts working with the pirates. Naturally. And soon enough, she robs her way to the top. Meanwhile, there's a slow-burn fling going on between her and the group's original leader that's slightly toxic but really sexy (*Promiscuous*, Nelly Furtado feat. Timbaland).

Eventually, the guy gets jealous that she's in charge now. So, like any fragile man, he hatches a plan to kill her.

Obviously, she figures it out—because she's the main character and anyone named *Gertie* can most definitely solve a puzzle. Mid-heist, she pushes him off a moving train while *get him back!* by Olivia Rodrigo blasts in the background.

He dies. (Rip. *Ish.)*

She rides off into the sunset with the hot blonde female Russian train conductor who was secretly helping her all along. They end up co-running a glamorous and mafia-like crime ring across the Western rail lines (*Femininomenon*, Chappell Roan).

"So what happens to her dad?" Peyton asks, wrapping the wired earbuds around her phone as we step off the bus. "Does he ever sell his inventions? Does he ever get to see his daughter again?"

I glance down at her screen; *Boulevard of Broken Dreams* by Green Day lights it up.

"No," I say, shaking my head.

Peyton frowns.

"But," I add, "he does end up healing from his wife's tragic death by running off with some exchange student who's just old enough to make the audience go along with it. He realizes that his true calling wasn't invention. It was finding love again."

She smiles at that.

"Come on." I wave her forward. "This way."

We walk along the sidewalk, disappearing into the early-morning fog. I think of Gertie for a while, and how this would be where the story starts—her lugging her suitcase stuffed with linens and books down the muggy street. I wonder if she ever goes to visit her mom's grave and decide that she does each year on the anniversary of her kidnapping. Streetlights cast halos on the dark, glistening concrete, and I try to tug my jacket zipper the rest of the way up to my chin to fight off the breeze.

Only, my fingers cramp.

I slip the tiny piece of metal between my thumb and forefinger again, squeezing them together, but a sharp pain slices through. I wince, pulling back. Peyton notices, but she doesn't say anything. She just leans over and zips it up for me without a word. Then she scoots closer, her arm brushing mine, probably trying to share body heat.

I can't help but remember the last time Peyton and I shared body heat.

"I'm starting to think this has nothing to do with hockey," she says, eyes flitting as we pass into a slightly hazy park.

A grin tugs at my lips. "Oh, but my young, overly ambitious Icarus—" I say, flicking her hair in mock affection that feels a lot less mocking than I had intended. "It has *everything* to do with hockey."

Through the fog, a massive white dome takes shape—the Oregon State Capitol, according to the map on my phone. We veer off the main sidewalk, onto a little paved path, which leads us to a tall, bronze statue. The metallic man stares out, gripping a cane in one hand, and a hat in the other. Behind him, his cloak flows in the imaginary wind that's blowing the opposite direction of the real wind.

We just stand there and stare.

After a moment, Peyton turns to me.

"I don't get it," she says.

I grin, a cocky, Peyton kind of grin, and point at the base of the statue with my toe. "Still need me to teach you how to read?"

She rolls her eyes. "Funny," she says, but leans down anyway, squinting at the engraving. Then she straightens up, still confused. "...Okay?"

I keep staring. Waiting.

She sighs, and asks in the most uninterested tone possible: "Who's Dr. John

McLouglin?"

A giant grin breaks across my face. "I'm so glad you asked!" I say, high-pitched and condescending like a kindergarten teacher.

She groans, which is my cue to continue.

"Johnny here was a physician turned fur trader slash colonizer who basically ran the Hudson's Bay Company."

Peyton blinks, unamused. "And you're telling me this because...?"

"Because ol' Johnny had a son. Johnny Jr. And one day, after screwing up basically everything in his life, JJ decides he wants to follow in daddy's footsteps and be a fur trader too."

I stop there, just to see what she'll do with it.

She raises an eyebrow. "Well? Did he?"

I nod. "Yeah." A beat. "Until he got blackout drunk, beat the shit out of some coworkers, and got himself shot to death."

Peyton recoils. *"Jesus, Darcy!* Why would you tell me that?"

I shrug. "Because sometimes trying to be like your dad gets you somewhere you don't want to be."

"You brought me all the way here to tell me *that?* To make me stare at the statue of a dead guy who has an even deader son?"

I tilt my head. "Can a dead person really be more dead than another dead person?"

She gestures to Johnny Sr. "Well, his son doesn't have a statue to commemorate him, so."

Another breeze cuts through, shaking the leafless trees, biting at my skin. I pull my hair back over my ears, makeshift insulation against the cold.

"I brought you here to tell you that," I say, voice firm, "and to stop you from getting on the ice. Practicing every morning isn't helping you get better. It's setting your body up to fail."

Peyton looks away instead of arguing. Which means she knows I'm right.

"If we're doing this, if I'm going to keep helping you, then no more early practices."

Now she argues.

"Four," she says.

"One."

"Three."

"Two. Thirty minutes, max."

Her amber eyes scan mine, searching for leniency. She finds none. A sigh escapes her lips, her shoulders sagging in surrender, but when our eyes meet again, there's a gleam there. A spark of something I can't quite decipher.

"Okay," she says. "Two."

I smile. "Two."

After another long pause, I add: "In a completely coincidental and un-planned circumstance, there just so happens to be a five-star coffee shop just down the—"

Before I can finish, she steps closer. Close enough that our bodies are, once again, touching. Her hand curls behind my neck, pulling herself onto her toes until our mouths are perfectly aligned.

I like when her mouth is parallel with mine.

"You're a pain in the ass," she murmurs, her smile soft and lopsided.

I can't stop staring at her lips as I reply, "Likewise, Icarus."

For a second, we stand there, her fingers tangled in the back of my hair, my eyes tracing her chewed bottom lip. I want to kiss her. I shouldn't want to kiss her.

"I can't—" I start, pulling back. My stomach sinks. "Sorry, but, after—"

"Yeah, no," she cuts in quickly, dropping back to her heels. I'm suddenly a whole lot colder without her pressed against me. "I know. Me too. I don't know what I was thinking. I'm sorry."

She shoves her hands into her pockets, awkwardly rocking on her feet. I shake my head.

"You don't have anything to apologize for," I say.

She flashes me a cocky grin. "But *you* do."

I frown. "What? Why?"

She hitches a shoulder. "You can't walk around with lips like that and expect me to not want to kiss them."

Heat creeps across my cheeks, and I curse its existence because Peyton is doing what every arrogant hockey player does, and I should be immune by now. I *am* immune. She just has a way of slipping through the cracks sometimes.

"Has that ever worked for you before?" I ask, head tipping to the side.

Peyton hooks her arm in mine, just like she did that night downtown. "Yes," she answers simply. "Yes it has."

A loud melody springs from her back pocket, startling the both of us, and she fishes out her phone as I navigate our way to the coffee shop. I don't make out the name on her screen before she swipes it away, declining the call.

"Everything okay?" I ask, brow creasing in concern.

She just nods, slipping it back into her pocket. "Fine. Spam call," she says lightly. Then spins around to face me, walking backwards down the sidewalk. I follow. "Hey, so, how did Icarus get to the sun anyway? Spaceship? Blimp?"

I glance at my phone's map and toss my head to the left to signal a turn. She pivots—still backward—without missing a step.

"You think a blimp could fly to the sun?"

She shrugs. "Maybe. Humor me."

"Wings," I answer, eyes flicking to hers. She's still walking backward, and some irrational part of me pretends it's because she wants to keep looking at me and not because Peyton Clarke does things simply because no one told her not to. Which is stupid, because I just turned her down. Because she drives me completely insane. Because I can't date people. Because I shouldn't want her to like me.

But for some reason, I do. I want her to like me.

Her brows lower over her hooded eyes. "Wings?"

"Wings," I repeat. "He and his dad were imprisoned on Crete. His dad was this genius craftsman and built them both a pair of wings out of wax and feathers to escape. But he warned Icarus not to fly too high."

Peyton exhales like she already knows what's coming. "Let me guess," she says, glancing behind her just in time to dodge a mailbox. "He wanted to be just like Daddy too?"

I shake my head. "No. That's the thing. He wanted to be *more* than his father.

He wanted to be a *god*. So he flew higher. Too high."

She frowns. "And then he burned to death."

"Actually…" I grin. "The wax on his wings melted, and he plummeted to the sea and drowned."

Her feet come to a sudden halt, and her pretty porcelain jaw *literally* drops open. "What?" Her voice is an equal mix of horror and disbelief. "What the *fuck* kind of stories are these, Darcy?"

I laugh. "The good kind."

She's shaking her head, but she's smiling. *"No.* Because apparently you either try to be like your dad and get shot, or try to not be like him and drown under the scorching sun."

I give her a long deadpan look. "There is a third option."

She quirks a brow. "Yeah? What's that?"

"Stop trying to be like or unlike anyone," I say. "Just *be.*"

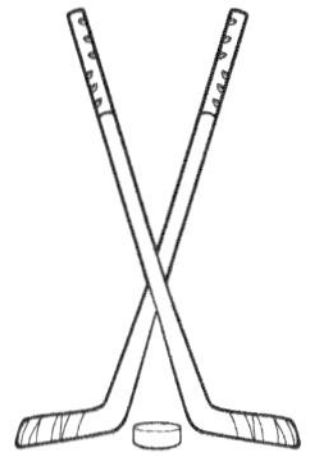

Peyton

THE SMELL OF VICTORY is sweet. Unless you play hockey.

Then, it's musty. Really, really musty.

Which is why, after our win today at the home game against the UMLR Warhogs, I spent a solid forty-five minutes in the locker room shower, scrubbing the scent of victory off me. Partly because Harlowe threatened to lock me out of the apartment until I did, and partly because the team's heading to the Puget Diner to catch a PWHL game to celebrate, and I'd rather not be the stinkiest thing in there.

The December wind catches my hair as I swing open the glass door, stepping into the diner. Everyone else is already here, huddled around the tiny box television. Sure, we could go to a fancy sports bar with seventeen 80-inch flatscreens scattered about the place, but they're always crowded, and trying to replace meat with cauliflower.

The diner is where we feel at home.

Cheers erupt through the restaurant as all my teammate's eyes snap over to me. They whoop and clap as I strut to the table, giving my best attempt at a catwalk and tossing my hair over my shoulder theatrically.

"Thank you, thank you," I say, bowing at the attention, like I at all deserve it. When my spine snaps straight, Harlowe pats me on the back, a little too roughly, and Indie's eyes sparkle.

"Great slapshot Cap!" she beams. I flash her a grin that I hope is opaque.

"Thanks Rose. You killed it out there. That breakaway was *insane.*"

"Good work today Clarke," Coach calls. My gaze snaps over to her, then falls to a large pint glass gripped in her hand, filled to the brim with what looks like flat beer. My nose wrinkles.

"You're a beer drinker?"

She flashes me a warning look. "With what you ladies put me through, you're lucky I'm not doing heroin."

A chuckle escapes me as I glance around at the team. Everyone's snacking on appetizers—glazed wings, mozzarella sticks—and Harlowe's got a milkshake the size of her head in front of her, sprinkled with Everything Bagel seasoning, obviously. But there's one person I'm not seeing. I scan the room again, eyes moving carefully over every head, bracing for that fiery mane of hair to pop into view.

But still, no sign of Darcy.

I'd have thought she'd tell me if she wasn't planning on coming. Especially given that since the retreat, she's been more and more invested in the team. And, I like to think, more and more invested in me.

Though, that's sort of how our agreement works.

For a fleeting moment, I consider asking about her. But better judgment floods my body.

"You gonna get in here, Pey?" Zayda calls, motioning to the baskets of food on the table. I nod.

"Yeah, just need to wash my hands real quick."

I head toward the bathroom, pushing open the heavy swinging door. The moment I step in, I freeze. Darcy's at the sink, sliding her gloves back on, her eyes meeting mine in the mirror. Quickly, I clear my throat, squaring my hunched shoulders as my gaze flicks down to the purple jersey perfectly hugging her body.

Damn. She's a vision.

Despite the fact that all I want to do is stare at her figure, remember how it felt in my hands, I force myself to speak.

"Oh, so you're like—" I cross my arms, leaning against the wall. "An *actual* Portland fan?"

In the mirror, Darcy pauses, those emerald greens flitting down my chest, locking onto my baggy pale blue jersey. She spins around, drawing a hand to her hip, pretty freckled face tipping to the side. "I should've known."

The Portland Porcupines and the San Diego Sabertooths are fierce rivals. Sure, there are less than twenty teams in the PWHL right now, so it's not like they have a ton of competition, but still—these two have been battling for the top spot ever since the league was founded.

The Porcupines are the worst.

Because they're *almost* the best.

Their goalie, Clover Solace, is the best goalie in the entire league. Hell, I'd argue she's the best goalie in all of hockey. Her stats are unreal, a .943 save percentage and a 1.56 GAA in two and a half seasons. If she keeps this up, she'll break every record in the sport.

She's the reason the Sabertooths lost the Walter Cup last season.

"Who would I be if I didn't rep the team I plan to play on?" I ask, stepping toward her with a grin.

Darcy's lips curl into a smirk. "A winner."

I try to fight it, but a suppressed laugh slips from my lips, and I take another step, the heat of her body radiating against mine.

"You're going down, Coach," I murmur, flicking my gaze up her body.

Darcy's brow cocks in challenge. Her eyes flick from mine to my lips, a breath catching in her throat. When her tongue brushes over her lower lip, she exhales, her jersey pressing against mine. My heart thrums against my ribcage.

And all I can think about is four days ago, in Salem.

How I tried—*very* clearly—to kiss her.

How she—*very* clearly—didn't let me.

I think about how hurt she sounded talking about Brenna. And how, no matter how much I want to show her I'm not like that, I could never risk pushing her into something she's not ready for.

So I take a step back. Repeating it like a prayer: *Don't kiss her. Don't kiss her.*

Don't kiss her.

The only problem is I back right into the grimy tile wall.

I shift to the side.

But Darcy moves with me.

Her hands land on my shoulders. Then her eyes drop to my mouth. And I stop breathing entirely.

Don't kiss her.

Don't kiss her.

Don't kiss her.

She looks back into my eyes, like she's telling herself the same thing, like she's about to pull away and apologize, just like I did.

"This is a bad idea," I blurt.

She nods. "The worst."

"We definitely shouldn't do this," I try again.

"Definitely," she breathes.

"You don't do this."

"And you don't have time."

"Right."

"Right."

But the moment that word leaves her mouth, I know it's pointless. And before I can even convince myself I meant it when I said we shouldn't—

She fucking kisses me.

It isn't slow. It isn't careful. It's a dizzying, enlightening jolt, like we both forgot this kind of euphoria was even a possibility. Our mouths part, tongues slipping together, hard and desperate.

Darcy makes me that way.

Kissing her is like a power play. You know the other team has the upper hand, but you still fight like hell, because in the end, the win is that much more deserved.

And I want to deserve her.

Her gloves are still on, the leather rubbing the back of my neck, and my fingers dive into her hair, tugging her impossibly closer. She tastes like strawberry lip balm. Her body presses into mine and the sheer feeling of it entices a moan out of me.

I always thought things were meant to be better in your head. That daydreams grow into impossible standards, leaving you nothing to reap but disappointment. But the moment my mouth parts open, and Darcy sucks my lower lip between the sharp cut of her teeth, I realize that I am not capable of inventing perfection like this.

Just as my hands start to drift down her spine, Darcy pulls back.

It's so sudden it knocks the breath out of me. She doesn't say a word. She just stares at me, wide-eyed, breathless. Then turns and walks out of the bathroom like she didn't just set my whole world on fire.

I blink at the door.

My god.

I catch a glimpse of myself in the mirror. My hair's a mess, lips swollen, cheeks flushed. *I'm a wreck.*

I wash my hands like I said I would, and when I come back out, Darcy's seated beside Coach Cole, gripping a ceramic mug. Her posture's relaxed at first glance, but there's a faint crease between her brows, and every so often, she shifts. They're small movements, barely noticeable, like she's chasing comfort and not quite finding it.

It makes me think of the other day in the locker room, the way she kept wincing. Of Salem, when she was struggling to zip up her jacket. I don't know if I'm just seeing it now because I know—because she told me she has Rumbustious Arthritis—or if she's actually getting worse. If all the extra time she's been putting in, before and during practice, is catching up with her. Just like the doctors warned it would.

But I know better than to bring it up.

And I should know better than to sit next to her.

In fact, judging by the rapid beat of my heart, I should keep at least ten feet between us at all times. But then she runs her gloved fingers through her ginger hair, flicks those pretty green eyes to me, and it's over.

I'm pathetic for her.

I grab the back of a chair, the legs etching lines into the grimy tile floor as I drag it. When I approach her, I spin the chair around, and toss my legs on either side of the seat, straddling it. Then I pull off my backwards cap, ruffle my hair, and plop it back on. Darcy's eyes stay trained on me, but the moment I'm beside her, I turn my attention elsewhere.

"Let me guess, you're a Portland fan too?" I ask, looking to Coach. She lifts her mug, carefully inspecting the glass before taking a heavy swig of her beer.

"Yup."

"Of course you are."

Darcy doesn't hesitate to cut in, sticking her big head in my personal bubble, just as planned. "And of course you're a Sabertooths fan."

I grin cheekily, casting her a fleeting glance. "Why? Because they're the best?"

Her gaze narrows. "Because they're *almost* the best."

An antagonizing laugh slips out of me, and I nod as my tongue traces the inside of my cheek. "That's the hill you want to die on?"

Darcy leans forward, her face inches from mine. "Yes, because it's the one at the top."

Coach's head falls into her hands and she rubs the inner corners of her eyes tiredly. "Oh Jesus," she mutters under her breath. But Darcy's got a fire in her eyes.

I move just an inch closer, so that my breath brushes against hers. I can hear the hitch in her throat. "How much are you willing to bet?" I ask lowly, tone sultry.

A small hand cuts in between Darcy's face and my own, forcing us apart, and Coach immediately begins shaking her head. "Uh-uh. There will be *no betting,*" she says.

Darcy frowns, jaw tightening as she pulls back.

Coach continues. "I'm serious. If I find out you guys put stakes on this, *any kind of stakes,* I'll have you both scrub the men's locker room showers." She pauses. "And put you on equipment cleaning with Kaiser."

I stop, watching Darcy's shoulders tense. I want to press. To push. To piss Darcy off because it seems like that's what entices her to kiss me. But upsetting

Coach in the process isn't a good idea.

"Fine." I surrender. "No bet."

"What about a game?" Darcy asks, almost desperately, her gaze flitting between Coach and me.

Her prerogative is simple: win, by any means necessary.

I've come to realize that winning is Darcy's ultimate game. Winning at making me want her, winning at being right on the ice, and now, winning at this.

I think it's time she learns how to lose.

Coach tilts her head back, letting out a dramatic groan. "Oh my god," she says, taking another drawn-out sip of her beer. Darcy and I lock eyes, and I bite back a grin. "Whatever. Just please, leave me out of it."

That freckled smile breaks across Darcy's face, and it makes everything in me flutter.

"What's the game?" I ask, folding my arms.

She grins. "Well, we don't have practice until Monday, so… Sabertooths score, I take a shot. Porcupines score, you take a shot."

I pause, considering as Coach pipes in.

"You really want to go down that road?" she asks, eyeing us both.

My eyes catch Darcy's before turning back to Coach, nodding and replying in unison: "Yes."

Her stare goes blank, and she lets out a heavy sigh, looking back at the screen without another word.

I lean in toward Darcy again. "What about blocks? Penalties?"

She shakes her head. "Just scores, Cap."

I study her for a moment and then nod. "Fine. Just scores."

"I**S SHE ALWAYS THIS** much of a lightweight?" Coach asks, watching Darcy lean forward, blocking half the screen with her giant head as she yells, "Oh, c'mon! That's not a penalty! What, are you blind?!"

Bailey reaches out and gently pulls her back into her seat.

"I don't know." I shrug. "She's your kid."

Coach sighs, glancing at the screen. Her brows furrow. "She's only had two shots and she's already... like *this?*" She gestures vaguely at Darcy, who's now throwing her hands up in disbelief as a Porcupines player gets sent to the penalty box with only a minute left on the clock.

"Does it run in the family?" I ask, grinning.

Coach shoots me a look that could salt the Earth. "Watch it, Clarke."

I laugh sheepishly. "Kidding."

The Sabertooths' center, Vivienne Kyro, lands a perfect icing shot into the net, and I cheer along with Harlowe, Bailey, Indie, and Lena. Everyone else groans dramatically. Darcy just turns toward me and taps the table like a flaming furious tyrant.

"Sure you wanna take it?" I ask, raising a brow. "There's only a minute left in the game. I'll let it slide."

Darcy narrows her eyes and jabs a finger at me. "Are you calling me a quitter?"

I can't help myself. I bring her a shot.

I love watching the way her face scrunches when she takes them. Her nose wrinkles and she makes this disgusted little "blech" sound before chasing it with a lactose-free peanut butter milkshake. A combination that's deeply concerning, and kind of adorable.

"How's that hill treatin' ya?" I ask, stealing a sip of her shake. She doesn't even flinch, just slumps deeper into her chair, arms crossed in surrender.

"That ref's blind, I swear," she mutters, inching forward like she can will the game to bend to her rage. I pat her on the back.

"You're gonna microwave your brain," I say, reaching under her chair and dragging it back toward me. The legs screech against the tile, and her body sways with it, but she doesn't resist.

That's when I notice it, that subtle shift again. The slight tensing in her shoulders. That faint crease in her brow returning. It makes my stomach sink and twist. Makes me want to trade places with her, so that she doesn't have to hurt anymore. I would live every day of my life in pain if it meant Darcy didn't have to.

Coach stands, pulling her purse over her shoulder. Her eyes land on Darcy and soften.

"I think she's probably tired," she says, voice gentle.

"I don't want to go home yet," Darcy replies quickly, shaking her head like even the implication of exhaustion is offensive.

Coach's brows lift, her gaze snapping to mine, tinted with worry. I wave a hand.

"I've got her," I say. "Don't worry."

She studies me for a long second, probably running through every argument Darcy and I have ever had. Every reason she shouldn't leave her daughter alone with me. But when she looks at Darcy again, casually sipping her milkshake, scrolling her phone, Coach exhales.

"You'll take care of her?" she asks, looking back at me. There's something in her expression I can't quite place. Something between a warning and a thank you.

"Coach," I say, catching her eye. "I won't let her out of my sight."

She watches Darcy for another beat, then gives me one last look. One that seems to say *I'm trusting you, don't make me regret it.*

"Alright," she says. "But *watch her*, Clarke. Or I'll have your ass."

I nod. "I haven't had a sip of alcohol, and besides, she'll probably be begging to leave in thirty minutes."

Darcy shoots me a piercing look. "No, I won't!"

Coach leans in, pressing a kiss to the top of her head. "Love you. Call me when you get home."

Darcy beams, big and goofy. "Okay Mom. Love you."

Coach turns to leave, the rest of the team trickling out behind her, still exhausted from the game. Harlowe and Bailey whisper to one another, casting me matching glances as they step out the door. Honestly, I could pass out right here in this booth, but if Darcy wants to stay, we're staying. Just before Coach hits the door, she spins around.

"Clarke?" she calls. My head snaps up.

"Yes, Coach?"

A subtle smile pulls at her mouth. "Thank you," she says. Then she's gone.

I glance back at Darcy, making good on my promise. She's still glued to her phone, thumbs flying across the screen. I peek shamelessly. She's texting Cleo.

"So, tough loss, huh?" I tease, and she just scowls.

"Do you actually think you're funny?"

"Of course." I grin. "But really, I just like making you mad. You're really cute when you're angry."

A faint blush creeps into her cheeks as she tries to hold back a smile. "Whatever, Icarus. You're obnoxious."

"And an amazingly good kisser."

The blush deepens. She scoffs, crossing her arms like a shield. "Whatever you're trying to pull, it isn't going to happen again," she says firmly.

I can't help it. I smirk. "Well obviously. You're drunk. But you weren't when you kissed me like you wanted it to."

"I—" She falters. Opens her mouth. Closes it. Repeats. Finally, she blows out a frustrated breath. "You know what? I don't have to explain myself to you."

I watch her nose scrunch in frustration. "No," I say. "You absolutely don't."

She just bobs her head triumphantly, tipsily unaware of the thoughts running through my head. If she weren't drunk, if I hadn't agreed to that stupid game, perhaps we'd be back in the bathroom right now, her hands in my hair, my face between her thighs.

"What?" She frowns.

Oh, just thinking about eating you out until your legs collapse.

I shake my head. "Nothing."

She's about to protest, her forehead wrinkling, eyes narrowing, but just as her lips part to speak, music floods the overhead speakers. It's a familiar sound, light percussion, a bouncing beat. *"Oh, Pretty Woman"* fills the air, and before I can blink, Darcy starts to move. Her shoulders sway first, then her hips, and soon enough, she's on her feet, pulling me with her.

"Darcy," I say, blinking as she tugs at my wrist. "What are you doing?"

"Dancing it out," she says simply.

I look around the diner. It's not popping, by any means, but there are definitely a couple other customers, chowing away in their booths. Darcy didn't even want to dance behind closed doors, and now, she's climbing onto a table, hopping around to the song. I stare at her, completely taken aback.

If I let her do this, she'll hate me in the morning. But if I stop her, I'll be depriving myself of this vision. She spins around, tossing her hands up as she hums along to the song. She's clearly caught the attention of the other diners, some of them grinning as they watch, others flicking judgmental brows. But Darcy either doesn't see them or simply doesn't care.

I really hope it's the latter.

"Hey. Are you sure that's a good idea? You've been in a lot of pain."

She pauses, giving me a wry smile. "The alcohol helps." She shrugs, tugging me upward.

"You said dancing it out was stupid," I call, still watching in awe.

"It is."

"Then why are you doing it?"

Her feet move offbeat, and when she smiles, revealing a little freckle on the inside of her bottom lip, my spine tingles. "Because you were right," she says. "It works."

I thought falling for someone was supposed to be subliminal, something you didn't even realize was happening. I thought you weren't supposed to understand why that ache in your chest existed, why someone you hardly knew could take up so much of your attention. But it's not like that. In fact, it's painfully, glaringly obvious. There is no confusion. There is no mistaking it.

I am falling in love with Darcy Cole.

I step onto the chair, pulling myself onto the table alongside her. That smile grows wider than I've ever seen, and as the music swells, I grab her hand, twirling her around, her purple jersey a blur of color. She lets out a nervous squeal as the table tilts beneath us, and I quickly pull her back in, pressing my palm to the small of her back.

Darcy spends most days trying to blend into the background, hiding what she's really going through. But right now, she's taking up space, and I can't get enough of it. She's lost in her own little world, and for some reason, she's letting me be a part of it. I want it to stay that way.

She lets out another bright laugh when I attempt a clumsy dip, her auburn hair flying as I pull her back up. But the sound cracks a little at the end. Her fingers clutch my sleeve a second longer than they should, and when I glance down, I see her jaw tighten, her breath catching as she steadies herself.

When the final notes fade out, Darcy carefully lowers one foot from the table. She wipes her hands on her jersey, breathing hard, chest rising and falling as if she just sprinted a mile. Her other foot hits the ground with a muffled thud, and she stiffens, like the impact shot straight up her spine.

The moment both her sneakers are flat on the floor, she lets out a low, sharp exhale and presses a hand to her thigh.

"Okay," she mutters, voice thin. "That was a really bad idea."

I hop down, my brows knitting. "You alright?"

She nods, but it's more of a wobble. "Yeah. I just... I need to lay down."

I offer her my arm, and she takes it with a quiet sigh, leaning into me. Not barely. Fully. Letting herself need me as we walk out of the diner toward my car.

I don't say it out loud, but I could get used to being the one she leans on.

If only she'd let me.

TWENTY SEVEN

Darcy

SOMETHING MOST PEOPLE DON'T realize about living with a chronic illness is how much of it feels like failure.

Not the pain. That part, I can handle. The full body aches, the stiff throbbing joints, the fatigue. That all becomes background noise after a while. A constant presence you learn to ignore best you can.

But the failure? That's harder to silence.

Failure for needing to cancel plans. For taking breaks. For saying no. For needing help. It doesn't matter how valid the reasons are, some part of me always believes I'm letting everyone down.

That part is worse than the pain.

Which is why I'm here, in the Hornets visitor locker room, sitting on cold yellow metal with heat packs stuffed under my clothes and double knee braces, instead of curled up in bed where I probably belong.

I slept through the weekend. Skipped Monday's practice, though not by choice. My mom physically hid my skates. Peyton didn't show for our early skate session the next morning, no matter how many times I said I'd be fine. And Professor Palit pulled me aside after class yesterday, offering me virtual lessons again.

But tonight is the biggest game of the season so far. I owe it to Peyton—and the team, of course—to be here. And besides, everyone would get suspicious that my "food poisoning" was lasting so long.

"Why are the most important games always scheduled when my ovaries are rioting?" Harlowe grumbles, adjusting her massive leg pads. She winces as Bailey yanks her short blonde hair into a painfully tight, completely ridiculous little bun on top of her head. Half her hair still spills out the bottom, but at least the bangs are secured, which, I suppose, is the whole point.

"Because the other team couldn't handle you at full power," Bailey replies, snapping the hair tie into place with a satisfying *pop*. She pats Harlowe's head like a well-groomed dog.

I glance around the room, mostly staying quiet. Faith looks locked in, focused and ready to play. I heard from Peyton that she patched things up with her ex, which probably explains the spring in her step these past few weeks. Caydence is... well, Caydence. She's currently leaned against the sink, slicking her hair into a ponytail so tight it gives me a headache just watching her. Indie doesn't look half as terrified as she did the first game of the season. She's still taking in slow, steady breaths, but now, she's got a smile on her face as she talks to Lena about something I can't quite hear.

It's kind of wild how much you can learn about people just by listening. Watching. Like, how I know Caydence is Catholic, and Lena was born in Ireland. Harlowe has two moms and Zayda has a twenty-pound cat. That Indie grew up on a ranch down in Sundown Sands, Oregon, and has seven siblings. *Seven.*

I didn't know any of that before. But I do now.

I don't know if word got around about Minnesota, or if maybe I was just too much of a bossy bitch in the beginning, but the more I listen, the more they seem to listen too.

Lena's been working on that low-angle wraparound shot I suggested at practice last week. Faith adjusted her stride pattern after I pointed out she was wasting speed on wide-angle turns. Even Caydence, of all people, accepted the electrolyte packets I gave her when she started to get dizzy during practice. She didn't say "thank you" or anything, but she's been using them all week.

Lately, practice hasn't felt like a job. It's felt like an escape. Like a reminder that, as much as I respect Professor Palit, I don't have to spend my life in a job I'll never truly love. Like finding version of myself that's old, yet new. The same as before, but also different. No one looks at me like I'm fragile, because no one knows that I am.

Well... Peyton knows.

But she doesn't treat me like I'm broken.

She just treats me like me.

I glance around the locker room and find her tucked into the corner by the bathroom, alone. She's staring down at her phone, thumbs tapping away. I've seen her do it before every game. I just never knew what she was doing until recently. Turns out it's her dad she's texting. He sends her a motivational message before every game, probably because she doesn't let him actually come and watch. She says it stresses her out too much and makes it harder to focus.

If my dad were Harrison Clarke, I think I'd feel the same way.

I saunter over and give her ponytail a playful tug.

"Flying low, or high tonight Icarus?" I tease.

But when Peyton whips around, the smirk that normally seems to be cemented to her face is gone. Her amber eyes are wide and glassy, her chest shuddering in rapid breaths.

My face drops.

My stomach drops.

My heart drops.

"Hey, are you okay?" I ask.

She nods, sucking in a breath, slower this time, but still shaky.

"I'm fine," she says, turning back to her phone. I scan the locker room, everyone else still caught up in their own post-warm-up rituals. When I look back at Peyton, her cheek is sucked inward between her back teeth as she gnaws a hole through it.

Clearly, she is not fine.

I take one last glance around the room, before grabbing her wrist and tugging her into a bathroom stall. She doesn't fight me. She doesn't say anything. She just flies into it with me, the lock clicking shut behind us. A crease etches between her worried brows, and she looks at me, bewildered.

"What are you doing?" she whispers, her breath grazing my chin. Her round eyes look up at me as she shifts back, though only an inch before the stall blocks her. I study her for a moment. The dip in her cheek, the stutter in her breath. I recognize this look. It's the one she had after that phone call with her dad. The one she had after reading that article last week. She gets it before every game. But this is the full, unabridged version of it. The extended edition, only, in the worst possible way.

Her throat bobs as she swallows, over and over like something's caught inside. I want to clear it away. To make whatever this is stop.

"What's wrong?" I ask. I hope she knows how sincerely I mean it. Peyton simply shakes her head, tossing a shoulder in an attempt to be cool. But I don't want her to be cool. I want her to be honest. "Peyton, I can only help if you tell me what's going on."

It's funny. That sentence has probably been spoken to me fifty times in the past year. I always rolled my eyes at it. But now that I'm the one saying it, I realize how true it is.

Her lips part as she sucks in another wavering breath, and her eyes drop to the concrete floor.

"I don't know," she says. "I'm... I'm just panicking."

I nod, my mind swirling helplessly. I can *tell* she's panicking. The only problem is that I don't exactly know what to do about it.

"Okay, umh—" I glance around the barren stall, as if the answers will be engraved in the bright yellow walls. My head shakes, and I look back down at Peyton, tossing my hands out in a gesture. "What are you scared of?" I ask suddenly.

A crease slips over her brow. "What?"

"Well, you said you're panicking—" I start, running a hand through my hair. "So what is it that you're scared of right now?"

What Peyton and I have, it's a give-and-go. One of us only makes the pass when we trust the other will be there to send it back. And right now, she needs to trust me.

"Okay, I'll go first," I say, watching the panic sink deeper. I swallow back the dry ache that's been throbbing at the base of my throat since I got off the plane yesterday and straighten my posture. "I'm terrified to see Brenna. Like, stressed the fuck out."

The furrow in her brow deepens. "Why?"

I hitch a shoulder. "I don't know. I feel like if she sees me like this—" I gesture down my body, back into my loose, baggy coaching clothes, because just being here puts me in enough pain. "It'll mean she won."

The corner of Peyton's lip twitches. It's subtle, almost nonexistent, but I catch it. "Darcy, you're coaching a D1 team. That's huge."

I nod. "Yeah, but she's reffing them."

Peyton's brow quirks. "Because even when you were falling apart, you got drafted, and even in the prime of her health, she couldn't."

A soft chuckle slips out of me, and I look down at her, brushing the hair from her eyes. "Your turn."

"It's..." She hesitates. "A couple of things. And they're not really all relevant right now."

"That's okay."

She falls silent for a moment, her breath steadying, then finally gives in.

"I'm scared that if I screw this season up, if the Sabertooths don't draft me this summer—*if we even make it to the finals*—it'll mean I only got here because of my dad." She pauses, her gaze dropping to her fumbling hands.

"And I'm scared that if I *do* make it to the Sabertooths, it'll be because of him too. But more than that..." She clears her throat, her shoulders shifting. Then, those amber eyes snap up, and everything else—Brenna, my flare-up, it all fades away.

"More than that, I'm scared that if I play like myself, like you said, I'll let people down."

"Like who?" I ask.

Peyton shrugs. "Everyone. The tabloids, the recruiters, the team, my dad." She pauses. *"You."*

My heart trips over itself, and the next words leave my mouth before I even choose them.

"Do it."

Peyton studies me, confused. "What?"

"Do it. Let me down. Crash and burn and miss every shot, because it doesn't matter. What matters is that you're on the ice because you love it. Not to prove something. Not to keep a stupid family legacy alive. Not to rewrite the headlines. But because there's nowhere else you'd rather be."

My hand brushes over her cheek, ignoring the hot flutter that transpires in my gut. "Let them write whatever they want. The only way you'll let us down is if you get on the ice and try to be someone you're not. Play for you, that's all anyone wants. If we make it to the finals and the Sabertooths are there, we'll deal with it then. You can only play one game at a time. Okay?"

Peyton nods, a soft smile tugging at her lips. Her body relaxes, and those warm, round, honey eyes look up at me. "Okay," she says.

I THOUGHT SEEING BRENNA would wreck me. That it would bring up all that heartbroken nostalgia and turn me right back into the mess I was when everything fell apart.

But it hasn't.

In fact, the hardest part of seeing her again is not yelling at her for the absolute *garbage* calls she's been making for the past two-and-a-half periods. And I'm not the only one.

"That wasn't a trip, *ref!*" my mom shouts, emphasizing the word like it's an insult as Bailey slams into the penalty box, frustrated.

Brenna just skates backwards toward the faceoff circle, cool and clinical.

I know she saw me when the game started. Her eyes locked on mine. But there was nothing behind them. No reaction. No nod, no hello, no acknowledgment at all.

And somehow, that feels like a win.

Because the old me would've needed it. The apology, the excuse, the closure. But I don't. Not anymore. My mom, however, is less content.

"That whistle only work one way?" she shouts, arms crossed, clearly done being professional.

I elbow her lightly, ignoring the creak in my joint as it collides with her ribcage. "Mom," I warn.

She shrugs, eyes glued to the rink. "What? It's her job to protect both teams. If she's not going to do it, then I will."

Caydence leans toward us. "Okay, I thought it was just me. She's like… getting in the way! I almost tripped over her earlier."

"It's not just you," Mom replies, shaking her head. "This ref's useless."

She's not wrong—but even with Brenna working against us, we're still up by three. Unless the Hornets score three times in the next four minutes, we've got this.

My eyes flick back to the ice. Lena looks tired, her strides starting to wobble.

"Brady needs out," I say.

Mom doesn't hesitate. "Wright!" she calls, already turning to Caydence. "Get in there."

Caydence hops the boards without hesitation, her skates hitting the ice with a *thud.* She's already in motion before Brady even finishes dragging herself off.

She drops beside me with a breathless huff, sweat trailing the side of her face. Her chest heaves rapidly as she leans forward, the low bun at the nape of her neck—woven from long, tiny braids—peeking from beneath her helmet.

"You good?" I ask, pulling her water bottle from the shelf and handing it to her. She takes it gratefully.

"Yeah," she pants. "Just gassed."

I shift forward, elbows planted on my knees, gaze locked back on the ice.

The refrigerated buzz of the rink dissolves beneath the roar of the crowd as the power play plays out. I scan the ice, searching until I finally spot her. Peyton's moving fast. So fast it's almost hard to track her.

She's a storm out there, darting around a Hornets defender, tapping the puck to Indie, then cutting hard to the inside like she's chasing her own pass. But its a calm kind of storm.

A contained hurricane.

A methodical tornado with only the ghost of Harrison Clarke making his appearance. The rest of it is her. Completely and entirely her.

And she's dominating.

Even with Bailey in the penalty box, even with Brenna getting in the way, even with the wrist shot Peyton missed a few minutes ago that I know is still eating at her, it's not even close.

We're going to win this game, and there's nothing the Hornets can do about it now.

Peyton's head is up, hips shifting, shoulders squared as she glides. The momentum is all hers.

Until it isn't.

It happens in a blink.

She pivots hard, *too* hard, and someone's in her blind spot.

Not Indie.

Not a Hornets player.

Brenna.

Their bodies collide mid-turn. Full speed. Full contact.

The sound is awful. A gut-wrenching thud followed by the clatter of a stick. I push off the bench. My mom pushes off the bench. Gasps surge from the stands as Peyton stumbles back, catching herself.

Brenna's not as fortunate. She drops to the ground, skidding backwards across the ice.

Everything stops.

The game, the sound, the breath in my lungs.

The rink goes quiet, frozen in time. All I can hear is the faint echo of Brenna's body hitting the ice, still replaying in my head.

I don't shake out of it until the medics lurch into motion, closing in on her, kneeling down, heads low, voices lower. One of them lifts her visor gently. Another checks her shoulder.

Peyton stands, frozen. She doesn't move until Brenna starts to.

Brenna stirs, then sits up slowly.

The whole bench shifts with her.

The medics try to steady her, but she waves them off with a stiff shake of her head. Pushing off the ice, she glides toward the edge of the rink with uneven strides. Her face is pale, and dazed, but I recognize the determination in her eyes. No stretcher. No help.

She always believed in independence. I think that's part of what bothered her so much about my disability.

A sigh of relief slips out of me as I watch her climb off, a new ref sliding out onto the ice.

"How the hell did that happen?" I ask, watching as they announce a ten-minute misconduct for Peyton. "Did she slip?"

The arena livens with a chorus of boos, though I can't tell if it's towards the ref's call or Peyton. Peyton doesn't flinch. She just turns and skates toward the box. Her shoulders stay high, her jaw locked in place. She collapses next to Bailey, who immediately starts frantically yapping.

My mom turns to face me, brows knitted.

"You think that was an accident?" she asks.

I pull back slightly, confusion flooding my body. "Yes."

"Then you didn't see the look on her face when she did it."

My stomach caves in on itself. That doesn't make sense. None of what just happened makes any sense. "Why would she do that?"

My mom flashes me an earnest look, tipping her head as she says, "You tell me."

I shake my head, trying to argue back. To point out how ridiculous the idea is. There's no way Peyton would get a misconduct just to ram Brenna off the icc... right?

"You need to call an Uber," Mom continues.

My eyes snap to hers. "What? But I—"

"Darcy," she says, so firmly it sends a chill down my spine. "When this game ends, you're going back to the hotel. I don't want this turning into a circus, and I definitely don't need the media poking around or Brenna trying to make a scene. This isn't the time for you to play 'Angry Coach'. Understood?"

Her eyes lock on mine, unblinking, and I know there's no room for argument. So I just nod, and look back to the penalty box.

"Okay."

"**C**AN YOU PLEASE STOP playing that?" I mutter, tipping my head into my hands as Cleo, for what must be the twentieth time since FaceTiming me, plays that damn video again on her laptop.

The clip's already gone viral. Peyton slamming into Brenna in slow motion, the frame spinning on impact. There's a dreamy haze filter over it, the audio some trending hip hop song, and Brenna hitting the ice right as the beat drops.

It's really fucked up.

Cleo smirks, barely bothering to hide it, and shuts her laptop.

"What?" she says innocently. "They said she's fine. No concussion or anything."

I glare at her through my fingers. She lifts her hands in surrender.

"Okay, okay. I will not play it again... in your presence," she says.

"Thank you," I mumble, shifting on the plush hotel bed.

"It's a really good edit though," she adds. Then, her expression shifts, her thick brow quirking. "So... is there something you want to tell me?"

I glance up at her, confused. "What do you mean?"

She rolls her eyes. "Darcy. Come on. First, you're ranting about how much you can't stand her every chance you get. Then, you start disappearing every morning, and now she *just so happens* to slam your ex to the ice?"

Cleo's got a point. But I don't know what she wants me to say. I don't even know what's happening myself. All I know is that it terrifies me.

"So?"

Cleo grins. "*So*, you've been practically glued at the hip since you hooked up."

I let out an exasperated breath. "Okay, *yeah*, but it's not—"

Wait, how did she...?

A smile breaks over Cleo's face and she jabs a finger at the camera.

"I knew it!" she squeals, jumping around like a child. The video feed shakes enough to make me nauseous. Or maybe, it's everything else that's happened. "I *fucking* knew it!'"

"No! No, it's not—"

"So you didn't hook up with her?" she asks, crossing her arms. I suck in a frustrated breath.

"Well, I *did*, but it was—"

Cleo tosses her hands in the air. *"Halleluja!"*

I grunt, hopping off the bed and grabbing a Seven-Up from the mini-fridge, using my foot to shut the door. "Will you knock it off? None of this is funny."

She's grinning so hard it's a miracle her face hasn't split. "No. You're right."

Her teeth sink into her bottom lip. "It's hilarious."

A frown pulls at my lips and I catch the time on the microwave clock. "Don't you have study group soon?"

Cleo rolls her eyes. "Nice try, but you're not deflecting."

She glances at the time.

"Shit," she mutters, then whips back to me, making eye contact with the camera. "Okay. I have to go. But we are talking about this when you get back."

"There's nothing to talk about!" I say, holding up my free hand like that'll make it true. "It happened once. And it is never, ever happening again."

"Just once?" Cleo asks, one brow arching as she slings her purse over her shoulder. Just as I'm about to admit that I might have also kissed her in a public bathroom, room service knocks at my door.

"Hold on," I say, strolling over to open it.

And when I do, I want to chuck myself in front of a semi-truck. Because there, on my hotel doorstep like a fucking 90's sitcom, is Peyton.

Her hair's wet, tumbling over her shoulders in slick waves, beanie pulled snug over her ears, and she's in a fresh set of clothes. The moment her eyes catch mine, she freezes.

"Peyton?" I ask, for some fucking reason.

On the other end of the phone, Cleo squeals.

"This isn't—I don't know what she's doing here," I blurt out. But Cleo's already made up her mind.

"Sure, Darce." She calls out through the phone. "Hey Pey!"

"Hi, Cleo," Peyton says awkwardly. Cleo blows two kisses through the screen, winks, then hangs up. The moment she does, Peyton's eyes find mine.

She looks... *beat up*. A fresh bruise is blooming along the edge of her chin, and as she shifts, she winces a bit, like her shoulder is still sore. But she's still, of course, annoyingly pretty.

"Why are you here, Peyton?" I ask, not inviting her in.

She stays in the doorway, hands buried deep in the pocket of her hoodie.

"You left," she says simply.

I let out a huff. "And why do you think that is?"

A sheepish smile creeps across her face as she begins rocking on the balls of her feet. "I mean, you did say 'crash and burn'."

"I didn't mean for you to ram full speed into my ex!"

"First of all, that was half-speed at best," she mutters. She takes one cautious step forward but stops short of crossing the line into the room. "And they're saying it was an accident."

I cross my arms. "Well? Was it?"

Those bright golden eyes meet mine. "Do you want it to be?"

"I want to know you didn't get a misconduct just to be petty!"

"Well, then I think you'll be happy." She gestures vaguely toward the settee behind me. "Can I come in now? This hallway is freezing."

"I thought you didn't mind the cold," I say, stone-faced. Then I sigh. "Fine."

She steps inside, peeling off her beanie as she does. Her hair's a damp mess, clinging to her face in awkward tufts. She tries to smooth it down as the door clicks shut behind her.

I don't move. I stay exactly where I am, arms crossed, spine straight, stare unrelenting.

"So it was an accident?" I ask. Or maybe declare? Insist? Plead?

Peyton presses her lips together, tips her head, and squints. "Well... I didn't quite say that. But we won!"

My jaw tightens. God, she's annoying. And gorgeous. Which is, frankly, the most dangerous combination.

"You better start making sense, Peyton, or I'm kicking you out."

"Okay, okay," she says quickly, and then steps closer. Too close. Just a breath of space between us. "It wasn't an accident. But it wasn't, like, *premeditated* either. I didn't step on the ice thinking I was gonna body your ex. But once the game started, and I saw her out there, and I thought about what she did to you..." Her jaw clenches. "I got pissed."

"So it was petty," I say.

She nods, unapologetically. "Yes. Absolutely."

I let out a long, exhausted breath, pinching the inner corners of my eyes.

She keeps going. "You said it yourself. They were going to write something either way."

I flash her a menacing glare. "Oh, so now it's my fault?"

She backpedals quickly. "No! No, I'm not saying that—" Her eyes widen, panic flickering. "I'm just saying... no matter what I did, they were gonna say something bad about me. Might as well control the narrative."

"You're self-sabotaging," I snap, frustration bubbling.

She gives a sly smile.

"I'm *guiding the future*." She adds. "Look, I didn't just do it because of you. I was sick of her trash calls, alright? I wouldn't have done it if I didn't know we were going to win."

I gape at her. "So we've been wasting our time training, then?"

She shakes her head, stepping closer, her voice husky and maddeningly sincere. "I wouldn't call spending time with you a waste." Then she grins, head tilted. "Maybe cruel and unusual punishment, but definitely not a waste."

A scoff slips out of me, and I roll my eyes so hard it physically hurts. "Why are you like this?" I ask, gesturing to her entire being. Peyton just smirks.

"You mean dangerously sexy?"

"I mean irritating as fuck."

Her eyes flicker. She's enjoying this. Me. My reaction. My unraveling.

"Why are you like that?" she asks. I prop a hand on my hip.

"Like what?"

"All haughty and avoidant when we both know you want to kiss me."

My breath catches, a silent scoff slipping out of me. My skin is tingly. My throat is dry. I can feel my pulse in places I definitely shouldn't.

"I—" I start, but the word sticks, wedged somewhere in my dry throat.

She just watches me, that smug expression tugging at her lips. She's looking at me like she's memorized me. Like I'm a play she designed, and she's just waiting for it to unfold exactly how she planned.

I want to erase that look. I want to devour it.

"What?" she asks, feigning innocence. Her head tilts, lips parting like she's daring me to say it.

"I might strangle you," I mutter. My voice is low. My cheeks are hot. My entire body is hot, ready to combust at just the thought of her.

She steps in, her chest pushing into mine. Those damn smile lines sink into her cheeks as she grins.

"I might be into that," she murmurs.

And then, she kisses me.

TWENTY EIGHT

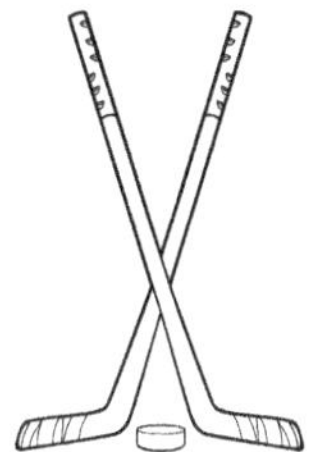

Peyton

NOTE TO SELF: MISCONDUCT=KISSING a pretty girl.

I'm unclear if that's a universal rule or just a me-and-Darcy-specific clause. Either way, I'm not complaining. Because her lips are still attached to mine, and my hand is still feathered through her soft, shiny hair, and we are walking—no, *stumbling*—backwards, staggered breaths and roaming hands.

Her fingers grip the front of my hoodie, pulling me impossibly closer. I think I bump into the wall. Or the door. Or the desk, I don't know. Because when her mouth breaks away, and those freckled lips attach to my neck, everything around me glows.

Still, I manage a breath. "Should we—" Her teeth sink into my neck. "Mmm—should we talk about this?"

Goosebumps flood my skin as she speaks against me. "Do you want this?" she murmurs. Something clenches deep inside me. I press my thighs together, tilting my head back as her lips return to that sweet spot beneath my jaw, her nose tracing the curve of my chin.

"Y—Yes," I answer, weaker than I care to admit. "Yes. I just—you said never again so I just want to make sure."

A soft hot breeze blows across my neck as Darcy chuckles. "Peyton," she says, and the moment it leaves her mouth, I'm suddenly reminded I have a name. I had forgotten that I exist outside of this. "Why do you have to make things so difficult?" *Kiss.* "It doesn't have to mean anything." *Kiss.*

My stomach sinks, but the pulse thrumming between my thighs amplifies.

"Right," I breathe out. "It doesn't mean anything."

So I kiss her like an agreement.

Even if my t is already traitoring its way toward more.

A soft sound escapes her lips, vibrating against mine. But she pulls back once more, her palms pressing softly against my chest.

"Unless you don't want to—"

"I want to," I say, cupping her cheek. I lean in and kiss her softer this time. Slower, tracing my thumb against her cheek as my lips memorize every inch of hers. "I want to."

And suddenly, we're on the bed. Darcy's straddling me, lights on, thigh grinding against my hot center as her tongue traces circles around mine. When she shifts her weight onto her knees, she sucks a sharp breath through her teeth. Immediately, I pull back.

"Are you okay?" I ask, a concerned crease popping between my brows. Darcy, of course, rolls her eyes.

"I'm fine. You don't have to baby me, Peyton," she says, leaning back in to suck on my neck. An unbridled moan escapes me, a slick heat emanating between my thighs, but when a tense jolt runs through her muscles, I pull back again.

"You're in pain," I say, searching her eyes. She just rolls them again.

"I'm always in pain," she breathes. She leans back in, but I don't let her kiss me this time. I pull myself up slightly, leaning my back against the headboard. She huffs, collapsing back against my shins, and even that makes her wince.

I look at her earnestly. "I don't want to hurt you."

Her brows furrow. "I knew this would happen," she exasperates, running a disappointed hand through her hair. "It's okay. I understand." She starts to slide off me, but my hands grip her waist keeping her in place.

"I said I don't want to hurt you," I vow. "I didn't say I don't want to fuck you."

Red spills across Darcy's cheeks as she looks at me, her hair all tangled and messy from my hands, her lips swollen. She looks at me confused.

I slip out from under her, and those wild eyes look up at me. I lean forward, just slightly, to once in my life, tower over her.

"Lay down," I order gently.

A puzzled expression conquers her face. She starts to turn her body, tilting her head against the headboard, but I shake my head, gesturing to the mattress. I know Darcy well enough by now to know that she's going to want to keep this on the down low again. And if the headboard is banging against the wall, we'll be caught. "Lay down right here."

She complies. When her head presses to the mattress, slowly, tentatively, I begin to crawl on top of her. My leg slips in between hers, her breath hitches, and I kiss her. As our mouths move together, I reach out and grab a pillow from her headboard.

"Lift your head up," I whisper, and when she does, I slip the pillow beneath her.

"You don't have to treat me like I'm fragile," she murmurs, letting out a moan as my tongue glides from behind her ear, down her neck, leaving a hot slick trail on her skin. Goosebumps rise one by one, and my core tightens. I suck her earlobe between my teeth, biting softly before whispering,

"I don't plan to."

"Fuck."

The word slips out so quietly, I hardly hear it at all. But even that, a single, breathy word, is enough to make me desperate.

My mouth slides against hers, fingers threading needily through her hair. "I haven't been able to stop thinking about this since the retreat," I murmur, pressing my thigh harder between her legs. She lets out a soft moan, her hips involuntarily bucking against me. I lean in closer, my breath tracing her jaw as my thumb grazes over her swollen bottom lip. "And I don't think you have either. Tell me you've thought about this. About me fucking you the way you fucked me."

Darcy shudders beneath my touch, one of her hands slipping beneath my shirt, tracing up my spine, as the other grips the back of my neck, anchoring it in place.

"I have," she moans. "I've thought about it."

The admission is more than it seems. Because Darcy Cole would never admit that I'm right, unless she had no other choice. And that, the fact that she too hasn't been able to get this off her mind, to stop thinking about that night in the cabin, with our slick skin pressed together, our sounds, our desperation, tangling in a wet hot mess of need, makes every nerve in my body spark.

I pull back, just enough to pry her hand from the back of my neck and cup it in mine. My eyes lock with hers as my fingers trace the seam of her glove.

"Can I take these off?" I make sure to ask it gently. No pushing. No pleading. Giving her every second of time she needs to decide. Her gaze falls to her hands, then flicks back up to mine.

She nods. "Yes," she says. There's a soft waver in her voice, something I'm sure she tried her hardest to push away. But as much as I want to see every inch of her, Rhinoceros Arthritis and all, even more, I want her to be comfortable.

"You don't have to," I say, a little firmer this time. But her eyes don't tear away from mine. Instead, they narrow. Her other hand moves from my back, and as she stares at me, almost like I've pissed her off, she rips off her gloves, one at a time.

My eyes fall to her hands.

They're beautiful.

Porcelain skin, soft in some places, calloused in others. Her knuckles are swollen just slightly, her pinky on one hand bent out at an angle.

They're not perfect. That's why I love them. Because they're hers. Because they hold on tight, even when they hurt. Because when they touch me, I feel like maybe I'm worth holding on to.

"Take it all off," she says.

And I do.

I want to be archaic about it. To move quickly. To rip buttons, and shred seams, and tear through every inch of space between us, punishing it for existing. But I also want to be careful. To make love to her softly, like candlelight and silk sheets. I want to slip my hand between her thighs and ride each sound wave that falls from her lips.

Up and down.

Slipping off her clothes is a compromise, not fast, not slow. Not overly gentle, but there's no torn threads either. She takes mine off just the same, pushing through the ache because for some incomprehensible reason, to her I am worth it. *This* is worth it.

I don't try to stop her. I don't tell her she's too fragile or too hurt for this. I know she doesn't want that. So instead, as her hands slide across my body, slipping underneath my clothes and tugging them off, I simply kiss each of her wrists.

Then her fingers.

Then her.

"God, you're beautiful," I murmur, tracing my fingers across her skin.

She's stretched out across the bed, pale skin, long limbs lit up in a soft gold glow from the dimmed overhead lights. Her freckles are everywhere, scattered across her shoulders, her chest, her thighs. Her hair's a mess, red strands tangled against the pillow, and her breath hitches when I say it. She looks away, like she doesn't believe me. Like there is a single part of her that I wouldn't spend my whole life staring at.

"Yeah, swollen ankles and unshaved legs are super sexy," she retorts. I shake my head, pulling back and standing up. I scoop her ankle into my hand gently, placing my lips against it.

"Yours are," I say. She rolls her eyes, but I ignore her, letting my mouth travel up her leg. I kiss her knee next. "And your knees," I say, then I keep going, placing my lips against every part of her. "Your hips." *Kiss.* "Stomach." *Kiss.*

When I reach her chest, I catch her eye. "These," I say, then I drag my tongue underneath the fold of her left breast, letting it travel up and circle around her nipple. Darcy lets out a moan, so I cure her ache by pressing my thigh against her bare heat. It's slick and warm against my skin, and she doesn't hesitate before slowly rocking against it.

"That's it," I coo, moving to her other breast. I suck on it, gently at first, then grow more desperate as her hands slip into my hair. "You like that?"

She nods, her teeth sinking into her lower lip as her back. "Yes," she breathes out. A smirk tugs at my lips, but before I can say anything back, a loud moan tumbles out of me. My hands grip the sheets, and for a second, my eyes flutter shut. When they open, Darcy's the one smirking, her head cocked to the side, brow raised.

"You like that?" she asks tauntingly, her thigh slipping against the raw ache between my legs. My body jolts as she moves it, another hitched breath tumbling out of me.

"God yes."

The words slip out on their own, but I don't regret it. Because the moment it leaves my mouth, Darcy begins rocking and grinding against me, and the more she moves, the more I need her. I let myself collapse onto her, catching my weight on my forearms. Our chests glide against each other as we move. Her pussy is wet and warm against my thigh, and when I press it harder, pushing against her clit, she curses again.

"Shit, Peyton," she moans, her fingers tightening in my hair. My head gives way to the pull, tilting back as we grind. I start to move faster, and when I do, her hips lift slightly off the mattress, back arching.

A low groan hums in my throat, vibrating against her ear as I rock and press and buck against her.

"You feel so good," I rasp, my movements becoming more urgent. The heat between us is intoxicating, and I can feel her clenching around my thigh. "So fucking good."

She throws her head back, a strangled cry escaping her. "Peyton... Oh, shit, Peyton... *Fuck...*"

Her words are a ragged whisper, lost in the rhythm of us. I press harder, focusing on the small, sensitive nub against my thigh. And the best part is that every time her clit rubs against me, mine receives the same pressure. Darcy's moans grow louder, more desperate and her nails dig into my back.

Short, sharp gasps slip out of me as my vision tunnels. I can feel the tension in my stomach, coiling tighter and tighter, but I don't stop. Not with her, gripping me like a lifeline, begging for the pressure in her body to release.

"Almost—I'm almost—" she pants, her body trembling beneath mine.

And then, with a final, shuddering cry, she arches off the bed, her muscles clenching around my thigh in a series of powerful spasms. The wetness against my legs becomes slicker, the heat radiating between us hotter. And when she lets out a final, pleasured sound, my body absorbs it.

I hold her tight, burying my face in her neck as the last tremors wrack her body. My own release follows quickly, the tight coil in my stomach unraveling. I collapse against her, our bodies slick with sweat, hearts pounding in unison.

"Fuck," I pant. I lift my head, my gaze meeting hers. Her eyes are glazed, her cheeks flushed, and a soft smile tugs at her lips. She looks utterly, breathtakingly beautiful.

"Yeah," she agrees, brows drawn tight as her chest still heaves.

We lay there for a moment, just catching our breaths, bare bodies pressed together. And when our eyes meet again, this time, laughs slip out of the two of us. I slide off her, letting my wet back fall against the mattress, running a hand through my damp hair. I blow a slow, steady stream of air through my lips.

"We should've been doing that this whole time," I say, flitting a finger between us. Darcy laughs, then tilts her cheek against the mattress to look at me.

"I don't know about that," she says, grinning cheekily. I raise a brow, dragging a hand up her thigh. Slowly. Intently.

"Oh?" I tease, flirting with the dip in her hip. "So you're saying you didn't enjoy yourself?" Her back arches just before she smacks my hand away.

"Okay, okay," she surrenders, pulling the pillow out from under her head. She lays it on top of her body, wrapping her arms around it like a koala to shield herself. "It was unregrettable."

I stare at her earnestly. "Unregrettable?"

She hitches a shoulder. "Yeah."

"Is that even a word?"

"Shut up." She rolls her eyes.

"So what does that mean, then?" I ask. "This being 'unregrettable'."

Something flares in my chest before I can stop it. That annoying little spark of hope, showing up uninvited. I shouldn't let it stay. Darcy's made it clear. She's not looking for anything real. Not with me. Probably not with anyone. And I thought I was clear too, but ever since I met her, everything has become blurry.

And that doesn't stop the part of me that wants her to say something. Something that sounds like "maybe," like "not yet", like "almost". Something that would make it okay for this to mean more to me.

"I don't know." She shrugs, then goes quiet. Her eyes catch mine, and something in them softens. "Look, I don't—I can't do anything serious," she says.

My throat goes dry. But I just nod, like it's nothing.

"Yeah, I know," I say. And damn, I should've majored in theater, because it rolls off my tongue, so smooth, so sure, like I wasn't just out here wishing on some goddamn star that Darcy Cole might change her mind for me, might be feeling what I've been feeling too. I almost believe it myself.

"I wasn't suggesting that. I mean, I can't either. I don't have time."

It's almost the truth, but it feels so far from it. Because if I had the choice, I'd spend all my time with Darcy. And yet, that's part of the problem.

Her head bobs, but something flickers in her eyes when I say it. For a second, I almost mistake it for disappointment. Almost. But I pull myself back.

"Yeah, no, I knew that," she says, turning her head away. She stares up at the ceiling.

I stare at her.

We sit there silently for a bit, as we always do. I usually enjoy the silences. These little stretches of nothing but breaths and heartbeats. But this one isn't as magnetizing as the ones before. It's not pulling us closer. And all I want to do is break it. To tell her the truth.

I know if I do, she'll just pull away. So I hold my breath and stare at the ceiling too.

"Are you staying in Seattle for winter break?" she asks after a minute. I shake my head against the sheets.

"Nah, I'm going back to the valley," I answer.

"Oh." In my peripheral, I see her tilt her head to look at me again. My heart pounds against my ribcage, and I swallow before turning to look at her too. Our noses touch.

"I should go," I whisper.

I watch the lump in her throat bounce as she swallows. "Yeah."

But I don't. Instead, I lay there until Darcy drifts to sleep, and I sneak out of the room just past midnight, wishing I had a reason to stay longer.

TWENTY NINE

Darcy

MY MOM'S NEVER BEEN great with crying. My dad's the soft one. He gets misty during raw dog food commercials, but my mom grew up in a bootstraps kind of household, where feelings were things you dealt with silently, or not at all. So, watching the face she's making right now? *Hilarious.*

"This is the nicest thing anyone has ever done for me." Cleo sniffles, her eyes glassy and overflowing. She's holding up the pajama set my parents just gave her, identical to the one I just opened. Including the size, which means hers will be comically long. But Cleo doesn't even seem to notice. Or maybe she just doesn't care.

The golden threads weaved throughout the plaid fabric glow in the multi-colored lights on the Christmas tree behind her. When she stretches the shirt out, to see the full style of it, her arm grazes a branch, sending a wave of fresh pine in my direction.

Cleo doesn't really talk about her family much. They're all the way in Chicago, and her relationship with them... it's complicated. So when she didn't have plans for Christmas, and since I live and breathe for this holiday, I invited her to spend it with us. We do Christmas on Christmas Eve. I don't really know why. It's just how it's always been.

My mom watches Cleo cry like she's got the plague. Her brows furrow.

"It's... *Ross*," she says confusedly, gesturing at the pajamas. My dad whips his head toward her, eyes wide. In the reflection of them, I can see the flames from the fireplace, and I have to stifle a laugh, because it's the scariest I have ever seen my father. And it's not scary at all.

"Paula," he hisses.

"Sorry!" she blurts, then immediately leans forward to pat Cleo on the back awkwardly. She looks like she thinks she might catch something if she lingers too long. "It was the least we could do. You've been such a good friend to Darcy."

Cleo just sobs harder, clutching the pajamas. I keep patting her back, biting down on a smile. I love her. I love Christmas. I love this ridiculous, slightly dysfunctional moment.

Something warm melts in my stomach, a feeling I don't think I've fully felt since March. I want to correct my mom. To say that Cleo and I are just roommates, nothing more. But I don't think that's true anymore.

Actually, I don't think it was ever true. No matter how hard I've tried.

My dad leans forward, handing her a tissue.

"Thanks," she manages, dabbing at her eyes.

My mom and I make eye contact as I reach into the pile and hand another gift to Cleo.

"Another one?" she asks, her voice already cracking.

"This one's from me," I tell her. My dad shoots my mom a quick warning look as Cleo crumbles all over again. Her fingers tremble as she works the ribbon loose, tears trailing down her rosy cheeks.

She pulls out a thick notebook and stares at it, confused. I can see the polite smile forming. The "Oh wow, thanks, I'll never use this" kind. I grin.

"Open it," I say.

She flips it open, and her hand flies to her mouth, the notebook dropping into her lap. Without another beat, she launches herself at me and squeezes until I hear my bones crack.

"What is it?" my mom asks, raising a brow.

Cleo pulls back, wiping her face with the tissue, which is now just a soggy, flaking mess. My dad hands her another. "It's a D&D planner," she explains, holding it up proudly. "It's a game I play."

I smile. "Do you like it?"

She nods quickly, eyes still glossy. "I love it. Does this mean you'll play with me now?"

"I'll consider it."

I push myself to my feet, doing my best to mask the pinch in my joints. It's been constant lately. So bad that I nearly pretended to have a fever so that I didn't have to get out of bed. But Cleo deserved to have a real Christmas. My parents too. "I'm gonna grab some apple cider. You guys want some?"

Everyone nods, a chorus of yeses.

"I'll come help you," my mom says, rising from the couch.

The moment we step into the kitchen, her eyes catch mine, glinting with amusement.

"Does she cry like that a lot?" she asks in a hushed tone. I pause, thinking about it.

"That's actually the first time I've ever seen her cry," I say, sounding just as surprised as my mom looks. "I don't think her family sent her anything."

Something sparks in my mom's eyes, and her brows furrow. "Do you have her mom's number?" she asks, crossing her arms. "I'd like to exchange some words."

I laugh. "Unfortunately not."

As I reach up into the cabinet, looping my fingers around a collection of mug handles, a fire spreads from my wrist, up my arm. It shakes as I bring the mugs down, setting them on the counter with a light clatter. In my periphery, I can see my mom staring at me, brow cocked, eyes judging. So instead of looking at her, I dig through a drawer for a ladle.

"When was the last time you saw Dr. Oswell?" she asks. The tone in her voice tells me that she already knows the answer. I hitch a shoulder, still avoiding her gaze as I move over to the crock pot of cider. She lifts the lid off for me, streams of cinnamon apple steam flowing out of it.

"I don't know, like two months?" I say, lowering the ladle into the pot. I do it slowly, watching the warm amber liquid pool into the scoop. I can't help but think of Peyton as I do it. Of those apple-cider eyes

"So those meds seem to be working then," my mom continues. She says it like a statement, but I can feel the question that lies beneath.

"Umh…" I falter.

Here's the thing: It's hard to know if the meds are working when you've been pushing yourself harder than before you started taking them. There's no baseline anymore, no steady control to measure against. It's like trying to judge an entire team when the lineup changes every game.

Mom steps closer, her voice growing firm. "Darcy," she says, and I curse myself for looking at her.

"Mom."

"You can hide it from the team, but you can't hide it from me. I know you've been struggling more than you're showing."

I let out a heavy sigh, pouring the cider into the cups. I've been trying really hard to ignore the pain. And when that's not possible, I've been doing everything I can to push through it. I made it to winter break, which means I have a week's rest before I'm supposed to meet up with Peyton again.

"I'm okay, Mom," I say. "Really."

My mom shakes her head. "That's what you said last time."

"Okay," I say pointedly. "Fair. But really, I'm okay. See?" I gesture to myself, proud at how well I hide the wince. "I'm resting."

Mom doesn't budge. "You're not stepping on the ice at practice again until you get a doctor's note clearing you."

"What?" I ask, brows furrowing. "But that's not fair! You're the one who wanted me to—"

"And I still do," Mom cuts in, swiping one of the mugs off the counter. "But I'm not going to watch you ignore all these warning signs again. You're not invincible, Darce. You can and will get worse."

My throat goes dry, a hard aching lump forming in the base of it.

"I know," I mumble. She lets out a heavy sigh, pulling me into a hug. It's gentle, careful. Mom knows how to hug me without hurting me, because once upon a time, she was me. The only difference is that she got treated in time to go into remission.

I look down at her, breathing in the familiar scent of her shampoo. "Can you schedule the appointment please? I really hate calling."

Mom chuckles softly against me, then pulls back.

"I already did last week. It's on the 27th at four."

"Such a meddler," I mumble, and she gives a half-shrug.

"It's my job." Both of her brows raise, and something in my stomach twists. I know that look. I'm scared of that look. "Speaking of meddling," she continues, leaning her back against the counter. She blows on the cider, then takes a long sip. "Have you talked to Peyton since the game?"
Ah fuck.

I hate lying to my mom. I'm also notoriously bad at it. So I tell her the amount of the truth I can manage. "*Yes,*" I say slowly, studying her. She smirks. "And I have no idea why you're looking at me like that."

Mom deadpans. "Oh really? You have '*no idea*'?"

I roll my eyes, failing to fight a smile. "It's not what you think."

 "And what do I think?"

I don't dignify her with a response. I just roll my eyes and snatch up the extra mugs on the counter, a limp in my step as I move.

"You know, it's not against the rules!" Mom calls out behind me. Something in my chest flutters, and I blink away the surprise before turning to look at her. The Christmas lights strung along the window behind her give her a multi-color glow.

"Doesn't matter, because nothing is going on."

Of course, that would have an effect on the situation, if there were a situation for it to have an effect on. But Peyton established that boundary, and so did I. I turn back around, but my mom is relentless. "Peyton is a lovely girl!"

This time, I don't stop. "So I've heard," I call back, pretending like I haven't spent the past few weeks living it.

I'M BACK AT THE apartment, two hours into doom-scrolling on the couch, animated Christmas movies flickering quietly on the TV. Cleo's head is resting in my lap, fast asleep, swimming in the plaid pajamas my parents gifted her. Innocently curled up on her legs, Socks is acting like I didn't have to fend him off from chewing her hair a few minutes ago.

My phone chimes, a banner flashing across the top of the screen.

ICARUS

Hey Kim Possible

My chest flutters, and I click on the notification. We've talked plenty in the few days it's been since I woke up to her no longer in my hotel room. We just haven't talked about what *happened*. I stare at the gray bubble for a few minutes longer than I care to admit, then my bare fingertips hit the cold glass, tying out a response.

ME

What, Icarus?

I don't realize I'm smiling until I press send, and even though nobody is around—or awake—to see it, I force it away. A short, descending sound slips from my phone as Peyton replies.

ICARUS

Merry Christmas!

ME

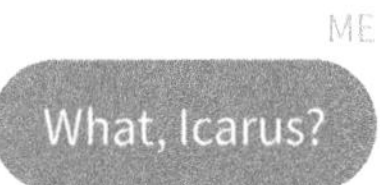

A few hours ago, Harlowe blessed us all with a photo of herself in a sexy Santa costume (beard included) flipping double middle fingers with the caption: "Ho Ho Ho, Hoes." She followed it up by declaring it was our Christmas present.

I read the message. Then I read it again. And then again. *What?*

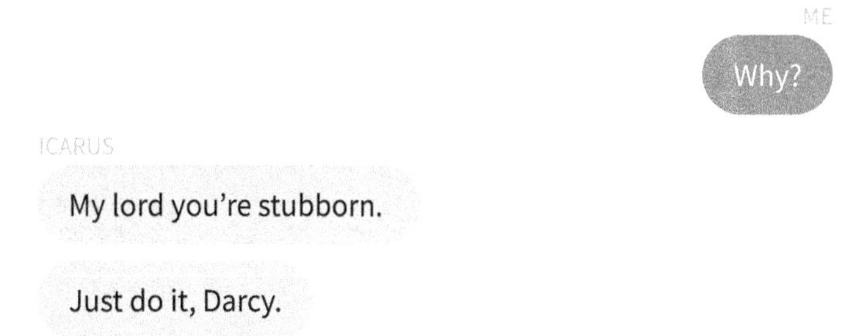

I don't know why, but my stomach flips when I see my name. When I imagine her fingers typing it out.

Cleo's still asleep, her head heavy in my lap, breath warm against my knee. Gently, I shift out from under her, catching her head and easing it onto the dragon-shaped throw pillow she got me. Socks stirs on her legs but doesn't follow me as I head to my room.

I'm a firm believer in systems. Specifically, organizational systems, and my bookshelf is no different. God bless Dewey and his Decimals. Every book has its home, and every home is sacred. Which is why I notice it immediately.

There, wedged beside my Lord of the Rings omnibus, is a book I don't recognize. A valley forms between my brows as I reach for it, fingertips brushing the spine. I pull it down and immediately notice the plastic edges. The light weight.

It's not a book at all.

It's one of those hollowed-out book boxes.

I shake my head, flipping it open. Inside is a Ziploc bag stuffed to the seal with green M&Ms. I laugh under my breath, setting them aside and looking back into the capsule. There's something else in there, and the moment my fingers graze the soft paper, I realize it's a book. A *real* book this time. I pull it out, studying the lime green cover, tracing the illustrated design with my finger.

A book inside of a book.

Such a Peyton idea.

I flip open the cover, eyes catching onto the message scrawled on the inside.

Kimmy,

A quiet chuckle slips out of me.

Merry Christmas. I hope you know the sacrifices I made to sort through all those M&Ms. I now have a stomachache. Anyway, I was walking Mr. Bubbles down-
town by the bookstore the other day and decided to grab you something. Y'know,
just in case cold-hearted bitches don't get happily ever afters. This should hold you

over.

~~Love~~ Affectionately,

Icarus

P.S. If you ever change your mind about dating, that store is crawling with cute

sapphic women. None as cute as me, though.

An amused huff escapes me. I set the book on my bed, still smiling, then reach for my phone and send her a message.

For the first couple minutes Peyton disappears, I'm excited. But after four minutes pass, then five, then six, I start getting anxious. It was a bad idea. A dumb gift. I had snuck it into the inner pocket of her bag before she left for break, thinking it was a good idea. Now, it just feels like too much.

I'm halfway through typing a humiliated "ignore that" text when the bubbles pop up.

ICARUS

Sorry. Harlowe and Bails are hammered and I'm trying to coax them out of the bar with a churro.

So far, unsuccessful.

Sounds about right.

ME

The bars are open on Christmas?

ICARUS

Monsey's is like a hospital. 24/7, 365 days a year.

Holy shit.

ME

What?

ICARUS

Apparently Harlowe and Clay fucked???

What dimension are we in???

ME

WHAT??

How?

When?

Why?

ICARUS

I have no earthly idea.

Look, I've got to get them home, but I'll text you when
I get back to my parents', okay?

I don't know why my stomach sinks a little. Or why a hot flicker in my chest I wasn't even aware of feels like it's extinguishing itself. I brush it off, shoot back a thumbs up, and toss my phone on the nightstand.

Then I grab a handful of green M&Ms, my brand new book, and curl up in bed, diving into it.

Nearly an hour later, I couldn't tell you a single thing about this book. I've read the first chapter three times now, maybe four. My eyes keep moving across the page, but all I can think about is Peyton, and that first morning at the rink.

The way Peyton smiled at me. How fast that smile dropped. The way her shoulder brushed mine when we hid, both of us sweating, breathing hard. The way those honeycomb eyes looked at me like I was something worth looking at. That morning turned my world upside down.

She turned my world upside down, and I'm starting to like how it makes my hair stick up.

I flip the page, confident that I didn't absorb a single sentence from the last one, when my phone lights up on the nightstand. I'm not going to talk about how fast I grab it. Or the stupid way my heart skips when I see her name.

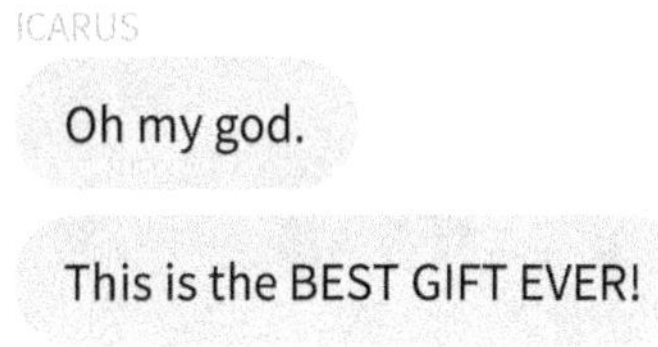

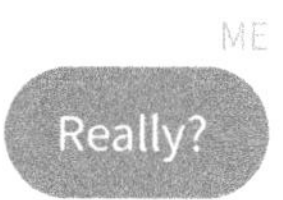

Sitting in front of a fireplace—six stockings hung across the mantle, expensive-looking garland and glass ornaments strung along the brick like something out of Pottery Barn—are Peyton and Mr. Bubbles. Both of them outlined in a soft orange glow from the fire crackling behind them.

Mr. Bubbles is proudly wearing his custom green Grizzlies jersey, reindeer antlers perched crookedly on his head. Beside him, Peyton is holding up her present.

The broken, jagged puck.

The smile on her face is cosmic. And she's wearing a red and white sweater-patterned onesie that clings to her body like saran wrap, the zipper stopped halfway up her chest.

Peyton always wears baggy clothes. The tightest thing I've seen her in is her jersey when the wind tugs it against her chest. And don't get me wrong, even in her dark baggy clothes, she's beautiful. But seeing the way this outfit hugs her body, the dip in her waist visible, the broad outline of her shoulders, the cleavage on her chest?

It strikes a match between my thighs.

"Fuck," I mutter to nobody but myself. My phone chimes.

ICARUS

I love it. Thank you.

My stomach flutters as I respond.

ME

Thank you.

The dancing dots pop back up on the screen, followed by another whooshing sound. I never thought I'd be the type of person to be smiling at my phone for hours, but with Peyton, I am.

ICARUS

Did you open any other presents?

ME

A throw pillow from Cleo, some pajamas and money from my parents.

Oh, and that photo of Yersie. Definitely a top contender.

ICARUS

That was a good gift.

ME

> What about you?

ICARUS
Nothing from my parents yet, I'll keep you posted in the morning.

But Harlowe and Bails pitched in and got me a gift-card.

ME

> Oh cool. To where?

Peyton sends a link attachment, and like the idiot I am, I click on it without thinking. Immediately, I'm greeted with a moving, uncensored video of a hyper-realistic dildo. Flustered, I quickly exit out of the tab and tap on our thread.

ME

> You just sent me a sex shop.

ICARUS

Indeed I did. Any recs?

I'm beginning to think that the photo she sent was no innocent act. A heavy pulse emanates between my thighs, my clit throbbing at the thought of it. Of Peyton touching herself. Pleasuring herself.

Of me helping her.

I do the mental equivalent of spraying myself with a water bottle, repeating in my head "Bad Darcy." Because the way Peyton makes me feel isn't something I could chalk up to just sex. And, as we established, rather bluntly, I can't let anyone be more, and Peyton simply doesn't have time to.

But it's useless. Because somehow, when I snap back into reality, my hand is moving between my thighs.

ICARUS

NM

I found just the one.

I want to ask which one it is. I want to know exactly what it looks like, the shape, the color, the vibration settings so I can picture it pumping in and out of her. So I can imagine it rubbing against her pretty pink clit in a rhythmic motion until she weeps. But while my hand seems to be following no instruction from my brain, I at least have enough self-control to not ask.

> Anyway, I've got to go. Thank you again for the present. Sleep tight x

I blink, reading the message a couple more times.

I'm unsure of her intentions, not that they matter. Because one way or another, I scroll up into the thread, click on that photo, and fuck my hand until I fall apart, moaning her name into my pillow.

THIRTY

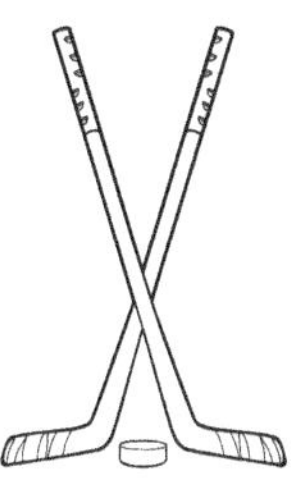

Peyton

"IT'S SEVEN!" I SING, popping my head into Avery's childhood room. He lets out a low, protesting groan, opening his sleep-stuck eyes to glance at the clock on his nightstand. I remember the birthday he got that nightstand. He was turning thirteen, and, as usual, requested a very specific set of items.

1) an encyclopedia of dogs

2) new socks from Reggie's Grocery in the clear and red packaging

and

3) the dog-shaped table

My parents scoured every inch of Greenrock Valley for a dog-shaped table, only to find that such a thing didn't exist. At least, not in the confines of the tiny mountain town. Eventually, my dad just paid my Uncle T to make one. It's a little lopsided, and one of the front feet is definitely an inch wider than the other, but when Avery unwrapped it, he was so excited he couldn't talk about anything else for a week.

"It's 6:57," he grumbles, tossing a pillow over his head and rotating in the opposite direction. I roll my eyes, lingering in the doorway as if I don't know that he isn't going to budge. Sticking my forefinger out, I flick it up in a quick motion to turn on the light.

He doesn't move.

"Come on!" I plead, like a child because even when we're eighty, I'll still be the annoying little sister. "Don't you want to open presents?"

Avery mumbles something that doesn't make it past the muffling of his pillow. I flip the light switch off.

Then on again.

Off.

On.

Off.

On.

Off.

"Isn't the spirit of Christmas not to be a fuckin' dick?" he snaps, ripping the pillow from his face. He sits up, his navy-blue comforter slipping off his chest as he glares at me with eyes identical to mine. Avery's pretty much the male version of me. We have the same inverted triangular build, the same amber eyes, and the same smile. Only, his is framed by a thick stubble.

"Actually, the spirit of Christmas is for people who don't talk to you all year long to apologize with monetary exchange."

He frowns. "Well seeing as you practically forced me to talk to you every two weeks can I be exempt?"

I shake my head. "Leaving voicemails is not 'force'."

"It is when you leave twelve of them in a week."

A short laugh escapes me. "I didn't leave *twel*—" When my eyes lock on his, my sentence stops, because I remember that Avery doesn't exaggerate. At least, very rarely. "I'll dial it back."

He nods. "Thanks."

A blaring noise erupts from his nightstand, and his frown deepens as he smacks the seven a.m. alarm to silence it. His eyes lock on mine. "I'm not sleeping here when you're in town anymore."

He pulls himself out of bed, raking a hand through his brown, messy hair.

I frown. "You have to. It's tradition."

He trudges up to me, an arrogant smile tugging at his lips. Is this what I look like to other people? This cocky?

"You know what else is tradition?" he asks. I tilt my head.

"The gingerbread house competition?"

He shakes his head, placing his hand on my shoulder and gently shoving me back through the door frame.

"This."

He slams the door in my face.

Yeah, I should have seen that one coming.

Honestly, I'm not sure how I'm not in the same boat. I should be exhausted after last night. Nothing in the world could keep my hand from moving to the slick heat between my thighs and relieving myself of the pressure that's been building from the last time I saw Darcy. It's only been a few days, and I swear, I'm going through withdrawal.

This might be worse than I originally thought.

IT'S ALMOST TWO O'CLOCK by the time we all huddle around the kitchen table. The recycling bin is stuffed full of wadded wrapping paper, the sink full of dirty dishes, and on the couch, Avery's past-expired, three-legged chihuahua Pumpkin is nestled on top of Mr. Bubbles. Her ginger fur is streaked with gray, her dry little tongue hanging out the side of her toothless mouth. I swear the Grim Reaper is scared of her.

So is Mr. Bubbles, which is why he whines every time she shifts.

"Do you have your house picked out yet?" Avery asks, reaching for one of the rolling pins on the floured surface. Every year, the four of us spend hours creating and decorating individual gingerbread houses. Then, we post them on social media and have our friends and family vote on their favorite.

The winner gets to pick the theme for the next year, and, of course, bragging rights.

I have yet to win those bragging rights. And judging by this year's theme, I won't be getting them anytime soon.

"*No.* And I feel targeted," I mumble, browsing a list of fictional houses in literature. Avery and my mom chuckle, while my dad casts me an agreeing glance.

"Definitely targeted," he adds. "You got anything good?"

I shake my head, scrolling past illustration after illustration of complex, architectural disasters. I flash him the screen. "Not unless you want to make a mansion."

"You can't do the Gatsby mansion; I'm already doing that," Avery cuts in. I blink.

"*You* are going to build *that?*" I ask, holding the screen out to face him. His amber eyes flick to the photo, then back to me, expression unwavering.

"Yes."

"I am *so fucked,*" I mutter, continuing to scroll. But only a few moments later, something catches my eye. It's a drawing of a circular door, planted into the side of a tiny hill. My chest tightens, and I tilt my head, studying it. Something about it is strangely familiar.

Where have I seen this door before? I scroll back up an inch, reading the caption.

Lord of the Rings: Hobbit House

A smile breaks across my face. It's perfect. Asymmetrical, kind of lopsided, and just low enough to the ground that I won't have to worry about structural integrity. I flash my dad a coy smile.

"You're on your own, Pops."

Dad sulks. He, too, has yet to earn bragging rights.

The kitchen fills with the scent of cloves and molasses as we roll out the dark, spicy dough and catch up on everything we've missed since the last time we were all together. We don't celebrate Thanksgiving, and I had a mountain of homework over break anyway, so I haven't seen them since September.

Avery, as usual, doesn't talk much. He's too busy taking a ruler to his stretch of dough and cutting out perfectly even shapes. This isn't a competition to him. It's an assignment. He takes it as seriously as he takes his job.

And he takes his job *very* seriously.

My mom dives into the latest releases from her hockey-fan boutique, a small business she started a few years ago that exploded. Perks of being a former *WAG*. She scrolls through photos on her phone, parading new embroidered hoodies and limited-edition decals she paid Avery's roommate to design. Afterwards, my dad confesses his new life as an unemployed empty nester. After he retired from the NHL, he coached Greenrock Valley's Bantam league, up until last year when he quit out of boredom. Said he wanted to try something new.

I don't think it's working.

"I never thought I'd be passionate about bread," he rambles. "But once you name it, it's hard not to get attached."

I tilt my head, tossing it toward the kitchen. "Are you talking about that jar of *guck* on the counter?"

He scowls. "Don't talk about Flower that way."

I squeeze the inner corners of my eyes with my thumb and index finger. "Did you name your sourdough starter after *Marc-André Fleury?*"

Hitching a shoulder, he runs his palm over his tamed beard. "He's resilient."

"You have *got* to find a new hobby."

He beams, pinching a bit of flour between his fingers and tossing it at me. I squeal, batting it off as my mom chimes in.

"So what about you, Peyton? How have you been?" she asks. Before I can respond, Avery adds:

"Yeah, why'd you bulldoze that ref on Friday?"

My dad's eyes flick to me. Then my mom's. Then they flick to each other, and I watch the silent exchange like it's a tennis match, his *Are we doing this?* battling her *Don't look at me.*

Classic Clarkes.

They weren't planning on discussing it. I figured as much. If they were, my mom would've led with it the second I walked through the door.

Thanks, Avery.

I clear my throat and shift in my chair, suddenly very invested in pressing a perfectly circular cookie out of my dough. I can feel all three of them watching me. Even the dogs are watching me. Hell, even the gingerbread man I decapitated two minutes ago is probably watching me.

"It was an accident," I lie. But if that's what all the tabloids are saying, is it really a lie?

My mother cuts in. "Well, at least she's not hurt," she says. Then, as an afterthought, "The referee, I mean."

I frown. "Thanks, Mom."

"Well, you too, Peanut," she adds quickly. "But you *did* hit her really hard."

"*Really hard,*" my dad echoes, almost impressed.

I look around. "Am I being ganged up on right now?"

Everyone says no, except Avery, who I can always count on to tell me the truth.

"*Yes,*" he confirms. He doesn't even look up, just tediously scores the cookie dough with a knife. "Dad thinks you're going through a crisis and Mom thinks you're hiding an injury because she snooped through your bag and found printed-out articles about joint issues."

Both of my parents' shoulders drop. They exchange matching looks of guilt, then flash Avery an unsurprised but disapproving look.

Avery just shrugs, unbothered. "What? It's the truth."

"Okay, first of all," I huff, turning to my dad, "I am *not* having a crisis."

It's not exactly the truth. But it's not exactly *not* the truth.

"We're just worried is all," he explains. "You just didn't seem like yourself on Friday. It was like you were a different player."

"Maybe I am." I shrug. "Is that alright with you, *Father?*"

I say it teasingly, but it's not really a joke. In fact, my heart is vibrating right now, buzzing in my chest, sending a nervous tingle through every limb of my body. It's like I've swallowed a pager, and I'm getting message after message warning me not to do this. Not to set myself up.

Because I already know what he's going to say.

And it's going to confirm the thing I've been trying really hard not to admit: that this stress, the pressure, the panic, *none of it* came from him. Or anyone else. It's me. It's always been me.

He wouldn't care if I never got drafted to a pro league. Or if I quit and became a tattoo artist. Or, I don't know, one of those people who farm worms. He'd still cheer me on like it was the Walter cup.

I know that. And yet, some part of me still doesn't believe it. Some part of me still acts like letting myself down means I'm letting everyone else down too.

Just as predicted, a smile tugs at my father's lips, and he turns back to his giant mess of cookie dough.

"Yes," he says. "That's quite alright with me."

"Good." I turn to my mom. "And *you*," I fume, and she's already shrinking a little, hands raised in defense. "A *complete* invasion of privacy—"

"I know," she cuts in quickly. "You just haven't talked to us about what happened yet, so—"

"—and also, a *wild* conclusion to jump to. I'm majoring in *exercise science*. Wouldn't your first thought be that it was for a class?"

She falters, considering it. In her defense, she's wound tighter than a triple-knotted skate. Having one kid building model animal lungs at gifted-and-talented science fairs, while the other was bashing her head into the boards every weekend will do that to a person.

"That's a good point," she admits finally, averting her eyes. "So is it? An assignment?"

"It's..." I trail off, trying to decipher how to explain this. I had planned to bring up AIHL to my dad later, when he's full and mildly buzzed on too much peppermint mud pie and spiked eggnog, ogling his trophies like he does every year. But I guess now's as good a time as any.

"*Kind of*," I concede, taking a deep breath. "Basically, there's this girl."

As a collective, my family leans back in their chairs, all at once letting out a synchronized "*Ohhh.*"

Immediately, I shake my head.

"Not like that. She's my student coach."

My mind flashes to what transpired at the resort last month. And the hotel last week. And my DMs last night.

Though, that was one sided.

"Okay, maybe *a little* like that, but not really. Nothing's going to happen. Anyway—" I shake my head, trying to steer the conversation back on track. But my family, as loving as they are, veer me off course.

"Hold on," my mom interrupts, leaning forward, eyes wide. "You can't just say *'there's a girl'* and not elaborate!"

"Wait, did you say she's your *Coach?*" Dad asks.

"*Student* Coach," I clarify. He grins.

"*Nice.*"

My mom continues. "Tell me about this girl."

Jesus Christ.

"There's nothing to—"

"You know, I had this gut feeling you were going to end up with a woman," Avery cuts in.

My parents are all about buying things in pairs. Two remotes, two vacuums, two refrigerators—one for the house, one for the garage. So, of course, they had two kids... who *both* turned out to be pansexual. Guess they like having doubles of everything.

"I'm not ending up with anybody!" I object. "Need I remind you all that I have yet to secure an *actual* relationship?"

"Well, that's by choice sweetheart," my mom rebuts.

"Yeah. Like, you could've said 'yes' when Miles Evans asked you out instead of telling him you were already betrothed to hockey," Avery adds.

"I was *nine!*"

He shrugs, unfazed. "Still could've." His eyes catch mine, and that antagonizing smirk tugs at his lips.

I love my brother, but sometimes I want to punch him in the fucking face.

"You're blushing."

I scoff and look away, swiping at my cheeks as if my fingertips are made of rubber and I can erase the color. "I am *not.*"

"Are too."

"No!"

"Yup."

"No, I'm irritated because my family has *no sense of boundaries!*"

That shuts everyone up. The silence is palpable, four seconds, then five, and when Pumpkin lets out a mitochondria-sized sneeze, we all burst into laughter. For the rest of the afternoon, as we bake the gingerbread and construct our houses, I tell them about Darcy. Not *everything*, but the important stuff. How we met, how she retaped my stick, AIHL. And how we will never turn into anything more. And as much as it hurts, it's nice to share it with them. I always forget how much I miss my family until they're back in my arms.

"**I** GOT ALL YOUR genes, huh?" I ask, eyeing the completed row of ginger-bread houses. Ours (mine and Dad's) look like we ran them over with a car, especially next to Avery and Mom's art-gallery-quality creations. My dad crosses his arms defensively, regarding our pitiful attempts.

"Uh-huh."

"Can you lend me twenty?" I whisper.

His brows furrow, and I quickly shift my gaze back to my sagging hobbit house. That's kind of how they looked in the movies, right?

"For what?" he questions.

"I wanna bribe all the cousins to vote for me."

My dad tilts his head back, chortling, and his arms drop to his sides. "That's cheating," he answers lowly. His amber eyes catch mine. "I'm stealing it."

With a scoff, I playfully shove my elbow into him, then snap a photo of my creation, sending it to Darcy. My phone pings immediately with a response.

KIM POSSIBLE

What the hell is that?

ME

What do you mean?

Can't you see that it's a hobbit house?

KIM POSSIBLE

Perhaps I could if you'd scrape away the pound of neon green frosting.

My tongue traces the dent on the inside of my cheek, fighting a smile.

ME

It's the hill.

KIM POSSIBLE

It looks like Flubber melted.

ME

You know, it's hard to imagine why people find you cold.

KIM POSSIBLE

I'm a ray of fucking sunshine.

So what is this for? Punishment?

ME

Gingerbread house contest. Wanna vote for me?

I send her the link.

KIM POSSIBLE

If I click that link is it going to take me to porn?

ME

Would you like it to?

A few moments later, I get a notification banner across the top of my screen.

Darcy Cole voted on a poll you're tagged in.

I click on it, skimming the census. A frown tugs at my lips as I open our thread and send her another message.

ME

You voted for the wrong one. Mine is number 3.

That one is Avery's.

KIM POSSIBLE

I have a moral obligation to stay unbiased. His is objectively the best.

ME

That is so fucked up.

KIM POSSIBLE

Rules are rules.

Even Jay Gatsby would be impressed.

ME

Who is that? The architect?

KIM POSSIBLE

Did you take eleventh grade english?

ME

Okay now you're just being mean.

> And of course I did. It's just that Bailey did all my summer reading annotations so I would do her pre-calc.

KIM POSSIBLE

> Why am I not surpri

I don't get to finish reading Darcy's message before I'm cut off by Avery dropping Pumpkin into my arms. I frown, cradling the yeasty little beast as my eyes meet his.

"She needs Auntie time," he explains.

Beside him, Mr. Bubbles nuzzles into his leg. One extremely irritating thing about my brother? He's basically Snow-fucking-White. Animals are obsessed with him. Since he got here yesterday, Mr. Bubbles has spent more time curled up in Avery's lap than mine.

He's a dog thief.

"You do realize I have to take him back to school with me?" I say, pointing at my dog with my chin. Avery glances down at him, a soft smile tugging at his lips as he scratches behind the pup's ears just right to entice a groan out of him.

"We'll see."

My gaze flicks around the room, catching on my dad who is now admiring his trophy case, as expected. He always gets nostalgic about his time in the league when he's tipsy. I huff a laugh, drawing Avery's attention. We both stand there, side by side, watching.

"Reminiscing the good ol' days," Avery mumbles, still petting Bubbles on the head. A sad smile tugs at my mouth.

"Yeah, that might be the both of us soon," I say. It's supposed to be a joke, but the way it comes out, Avery can tell that I mean it. His eyes flick over to me, only briefly, before he looks back to Dad.

"You know, Dad doesn't care if you make it to the PWHL," he says, softer this time. A metallic taste floods my tongue as I chew on the inside of my cheek.

"I know."

My hand glides over the top of Pumpkin's soft fur, and she lets out a little sound of contentment as she melts into me.

"Then why do you act like he does?"

When Avery asks you a question, it's never to corner you. He's not being malicious, or even passive-aggressive—though sometimes it feels that way. He just genuinely wants to understand why things are the way they are. Which is funny, because he already seems to understand things better than most. My dad sips from his mug of eggnog, head tilted as he stares at his trophies.

"I don't know," I answer truthfully. "I think there's something wrong with me."

Avery's hand rests on my shoulder. It's quick but warm, and he scrunches his brow at me as he pulls it back.

"You say that like it's new."

My brows pinch. "What?"

"You've been saying there's something wrong with you since, like, eighth grade when you stopped letting Dad come to your games."

My stomach tightens. My fingers twitch against Pumpkin's fur.

"That's not the same thing," I mutter, my heart beginning to pound.

"Isn't it?" he challenges. "You keep acting like this stuff is a mystery. Like no one's figured you out yet. But you've been assessed. Imposter syndrome doesn't mean there's something wrong with you." He pauses, long enough for me to feel the lump in my throat harden. "Also, you have a therapist. Who is *very* worried about you, by the way. If you're going to make me your emergency contact, at least pick up the phone when she calls. It's been three months now. It's like you're determined to be miserable."

His words sink into the pit of my stomach. Growing up, his candor always irritated me. He never bothered to sweeten his words. He just served them raw, no sugar to soften the taste. But over time, I've come to appreciate it. To love the sour twang, because even if it's not what I want to hear, or what I want to acknowledge, it is the truth.

Maybe that's what I like about Darcy so much. She doesn't occupy herself with artificial sweeteners. She just tells it like it is.

"Have you told Mom and Dad that I haven't been going?" I ask hesitantly, my voice embarrassingly small. There's something hard and swelling, weighing over my vocal chords, tugging them down. He shakes his head.

"No, but if you keep ghosting her I will."

I smile briefly. "Thanks."

He just nods.

We're quiet for a beat, but of course, I never let the silence sit too long. Not unless it's with Darcy.

"Do you think he really misses it?" I ask. Avery hitches a shoulder.

"Yeah," he responds. "I think he does. But there wasn't a whole lot he could do about it."

I nod, sucking my cheek back between my teeth. "Yeah. I mean, Mom was practically a single parent. Your diagnosis is probably the reason we don't have daddy issues," I joke. Avery doesn't get it. His brows furrow, and he looks at me, puzzled.

"What do you mean?"

"Because if you didn't," I explain, "Dad probably would've played until he was like, sixty, and we would've never seen him."

I expect the crease between Avery's brows to smooth out, which is what normally happens when I explain a joke he didn't catch. Instead, it deepens, and his head tips to the side.

"Wait, you think dad quit hockey because I got diagnosed with autism?" he asks.

"Yeah." I hitch a nonchalant shoulder. "The same summer you got diagnosed, that's when he quit."

Avery's hooded eyes narrow, and a chill shoots through my chest. "Peyton, Dad didn't quit hockey."

I blink. Then I blink again. Then again. A confused laugh escapes me.

"What are you talking about?" I ask, brows furrowing. "Yes, he did."

Avery shakes his head. "Who told you that?"

"Nobody *told me,* I just connected the dots."

Avery just keeps staring at me, his hand smoothing up and down the thigh of his pants to steady himself. He clears his throat. "Peyton, Dad didn't quit. He got *cut.*"

"*What?!*" My brows shoot to my hairline, and I whip around to fully face him, propping my free hand on my hip. "What are you talking about?"

"How do you not know this?"

"Because *every article* I've ever read says he retired?"

Avery tucks his hair-covered arms over his chest. "Do you believe everything you read on the internet?"

I roll my eyes, letting them descend onto my father, who is now in the kitchen with my mom, feeding "Flower". Avery continues.

"The team was going in a different direction. Dad wasn't getting the minutes he used to. And honestly, he was barely hanging on. He knew he wasn't going to last much longer, and then when they told him... well, he had to make the call."

My eyes squint, like maybe if I shift their perspective, I'll be able to see things more clearly. But everything remains blurred. "But he always talks about it like it was his choice. Like it was his decision to leave."

Avery nods. "It *was* his decision. His choices were to retire completely, or try to get drafted by another team. But he'd been playing for like, fifteen years at that point."

My breath stays caught in my lungs, and I rub the inner corners of my eyes, still trying to process. This entire time, my *whole life*, I believed that my dad gave up his career for us. I believed, in some twisted way, that I owed something to him because of it. That because he was the best, I had to be the best too. And it was built on... an *assumption?*

"My brain hurts," I mutter, rubbing my eyes. Avery pats my back awkwardly.

"Yeah, I don't know how you jump to conclusions like that."

From the kitchen, my dad cuts in, calling out to me, "Hey! You gonna show me that AIHL shit?"

I give him a slow nod, my mind still whirling. "Yeah," I answer, finally releasing the air I've held hostage in my lungs. "Yeah, I'll go get it."

THIRTY ONE

Darcy

I T'S A UNIVERSAL TRUTH that winter break ends too quickly. I swear the space-time continuum has a grudge against respite.

Unless, that is, you have something worth returning to.

The rest of the break has been agonizingly slow. A doctor's appointment. A blood draw. An ultrasound. A New Year's party that was wrapped up by 10pm. Every hour that ticks by, I can't help but miss GU. Professor Palit. The rink. *A certain captain who lives in that rink.*

Peyton and I have stayed in touch, though I'll admit I muted her a couple times. Once for sending me endless live updates about a PWHL game while I was reading. Again when she got drunk with her brother's friends, and sent me seven consecutive videos of her doing Bee Gees karaoke. And the next morning when she was updating me on the color of her vomit, though I ended up unmuting her later that day to update her on my progress of the book she gave me.

Welcome back.

That was, in fact, the goal.

ME

Have you read it? It's pretty good.

ICARUS

No. I just asked one of the booksellers to guide me to the horniest sapphic options with happily ever afters.

But if you still want to "teach me to read" I'll happily start with that one.

ME

Why?

ICARUS

Inspiration.

Then the next day, in the group chat:

FINAL CHAT FR THIS TIME

ICARUS

LNHL Countdown: 8 1/2 weeks

Z

anyone know who we're playing against in the first round?

ME

The schedule won't be released until February.

YERSIE

Better be Glacier. I want their asses out in the first round.

ICARUS

Trouble at home?

YERSIE

If I told you Clay Matthews was even more of a dick than we originally thought, would you believe me?

CAY

Yes.

HAMMIE

Yes.

BRADY:

Yes.

ME

I could see it.

Then, just now:

ICARUS

Morning Kimmy!

ME

Morning.

ICARUS

Whatcha doin' this morning?

ME

Many, many things.

ICARUS

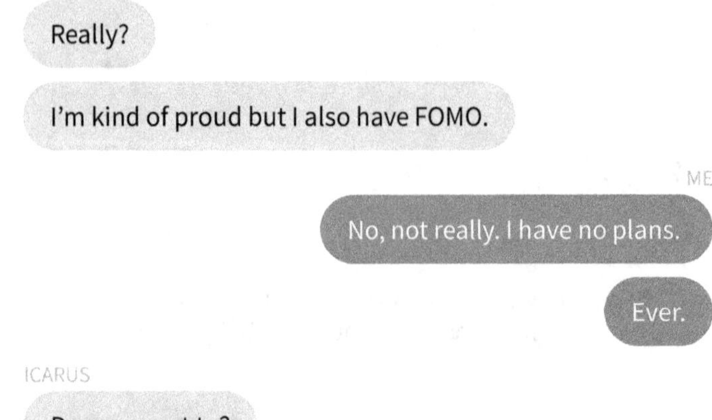

I read the text a second time, then a third. My heart flutters, and I consider, for a moment, admitting that I do. That I want to get out of the house. That our early mornings twice a week are something I now look forward to. That ever since she pulled me back up onto the ice, since she's been applying all of my coaching advice, I've been getting this feeling in my chest, right where that hole used to be. Something warm. Fulfilling.

I think I see pieces of myself in her that I thought I'd lost. And when we're together, it feels like she shares them with me. Like for a moment, we're whole.

When my eyes flit across the text, my stomach sinks. I haven't gotten my test results back from Dr. Oswell yet, but the break hasn't been as kind to my body as I'd hoped. I thought, by now, that I'd feel better. Not cured by any means, but at least figured the persistent burn underneath my kneecaps would have soothed some, or that the rash forming on my left ankle would cease. Instead, both of my patellas throb with each step, and the erythema has spread faster than misogyny in the PWHL Instagram comment section.

I haven't told Peyton about it yet. And I haven't breathed a word of our sunrise skates to my mother either. I like the separation between my worlds. Peyton knows about the diagnosis, but not the current degree of it like my mother. And my mother knows that Peyton and I have stayed relatively in touch, though not the extent of how it makes me feel.

I like that. I like that Peyton sees me as strong enough to glide across the ice with her, in spite of my RA. I like that she thinks I'm good at coaching. I like lingering in this limbo.

But my mom was right. If I keep ignoring this, if I keep pushing myself like I did before, I *can* and *will* get worse.

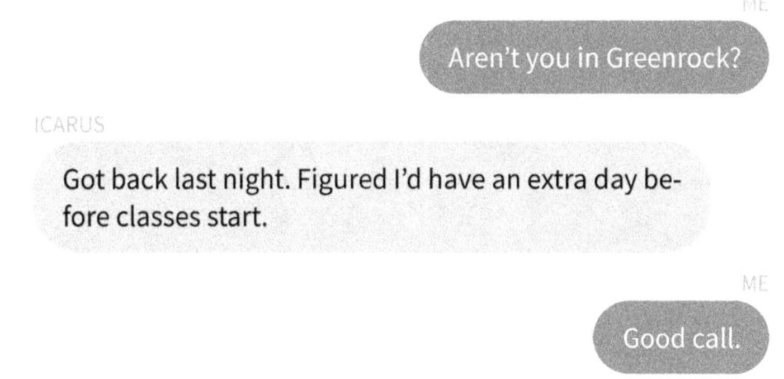

I click off the screen and drop my phone onto the nightstand, giving myself space to think. Which was pointless, really, because it only takes me two seconds to realize that if I declined entirely, I'd just lay here staring at the ceiling, wishing I hadn't. Still, I'm not ready to tell Peyton that I'm getting worse. I still haven't fully accepted it myself. I grab my phone and click on her thread again.

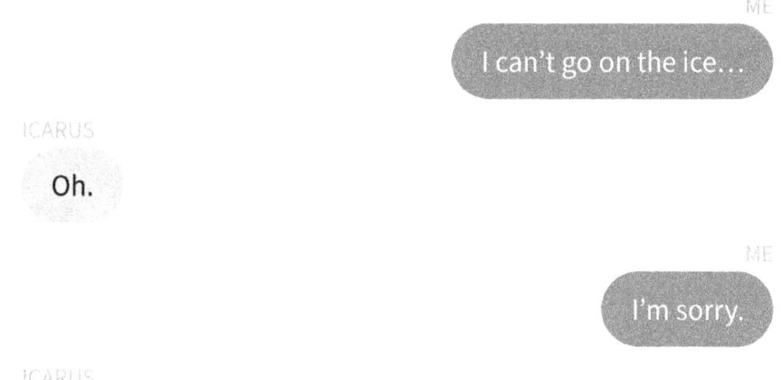

A smile—equal parts sad and mused—breaks across my face.

I FEEL LIKE I'M home. I've been "home" for the past week, but here at the rink with Peyton?

It's become my sanctuary.

Even just sitting on this slab of green foam, watching her whirl around the cones, and sink shots into the net, feels comforting. I never thought watching would be enough. It still isn't. But for now, it satiates me.

"You know," she pants, dragging the back of her wrist across her cheek to wipe away a bead of sweat. "I'm kind of relieved you can't show me up today. My ego was starting to take a hit."

Under the sickly pale stadium lights, her salt-slicked porcelain skin glows, beads gathering along her forehead like a crown. It's hard not to look at her for too long.

Harder not to think about the hotel.

About how she sounded.

How she felt.

Hardest of all is that I want to happen again.

I smile something bittersweet. Not just from Peyton's words, but from this aching realization:

I missed this. Missed *feeling* something.

Even if it comes with pain.

"You should've seen me in my prime," I say.

Her damp hair sticks to her gloves as she drags them over her head, smiling. "I would've liked that." A pause. "Hey, whatcha doing later?" she calls, tapping her stick playfully against the ice.

"I have plans," I say.

Surprisingly, it's true. And thank god, because if I didn't, there'd be nothing stopping me from jumping Peyton's bones all over again. Well, nothing but my swollen joints. I said it in the beginning. She's magnetic. I just didn't realize I was made of iron.

Peyton looks just as surprised, her dark brows raising as I shift on the cushion.

"Oh?" she teases. "Miss trust-issues made friends?"

Despite myself, a half-annoyed laugh slips out. "Fuck you," I say, but the chuckle in my tone drowns out the sting.

Peyton just shrugs, grinning like an idiot. "When and where?"

"No, not—" I rub my eyes with a frustrated groan. Heat flushes up my neck as I stumble over my words, using every ounce of restraint not to strangle her. As much as I'd like to, getting involved with Peyton would only hold her back. She has goals. Plans. *Achievable* plans. She's headed somewhere, and I'm not. And *this,* whatever it is, isn't worth slowing her down. "You better watch it. You're skating on thin ice, *Cap.*"

Her grin only widens, those infuriatingly pretty amber eyes flicking upward in mock thought.

"Really?" she muses, tapping the blade of her skate against the ice. Her head tips. "Feels about right to me."

God, how can someone be so endearing and so fucking annoying at the same time?

"Don't forget your cool down stretches," I order, pushing off the bench.

And I walk away before she can see the smile breaking across my face.

THIRTY TWO

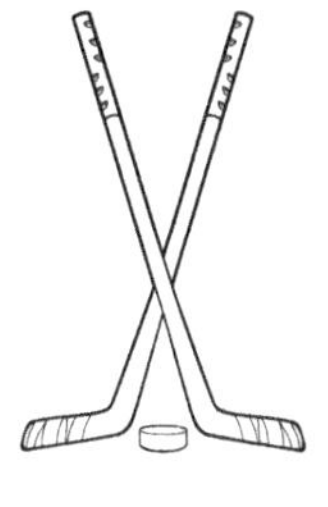

Peyton

FINAL CHAT FR THIS TIME

What's going on?

CAY

Kaiser

ME

Oh come on, people. She's not THAT bad.

YERSIE

She's evil.

HAMMIE

I can confirm that I've felt evil spirits in that room.

BRADY

She's out for blood today. I saw her in the hall and I swear her eyes were glowing RED.

KIM POSSIBLE

Wait, what's Kaiser's deal?

ME

She's…

YERSIE

Evil?

BRADY

Aggressive!

Z

vociferous

CAY

Egregious.

HAMMIE

Perpetually angry…

ROSE

Unpleasant.

ME

Pretty much what they said.

KIM POSSIBLE

Have you filed a complaint with the board? Or with my mom?

ME

Do you know how hard it is to get coaches for women's teams?

KIM POSSIBLE

Fair enough.

YERSIE

Anyway, I don't feel well so I'm actually going to stay home.

CAY

Same.

ROSE

Same.

ME

Gym. Ten minutes.

I'll bring Monsters.

"**I** TOLD YOU SHE'S evil!" Harlowe groans, her arms trembling, shoulders quivering as she holds a plank. Her fists are clenched so tight her knuckles might burst through the skin, and the flush creeping up her neck tells me she's probably got about thirty seconds left before she collapses.

I let out a slow, controlled breath, my own body starting to give in to the burn. My legs are shaking now, every muscle screaming for mercy, but I force my focus back to the clock on the wall.

"First day back," I mutter. "And she's putting us through hell already."

Meredith Kaiser knows no mercy. Where Coach Cole is a little more... accommodating, Kaiser is an absolute *monster*. She doesn't care if we've just returned from break, or if we're running on three hours of sleep, or if we've maxed out every muscle in our bodies. Her workouts are relentless.

And she is *terrifying*.

Normally, I'm all for it. You can spend hours on the ice, but you won't see real improvement without putting in the work in the training room. It's part of the sport. But today?

Maybe it's just because Darcy made me cut back on ice time, but after squats, deadlifts, box jumps, and RDLs, this feels excessive. I haven't lifted a weight in a week, and instead of easing us back in—just a little, for the love of god—*Meredith's* thrown us straight into the deep end.

"Shut up or she's going to make us do T-Drills!" Bailey hisses. I force a tiny chuckle through my clenched teeth, but it quickly turns into a strangled gasp as another round of pain shoots through my abdomen.

In sync with the sporadic twinges in my muscles, the fluorescent lights above flicker, once, twice, before giving up entirely, plunging into darkness. A collective gasp ripples through the team, followed by an uneasy shuffle of feet. Someone lets out an embarrassingly shrill scream.

"Oh my god!" Bailey shrieks. "It's the ghost!"

Harlowe's voice breaks through the dark, pleading. "Does this mean we can stop?"

The darkness looms over us, deceiving me into the relief that I can stop. But just as I'm about to drop, a low, menacing voice cuts through the gloom.

"No!" Kaiser calls out, her tone unwavering. "Clarke, keep everyone on track. I'm going to go see what's going on."

I glance around the room, but all I can make out are the faint silhouettes of my teammates. A sigh slips from my mouth, my abdomen ablaze as I nod.

"Yes, Coach."

As the seconds tick away, all that can be heard is the struggling sounds of our breathing. I want to give up. We *all* want to give up. But no one dares. Because if Kaiser comes back to any of us collapsed, hell will burn a fuck of a lot hotter.

Though, right now, I don't know that anything could burn more than my abs. I suck in another slow breath, the flame from the plank relentless, when a familiar voice rings out from somewhere near the front of the room.

"Why are you guys sitting in the dark?" it asks.

I can't see anything, but I don't need to. Because the low, smooth tone of Darcy's voice is unmistakable. My body betrays me, and I collapse onto my stomach, groaning, *"Fuuuuck."*

The light snaps back on, blinding everyone in an instant, the sudden shock sending the rest of the room crashing down too. I rub my eyes, trying to adjust to the abrupt brightness, fighting to clear the swirling spots in my vision.

"What are you doing here?" I ask, blinking away the floaty remnants of the light burn.

Darcy looks gorgeous as always, wrapped in her new coaching jacket, complete with the GU logo on the shoulder, and soft, flowy pants. I have to say, while I miss her old, tattered look, I'm not opposed to this one. She looks happier. More confident.

Beside me, Bailey points at her, yelling, "Witchcraft!" Darcy's brows furrow in confusion, and a laugh slips out of me before I can stop it. She adds quickly, "In a good way."

Darcy tilts her head, as if weighing the ethics of witchcraft, before answering me. "Coach wanted me to check on you guys. Said you're supposed to be on the ice already."

At that, everyone turns to Harlowe. She shrugs, her sweat-slicked hair sticking to her cheeks. "What?"

I sigh. "We *are,*" I reply, shooting Harlowe a disapproving scowl. "But *Yersie* decided to talk trash, and now we're being punished with planks."

"What the hell is going on in here?" Kaiser snaps, propping a hand on her hip as she steps through the doorway. Immediately, everyone cowers. And that's not even a slight exaggeration.

Well, *almost* everyone.

Darcy stays unfazed, her posture steady as she meets the glare. "Coach Cole needs them on the ice," she explains coolly, the glint of the silver whistle around her neck catching the light as she shifts, putting herself between Kaiser and the rest of the room. She used to carry that thing around in her pocket, or have it looped around her clipboard.

Seeing her wear it... well, it does something to me.

If possible, Kaiser's scowl deepens. "And I need them *here* until they're done."

Darcy pauses for a split second, her gaze flicking briefly to me. I blink at her, confused at first, then finally realize what she's silently communicating.

This is it. This is *part* of it. Part of my role as captain.

Standing up for my team.

I take a breath, pushing myself to my feet. My legs scream in protest, the burn from the planks still fresh, but I stand tall, locking eyes with Kaiser.

"With all due respect, Coach," I start, my voice steady even though she's already trying to smite me with her eyes. "We already have limited time on the ice, and you're taking it away from us."

Every muscle in the room tenses, and Kaiser's eyes narrow, her jaw tightening as she stares me down.

"That's not up to you, *Clarke,*" she growls.

Heat creeps over my cheeks, but I don't back down. I clear my throat, ready to stand my ground, ready to fight back for my team and make up for all the lost passes, all the selfish moves, all the times I let them get into trouble because I was too focused on myself, but before I can, that firm, beautiful voice cuts back in.

"It is now," Darcy insists. "If you want to keep them here, take it up with Coach Cole."

And with that, she spins around. It only takes one silent second for everyone to follow, funneling out of the room in an animated rush of apprehensive exhilaration. Lena's cheering, Caydence looks begrudgingly pleased, and though Indie's hazel eyes are so wide they might fall out, she lets out a tight, nervous giggle. As we parade to the locker room, I see Faith pat Darcy on the back.

"That was sick," she praises, and Darcy's face flushes.

As we all get ready for practice, the team is a bundle of excited murmurs and laughs. I'm sitting on the bench, tying my skates when Darcy approaches me, clipboard in hand. I tilt my head curiously, letting a grin take over my face.

"Haven't seen that in a while." I point to it with my chin. Darcy's freckled lips quirk.

"Well, I figured I should probably start using it for actual plays and stuff," she says. "You know, as coaches do."

"Yeah, that's probably a good idea." I laugh, the sound trailing off awkwardly at the end. It's like I've forgotten how to exist next to her. Every word that comes out of my mouth that isn't "I am definitively and helplessly falling in love with you" just feels like the wrong ones to say. Gnawing at the dent in my cheek, I catch her eye. "You feeling okay?"

Her expression drops briefly, before she catches it, and schools herself into apathy.

"I'm a little banged up." She shrugs. "Double knee braces. Rash cream. My finger might fall off. The norm." She cracks a smile.

I'm about to ask if there's anything I can do—even though, from the research I've done, I'm practically useless—when a vexed voice booms through the locker room.

"I'm sorry?" Coach Cole snaps. "Did the Grizzlies turn into *Sloths* during hibernation? Clarke, why is your team not on the ice?"

Everyone's eyes snap to me, and I immediately jump into mediation mode. "Sorry Coach!" I answer, hopping off the bench. Darcy takes a step back from me, clutching her clipboard to her chest. "My fault. We're coming!"

Her gaze narrows onto me, sternly, but she grants me a sharp nod before disappearing out of the locker room. I slam my dry stall closed, gesturing for everyone to vacate as soon as possible.

"Code MB!" I yell, pushing everyone toward the door. Darcy looks at me, red brows furrowed.

"What's code MB?" she asks.

I grin. "Code Mamma Bear."

Darcy erupts into a fit of giggles, slapping a hand over her mouth. Then, her expression turns warning. "Don't let her catch wind of that. I won't be able to save you."

"Oh, come on Kimmy." I flash her a toothy grin. "Don't underestimate yourself."

Voices echo as the team travels through the tunnel, a cluster of green already moving like a school of sweaty fish. I'm walking side-by-side with Darcy, like we did downtown, and in Salem. I only realize she's stopped when I feel a light, familiar tug on the sleeve of my jersey.

The smile breaking across my face is unstoppable as I turn to face her. Bodies move around us like we don't exist; only Harlowe seems to notice, patting me silently on the shoulder as she passes. We just stand there, staring at one another.

When everyone else is far ahead, funneling onto the ice, I can't help but feel like this is my moment to say something. To *do* something. To ask if I've been reading between lines that don't exist, or if that night in the hotel, when she said it didn't have to mean anything, she was doing what I've been doing this whole time.

Claiming I'm too busy. Calling it bad timing. Making excuses to prevent what had already begun. But when you bury something that has already taken root, it only grows.

The tunnel is vast, and all-encompassing, but the silence is even more so. And just when I gather the courage to open my mouth, Darcy speaks.

"You deserve to be here," she says firmly. The weight of her hands sink to either side of my shoulders, and her eyes study mine like a map. I think back to the night of the party, when she was drunk in my room, standing in the same position.

I wanted to push her away then. All I want now is to kiss her.

"You deserve to be here," she repeats. "I know you don't believe it. I know that voice in your head keeps telling you you're a fraud. But it's proof you're not. People who don't care don't question themselves. You *do*. Because this matters to you."

I've heard that phrase a lot.

You deserve to be here.

It's something my therapist has had my family tell me for years, and not that it doesn't help, but it feels different coming from Darcy. Maybe because she owes me nothing. Maybe, it's what she follows them up with. The reasoning behind it. Or maybe, it's just the way it sounds when she says it.

There's something about her that turns the pieces of myself I've always resented into pieces of myself I don't. It's like she sees the darkest parts of me and calls it light.

I smile softly, reaching my hand up to brush her hair out of her face, when suddenly—

"*Clarke! Darce!* Get your asses out here!"

I pull back quickly, blood pooling in my cheeks. Judging by the deep crimson spreading across Darcy's face, she's feeling the same sheepishness. We both stumble into motion, scrambling down the tunnel and bursting out into the harsh stadium light.

I rush onto the ice, surveying my team as they warm up. *My* team. My family. One that I deserve.

Maybe, if I say it enough, I'll keep believing it.

"Cap!" Coach calls, tossing her head toward me. I lock eyes with her. "Lead regroup drills. Your choice."

"Yes Coach!" I call.

I quickly turn back to the ice, clearing my throat. My voice comes out strong and steady, like I've done this all my life. "Circle up!"

Skates cut across the ice as players rush in from every direction, and for once, I don't flinch under the gravity of their attention. Most people might hate that kind of spotlight.

But not me.

Not anymore.

I love being around my people. I'm even learning to love leading them.

We huddle close, arms thrown around shoulders, jostling and laughing. I suck in a steadying breath, lock eyes with Darcy one last time, then look back to my group.

"Alright team." I grin. "Here's what we're gonna do."

THIRTY THREE

Darcy

I thought I found Lachlan's mouthguard case but it was a container of icebreakers :(

Btw LNHL Countdown: 6 weeks.

Dammit! I've been looking everywhere. Still nothing.

Yeah me too.

Same :(

What flavor?

Wintergreen.

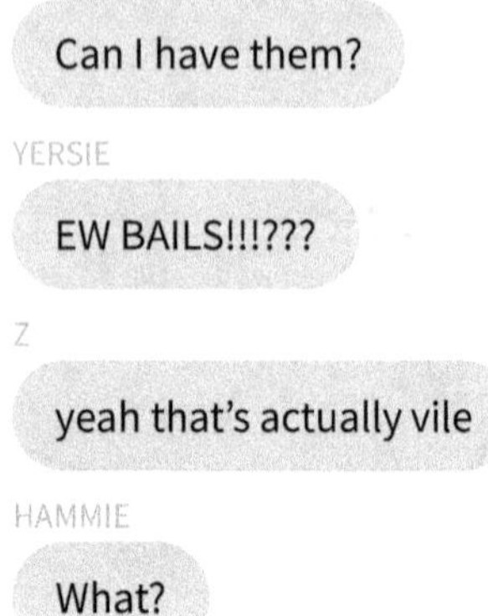

"**W**OAH."

Cleo's gray eyes scan the union building, flitting booth to booth in agitation. There must be fifty tables, all clamoring about internships and career paths and "building your future" like there's a future to build on.

The world is on fire. And so are my kneecaps.

I really didn't want to come. Every time I think about the future, I feel this impending sense of doom.

This Autoimmune Hockey project—AIHL, as Peyton calls it? It's a fantasy. A beautiful, reckless distraction. Just like Peyton. An excuse to keep moving instead of giving up completely. I know that. I'm not delusional. And sure,

Professor Palit is great, but every hour I spend on the ice just confirms what I already know:

I don't want to be a sports physical therapist. I want to be a hockey player.

My body just won't let me.

I've been coaching Peyton's morning sessions from the bench for the last few weeks. And my mom has stuck to her word, barring me from the rink just like she said. Even though I've been careful—wearing my braces, taking short walks, stretching—this flare up is still hitting me like a truck. My body feels like one giant cramp. Breathing's a full-body exercise. My knees ache, my spine is on fire, and if I hadn't been on bed rest for four days in a row, I'd be completely unable to function.

But Cleo needs me. So here I am.

"You okay?" I ask, studying her concernedly. She looks perfect, as always. The soft swoops in her pixie cut, her olive skin glassy and bright. Jewelry drips from every limb, bracelets, earrings, chains, things looped through her belt like charms on a key ring. Every step she takes, her own brassy theme song follows her.

It's pretty fitting if you ask me.

"Yeah. No, I'm great," she replies, eyeing the maze of tables cautiously. "I just don't know if I'll have time to get through them all."

I plant a hand on my hip.

"If you can binge season two of Bridgerton in one day," I counter, squinting at the clock on my phone, "you've got time for fifty booths in... *two hours*."

Cleo grins proudly.

"Look at you," she teases, patting my back gently, but not gentle enough to stop the burn in my skin from spreading. "The optimist."

I roll my eyes, waving her off as I hobble behind. "Yeah, yeah."

The first booth we approach is drenched in blue. Pens, face masks, even the banner is some shade of muted navy. Definitely medical school. Which is ironic, considering half the existential crises Cleo's been having stems from deciding she *doesn't* want to go to medical school anymore.

But I'm not about to bring that up while she flips through the pamphlet.

Cleo can change her mind a thousand times if she wants. She'll be great at whatever she ends up doing. I haven't yet found anything Cleo Mardas is bad at.

Except maybe minding her business.

"What's the average GPA for accepted applicants?" she asks the man behind the booth.

"3.8," he answers with a smile.

Cleo nods, then places the pamphlet neatly back down. "Thanks."

With that, she's on the move again, weaving toward the next table, and I follow, though my steps lag slightly behind. There's a limp creeping into my walk, bordering excruciation that makes me thoroughly impressed I'm even here. I give credit to the remorse from cancelling on Cleo three separate times last week because my body still hadn't let up.

"Tomorrow" turned into "tomorrow" turned into "tomorrow".

And even though I felt guilty, Cleo never made me feel like I should. She facetimed me while out the first night, brought me takeout the second, and refunded our movie tickets to stream it from the couch the third.

Being deliberately considered is a virtue. Especially when you've been denied it despite begging.

It's something I never realized until I became disabled. This world is built for those who can help themselves, and no one else. But humanity? Friendship? That's for everyone.

Cleo helped me see that.

"Why'd you leave so fast?" I frown. "You have a 4.3. Which, honestly, I didn't know was even possible."

She lets out a soft laugh. "Yeah... I don't know. I thought maybe I'd feel something reading that brochure, but..." Her shoulders rise and fall in a shrug.

It takes more effort than I'd like to lift my arm, but I do it anyway, resting my purple gloved hand lightly on her shoulder. "That's okay."

Her eyes flick to mine. "Am I crazy?" she asks, thick brows drawing together. "For suddenly changing my entire career path junior year?

"No," I reply reflexively. "People change careers all the time, even *after* graduating. If anything, I think you're smart." I scratch the back of my neck awkwardly, like the next part doesn't mirror my exact dilemma. "You never know what'll happen. And if you already know you don't want to be a surgeon, then—" I shrug, "why keep pouring time into something that isn't what you really want?"

She smiles as we step up to the next booth. "Thanks, D."

Cleo has never called me "D" before. I don't know if I'm particularly a fan, but the way she said it, so casually, thoughtlessly, like she's called me it forever, makes my chest warm.

We trail through a plumbing exhibit, skim a study abroad program, and duck past the preying military recruiters in the corner. Eventually, we end up at a table draped in a paw-print patterned tablecloth. Cleo's eyes catch on a little ceramic dog propped beside a QR code, and she lights up.

"That looks like Mr. Bubbles," a voice behind me chimes.

It's smooth. Familiar. I'd recognize it even if it weren't wrapped in that soft, powdery lavender scent.

I turn, facing Peyton.

Damn.

Something they don't tell you about being a lesbian: it's confusing as *hell.* Sometimes when you see a pretty girl, you can't tell if you want to *be* her or *kiss* her.

Don't get me wrong, aside from the swollen knees, crooked fingers, and occasional rash, I'm a damn sight to behold. But Peyton?

It's like all the wonders of the world live within her.

She's got canyons in her cheeks when she smiles and molten honey in her eyes. Her shoulders are boulders, and her arms ripple with a river of muscles, only half-hidden beneath the oversized tee she's swimming in.

There's a stereotype for hockey players: strong, scruffy, hot.

I hate to admit it, but she doesn't just meet expectations, she exceeds them. Far, *far* exceeds them.

"What are you doing here?"

The words blurt out faster and louder than I intend. I don't even know I'm saying them until they're already echoing. It startles even me. My head jerks up like someone pulled a string in my spine. Like I'm Woody the Cowboy and suddenly, there's a snake in my boot.

"Darcy!" Cleo hisses, shooting me a look like I've just kicked a puppy. Which, I guess, isn't too far off.

I raise both hands in surrender. "Sorry! Sorry, I didn't mean it like that, I just…" I suck in a breath. Why is it shaky? "I just wasn't expecting to see you. I'm confused."

Peyton's gaze flicks between me and Cleo, and the corners of her lips tug into a sly smile. "Yeah, I decided to trade in my hockey career for veterinary science," she deadpans.

I let out an awkward laugh, probably half a second too late.

"Right," I say, rolling my eyes in an attempt to regain control of myself. I turn back to Cleo, but she's already deep in conversation with the woman behind the table, enthusiastically talking about Socks.

That demon.

"I'm actually here for the physics club," Peyton clarifies, stepping what feels impossibly closer. "Indie's doing a presentation at five, and I promised I'd show up."

I pretend to glance around the giant room to disguise the smile tugging at my lips.

This is the third time this month she's mentioned some obscure campus event she's "promised" to attend. A couple weeks ago, I accidentally liked a picture of her sitting on a football player's shoulders after their win. I unliked it immediately, then blocked her for three hours hoping the notification would disappear. She hasn't said anything, so I'm assuming she never saw it.

Close call—especially since we're not mutuals, which means I had to search her up specifically.

But the only reason I looked her up was because she bailed on our practice plans to go to some campus poetry slam, and I wanted to make sure she wasn't lying.

That's the *only* reason.

"Oh." I force a shrug. But after a second, I feel my expression shift, so I play it off with a taunt. "Planning to be a rocket scientist, Icarus? That'll get you closer to the sun."

Peyton grins. "Something like that. You should come watch. Maybe kinematics will help you block my shots better."

Her cheek bulges slightly as she tries to bite back a full smile, tongue pressing to the inside of her lip. I take a step closer, watching her pupils dilate as I loom over her. There are two things in this world that have made me appreciate my height:

Hockey, and Peyton Clarke.

"Maybe *you* should—"

A buzz interrupts me, vibrating through my back pocket into my left ass cheek. My body tenses, and I pull my phone out, glancing at the screen.

MyChart: You have new test results.

Promptly, a lump rises in my throat. I clear it, making just enough room in my esophagus to speak.

"Hold on." I lean toward Cleo, cutting into her conversation. "Sorry to interrupt, but I have a... *thing*. Do you mind if I take a break?"

Cleo smiles, though her forehead creases in concern. "No, I'm good, D." She waves me off. "Do your thing."

I nod, casting Peyton a look that says *this conversation isn't over*, then glance around the union building, searching for an empty space. In the far, right corner of the outrageously large room, I see just the spot.

With each step, I feel these painful balls in my knees, smacking against one another like a torturous Newton's Cradle. Once I'm semi-isolated from the chaos, I click on the notification, and log in to my patient portal.

You have new test results, it says.

Lucky me.

After staring at the sentence for what feels like forever, I suck in a breath, and scroll down.

Once I read these results, everything becomes real.

Of course, I know, it already is. The pain is real. The unpredictability is real.

The unraveling of every plan I ever had for my life is real.

But this places the gravestone.

It confirms that the meds aren't working. It confirms I'm getting worse. It's going to dictate what happens to me next.

I'm no stranger to pain. Not just from RA, but from a lifetime on the ice. I'm used to ripping off Band-Aids that have fused to the skin.

And that's what I need to do now.

I shift my gaze back to the luminescent screen, and read the results.

Ultrasound Examination

View: Adequate

Findings: Presence of boutonnière deformity in the right fifth digit. Synovitis and joint effusion noted in both patellas. Left wrist shows moderate tendinopathy. Structural damage identified in the right medial patellofemoral ligament.

The upside of being a bio major is that I can actually understand all of this.

The downside? I understand all of it, and it's *bad*.

My finger's shot, which isn't news. There's fluid pooling in both knees. The tendon in my left wrist is either inflamed or starting to break down, and the ligament that's supposed to keep my kneecap in place is falling apart.

My throat tightens, an itching sensation spreading down my esophagus like I've put a whole kiwi in my mouth and swallowed. In my chest, a sinkhole forms. I know it could be worse. The report could've said my knees were breaking down completely. It could've told me my elbows were past saving, or that my shoulders were beginning to disintegrate.

But just because it's not the worst-case scenario doesn't mean it doesn't fucking suck.

I look back at the screen, scrolling down to the blood tests. Before I even begin reading them, my vision blurs, and I feel a sharp pain in my lungs. Taking in a breath that's not nearly soothing enough, I blink away the tears and press on.

Blood Test Results:

CRP: 38.2 mg/L   Normal Range: <10 mg/L

CRP is C-Reactive Proteins. Elevated proteins indicate inflammation, which is exactly what you would expect with Rheumatoid Arthritis. What I didn't expect is for the levels to be over ten milligrams higher than my last test.

CRP: Worse.

Next is the Rheumatoid Factor. Those are antibodies that are self-destructive. They get confused and attack your own healthy tissue instead of *doing their damn job.* If you have RA, you likely have a high Rheumatoid Factor, hence the name Rheumatoid Arthritis. My last result was at 87.6 IU/mL. Now, it's at…

RF: 122.9 IU/mL

The normal is below 20. *Awesome.*

Rheumatoid Factor: Worse.

I check the ESR next (The Erythrocyte Sedimentation Rate), then the Complete Blood Count., all of which are elevated.

As I read result after result, that coarse, itchy lump in my throat swells.

Worse.

Worse.

Worse.

My eyes move to a boldened word from beneath the list of labs.

Surgery.

What a terrifying word. At least to me. The thought of going under anesthesia, of being poked, prodded, and cut open is terrifying. Spending months recovering in a way that is visible to the world around me terrifies me even more.

I have spent so long trying to be normal. Trying not to let people see how broken I am. And while I know the only way for it to get better is to treat it, I'm still not prepared for everyone to know.

A disability isn't something people should be ashamed of. I believe that, truly, I do. But just like Peyton struggles to believe she deserves to be Captain, I can't seem to believe I'm not broken.

"Everything alright?"

My eyes snap up, landing on Peyton. The moment I blink, the tears that I had fought to hold back start to fall. I quickly swipe them away, sniffing.

."I'm—" A sigh slips out of me, my gait uneven. The limp's getting harder to hide. Peyton's brow pinches as she watches me.

"Do you need to sit down?" she asks, tone shifting toward worry. Before I can respond, she disappears toward one of the booths and comes back hauling a folding chair over her shoulder like a firefighter. She sets it down in front of me and unfolds it.

"Sit."

And because everything hurts, I do. The second I lower myself, the burn in my knees flares like it's punishing me for giving up. But slowly, it eases.

"Do you need water?" she asks.

"I'm *fine*," I snap, then soften. "Thank you."

She nods and drops down beside me on the cold, hard floor.

"Aren't you gonna miss your physics thing?" I ask, still sniffling.

She shrugs. "Nah. I've got time." Her chin rests in her palm, and her eyes meet mine, round and curious. "So... you finally gonna tell me what's going on?"

Peyton's pushy, but in this strangely respectful way. Like she's always listening, even when she's needling me. She asks but never demands. At Pineview, when I needed space, she gave it to me but sat closely. Waiting. Not prying, just present. When I told her about the RA, it was the same. No fixing. No claims of alternative medicine that have been proven by nobody but a church in Arkansas. She just listened.

It's terrifying.

I'm scared that she's filling the void that helped me keep my balance. That the weight of her presence in my life has tipped the scales of my cynicism, pushing me toward something dangerously close to contentment.

You know, when she's not completely driving me up a wall.

"It's stupid," I say.

She grins crookedly. "Stupid's my favorite."

I narrow my eyes. "What does that make me?"

"Are you suggesting you're my favorite?" Her brow arches victoriously.

Fuck.

I roll my eyes, biting back a somber smile. "Whatever."

My fingers dance nervously along the edge of my phone, and I gather the courage to look into those golden, glowing eyes.

"I got some blood tests done," I admit finally, my voice dropping at the end. I straighten my posture best I can, and continue. "And an ultrasound."

Her expression drops even more than I expect. But the strange thing is, it doesn't bother me this time. Maybe it's because I know Peyton doesn't pity me like others. She feels bad, sure. But she doesn't let me wallow. She doesn't let it consume me.

"How bad is it?" she asks softly.

I shrug. "Not great. I haven't read the full treatment plan though. I'm... *scared*."

Admitting that for the first time makes me nauseous, but it's also relieving. I'm tired of pretending that this isn't scary. That waking up every day not knowing to what extent you'll be able to function is daunting. It's not just about pain, or exhaustion. It's about how much of life I will miss out on because my vessel hates me.

Peyton places a palm over the top of my hand, tracing her thumb over the seam of my glove. "Do you want me to read it to you?"

My eyes snap to hers in surprise. "You would do that?"

She smiles. "For you, I'd read the goddamn dictionary."

My eyes begin to well again, so I look away as I hand her the phone. The entire time I stare at a crevice in the hardwood oak floors, her hand stays on top of mine, smoothing across my gloved knuckles.

"Ready?" she asks.

I nod.

"Following the review of blood labs and ultrasound results, my findings conclude that the patient continues to show evidence of active Rheumatoid Arthritis, indicated by—"

"Could you, maybe, just read what it says about treatment?" I ask hesitantly. I feel bad. She's trying to help. But listening to all the medical talk is something I just can't handle right now.

"Right," she says, fingertips tapping against the screen as she scrolls. She clears her throat. "The plan is to increase your DMARDs, start physical therapy, and get an arthroscopy for the knee effusion and tendon damage. Also surgery on the pinky, and a brace for your wrist."

Everything goes numb. I stare blankly at the sea of people moving through the room and wonder how many of them are doing the same. How many are shutting out their pain, hiding the broken parts so no one looks at them differently. I wonder how many had their dreams stolen by a diagnosis, and if any of them have found new ones worth chasing.

Even though it was naive, some small part of me believed AIHL could be it. That I could re-form hockey to something that included people like me. But I've heard nothing from Peyton's dad. And asking would only invite disappointment I'm not prepared for.

"Do you want me to give you some space?" Peyton's voice snaps me out of it, and I turn to face her.

"No," I answer quickly. Maybe too quickly. Quick enough to imply the truth:

That I want her here. That I trust her with this. That somehow, even without fully knowing what I'm going through, she makes me feel understood. She doesn't ignore my limits. But somehow, she makes me see what I can still do in spite of them. And being around her doesn't just make me miss who I was before all this. It makes me want more for who I am now.

"I want you to stay."

The corners of her full, pink lips pull up. "Okay," she says. "I'll stay."

Her eyes fall back to my phone, and her hand slips from mine, thumbs moving dynamically across the screen. A furrow creeps into my brow.

"What are you doing?" I question.

She glances up. "Research."

"For?"

"This is a part of you," she says simply, those soft golden eyes flicking back and forth between mine. "I want to know everything about it. How it works. How I can help. You need physical therapy? Cool, I'll drive you. Your ankles hurt? I'm going to find the best compression socks on the market. Send me your grocery list, and your favorite scent of Epsom salts. I'll get you one of those sponges on a stick."

A laugh spills out of me, and I stare at her as she keeps rambling.

"I want to understand what causes flare-ups. I want to know what 'no spoons' means and why people tweet about it at 2 a.m. I want to know all of it—because it's you. And no, it's not all of you. It's not even close. It's the least interesting part. But if I learn this, I get more time to learn the rest."

Still smiling, I shake my head. "All of that, and you still cant pronounce the damn word."

She scrunches her nose. "I *can*. Rheumah—roo... no. You know what, spell it for me again. Slowly."

THIRTY FOUR

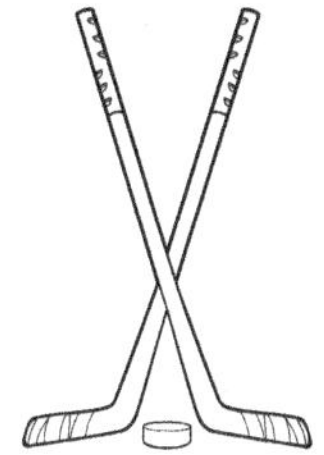

Peyton

"**E**XPECTING A CALL?"

I glance up from my phone to find Harlowe hauling two inflatable sleds behind her, round cheeks flushed, her purple beanie slipping over her snow-dusted brows. Those ocean eyes squint at me as we trudge up the Snoqualmie Summit.

I slip my phone back into my bra, adjusting my grip on the rope of my sled. "No."

Behind us, Bailey gives an amused huff, dragging her mittens to brush the dark hair out of her eyes as Mr. Bubbles plods beside her. It's been like this since we were kids. Bailey loves the *idea* of anything outdoorsy, as long as someone else is doing the work and she doesn't get dirty.

Picnics? Great, until she has to carry the basket. Paddleboarding? Absolutely, until it's time to inflate the board. She's our little royal pain, but she cooks us breakfast every morning so it's a pretty fair trade.

"That's like, the *thirtieth time* you've checked your phone since we got here," she says, hand propped on her hip. She's wearing these soft pink earmuffs, almost identical to the ones Darcy had on the first night we kissed. It's ridiculous how something so small can pull her right back into my head.

Not that she ever really leaves.

She has infiltrated every inch of my brain. Every atom in my mind has her name engraved on it.

I'm not normally someone who does the feelings thing. And now, I'm... *feeling*. Relentlessly.

February's been a blur of training and her.

With the LNHLs around the corner, my focus should be locked on the Sabertooths. On getting us to the finals. On securing a shot at the NCAAs.

For most of the season, that's been the only thing that mattered.

It's just, lately, nothing feels more important than her.

I don't know when that shifted. Maybe it was Pineview, when I kissed her. Maybe it was when I opened up about my dad and Avery. I didn't fully realize it until we were dancing in that diner, but now I can't shake the feeling that I've been falling since the beginning, and now I'm scraping my knees for just a shred of her attention, because hers is the only kind that ever made me feel like I deserved it.

"Just checking the time," I lie, focusing on the soft crunch of snow beneath my boots. Seattle doesn't get snow like this, which is why we have to drive to the mountain. I've used that fact to try and lure Avery out for a visit, but he insists he won't leave town unless it's for somewhere perpetually warm. Which is his personal motivation behind me being recruited to the Sabertooths. He'd thrive in San Diego.

I don't see it, but I swear I can feel Bailey and Harlowe exchange a glance behind my back. My brows knit as I glance over my shoulder at them.

"What?" I ask, already sighing.

Harlowe hitches a shoulder. "Nothing."

Bailey mutters something under her breath. The snow kicks up under my boots as I spin around, arms crossed.

"Okay, you're both being weird. What's going on?"

Bailey just looks at Harlowe with a shit-eating grin, hand outstretched, palm facing the sky. "Pay up, Yersie."

Harlowe shoots her an icy glare. "Not a chance. Nothing's been confirmed or denied."

Bailey scoffs. "Oh, come on. We both know that's BS."

"Is not."

"Is too. And Mister chewed through my earbuds, so I need that hundred."

"Okay!" I raise both hands, my head whipping back and forth between them like a ping-pong ball. Snowflakes settle on my lashes, but I blink them away. "Can someone tell me what the hell you're talking about?"

Harlowe finally stops, tugging at the stuck zipper on her plum downy coat with her free hand. "Will you *please* tell Bailey you and Darcy aren't a thing so she'll let it go?"

I open my mouth to shut it down, to roll my eyes and say how ridiculous that is, because just a few months ago, I could barely stop myself from strangling Darcy.

But nothing comes out. The words catch in my throat, the only think to escape a pathetic, "eh?"

"Ha!" Bailey crows, pointing an accusing finger at me. "You are!"

Instinctively, I toss my hands up in defense. "What? I didn't even say anything!"

"Exactly." Harlowe sighs defeatedly, crossing her arms.

"You always have something to say," Bailey adds.

I shake my head and pat my thigh, beckoning Mr. Bubbles to my side. He lumbers through the snow, lifting his feet like a baby giraffe in his new boots.

"We are *not* a thing," I say, rolling my eyes as I start walking ahead of them.

But the words taste weird in my mouth. My chest tightens.

Because as true as it might be, part of me wishes it wasn't.

Part of me wishes I had a reason to anticipate her texts. A reason to have her constantly on my mind. A reason that isn't one-sided.

I hear the shuffle of boots and the soft drag of their sleds catching up.

"Then why have you been spending so much time with her?" Bailey asks breathlessly, vapor clouding in the cold.

I hitch a shoulder. "She's been helping me prep. Giving me tips on leading the team."

What I don't say is that for the past few weeks since Darcy has started physical therapy, I've been squeezing her into my never-ending schedule. Every Monday, I've been taking her to and from the PT on campus so she doesn't have to take the bus. More often than not, we've ended up spending time together after.

"Is that why you stayed behind with her after the Warhogs game?"

"She was drunk."

"And after the Hornets game?" she presses, flicking a sculpted brow at me. "You weren't in your room."

I glance over. Her cheeks are pink from the wind, black hair whipping across her face, and suddenly, it hits me.

"Shit," I mutter. My stomach folds in on itself, over and over until it becomes tungsten and sinks to the bottom of my body. "I forgot you wanted snacks."

"And you promised to walk with me to the store," she finishes for me.

My feet slow to a stop, snow piling over the tops of my boots as I blow out a breath. "I'm really sorry, Bails."

"It's fine," she replies with a little smirk. "Harlowe took me."

But it's not fine. Not to me.

This is exactly why I don't do this. Between practice, games, and school, my time's already sliced to pieces. Whatever's left, I owe it to my people. To the ones who don't have a family like mine. Bailey, whose parents treat her hockey career like a cute little detour on the way to something "real". Harlowe, whose moms split their attention so thin, she sometimes vanishes right under their noses. Indie, whose family is stuck in Buttfuck, Oregon, and my brother, who, no matter how many times he ignores my texts, is my best friend.

But Darcy has become my people too.

I shake my head and rub the heels of my hands over my eyes. "No, seriously, I'm really fucking sorry." I look up at Bailey, my voice dropping. "I promised I'd take you. I always keep my promises."

Her smirk falls. She steps forward and puts a mittened hand on my shoulder. "Hey. It's okay. It was just a trip to the store. I could've taken the bus if I had to."

"Still." I shake my head again, sucking in a slightly shuddered breath. But before I can spiral into a mental disaster, Harlowe reaches out, tugging my beanie teasingly over my eyes.

"Chill, Pey. Nobody's perfect," she cuts in, flicking me on the nose. I scowl, rubbing it to soothe the sting as I pull the hat back up, but when I catch sight of her, I can't help but smile. "Not even you."

I give her a light shove, positioning my tube at the top of the hill. She huffs as she drops the other two.

"Yeah, yeah, I know." I sigh. "I just hate that."

"I don't know," Bailey chimes lightly, tipping her head to the side. "I feel like I'm pretty close to perfect."

Her wide brown eyes flick between us, and we all break into laughter, clouds forming from our amused breath.

"Such a princess," Harlowe tuts, brushing the snow off Bailey's tube. She beams.

"My gallant knight." She pauses, turning to me, popping a hand on her hip. "So, you never answered my question," she presses, the corners of her glossy lips quirking.

My brows furrow. "What question?"

She rolls her eyes. "Where were you?"

"I was... *busy,*" I deflect, waving her off. I crouch to adjust the velcro on Mr. Bubbles' boot, mostly so I don't have to meet their eyes.

"Busy doing what?"

"Darcy," Harlowe chimes, grinning.

I shoot her a pointed look, but again, when my lips part to argue, nothing comes out. My heart begins palpitating as my mouth snaps shut.

Bailey's brows shoot beneath her bangs. *"Oh my God."*

"Don't—"

"You *did!*" she gasps, pointing at me with her mouth stretched wide. I can see every single one of her perfect white teeth.

"No!" I lie, my tone betraying me. "I—We—"

"Oh my God," Harlowe echoes, her face blank with shock, pouty lips parted as she stares at me.

I shake my head furiously, a nervous laugh slipping out. "It—I—" I stammer, blowing out a breath. Why am I such a bad liar? My shoulders sink. "Okay, fine," I say, holding my hands up, then lifting one finger. "But it was only one—"

A piercing shriek cuts into my eardrums as Bailey squeals so loudly, birds in the distance begin to flee for their lives. She bounces around like there's springs in her joints, clutching Harlowe's shoulders and dancing in circles. Harlowe joins in, an amused grin sewn into her cheeks as an equally loud, but lower squeal erupts from her lungs.

I just watch them, unamused and slightly puzzled, tucking my arms over my chest.

"Okay," I say slowly, narrowing my eyes at them. "Not exactly the reaction I was expecting."

They freeze mid-bounce and swivel toward me in perfect unison.

"Are you kidding?" Bailey exclaims. "I've been rooting for this since day one!"

Harlowe smirks, pressing her lips into a smug half-smile. "She has," she confirms, jamming her hands into her jacket pockets. "You should've seen your face when I let her borrow my hoodie."

My jaw drops. "You did that on purpose?"

A low laugh slips out of Harlowe. "Obviously." She grins. "Bailey wanted to fuck with you. Now spill. Details. Stat."

A flush creeps up my neck as the memories flash in my mind. Her hands on my waist, the rasp of her voice in my ear, the faint taste of strawberry lip balm. How she kissed me against the bathroom wall like there was nothing else in the world but us.

Bailey, Harlowe, and I don't have boundaries. We overshare. Always have. Always will. Hookups, heartbreaks, bowel movements. But back at the cabin, Darcy had asked me not to tell anyone. And they don't know about what's really going on with her. With the Regurgitated Arthritis. I already feel like I've betrayed something just by saying her name.

So I shrug, avoiding their eyes.

"There's not much to say," I mumble, chewing on the inside of my cheek. "It happened. And it's not going to happen again. That's all."

Harlowe's eyes narrow, and she exchanges a glance with Bailey. "And you said just once, right?" she asks, but the glint in her eye tells me she might already know the answer.

"Twice," I admit, voice muffled as I hide my mouth behind the collar of my snow jacket. "And we kissed in the diner bathroom."

Harlowe lets out a low whistle. "Damn. Peyton Clarke has finally fallen in love."

"I have not 'fallen in love'," I shoot back, knowing damn well I'm lying. "I'm just... *mildly disoriented.*"

"You never hook up with the same person twice," Bailey points out. "You're *totally* in love."

I roll my eyes back so far I can see each nerve ending in my brain. "I don't fall in love."

"I hate to tell you this, bud," Harlowe starts, forcing an apologetic wince. "But you've been talking about her since the day you met. You snuggled on the bus on the way home from the retreat. And we know she's been practicing at the rink with you in the mornings. Cleo told us. Every time you score, you immediately look for her on the bench. And what happened at the Hornets game? I'm sure that has something to do with her too."

My cheeks warm, the skin stinging against the frigid contrast of the cold winter air. I don't understand how it could be so obvious to them, when I only figured it out a few weeks ago myself.

"I don't fall in love," I repeat, this time even less convincing than the first.

Harlowe smiles, softer now as she pats my shoulder sympathetically. "Peyton," she says with earnest. "You already have."

I tip my head into the pine green gloves Avery's roommate knitted for me and rub at my temples. "Yeah." I sigh, defeated. "I know." My stomach flips, and I press a hand to it.

Harlowe rubs slow circles on my back. "You okay?"

I nod. "Just nauseous."

"Lovesick," Bailey chirps.

I groan. "God! How did this even happen?"

I glance at both of them like it's their fault. Like loving them made me soft enough to be capable of this. But the truth is, I've always been capable of it. I've had love for every person I've met. I just thought Darcy was the exception—with her obnoxious voice, that maddening smirk, her relentless need to be right. I thought I couldn't stand her. But I love all of it. And I didn't realize it sooner because it isn't just love. It's being *in* love. And that feels completely, terrifyingly different.

"Yeah, it sucks," Harlowe deduces. "Love has no regard for convenience. It does what it wants."

Bailey's pink tube tightens as she plops down into it, nodding. "Can confirm." She looks at Harlowe. "So, you gonna pay up now?"

Harlowe's gaze flicks to me, a devilish grin tugging at her lips, a glint of mischief in her eyes. Without breaking eye contact, she lifts her foot and swiftly kicks Bailey's sled, sending her flying down the hill before Bailey can stop it. Bailey's scream echoes all the way down, and I can't help but laugh as I watch her arms flailing at her sides, her head bobbing over every bump in the snow.

"She's going to kill you for that," I manage to say between fits of giggles.

Harlowe just shrugs. "Worth it." She pauses, her eyes flicking between me and Bailey. There's a soft, almost knowing smile playing at her lips. "So... what about Darcy?"

I shrug. "What about her?"

Harlowe gives me a look I've known for years. One that tells me she's not buying my ignorant act. "Does she feel the same?"

Despite the brittle chill of the winter air, it starts to feel thick. Too dense to fill my lungs, too heavy to reach my mind. My tongue drifts over the dent in my cheek, grounding me as I search for the right words.

"I don't know," I admit, voice quieter than I intend. My eyes fall to the ground like maybe if I look hard enough, I'll find a new answer buried in the snow. "I thought maybe she did. But she told me she's not into the whole dating thing. And now..." My words fumble. "I don't even know anymore."

Harlowe grows quiet for a moment. She drops into the tube beside mine, her hands planted behind her, eyes on the slope where Bailey's still screaming all the way down.

Then, those pretty blue eyes flicking to me, she says, "So go ask her."

A sarcastic laugh tumbles out of me. "Yeah, okay. I'll just show up to her apartment like some crazy stalker."

"You're not a stalker," Harlowe says calmly, though she rolls her eyes. "You're confused. And a little pathetic."

I shoot her a look.

"I say that with love," she adds quickly. "But seriously, Pey. I know this is a first for you, but we both know I've been through this more than once. Remember Odette from freshman year?"

A small gasp escapes my mouth, and I collapse into my tube beside her. "Oh my god, *Odette!* I hope she's doing well. I loved her."

Harlowe's frown deepens. "Yeah, me too."

I give her a sheepish smile. "Sorry."

"Anyway," she continues. "Remember how I basically went feral for five months because I wasn't sure if she liked me back?"

I nod, the memory flooding back. "Yeah, and then I had to come drag you out of a party on frat row because you'd watched *Pitch Perfect 3* and were mad that Beca and Chloe still didn't end up together."

"Bechloe is real, and I'll die on that hill," Harlowe says with a pointed look. She sighs, getting back to the point. "The thing is, this—" she gestures toward me, "—if it's real, it doesn't just go away. You can ignore it, but it'll always be in the back of your mind." She gives me a teasing grin, her tone softening. "And listen, I'm not losing the playoffs 'cause you're out here emotionally concussed over some girl. So you better go talk to her."

Harlowe and Bailey have both had their fair share of heartbreak and pitiful pining. Which is ironic because both of them are the type people pine after. I remember each and every one, pushing them to have the same conversation that Harlowe is pushing me to have now. But it feels different, being on this side of it. I now suddenly understand why they'd have so much resistance. Why they said they couldn't, or that it was a bad idea.

Some things are better left unknown.

"It really sounded like she meant it when she said she was done," I say.

"Maybe she's scared," she replies. "Or maybe she really doesn't like you. But either way, don't you want to know for sure?"

I don't answer. I don't need to, because we both know the truth.

We look out over the summit at the crowd of bodies below. We don't say anything. We just stand there in silent acknowledgement.

"Mister," she calls after a moment, patting the icy slope beside her. Mr. Bubbles trots over, watching intently for her command.

"And I just... say it?" I ask hesitantly, glancing at the bottom of the hill. Bailey is a baby pink ant, but I can make out her tiny little arms propped on her hips, waiting. Harlowe nods.

"You just say it," she says. Then she whips her head toward Mister, and, with a snappy command, shouts, "Go!" The big dog springs forward, his belly brushing the snow as he slides down the icy slope, following Harlowe's lead.

I watch them for a beat, my heart picking up speed. I glance back at Bailey, her impatient stance stagnant. I take a slow breath.

Just say it, I think.

Then I nudge myself forward, hesitating for a split second before the edge of the hill gives way beneath me.

THIRTY FIVE

Darcy

T HERE'S SOMETHING PEYTON SAID in the cabin at Pineview that I'll never forget.

I just don't enjoy the anticipation of the sting.

It was such a throwaway line. Just a few words that slipped out of her in a moment of fear. But now, I can't stop thinking about it, because lately, that's exactly how I've been feeling too.

Every morning this cold February, I've woken up another day closer to the surgery. And to be completely honest, it terrifies me.

Thankfully, I've had a lot of distractions. Physical therapy isn't nearly as bad as I had thought. Thanks to my job, I get free PT through the university. So three times a week I go to the big room across from Kaiser's office, and do various exercises and stretches with Dr. Ramirez. Sometimes, she sends her assistant Aniyah—a junior in my chemistry class—with me to the indoor pool, and I get to swim.

I won't lie and say that swimming is comparable to being on the ice, but it's not terrible, and it does help. The wrist brace (which I've been playing off as a sprain) and increase in my medication have been helping too. My morning stiffness isn't nearly as brutal as it was a month ago, and I've had a lot more energy. Which is a relief, because there's been *a lot* going on.

Finals are coming up in two months, and even though I'm still not entirely sure what I want to do with my degree, I know that finishing it is important. I've started attending study sessions with Peyton and Cleo, which have moved to the library now that Zayda and Kai are joining in too.

Speaking of the library, when I'm not in PT, class, or coaching, I'm practically living there. It's a haven. The mahogany shelves stretch toward the ceiling, lined with thousands of books, and sliding ladders that glide along the walls. Large arched windows look over the courtyard pond, and it always smells like coffee and nutmeg. It's not all textbooks either. As it turns out, the library has an impressive collection of queer literature. The librarian, Robyn (a forty-year-old non-binary demisexual, who is loud in their belief that "the library is humanity's prevailing resistance" has become my new favorite source for recommendations.

And of course, there's the team. Since break ended, we've played ten season games. We've won eight of them, and lost the other two. The LNHLs kicked off this week, and we were the first team to notch two wins, which put us ahead and into the semifinals. Next weekend, we'll face the Cougars, while the Giants will go up against the Warhogs in the other bracket. It's single elimination now. If we lose, that's it.

But if we win? We move on to the final round.

And if we win *that*? We get an automatic bid to the NCAA championship.

It stings a little, knowing that if we *do* make it to the championship, I won't be there to see it. Surgery's scheduled for the same week that they start. But if any team deserves to be on that ice, it's this one.

I try to push the thought out of my head as I step through the door of Professor Palit's class and into the hallway, Bailey trailing beside me. I hear the quick shuffle of her boots and the jingle of keychains bouncing against her bright pink Hello Kitty backpack.

"Is it just me, or is Palit like, *four times hotter* with his beard grown out," Bailey whispers, albeit loudly. We get a few judgy glances from nearby students, but Bailey either doesn't notice or doesn't care. She's kind of... *whimsical*. Not just in a quirky, fairy way, but also like she is who she is, and whoever doesn't like it can, kindly, fuck off. I think I kind of admire that.

"Strangely," I say, remembering his clean-shaven face before winter break, "I agree."

She boasts a perfect, Barbie-like grin. "It reminds me of *Infinity War* Captain America!" She presses the back of her hand to her forehead, pretending to swoon. "He could be my Indiana Jones-slash-Steve Rogers."

My laugh echoes off the forest green lockers. "I see that for him, actually."

"Right? Hey, are you busy tonight?"

Caught off guard, my feet slow. I clear a tickle high in my chest, studying her face. "No," I answer hesitantly. "Why?"

"Well," she starts, voice soft but picking up speed. "I was going to ask again, but seriously, *only* if you want to. Tobias dropped out of our campaign. He said he needs to focus more on school." She rolls her eyes and lets out a disgruntled huff. "I mean *I get it*, but we're in the middle of a *disaster*. I'm scared it's going to end in a TPK. We could *really* use another frontliner."

I stare at her, puzzled, until finally, it clicks.

"Your D&D campaign?" I ask.

She nods, a blush creeping over her alabaster cheeks. "Yeah," she says, then rushes to explain. "I mean, a lot of people think it's dumb or whatever, so if it's not your thing, that's totally okay."

I shake my head. "I don't... really know how to play."

Bailey nods, disappointment flickering in her eyes. "Yeah. Right. No worries."

"But," I add, feathering a hand through my hair. "If you don't mind a rookie, I'm all in. You said it's *Lord of the Rings* themed, right?"

"*Yes!*" she squeals. Her arms fly out toward me, like she's about to pull me into an aggressive hug, but she stops herself just shy of my body, letting them fall to her sides instead. "You can pick your name, and species, and—it's like you're *actually* in the Fellowship. Or *not*, if you want to do something else! We're totally relaxed on the rules. Not like the group Jamison runs."

I have no idea who Jamison is, or what the rules of their role-playing group might be, so I just flash her an awkward smile. As I do, my eyes catch on a small, rectangular object dangling from her backpack zipper. I narrow my gaze, realization flooding in.

"Is that a mini version of *Pride and Prejudice*?" I gasp. At first, Bailey looks confused. But when she follows my line of vision over her shoulder, her eyes widen excitedly, and she spins around so that her back's facing me, presenting the keychain.

"Isn't it great?" she gushes. "I got it over at the romance bookstore on Blanchard. They have, like, a *million* different versions."

My jaw literally drops. "You read romance books?" I ask.

Bailey spins back around to face me. "Uh, *yeah*!" she says, the "duh" implied. "Romance books are the only PR men have left."

A laugh spills out of me, and I clasp a hand over my mouth to suppress the giggle. I think back to what Peyton said in the locker room that day. How she thought Bailey and I would get along great.

I'm starting to realize Peyton is right a lot more than I give her credit for.

We continue down the hallway, side by side. Now that Peyton's on my mind, I don't think I'm going to get her out of it. There's no cure for Peyton Clarke. When she's not around, my thoughts chase her. And when she is, they scatter.

"So," I say, already knowing that this isn't going to come off nearly as indifferent as I want it to. "Peyton isn't part of the campaign by any chance, is she?"

Yeah, I could not have worded that worse.

Bailey's eyes flick to me, knowingly, and a sly smirk tugs at the corners of her lips. "*No,*" she says, drawing out the word and flicking her tone up at the end. "She's not into the whole role-play thing."

She pauses, drawing her gaze from my feet to my head.

"*In the game setting,*" she clarifies, and heat floods my body at the implication. "Otherwise, no clue. You'd have to ask her."

I don't even know what to say. A strangle noise slips from the back of my throat, and I quickly snap my mouth shut.

"*Shit!* Sorry, I shouldn't have said that," she says, scrubbing a hand over her face. "For what it's worth, I'm pretty sure she'd do anything for you. You're like, one of her favorite people."

A flustered half-laugh tumbles from my mouth, and I look away, inhaling slowly to soothe the flare in my cheeks. "Yeah, well," I say, tucking my hair behind my ear. "You know. She says that about everyone."

But Bailey shakes her head, her brows drawing together. "No," she says slowly. "Not like this. Not like *you*."

My eyes flick up to meet hers, heart thudding mercilessly in my chest. She continues.

"Look, I probably shouldn't tell you this," she says, wetting her lips. "But the only reason Peyton hasn't said anything is because she thinks you're like—" She stops, tilting her head. "What's the word for celibate, but for like, relationships? Whatever that is."

An awkward laugh slips out of me, and I clear my throat. "Um..."

Bailey's eyes go wide. "Which is totally fine if you are!" she adds, almost frantically. "I mean, *trust me*, I've been there."

I shouldn't open up to Bailey. Even spending a whole season with the woman, I hardly know her. But that's kind of how you make friends, isn't it? You just decide one day to randomly trust this person with a piece of information and pray they don't break your heart.

That takes a lot of faith. Something I didn't think I'd ever have again. But in this moment, in this hallway that reeks of coffee and sweat, I feel it.

"I don't really know what I am," I admit. "Maybe just... slightly traumatized?"

Bailey huffs a laugh, pushing open the door to the courtyard. It's a pretty dreary day. A cold one. The sun is hidden behind the clouds, and yet, it feels like it's right in front of me.

"Make that two of us." She smiles. "Are you ready for the semis?"

"I wouldn't miss it for the world."

THIRTY SIX

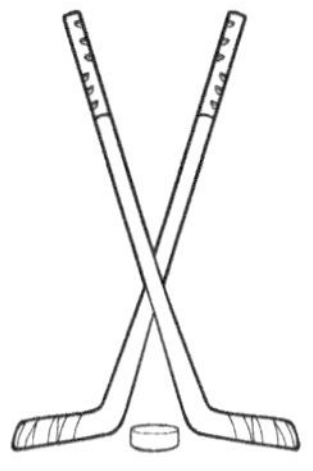

Peyton

M Y NIPPLES ARE SO hard I fear they might fall off. The pool of ice water shrouding my nearly bare body vortexes, my prickled left arm developing little whirlpools beneath the surface of the bath. Cubes of ice clatter against one another as they move, and I release an anchoring breath, using my free hand to type on my phone.

FINAL CHAT FR THIS TIME

I huff a laugh at Harlowe's message. Her and Clay are back on hating terms *again*. I swear, every other day, she goes from hating them, to being desperately horny for them. Right now, Harlowe says she's over it, but it's clearly affecting her more than she lets on. If not from her sour mood, then from the fact that she seems to be unable to stop bringing it up.

Honestly I'm still lost on how they ended up on *fucking terms* in the first place but hey, who am I to judge?

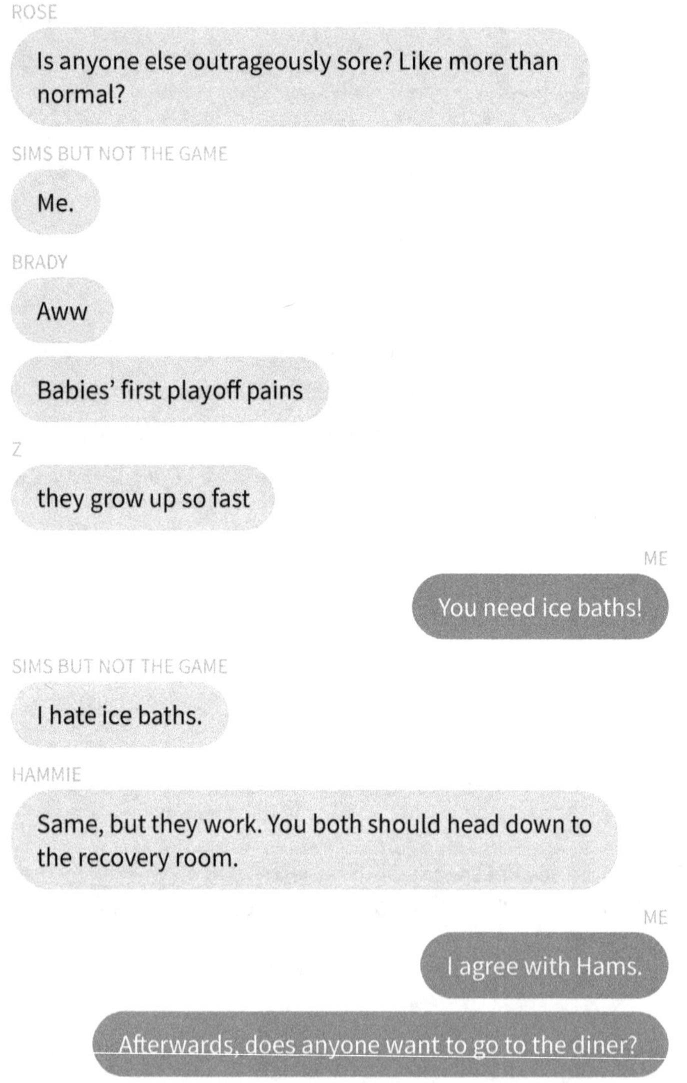

The avalanche of "no"s that follows is fatal to my ego.

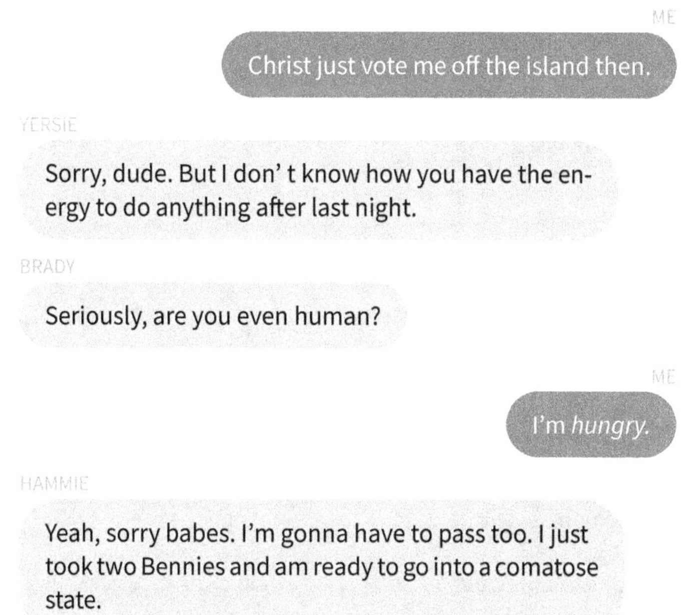

Just as I'm ready to make a dramatic exit from the chat (knowing I'd be immediately added back but it's the statement of it all) a banner flashes across the top of my screen. It's a private message, and when I read the name, I don't waste another second before clicking on it.

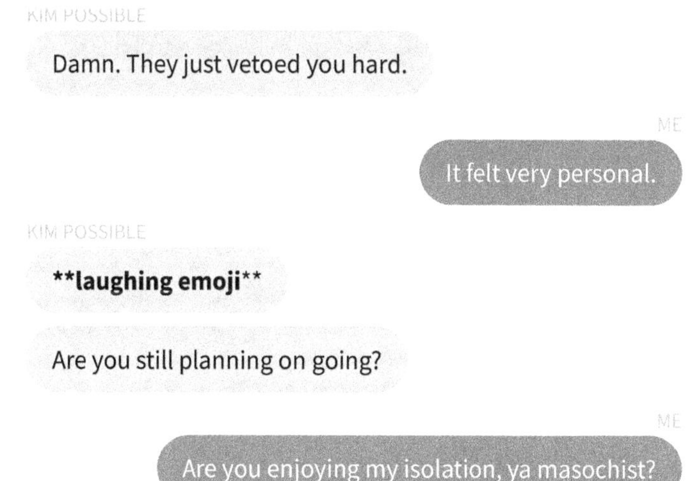

KIM POSSIBLE

Gotta find happiness wherever I can.

wink emoji

ME

Wow.

You really are evil.

KIM POSSIBLE

Oh, don't be dramatic Icarus.

I'll come eat with you. It's downtown, right?

My heart does this weird, fluttering, palpitation thing that makes me speculate the presence of winged insects inside my chest. My free hand travels through the miniature icebergs in the tub as I type my response.

ME

Yes, but I can pick you up.

KIM POSSIBLE

Make no mistake, I was fully intending on demanding a chauffeur.

That isn't why I was asking.

The corners of my lips curl up, intrigued.

ME

Why were you asking?

KIM POSSIBLE

A spy never reveals her secrets.

ME

By the time we're stepping out of The Puget Diner, my stomach is packed full of biscuits and gravy, and Darcy's of some strange, banana oat "pancakes" that were hard enough to double as a puck.

I know I've said it a thousand times, but she's truly stunning.

The off-white turtleneck underneath her brown plaid pinafore fits her perfectly snug. Not like Harlowe's sweatshirt, but like mine. Okay, maybe *better* than mine. Matching off-white socks hug her long, pale legs, and on top of them, brown boots sit just under her knees. Darcy's never shown her knees in public.

At least, not that I've seen. I think she's self-conscious about the redness in her skin, but I don't know how anyone could look at her and see anything other than perfection.

Next to her, in baggy gray pants, a white long-sleeved shirt, and a black tee I jacked from Avery's room before leaving home, we probably look like day and night. Which makes sense because being with her feels like the sky, the moment it softens between the two.

I pull my keys from my pocket, holding them out toward my car parked by the meters. But when I glance over my shoulder, Darcy's still standing in the middle of the sidewalk, staring at me. My brows furrow, and I turn to face her, confused.

"What are you doing?" I ask. "We parked this way."

Darcy waves her hand, a smile tugging at her lips. She clears her throat, then says, "Follow me."

"Why?" I ask suspiciously, not yet moving. She rolls her eyes, hobbling over to me, wrapping a white glove around my wrist and tugging.

"Will you just listen for once?" she huffs, blowing a strand of hair from her eyes. I flick a brow, pressing a hand to my chest.

"I'm sorry, can *I* listen for once?"

She nods. "*Yes.* Can *you* listen for once."

I feel like the joke just wrote itself, but I don't dare point it out. Instead, I just let my gaze shift from one of her eyes to the other, mentally reminding myself not to kiss her.

"Okay," I say finally.

We walk a few blocks in silence, the streets strung with St. Patrick's Day decorations and green lights, blinking against the gray early afternoon. The air smells of salt and wood, like it always does down near the water. Darcy's a step ahead of me, her limp more noticeable on the slight decline, but she doesn't slow down. I watch the way her hair blows behind her, how her lips tug into a smile as she points at a cute pair of gloves through a shop window. I could follow her like this for blocks. Maybe forever, if she asked.

When we approach Pike Place Market, Darcy weaves us through the crowd like she's done it a thousand times. We pass stalls packed with handmade soaps and freshly caught fish. She stops for samples at every table, handing me dried mango, lavender honey, and some kind of spicy chocolate that I'll see in my dreams.

I've lived in Seattle for years now, but I've never actually shopped Pike Place. I only ever come downtown for the diner and the occasional night out. So I just follow her, wide-eyed, like a tourist in my own city.

We pass a flower stand, and I stop short. Buckets of tulips spill out onto the sidewalk. Thick stemmed with yellow, red, and pink petals. like a flower field right on the water.

Tulips are my favorite.

"Only five dollars!" the woman behind the stand says, clipping a fresh bundle without looking up. I shake my head.

"Thank you. Maybe next time."

Darcy frowns, then pulls a five from her pocket and hands it over. She circles the rows of buckets, tapping her finger against the little dent in her chin, until her eyes lock on a gorgeous bouquet of pink and yellow tulips. Without another beat, she scoops them up, and strolls on.

As we walk away, she pushes it into my hands.

"They're for you," she says.

Taken aback, I blink. "What? Why?"

She shrugs. "Because you stopped walking." Then she pauses, her brow furrowing as she catches the look on my face. "What?"

"I just—nobody has ever bought me flowers before, is all."

A valley forms between her brows. "What?"

I hitch a shoulder, gesturing to myself. "Relationship-less, remember?"

"Yeah, yeah, but still." She waves me off, looking forward. "It's criminal. Pretty girls deserve pretty flowers."

My fingers tighten around the stems as warmth pools in my chest, and my face, and my stomach. I don't say anything else, but I don't stop smiling, either. I just walk beside her, weaving through the sea of people.

You know how they say love is in the little things? The small gestures in everyday life?

I realize it when she stops on the sidewalk, pulls off one glove and tucks it into her armpit, then takes a cautious, excited bite of honeycomb she bought from a local beekeeper. The honey clings to her teeth as she pulls it away, and without thinking, she holds it out to me to try, like we've always shared food and germs and laughter.

It's in that moment I know for a fact I'm not falling anymore.

I am fully, helplessly, unconditionally in love.

The honey's thick and treacly, sticking to the roof of my mouth. I finish licking the sugar off my lips, my tongue smacking like a dog with a mouthful of peanut butter, and continue on. I know she's probably tired by now. She's been doing a lot better since the new treatment plan started, but that doesn't mean she's invincible. Burnout sneaks up on you. I'd rather step in early than wait until she's struggling and pretending she's not.

"We should probably head back," I suggest, tugging my sleeves down as a salty breeze pushes past. She doesn't stop.

"We haven't even gotten to the best part," she says.

I frown. "What are you talking about?"

She just grins a devilishly pretty grin. "You'll see."

We walk side by side down the street, trading bites of homemade sweet chili jerky and reminiscing every moment of how we destroyed the Cougars in the semis last night. Eventually, the sidewalk spills out onto the waterfront. The scent of the ocean deepens, laced with caramel and buttered popcorn. The wooden planks of the pier creak faintly beneath our feet as Darcy guides me onward.

That's when I see it.

At the end of the dock, illuminated in soft blues and golds, the Seattle Great Wheel towers in the dreary sky. The lights flicker across the top of the glassy water of Elliott Bay, and in the distance, ferry boats sound their horns. I stop in my tracks, just staring at the sight, wondering why on Earth it took me this long to explore the city. The next thing I know, Darcy's fingers are wrapping around my wrist, and tugging me forward.

My heart thunders in my chest as I trail a few paces behind her, eyes locked on the top of the towering ride. By the time I manage to tear my gaze away, Darcy's already bought the tickets, pressing one into my hand with a triumphant grin.

"Are you excited?" she asks, her evergreen eyes scanning my face.

There's one minor detail I may have "forgotten" to mention when I first brought up the Ferris wheel all those months ago.

I'm absolutely terrified of heights.

"Super," I lie, my smile tugging a little too tight at the corners of my mouth.

My heart's pounding faster with every step as we join the short line. I take a shaky breath, then another, wiping my sweaty palms down the front of my jeans.

Darcy's brow creases. "What's wrong?"

I shake my head. "Nothing." But my eyes flick up to the top of the now-slowly-turning wheel, and I gulp.

Darcy gasps. "Oh my god," she whispers. "You're *scared of heights!*"

"I'm not *scared,*" I defend. The line shrinks as group after group loads into the cabins, the wheel creaking softly as it rotates. We inch closer to the operator, and panic begins to set in.

"Okay," I blurt, turning toward her. "Yes. *Fine.* I'm scared of heights. *Terrified*, actually."

Darcy throws a hand up. "Then why did you say you wanted to go?"

"I did!" I insist. "I mean—I *do.* But..." My voice trails off as I glance back up. The top of the wheel looks even higher now, and I swear, my ribcage is rattling from the intensity of my palpitating heart.

"Tickets, please," the operator says, motioning us forward.

Darcy hands hers over, then turns to me. I don't move.

I'm frozen.

Darcy looks down at my hand, threading her fingers between mine. "Where I go, you go."

Despite the tremble in my chest, a soft smile tugs at the corners of my mouth at the reference. "Where I go, you go."

She steps into the cabin first, sliding into the corner by the back window. I put one foot in at a time, prying them from the pier like they've been cemented down. I'm pretty sure I'm imagining the shake of the gondola as I step, but it doesn't help solidify the muscles in my legs. I quickly collapse onto the seat beside her, fingers clutching the edge of the bench.

"Hey," she says, and my eyes flick up to meet hers. "It's okay. You're doing good."

I nod, exhaling another shaky breath. When the wheel jerks to life, an embarrassing sound slips out of me, and my fingers sink deeper into the bench.

"Oh my god," I whimper, watching the ground shrink beneath me. Darcy places her hand over mine again, squeezing.

"We're okay," she repeats. I nod again, like the more I do it, the more I'll believe it. It starts slow at first, just moving a few feet to funnel in the last of the line. But once everyone is on board, it speeds up, and before I know it, I'm a hundred feet off the ground, breathing like I'm in dire need of a paper bag.

Darcy doesn't let go of my hand the entire time.

After a few minutes, going round and round, the wheel jerks to a stop. My grip tightens, and my eyes squeeze shut.

"Peyton," Darcy says. Hearing her say my name, my *real* name, does something indescribable to the inside of my body. Every organ, every nerve, perks up. *"Look."*

I'm truthfully terrified, but my eyes flutter open anyway. Through the crystal-clear gondola window, the water stretches out forever. As the sun breaks through the heavy clouds, streaks of gold illuminate the waves, ant-sized ferries drifting in the distance.

"Woah," I murmur.

Darcy's smile grows. "And this way."

She juts her chin in the opposite direction, and I follow her line of sight. We're front-and-center of the city, and there are numerous skyscrapers reaching above us, but still, in here, with her, it all seems quiet. Windows upon windows decorate the view. I look at the buildings and think how wild it is that someone, right now, could be looking out at us the way we're looking out at them.

"It's so pretty," I say, almost sounding surprised. I think I knew Seattle was pretty, but I guess I've never taken the time to really see it beyond the apartment. Beyond whatever views I've happened to catch while focusing on everything else. I never stopped to admire details.

Not until her.

"Yeah," Darcy agrees, shifting closer. Right as I turn to look at her, the wheel jerks to life again. My body tenses as our gondola moves, and Darcy's nose brushes against mine as our bodies sway with the movement.

"You okay?" she asks, her breath brushing against my lips.

I nod, swallowing. "Yeah," I manage.

Darcy's eyes flick between mine, then, without warning, drop to my mouth. She just stares, breath hitching, like she's about to say something. But she doesn't.

She leans in and kisses me.

It's quick and soft. Just a simple, regular kiss, but then, nothing about Darcy is simple or regular. And nothing about her makes me feel simple or regular either.

When she pulls back, she looks bewildered. "Sorry, I—"

I cut her off. My hand finds the side of her face, and I kiss her like I mean it. Like I've wanted to for a while. Like I've never kissed another person.

With love.

Darcy tenses, just for a beat, then melts into it.

We don't say anything else. We just kiss, all the way back down to the ground.

THIRTY SEVEN

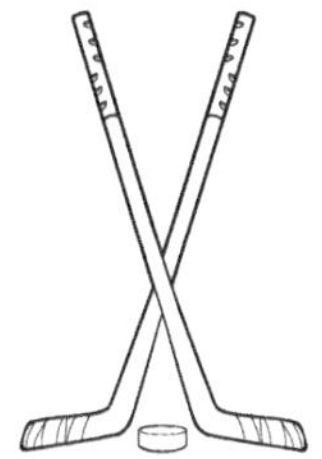

Peyton

MY STOMACH IS EERILY still.

I can't remember the last time it wasn't doing somersaults before a game, let alone the *finals*. Something's got to be wrong.

I stretch my arms out like a starfish basking in the sun, then bounce through a few jumping jacks, trying to rouse my body. When I stop, my arms flop back to my sides, and I press a hand over my stomach.

Still nothing. No tremors. No water. *Zilch.*

I'm supposed to be panicked right now. I'm supposed to be spiraling about the Sabertooths, and the media, and my dad, who is currently posted alongside the rest of my family in the stands. But I'm not. In fact, I don't think I have ever been more relaxed in my entire life.

"I swear I smell funnel cake," Harlowe says, sticking her nose up in the air and inhaling deeply. "Why doesn't our tunnel smell like funnel cake?"

"I think your sniffer's broken," Lena replies, pulling her twists into a low bun before tugging her helmet back on.

"That tracks," Bailey chimes in, redoing her own straight ponytail. "She has long COVID."

Beside me, Indie picks at a frayed strip of tape springing off the handle of her twig. She's not looking at anything specific, just staring straight out ahead, blank-faced. I give the top of her helmet a light pat.

"How you feeling, Rose?"

Startled, she snaps out of it, looking up at me and offering a soft smile. "Good."

"Yeah?"

She nods. "Still nervous, but—" She shrugs. "I'm excited."

"Good." I smile. "That's all that matters. You remember what we talked about? The signal?"

That's when her smile—her *real* smile— deepens. I don't think I've ever seen her grin like that. She's got these tiny sharp canines peeking out that make her look a little mischievous.

"I remember," she answers, then sucks her cheek between her back teeth. "Do you have family here?"

A thousand little fireflies flutter in my stomach, and I nod. "Yeah. My parents, and my brother." I squint, then add, "And I think his roommate? For some reason?"

I laugh a little at that, then glance over at Indie. "What about you?"

She shakes her head.

My stomach dips. I'd kind of assumed her family would be here. Oregon's not far, and it's the biggest game of the season. But I guess that was just me hoping.

I knock the top of her helmet again, gentler this time. "Sure you do," I insist, grabbing her hand before she can argue. I tug her toward the edge of the tunnel until we can peek out at the stands.

The crowd's huge, even bigger than I expected. I can barely spot an empty seat in the entire arena. And when the fans catch sight of us, the place *erupts*. A wave of thunderous cheers crashes over the rink, bouncing off the walls and amplifying.

Usually, that kind of sound would fill my lungs with water. All that attention, all that noise. But not anymore.

Not since Darcy.

It's funny. Proving myself to the world got a whole lot easier when she became it.

I point to the stands, waving. "See all of those people?" I ask.

Indie nods.

"*That's* your family. They're here for you."

Her brows drop into a furrow, and she glances at me. "I'm pretty sure they're here for *you*," she counters. "Or Clay Matthews."

I shake my head. "They're here for all of us."

I scan the stands for just a second longer. It's probably best that I don't locate my family. That way, I can't feel their eyes burning into me while I skate. But just as I'm about to turn away, I spot them.

My dad's wearing the biggest smile I've ever seen. If it were a convertible source of energy, it could power the stadium. Beside him, my mom's got a footlong hot dog in one hand, and a sign in the other that reads "Grizzlies Eat Giants." I laugh silently to myself, then let my eyes wander further. Avery's next to her, headphones on, mumbling something animatedly to his roommate Adrian, who, *naturally,* is crocheting. I swear, they're good at everything.

"Two minutes!" Coach calls out, snapping me out of it.

Indie peels off toward Faith, who's motioning for help with her cage. I head past them, back toward the end of the tunnel.

Which is where I find Darcy.

She's standing alone, completely absorbed in her clipboard, eyebrows furrowed in focus. I stroll up beside her, casually.

"Playing *M.A.S.H.*?" I ask, flashing her a crooked smile.

Darcy's brows draw together. "What?"

"*M.A.S.H.,*" I repeat. "You know, the game where you figure out who you're gonna marry, and how many kids you're gonna have, and if you're gonna live in a cardboard box under the freeway next to your Ferrari?"

She huffs a laugh, shaking her head. "No kids for me," she says. "At least, I'm not pushing the fucker out."

I should laugh. Acknowledge what she said. Do anything other than stare at her like I've just turned to stone, but I can't. All I can do is marvel. Because the way the overhead lights catch in her hair, and that little disappearing freckle between her brows when she's focused, and the ***ASSISTANT COACH*** patch embroidered on her tightly-fitting jacket...

When her eyes finally flick up from the clipboard, everything inside me stirs to life.

Pounding.

Shaking.

Ah. There it is.

I clear my throat, trying to steady it. I thought I didn't have pre-game nerves this time. I was feeling good. Confident. So why the hell am I suddenly vibrating?

"As for marriage," she continues, glancing back at her clipboard, "that's a possibility. But I'd *never* buy a Ferrari." Those freckled lips pull into a perfect smile. That golden septum ring catches the light. And god, I can't hold it in anymore.

"Alright it's game time! Let's go!" Coach calls, her voice cutting between us.

I want to reach for Darcy. I want to grab her by the collar and kiss her stupid. I want to tell her that since the day she barged into my life, everything's changed, undeniably and irreversibly, for the better. I want to tell her I don't care about Ferraris or the Sabertooths or all the kids she doesn't want. I just want her.

I want to tell her I love her.

But when *Queen of the Night* starts blaring through the arena speakers, and the entire team surges forward, I know it's not the time.

Now isn't about me.

It's about *us*. About the team.

And dammit, I'm going to lead us to *victory*.

I sprint as fast as I can in my skates, weaving my way to the front. Coach always likes me to step on the ice first. I never really understood why until now. I glance behind me briefly, looking at my team, giving them a sharp nod.

"Alright fuckers," I grin. "Let's do this."

We flood onto the ice. I don't let myself look at Darcy, even though I want to. I stay focused, chatting with the ref, rallying near the bench, keeping my head where it needs to be.

I just keep repeating it:

I deserve to be here.

I deserve to be here.

I deserve to be here.

By the time the lineup's called and I glide into position for the face off, I've said it enough times that I believe it.

My fingers tighten around the multi-colored tape, a grin pulling at the corner of my lips as I square my shoulders. My eyes flick down, just for a second.

And that's when I see it.

There, just below the grip, something catches my eyes: little black squiggles bleeding into the fiberglass.

I squint, tilting my head to get a better angle, which is when I realize:

These aren't meaningless squiggles. They're letters. *Words.*

Scrawled just beneath the handle tape, in unmistakably familiar handwriting are the words:

Mind the sun, Icarus.

A quiet laugh slips out of me, and I shake my head, glancing back up at Clay. They're watching me, brows knitted, eyes blazing.

"What's so funny?" they ask.

Before I can answer, the ref blows the whistle, and the puck drops.

My hands move before my brain even processes it, stick grappling messily for the puck. But Clay was distracted by my chuckling, their movements much messier than mine, and I'm able to wrestle it, darting toward the other end of the ice.

The rink feels the same beneath my feet. The cold air feels the same against my face. But I don't hear the loud roar of the crowd as I barrel forward, dodging one of the Giants' defense-women. I don't hear my own either. I just hear Darcy's.

You deserve to be here.

I'm not far from the net. I could carry it the whole way, take it in myself, dodge the other defender, and set up a shot. It would impress my dad. It would impress the media. And it sure as hell would impress the Sabertooths recruiters.

But out of the corner of my eye, I see her.

Indie's blazing in like a bat out of hell, grinning wildly, eyes ablaze. There's a slight lean in her posture, her stick angled, her body ready.

For a second, everything slows. My skates. The puck. My breath. I lock eyes with her.

She gives me a sharp nod.

I don't consider taking the shot for another second. I wind back, powder flying behind me as I fake the puck to Bailey, then hit it in Indie's direction, the rubber gliding across the ice right into her clutches.

It's like a goddamn movie, the way those sharp little canines conquer her face as she flies forward. How the Giants are just now figuring out that Bailey doesn't have the puck. How the goalie is positioned right in the center of the net, where she shouldn't be. And how Indie pulls her stick back with her top hand, thrusts it in with the bottom, and sends the puck hurtling through the air, smacking into the net with a snapshot, causing it to ripple.

I've been playing hockey my whole life. And it could be the acoustics, but I've never heard a crowd scream this loud for a rookie. Indie slowly turns to face me, her jaw slack, eyes wide, like she's still processing what just happened.

She better start soon, because every single one of our teammates funnels off the bench, pouring onto the ice, cheering and screaming and shaking her so hard I fear she might get whiplash. Finally, after a moment, the biggest smile I've ever seen breaks across her red, splotchy face, and she lets out an excited scream. One that randomly cues me in to who might have screamed when the lights went out in the training room.

"Holy *fuck!*" she yells, grinning wildly. "Did you see that? I can't believe I did that!"

I let out a clipped, surprised laugh, mouth stretched wide as I glance over at Bailey and Harlowe. They both blink in shocked unison.

"I didn't know she knew cuss words!" Harlowe yells, beaming.

Bailey shakes her head. "Me neither!"

The rest of the game is the best I've ever played, and I didn't score once.

Instead, I racked up five assists, helping bring our total score to seven. The

Giants only managed four.

I know that's not usually what the Sabertooths pay attention to. They like flash. They like stats and stars and scorers with recognizable names.

But I don't care.

Because this has never felt more like a team. And I've never felt more like a captain.

What follows is a whirlwind of press interviews and locker room shenanigans. Faith carried Indie around on her shoulders for a solid twenty minutes while Indie screamed like she'd just won the lottery. Which, in D1 hockey terms isn't too far off. Zayda and Caydence already began theorizing who we might go up against in the NCAA playoffs.

Harlowe vanished completely. I still don't know where she went. Meanwhile, Bailey had already made her way over to my family, wedged between my mom and dad like she's one of their own, and devoured the cold hot dog Avery refused to touch because the concession worker "scratched his ass, I swear to god." His words.

I weave through the throng of bodies, the scent of extortionately priced concessions and dank hockey stench filling the arena. People pat me on the back, and even tug at my sleeves as I push through, but I ignore them. I'm looking for one person. Well, two if you count Harlowe.

My thighs stick together from the heat when I push myself up onto my toes, muscles still buzzing, fingers threading through my damp, salty hair. I scan the tops of a thousand heads, but none come up as that sleek, bright, fiery mane. That is, until I turn toward the bench. There, leaning against the short gate, chatting with the ref, is Darcy.

That fluttering in my chest returns, slipping right beneath my collarbone, wrapping itself around the base of my throat, tickling. I try to clear my throat, but the feeling is insistent, like it knows something's about to change.

I've only felt it once before.

The first time I ever stepped onto the ice.

This is that moment. One of those moments in life that, no matter how much time passes, you'll always remember, because it became a fundamental part of you.

This is the moment I know I can't hold it in anymore. I can't spend another second swallowing words or hiding behind semi-mean banter.

I need to say it.

All of it.

The full, messy truth.

I keep slipping past bodies, faster now, more intent in every step. My heart hammers loud enough to drown out the noise of celebration, my hands trembling and sweating like the guilty on trial.

Then, just as I'm about to close the distance, about to call out her name, a woman steps directly into my path and stops me cold.

"Excuse me," she begins, her voice sharp and authoritative.

Thinking she's one of my dad's fans, I glance back over my shoulder and gesture vaguely. "He's... um, over there."

But the woman doesn't avert her eyes from mine. She just smiles. "That's nice. But I'm actually here to talk to you."

She pulls a business card from the pocket of her tailored slate-gray blazer and holds it out to me. Confused, I take it, noting her perfectly manicured nails. Her white-blonde hair is cut into a precise bob that grazes her jawline, and her lipstick is the exact shade of red that my jaw bled when I got punched by that Giants player at the beginning of the season.

"I'm Sally," she introduces. "Head recruiter for the Sabertooths. I'd like a moment of your time to talk about your plans after graduation."

Furrowing my brows, I study the business card gripped between my fingers, flipping it over to verify the information. The glossy paper feels slick beneath my fingertips as I trace the famous Sabertooths logo.

The Sabertooths... want me? Even after last summer's draft silence? Even after I spent the whole game setting up goals instead of scoring?

"We've always admired your father's career, and it's clear you've got that same talent. Even though you didn't score tonight, your stats show you play with real intensity, and you definitely know how to find the net. We've got some of the *biggest names* in the league on our roster—"

My stomach drops, and I suddenly feel cold and alert, like someone just doused me in ice water.

"Solace, Wang, Lexington. You belong with *them*. We have a—"

"Sorry," I cut in with an awkward, almost annoyed laugh. I shake my head, the next words coming out a little clipped. "Do you have my coach's contact info?"

Sally blinks, clearly not used to being interrupted. She hesitates, then gives me a slightly disapproving, "...yes?"

I flash a tight smile and shove the card into my pocket, the edges crumpling under my grip. "Awesome. I actually have to go do something, so—" I pat her shoulder and push past.

Turning, I jog toward Darcy, not waiting for Sally's reaction. Honestly, I wouldn't be surprised if her jaw hit the floor.

Was this a career-altering decision? Probably.

But listening to her drone on about the "big names" and wanting to see my name—my *dad's* name, really—up there with them made one thing in my mind clear: I don't give a damn about the Sabertooths. They can take their overdue draft papers and shove them up their—

"Was that Sally Rosenfield?" Darcy's eyes go wide, her rosy brows nearly touching her hairline.

I'm panting pathetically, which I'll blame on the ten feet I jogged, and not on the fact that my heart might burst out of my chest.

"Yes," I answer, still catching my breath. My gaze wanders helplessly over her, those emerald eyes, strawberry hair, the slender curve of her nose, the freckles scattered across her cheeks, her soft, gloved hands. I'm erratic: my breathing, my thoughts, everything.

"Was she—I mean, did she... say anything?"

"I don't want to live in California," I blurt.

Darcy's brows fall in confusion. "What?"

"I don't want to live in California. It barely rains there. It's too far from Bailey and Harlowe. And my brother. I don't like the heat. And pine trees are *way* prettier than palm trees."

She blinks. "Okay, you're losing me."

I shake my head, pushing forward. "I didn't know it before, but I realize now, that the only reason I wanted to be recruited by the Sabertooths was to prove something."

"That doesn't make any sense," she says skeptically. "It's been your dream since the team started. *You* told me that."

I nod. "I thought it was. But then it wasn't anymore. I mean, have you seen their roster? It's full of people like me. Kids with pro parents, kids from legacy programs who got scouted at eighteen. I don't want to be another second-gen athlete coasting off a name. I just want to be me." I pause. "They said it themselves. They only want me because of my name."

Darcy gives me a soft, sympathetic look. "Peyton, I'm sorry. They—"

"Wait." I cut her off, breathing hard. Her emerald eyes lock with mine, and I blow out a shaky breath, trying to remember the script I practiced in my head.

I think I might throw up.

"I'm not done. You don't have to say anything," I say, holding her gaze. "Just listen. Okay?"

Still slightly puzzled, she nods. "Okay."

I clear my throat and inhale again, letting my lungs take in as much air as possible.

Just say it, I think.

"The first time you opened your mouth, I wanted to stab myself in the eardrums."

What? That wasn't in the script!

Darcy looks at me, her brows drawing together. "...Okay?" she says hesitantly. Frantically, I shake my head.

"Hold on, hold on," I falter, sticking my hands up. "I'm not done."

She tilts her head, quirking a brow, but waits for me to continue. I suck in a breath.

I guess we're freestyling.

"I wanted to stab myself in the eardrums because I was angry, and defensive, and insecure, and I didn't want to listen to anything you had to say. I thought you were just another voice in the noise, tipping me over the edge."

My throat constricts, but I swallow back the lump forming in the base of it. "I've spent my entire life drowning in voices. In magazines, and gossip, and my own damn head, telling me who I should be and what I should want. I got so tired of listening to them. Tired of believing them, but I couldn't help myself. And then—"

I pause, flicking my gaze from one of her eyes to the other, wondering if it's just the light—or if one of them is a slightly lighter shade of green than the other. "And then you showed up. And even when I fought you on it, even when I made an absolute *fool* of myself, you helped me anyway. You showed me what a waste it is to be stuck in my head when there's a whole world out there. And sure, I still have my doubts. Anyone would. But the difference is, I don't listen for them anymore. Not the magazines. Not myself. I just listen for *you*."

A thick, glossy coat forms over Darcy's eyes, the light reflecting a golden ring in the puddle. She sniffs, bottom lip trembling. I don't know if this is my cue to stop, or to keep going. If she's crying because being with me sounds like the worst possible ending of *M.A.S.H.*, or if it's because, this whole time, she's felt it too.

So I don't stop. In fact, I think I get louder.

"I love you, Darcy," I announce. "Like, complete, total, Caspian-Susan in love and I know that wasn't supposed to happen, but it did, and frankly I'm not sorry. Because even if I didn't fall in love with you, I would love you anyway. For everything that you are."

I take a breath, and when Darcy blinks, the tears trickle down her perfect, porcelain cheeks. "And you've been hurt, and I get that. But I'm not asking you to do anything you aren't ready for. You just deserve to know that you're loved. And, god—" I laugh. "I kept telling myself I didn't have time to love you, but the truth is, I've loved you in every minute we've ever had. And even if I didn't have time," I breathe, "I'd invent time for you. I'd go minor, or even beer league. I'd build a quantum machine—*whatever it takes*. I'd rather have nothing with you, than have everything without you."

Darcy's a puddle now, or maybe a river. Tears are steaming down both sides of her cheeks, but her lips are pulled into a bright, quivering smile. She lets out a stuffy laugh, swiping at her eyes, the salty drops absorbing into her gloves.

"You know they're only in love in the movie, right?" she chokes out in a chuckling sob. I grin, shaking my head.

"No," I admit, a short laughing slipping out. "I didn't know that."

Her hand reaches out, caressing my cheek. Those soft, teary eyes search mine, freckled lips parting to speak. But just as she opens her mouth, her chest collapsed.

It's an agonizing, wet sound caught in the back of her throat, and dragged down, down, down. Her jade-toned eyes go wide, an unfocused glaze pooling over them. She blinks once, then again, then faster and faster like she's trying to get them to work while she sucks in ragged, shaky breaths.

I barely react in time when her knees suddenly buckle. I lunge, wrapping my arms around her just as she crumples into me, all of her weight pressing against my body.

"Darcy?" My voice comes out high and desperate. "Darcy, hey—look at me."

She doesn't move. Her head lolls forward, breath ragged, eyes shut.

"Help!" My voice rips from my throat, louder than I've ever heard myself scream. *"Somebody help!"*

THIRTY EIGHT

Darcy

*B*EEP! *BEEP! BEEP! BEEP!*

I groan, rolling over in bed, my blanket winding around me like a cocoon. My hand slaps around vigorously in an attempt to silence my alarm, but it flies past my nightstand, crashing into my bedframe.

"Ow."

Sunlight floods my vision as my eyes flutter open. Rubbing them, I try to sit up, but the chrysalis of blankets traps me against the bed. My chest aches, a strange, tender feeling like ropes are pulling my arms apart, stretching me wide until something's about to split. As my sight clears, my bedroom comes into view.

It smells sterile. The illustrated posters of Middle Earth and the Isle of Berk are gone, replaced by abstract, shape-blocked paintings on beige walls. My bookshelf has vanished too. In its place sits a sleek mid-century modern armchair that doesn't look like it belongs here... or to me, for that matter. And where my nightstand once stood, a vitals monitor now beeps steadily, its wires trailing down into me.

Wait. This isn't my bedroom.

"Oh! You're awake!" a gentle voice coaxes.

My eyes drift toward a tall, slender woman, her curly blonde hair pulled back in a ponytail that sways as she moves. She's wearing black scrubs dotted with glittering green shamrocks, and little rainbow clippies in her hair. As I try to grasp my surroundings, she lifts a clipboard from the foot of my bed, approaching my left.

With a shimmering pink Truffula-Tree-looking pen, she jots down notes, studying the waves on the monitor. "I'm Nurse Eva," she introduces with a soft smile. "I'm just going to take your vitals, okay?"

I open my mouth to respond. A weak *"oh-kay,"* slips out, ragged and scratchy. I lift a shaky hand to my throat, attempting to clear it, but it sends a deep, tender ache through my chest when I cough.

Eva lowers her clipboard, peering at me with careful eyes. "Don't move too much," she warns. "You've got a chest tube."

My heart rate begins to quicken, hammering relentlessly, which is obvious not just from the jittery thudding in my chest, but from the beeps on the monitor, now speeding up. The green spikes on the screen inch closer together, stretching taller with each beat.

A chest tube? What the fuck happened?

Eva glances at the monitor, then back at me, her expression softening. "It's okay," she says. "You're okay. Dr. Hughes will be here soon. In the meantime, let's take some deep breaths."

Eva's eyes catch mine and she brings a hand up, breathing in slow and steady, showing me how. I try to match her, but my chest pangs with each one.

In. Wince.

Out. Wince.

In. Wince.

Ou—

"Where's my mom?" I croak.

Eva pushes her sleeve up, checking the time on her sparkly watch. "She ran down to the cafeteria a little bit ago. She should be back any minute."

I nod, calming just a bit, when a soft knock at the door draws both of our attention.

"Hi, Darcy," the woman greets kindly. She's curvy and small, even smaller than Peyton, with short, coily hair and a saccharine smile. She approaches the bed, holding her hand out for the clipboard, which Eva promptly hands her.

"Hi," I manage.

"Thanks Eva," Dr. Hughes murmurs, flipping through the chart. Eva's pager starts beeping and she gives me a little wave before walking out.

Dr. Hughes studies the papers, then looks up at me, raising her brows over her round metal glasses. "How are you feeling?"

I huff what's supposed to be a sarcastic laugh, but the contraction of my muscles makes it feel as though a crowbar is wedged between each side of my ribs, leveraging painfully against me.

"Like shit."

The corners of her plum lips lift and she lowers the chart to her side. "Do you know what happened?"

I pause, sorting through the fog, trying to trace my memory back to the last thing I can remember.

"I passed out, I think."

She nods, pulling a pen from the collar of her scrubs and clicking the light on. She shines it into one eye, then the other, the intense beam causing my stomach to swirl.

"Your mom mentioned you have Rheumatoid Arthritis," she says.

I rub the side of my nose with my knuckles, only to realize my little gold septum hoop is gone. My hand drops back to the blanket.

"Yeah. Stage three," I murmur. "But my doctor said with the new treatment plan, it looks like I might be heading back toward stage two."

"I have your records here," she gestures to the clipboard again, flipping through a few pages. "Your Methotrexate and Sulfasalazine dosage got increased in..."

"January. And I started physical therapy too." My throat hurts with each word, but I press on. "I'm supposed to get surgery in a couple weeks."

Pressing her glasses up the bridge of her beautifully broad nose, she asks, "Have you ever heard of pleurisy?"

I frown. It sounds familiar, probably something I read in a biology textbook.

But whether it's from passing out or just not paying enough attention in class, I can't remember what it means. I shake my head.

"Pleurisy is inflammation of a lining in the chest," Dr. Hughes explains. "Same idea as what happens in your knees or fingers. When it gets inflamed, fluid builds up, which is why you were struggling to breathe, and subsequently, lost consciousness. The chest tube's there to drain it."

My frown deepens. Frustration starts bubbling in my chest, which is a problem given that there's a *hole in it*. I get what she's saying. I just don't understand *why*.

"But I was doing better," I insist. "I was hurting less. I could move more. My morning stiffness wasn't even that bad anymore."

She nods. "That can happen. Some of the treatment *was* helping. But DMARDs can increase the risk of pleurisy. I think when your doctor upped the dose, your joints improved, but your chest started reacting."

The monitor between us starts beeping faster.

"So what now?" I ask frustratedly. "I take the meds and get fluid in my chest, or I don't, and my knees fuse?"

Dr. Hughes flashes me a sympathetic look. "There are other options," she answers. "Plenty of them. First, we'll take you off the DMARDs, if that's what you want. There are newer biological treatments we can try. I'll make sure you have everything you need to make whatever decision feels right to you. But right now, the most important thing is rest. Okay?"

Tears sting at the corners of my eyes, and a couple of them fall before I have a chance to blink them away. Not that it matters. I'm lying alone in a hospital bed with a tube in my chest, after doing *everything* right. I stopped practicing. I went to PT. I took the meds. I did *all of it*.

And still, here I am.

I don't know if there's ever going to be an end to this. I don't know if I even care about "options." Right now, I'm just tired. Too tired to pretend I have hope.

"Okay," I whisper.

Dr. Hughes asks if I want her to stay for a bit. She seems like a good doctor, but right now, I can't take another minute of being someone's patient.

I just want my mom.

I want my bed.

I want Peyton.

Only a minute or so after Dr. Hughes leaves, my mom walks into the room, balancing a teal tray with what looks like a piece of cardboard draped in half-melted cheese. Her emerald eyes land on mine, and her whole face lights up.

"Hi, baby," she coos.

The second she calls me *baby*, I fall apart like one. She climbs into the bed beside me without a word, and for twenty minutes, she just holds me while I sob. Which only makes me more irritated, because the more I cry, the more my chest hurts.

When the tears finally dry, and the sad excuse of a slice of pizza has disappeared into my stomach, I come to a realization.

I passed out in an ice arena packed to the brim with people. People I *know*. People who believed the worst I'd dealt with was a sprained wrist and a rough bout of food poisoning a few months ago. People who'd heard about my past in Minnesota and thought I quit because I lost the passion and not because I lost the ability.

"Does the team... know?" I ask quietly.

She tucks a strand of strawberry hair behind my ear. "I told them," she answers hesitantly. "I'm sorry, sweetie. I just—they needed an explanation, and—"

"It's okay," I cut in. "It was probably the right thing to do."

"You're not mad at me?"

I shake my head. I don't know how I could be. What else was she supposed to do? Lie? Leave them with no context, knowing they'd figure it out eventually anyway? I don't want to be seen as weak. But I'm tired. Tired of pretending things work the same for me as they do for them. Tired of making up stories about stomach bugs and imaginary trips down the stairs. Tired of feeling like I don't deserve to live my life the way I need to in order to survive.

"No," I say. "I'm not mad."

"Good." She smiles comfortingly, sending a flood of warmth to my aching chest. "Because they're all here to see you."

"What?"

She laughs. "They're wreaking havoc in the cafeteria right now. Probably eating the hospital barren. A few of them went home to shower, but I think most of them are back."

As if on cue, a familiar pair of blunt black bangs peek through the window. *Bailey.*

"If you're not ready to see them," my mom says gently, "I can tell them to come back later."

I hesitate. I know I want to see *Peyton.* That's easy. She's used to all of this by now. But the rest of them?

I'm scared that once they see me like this—in a gown, with a tube in my chest, eyes swollen from crying—it'll be the only version of me they remember.

But then I think about how they rallied when I stood up to Kaiser. How they made space for me at the diner when we watched the Sabertooths destroy the Porcupines. How they started calling me "Coach" like I deserved the title, even though I was kind of a dick in the beginning.

At this point, if all they see when they look at me is someone fragile, then they haven't been paying attention.

"I want to see them," I say, sitting up.

My mom smiles, then turns and waves them in.

Nothing could have prepared me for the parade that is the Grizzlies.

Not only do bodies flood the room, but with them comes an explosion. Balloons bob along the ceiling. Every flower I know the name of is being carried in someone's arms, filling the once beige, sterile room with color and soft floral scents. Zayda has a party hat on, for some reason, and one of those paper blowers that unrolls when you put air into it. She presses her hands into a heart shape and aims it right at me.

Bailey is the first to make it to my bed. She pushes past everyone, her dark bangs still damp from her shower, Kiki's Delivery Service pajama pants hanging from her waist. In one hand, she's carrying a bag of watermelon Sour Patch Kids, and in the other, a pink, vintage-looking gift bag with gold handles.

"Oh my god," she breathes, collapsing onto the edge of my bed. Her big, brown, worried eyes bore into mine. "Are you okay? *Please* tell me you're okay. You had us *so worried.*"

"I'm okay," I say coolly.

She lets out a huge exhale, her entire body relaxing as the air evacuates her lungs. "Good," she chimes. "Because I brought you this." She drops the candy on my tray, then shoves the gift bag urgently into my lap, gesturing for me to open it.

Humoring her, I reach past the crinkled eggshell tissue paper until my fingers—*my bare, bent fingers*—graze something smooth and rectangular. Bailey keeps rambling while I pull it out.

"It's my new favorite book, and I *need* someone to talk about it with, so I nominated you," she explains.

I turn the paperback over in my hands: a gorgeous lilac cover with an illustration of two voluptuous Victorian women, both dramatically posed, clearly on the verge of making lust-driven decisions. A grin breaks across my face as I look back up at her.

"You're kidding!" I exclaim, and instantly regret it as a jolt of soreness branches out in my chest like bolts of lightning. I wince. Bailey catches it and flashes me an apologetic look, but doesn't hold it for too long. She just waits for me to be ready to finish. "I've been dying to read this."

"Well, you better hurry up, because *I* am dying to talk about it." She grins sunbeams, pulling her knees up on the bed.

Zayda and Lena barrel in next, both wearing their numbered Grizzlies hoodies and balancing paper cups of gross hospital coffee. They nearly spill it over the end of my bed arguing about whether one of them saw Dr. Hughes in an episode of Grey's Anatomy once. Lena hands me a bouquet of bright yellow flowers, while Zayda pops open my box of Sour Patch Kids and pops a handful into her mouth. They talk about the game, how I looked "almost definitively dead" and tie balloons on the railing of my bed. After comes in Indie, then Faith.

As the room clamors, and my mom retreats to the cafeteria *(again)* because she "needs a fucking break from these monsters" *(again)* someone else approaches my bed.

Someone I honestly imagined would be the last person to show up.

"Hey."

Caydence stands awkwardly beside me. She's clutching a small brown bear wearing a yellow shirt that reads *Get Well Soon.* Her eyes flick down to it, like she had forgotten she had it, then she places it gently among the pile of gifts crowding the edge of my bed.

"Hey," I echo.

For a long, awkward minute, she just stands there, staring at the tubes running in and out of me.

Everyone else is preoccupied. Zayda brought her PlayStation and somehow hooked up NHL 21 to the hospital TV. Honestly, it kind of feels like we're just hanging out in the lounge back at campus. You know, if Caydence wasn't staring at me like I'm half-cyborg.

"Why didn't you tell us?" she asks finally.

A hole not unlike the one in my chest sinks deep into the pit of my stomach. My eyes fall to my nervously fumbling hands.

"It's... complicated. I guess I didn't want you guys to see me as... broken or whatever."

Admitting it feels dumb. Especially to someone like Caydence, who already excels at making you question yourself. But instead of proving my hypothesis, rather than moving on awkwardly like she never asked, she says, "We don't think you're broken."

An wet ache wells in my throat, tugging at my vocal cords. She goes on.

"I was a bitch," she states. Then pauses. "*Am.* I *am* a bitch. I know that about myself. It's not a secret I try to keep."

The corners of my lips twitch slightly.

"And I'm not apologizing just because you're all—*Winter Soldier.* I've been meaning to say it. But—" She huffs frustratedly, though I can tell it's aimed at herself. "I seem to be incapable of doing it like a normal person. I don't—*whatever.* The point is, I'm an asshole. And I'm sorry I made you feel like you couldn't tell us."

I try to fight the smile pulling at my mouth, only because I know it'll make this already-awkward moment *so much worse*. I avert my gaze, toying with the seam of my blanket.

"Thanks," I manage. Then add, "You know, I'm something of a bitch myself."

Caydence lets out an airy laugh. "Oh, I've noticed."

Now, it's my turn to laugh.

"Did you drop a Bucky Barnes reference while apologizing to me?" I ask after a moment.

Her face goes beet red. "Uh... yeah. I guess I did."

"Huh." I nod, considering it. "I think I'm going to make a mandatory element of any future apologies I receive from anyone."

After a few minutes of discussing the moral nuances of Buchanan James Barnes, Caydence pulls away to battle Bailey on the PlayStation. As my eyes survey the room, I find myself searching for one player in particular. Someone with a stellar wolf cut, and amber eyes. Someone who was the first to *make me feel like this.*

Accepted.

My eyes quickly sweep the room in anticipation, like I can will her into existence if I just look hard enough.

Left, right, nothing. Again. Left, right, nothing.

So I slow down, forcing my gaze to drag across every inch of the room. I count each ceiling tile, one by one, until I'm sure not a single corner has gone unseen.

Still, I don't see her.

That is, until I look back at the door one last time.

There, standing in the wooden frame, is Peyton. She's got Mr. Bubbles beside her, saddled in his green "therapy dog" vest. In her arms, she's carrying a wicker basket the size of him. And suddenly, it all floods back.

The Sabertooths. The words "I love you". The Narnia reference.

Oh my god.

You know they're only in love in the movie?

Really?

To be fair, there's no official guidebook on how to respond to sudden love confessions. Though, I'd assume the correct thing to do if the feelings are reciprocated would be say it back. Or kiss her. Or do anything other than point out the discrepancies between movie adaptations and the original literature, then *pass out.*

But I panicked. I didn't know what to say. The second she looked at me, I realized I was done for. Telling myself I couldn't trust her was like telling a fish not to swim. Telling myself not to love her was like telling myself not to breathe.

I like having options. Different books for different moods, new dinners every night.

But loving her? I had no say in that. And for the first time, I don't want one.

Peyton makes me feel like I can do anything. The anger, the grief, they don't disappear. Some days they're stronger than others. But even more, I have hope. I have drive, and passion. And that's something I never thought I'd get back.

But I don't just love Peyton for how she makes me feel.

I love her for who she is.

I love that she remembers the details about people. That she shows up for the ones who have no one. That she abducted a neglected puppy on the sidewalk, and that she took a punch to protect the most vulnerable member of the team. That she dances and sings to music, no matter who is watching, and paints her body green for Halloween. I love that she texts her brother twice a day, even though he rarely responds, and I love that she knew exactly how to get me back onto the ice after only knowing me for a few weeks.

I love every fucking thing about her.

And I said *"You know they're only in love in the movie?"*

Only a second after our eyes lock, everyone else in the room realizes she's here. Not because of the usual cheering that erupts around her, but because the whole room falls silent.

Except for Bailey.

"Dude, what the frick?" she blurts, turning toward Caydence. "You can't just stop in the middle of a—"

Caydence elbows her in the ribs, enticing a scowl out of her. Then she nods toward Peyton and me with a pointed glance.

"Welp," Harlowe announces, pulling herself to her feet and clapping her hands once. "I'm hungry. Who's coming?"

Bailey squints. "But we literally *just*—"

"Dude," Zayda cuts in, tone dry.

Bailey sighs as Harlowe loops an arm through hers and starts ushering her toward the door.

"Come on, Princess," Harlowe urges, tugging Bailey past my bed. As she gets close, she leans in and mutters, "Pro tip: don't roll on top of your tubes. If they kink, it sends an emergency signal to the nurse and stirs up all kinds of shit."

Slightly thrown by the oddly specific piece of advice, I manage a quiet, "Thanks," as she herds Bailey toward the door.

The rest of the team trickles out behind them, tossing waves and salutes in my direction, a few of them bumping Peyton's fist or ruffling Mister's head on their way out. Once the door clicks shut behind the last one, Peyton turns to me with a concerned smile.

"Are you okay?" she asks, worry evident in her tone.

I theatrically gesture to the tubes connected to me. "What, these old things?" I swish a dismissive hand. "Please. It's a cakewalk compared to dealing with you."

Peyton flashes me a sarcastic smile, scrunching that perfect button nose as she steps closer. She drops the basket to the floor beside my bed and collapses into the chair.

"I should've let you hit the ground," she jokes. "Teach you some gratitude."

"Thank you," I reply, making sure I sound just sarcastic enough.

She motions vaguely around her own head. "Is your—like—*head* okay? What's the deal with that thing?"

I frown. "What the hell is that supposed to mean?"

"What?" She throws her hands up in defense. "You hit your head, so I'm just wondering if it's still working. Like—did you forget anything? Or remember something weird? Or…"

"Ohhh." I nod slowly, narrowing my eyes. "You're just trying to find out if I remember you completely *fawning over me* with fantasy movie references."

She scoffs, but there's a smile tugging at her lips despite herself. "Nah, I'm just curious because you shattered the concrete floor with that wrecking ball of yours," she teases, pointing to my head.

I gasp, covering it protectively. "I did not!"

She nods, dead serious. "You did."

"No."

"I'm telling you. They might make you pay for damages."

I flip her off. "You're obnoxious."

"There's like a twelve-inch crater out there." She shrugs.

"...Wait. Really?"

She breaks into a shit-eating grin. "No. I'm fucking with you."

I grab a pillow and launch it at her. "Asshole."

She catches it, giggling brightly. "Yeah, but you like it."

After that, the room goes silent, save for the soft whir of machines and the steady beep of my monitor. Except it's not steady anymore. It's climbing. Fast. And I pray Peyton doesn't notice.

She doesn't say anything right away, just watches me carefully, like she's waiting to see if I'll talk first.

"So... you do remember," she says eventually, when I don't.

I nod. "If I recall correctly, you said you'd 'invent time for me.'"

Her face flushes. "Look, if you don't want to talk about it—"

"I do," I cut in breathlessly. It's true. I want to talk about it more than I've ever wanted anything. "I've been wanting to talk about it for so long it's just—" I sigh. "You said you'd invent time for me." I pause, struggling to keep my breath even. "Well, I'd *destroy it.* I'd break every clock. I'd smash every watch. I'd burn every calendar. I'd make sure time couldn't touch us. I'd—"

I falter. My throat tightens. *Jesus, how did she make this look so easy?*

Heat rises in my cheeks, and I blow out a breath that matches the vibration of my hands.

"I don't know how to do this," I admit, motioning awkwardly between us.

"How to be with someone without constantly wondering if I'm too much. Or not enough. Without bracing for the moment it all unravels because I'm too broken, or boring, or sad. But I want to try. I want to try with you."

Tears prick her eyes, and before I can say another word, she's out of the chair, leaning in, crashing her lips against mine. It's warm, and soft, and—

BEEP! BEEP! BEEP! BEEP! BEEP!

"Shit, sorry," she laughs, pulling back, her hands still gently cupping my cheeks. There's color blooming in her face, but her eyes stay locked on mine.

"Don't be," I whisper, breathless. Then I pull her back in and kiss her all over again.

It's slower this time. Steady and smooth.

Eventually, when she insists she's not risking me flatlining just for a make-out session, she pulls back with a grin and pats the end of my bed. Mr. Bubbles hops up obediently, spins in three tight circles like he's been training for this exact moment, and flops down with a dramatic sigh.

"Okay," Peyton says, nudging the wicker basket toward me, a glint in her eye. "Wanna see what I got you?"

I nod, scooting to the edge of the bed. "What is all that?" I laugh, eyeing the basket and tucking a strand of hair behind my ear.

"Well, at first I was just going to get you some hot chocolate—dairy free, *obviously*—but then I kept finding more stuff, and..." She gestures to the beast of wicker. *"Yeah."*

She plops the massive thing onto the chair. I shake my head, still confused.

"Why?" I ask, tilting my head. The light catches the flecks in her eyes as she stares down at me with a challenging grin.

"Why not?"

She proceeds to pull out each item, one at a time, holding them up and announcing them like she's filming a YouTube video.

"Okay, first, like I said—" She holds up a giant container of dairy-free hot cocoa powder. "With extra marshmallows, of course. Then," she reaches back into the basket, "they had like *seven* different kinds of pain reliever cream and I wasn't sure which one was the best, so I got all of them. *And,*" she pulls out a collection of items this time, dropping them onto my quilt, "heating pad, freezer gel packs, epsom salts, glittery pink nail polish—"

"Is that a *jar of peanut butter?*" I ask, quirking a brow. She nods, holding it up like a trophy.

"Yes."

My eyes drop into the mess of the basket. Items are piled over one another, an intricate mess of everything that is me. But my eyes lock onto one item in particular. It's pink and metallic, and I have no idea what it is. I tilt my head, pointing to it.

"What is that?" I question.

Peyton's eyes fall to the basket, then a giant grin conquers her face. She pulls out the object and hops off the bed, presenting it to me like a show-woman.

"*This,*" she starts, grabbing one of the folded metal rods and snapping it in place. After she secures the second one and rotates it vertically, the realization hits me.

"You did *not* get me a cane," I say defensively, crossing my arms. Peyton's grin falters, a valley forming between her brows.

"Okay, just listen," she explains, but I'm already shaking my head. "I read online that canes can really help with the pain, and—"

I cut in, firmer this time. "Peyton, I am *not* using a cane."

I should know better, by now, that nothing I say will ever deter Peyton Clarke from speaking her mind. She looks me up and down, propping a hand on her hip. "Do you enjoy making yourself miserable?"

I scoff. "I am not making myself miserable. I just—"

"Okay, riddle me this, Kimberly," she interrupts. I roll my eyes. "If I had a fever, and I refused to take Tylenol, would you not question my intelligence?"

"I—" I start, but nothing else comes out. Because yes, I would. I sigh. "Okay, yes, but—"

"But nothing," she shoots, clapping her hands. "We both know you're not going to be able to get surgery until you heal from your—*whatever this is.* You're going to need something to help you in the meantime. So stand up."

"Peyton, I really don't want to—"

When she cuts me off with a grating meow, I have no choice but to comply. I pull myself off the bed, the ache echoing in my chest when my socked feet hit the cold tile. My tubes tug slightly, like the wires of her earbuds, and she rounds the other side of the bed, pulling my IV pole along with me.

"Okay fine," I huff, gesturing to her face. "Just stop meowing."

Peyton beams proudly. I add, "You know you're annoying as hell?"

Her grin widens. "Yes," she answers, handing the cane over to me and taking a step back. "All I'm asking is for you to try it out. If it doesn't help, we never speak of it again."

I stare at her, processing. This moment, right here, kind of reminds me of Cleo, pushing me to take the coaching position. It's crazy to think about what I would be doing instead if I hadn't. To know that I wouldn't be here, with Peyton. And because of that, I try.

The foam padding is cool in my hand, brand new and uncreased. I watch the material crinkle when my grip tightens around it. At first, I just hold it, staring at Peyton with annoyance. She leans against the wall, crossing her arms over her chest.

"You have to actually put weight on it for it to—"

"Yeah, yeah I got it," I mumble, shifting slightly. I put a little more weight on it, taking a step. It feels ridiculous, and I almost stop immediately, but when I look at her, at everything she's done for me, I feel obligated to try. So I take another. And then another. And funny enough, with each step, the throbbing in my knees and ankles eases, just a bit.

"This is so not sexy," I mumble. Peyton smirks.

"Are you kidding?" she asks. "This is *incredibly* sexy. You're like..." She pauses, and nothing could have prepared me for what she says next. "A catty teacher in the 1800s." She turns around, pressing her stomach to the wall so that her perfect, muscular ass is facing me. "I'll be the naughty student if you—"

I laugh despite the pain in my chest. "Shut up," I say, now walking in circles. She turns back around, hitching a shoulder.

"It's the truth. Is it helping?"

I hobble back over to the bed, using the cane to lower myself. "No."

Peyton rolls her eyes, strolling back over to me. She leans in so that her face is inches from mine. "Liar."

A reluctant smile takes over me. "Yeah," I admit, scrunching my nose. Peyton collapses next to me with a sigh, rubbing her hands along the thigh of her sweats.

I study the pile of stuff for a moment. Every single thing Peyton picked for me has a back story. A meaning.

She knows me in specifics. Not in general. Not in theory. But in the details that weave the fabric of my being. It's not a rare way to be known. But I think it's the most important.

"Hey," she says. My eyes flick up to hers as she reaches into the basket and pulls out a bottle of nail polish. "Can I paint your nails?"

We spend the rest of the afternoon doing just that, talking, and drifting in and out of sleep. The team pops in and out, slowly trickling down to just Peyton and me after I finally convince my mom I'll be okay. Harlowe swings by to steal Bubbles away. It's a bittersweet goodbye, softened only when Cleo reveals she smuggled Socks into the hospital in her backpack. He takes Bubbles' place at the foot of my bed for a few hours, until he begins to demand dinner, forcing both him and Cleo to leave.

Eventually, I fall asleep in Peyton's arms, my thumb brushing over the curve of my freshly painted pinky.

THIRTY NINE

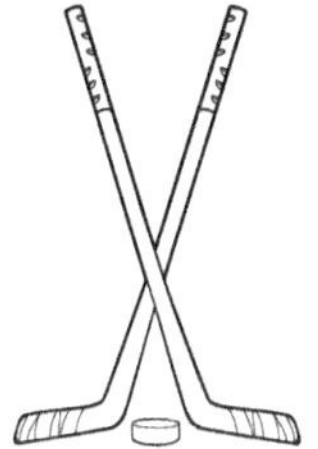

Peyton

IS THAT ANATOMICALLY POSSIBLE?" Clay (yes, *that* Clay) squints at the pair of ice skaters flying over the outdoor GU rink like the forces of gravity are optional. Their rhinestone-speckled outfits catch the late-afternoon sun, blades cutting into the ice as they land cleanly.

Harlowe threads her fingers through theirs, furrowing her brows.

"Jesus," she mutters, rubbing her reddened eyes. "And I thought *we* abused our bodies."

I glance down at their hands tangled together and chuckle quietly. No matter how many times Harlowe's told me the story, I still can't quite believe she and Clay *fucking* Matthews are a thing. Though I have to admit, they're cute. Harlowe towers a full ten inches over them in her pastel green zip-up and light-washed denim, while Clay, boasting a black muscle tee and complimentary moto jeans, leans into her side.

I turn my head to the left, toward Darcy, her cane wedge between her thighs as she sits.

"So you... *died?*" I ask, letting myself soak in the sight of her. She looks like autumn. Like peaches soaked in sunlight. When the sun hits her lashes just right, they catch fire, soft red-gold flames flickering around those emerald eyes. I never noticed before how each freckle on her skin is its own shade of orange.

I think it might be my new favorite color.

She nods solemnly.

"Yeah," she sighs, crossing her arms. "Disintegrated. *Poof.*" She puffs out her cheeks, mimicking an explosion with her hands.

"Damn. Brutal," Harlowe deadpans, tearing off a generous chunk of Everything Bagel–seasoned soft pretzel and stuffing it into her mouth. She licks her salt-flaked fingers, and when her eyes catch mine, they're dry and glassy, like she hasn't slept in a week. Really, it's just from the edible she took an hour ago. She blinks repetitively, trying to rehydrate them.

"Hopefully Bailey can revive me next week," Darcy continues. "Because having to watch them lead us into Mordor completely unprepared is *torture.*"

"Wait." I frown. "If you can be revived, what's the point of dying?"

"That's kinda deep," Harlowe drawls.

I roll my lips inward to bite back a laugh.

"I dunno." Darcy replies, hitching a shoulder. She turns back toward the ice. "Guess I'll find out."

Her bare fingers brush against mine as she reaches into my bucket of popcorn. She's more comfortable with people seeing her hands now. She only wears the gloves when her circulation acts up. Thankfully, spring's finally here, and the warmer weather hasn't been flaring her Raynaud's as much. She tosses the popcorn into her mouth, crunching thoughtfully as she watches the next line of skaters take the ice.

A series of "ope"s and "whoop"s and "excuse me"s echoes nearby as Bailey descends the steps, squeezing past a row of knees to reach us. In her hand is a comically large fountain soda, the straw wedged between her lips as she slurps obnoxiously loud.

"What'd I miss?" she asks, wiping her mouth on the sleeve of her hoodie.

"The debunking of physics," Clay replies dryly, nodding toward the skaters on the ice. Then they lean forward slightly to glance at her. "Also, sorry about the championship. That sucks."

She exhales sharply. "Yeah, tell me about it."

"I mean, first-round elimination is kinda—" Clay winces dramatically, pressing a palm to their heart.

Harlowe shoots them a daggered look, but doesn't let go of their hand. "Says the one who didn't even make it to finals."

Darcy and I exchange a knowing glance.

"*Uh-oh,*" I mutter.

"*Here we go,*" she echoes under her breath.

Clay opens their mouth. "Well if your *captain* hadn't—"

"Guess what?" Darcy interjects suddenly, halting the oncoming bickering match. Both Clay and Harlowe swivel their attention to her, and I find myself equally curious about whatever diversion she's just manufactured.

"What?" I ask, raising an eyebrow.

Her eyes glint mischievously. "You have to *guess.*"

Everyone groans in unison.

"Now *that's* torture," Harlowe grumbles, slumping into Clay's side.

Clay nods. "Yeah, I'm not doing that shit."

"Oh, come *on,*" Darcy pleads, face scrunching with faux offense. "It'll be fun."

"I'll play!" Bailey pipes up, still nursing her soda.

Darcy lights up, spinning toward her with a grin. "Okay, okay. I'll give you a hint: *S.*"

"*S?!*" Harlowe and Clay shout in horrified unison.

"'S' is a letter, not a damn hint," Clay protests.

Harlowe waves her pretzel in objection, adding, "Yeah, what are we supposed to do with that?"

"S... S..." Bailey repeats, tapping her chin in concentration.

I take a solid thirty seconds to ponder the hint, before ultimately coming to an impasse. "Yeah, sorry babe," I say to Darcy, "I love you, but I have *no idea* what that's supposed to mean."

"S... S... S..."

"It's the only hint you're getting," Darcy replies smugly, crossing her arms as a coy smile etches in the groove of her mouth. *Clair de Lune* drifts over the speakers, a comical choice for this argument's soundtrack if you ask me.

"What kind of hint is 'S'?" Clay continues. "I mean, I'm not Alex Trebek—may he rest in peace—but I'm pretty sure hints are supposed to... I don't know... *help.*"

"Don't get me started," I mutter. "Last week she refused to hand me my coffee until I guessed the syrup flavors."

"How long did that take?"

"Twenty minutes," I deadpan. "Three flavors, by the way? *Total* cheating."

"*YOU FOUND LACHLAN'S MOUTHGUARD!!!*" Bailey yells, so loud a couple people in front of us turn around and shush us. I flash them an apologetic smile.

"I *knew* you'd get it!" Darcy squeals, diving into her messenger bag. She pulls out a scuffed blue case with a big white *S* stamped on the front and holds it up like a trophy.

"Wait—*whose* mouthguard?" Clay asks, a little "v" etched between their brows.

"Lachlan Hunt," I answer.

Clay blinks. "Okay, but like... he *lost* it here? Or—wait—how the hell did you get *that* from the letter 'S'?"

Bailey grins triumphantly. "Easy. I just kept repeating 'S' and then it sounded like 'ssss' like a snake. Which made me think of boas. *Boa constrictors.* And *that* made me think of the Boston Boas, which made me think of Lachlan!"

I swear, if this were a cartoon, the following sound would be the *tink tink* of our eyelashes as we blink. We all turn to Darcy, trying to figure out if this Nancy Drew-level Easter egg was actually her plan. She frowns.

"I just said 'S' because it's a *Shock Doctor* mouthguard," she replies casually, holding up the case and tracing her finger over the big white "S" printed on the front. "See?"

Bailey stares at the mouthguard case for a minute, then, without a word, turns back to the rink. I reach around Darcy, patting her on the shoulder.

"Good thinkin' though Hams," I reassure her. Then, suddenly remember, "Hey, is Rose still coming?"

She nods. "She's finishing up a final but she should be here any minute."

Indie's been tagging along to a lot of campus events with me lately, ever since we lost in the first round of the NCAA championships. So far, we've hit up a drag show (which she loved), a swim meet (which she definitely didn't), and even volunteered at a voter registration drive—where, to my surprise, she ended up running the whole thing after the original organizer went home sick. Since scoring that first shot in the finals, she's been an unstoppable force, just like I knew she would be.

If the Sabertooths knew what was good for them, they'd stop spamming Coach with messages begging me to reconsider their offer, and start asking about Indie instead.

A soft vibration buzzes in my back pocket, and I pry my eyes from the impressive axel on the ice to look at my phone.

An unknown number is calling you.

"You okay?" Darcy asks, cocking a brow.

I nod, pinching mine together. "Yeah. Just... an unknown caller? I'm gonna—" I motion to the patch of grass over by the gate.

She nods, and I weave my way out of the stands, pressing the phone to my ear just before the call goes to voicemail.

"Hello?"

Immediately, a smooth, mellow voice fills the other end. "Hi. I just would like to confirm that I'm speaking with Peyton Clarke?"

My eyebrows furrow, and I clear my throat. "The one and only!" I joke. Then I pause, considering. "Actually, probably not. Sorry, how can I help you?"

"This is Alvie Lippencott," she responds. There's something about her voice that scrubs goosebumps down my body. Something that makes the hairs on the back of my neck stand up. Wait—*Lippencott?* "The head coach for the Portland Porcupines. How are you doing today?"

My brain sputters for a second, like an old engine running low on oil as I try to process what exactly is happening. "Yeah, I know who you are!" I blurt out, probably way too eagerly. "I'm—I'm *good,* how are you?"

"I'm doing well, thank you for asking." Her voice softens, just slightly. "I'm going to cut to the chase. To make a long story short, we're in a bit of a pickle here, and I wanted to contact you personally about an opportunity with our team."

I blink, my pulse suddenly hammering. I grip the phone tighter. So tight it almost pops out of my grip. "Sorry, *what?*"

She continues. "One of our star players has unfortunately suffered a pretty serious injury. She won't be returning this upcoming season."

A gasp slips from my lips. "Oh my god, that's awful!"

"Yes, it's quite unfortunate," Alvie acknowledges, her tone sympathetic but professional. "But it's fortunate for *you*." She pauses, just for a moment. "I've been following you at Greenrock University since your freshman year. I have to say I'm a big fan."

My pulse spikes even faster. I can hear it, feel it, *everywhere*. My hands. My throat. My stomach.

"Because of my dad?" I ask, hesitantly. The lump in my throat solidifies during the long pause on the other end, stomach twisting into untamable knots.

"Because you're a ruthless player, and I like *grit*," she clarifies firmly. Her tone is sharp, defensive even, like I've offended her with the implication.

The embarrassment only lasts for a beat. Because the moment it fades, I feel a surge of validation, of confidence flowing through me.

And *I like it.*

"Really?" I ask, utterly confused. But then I remember who I'm talking to. "I mean, *thank you.* Thank you so much! That means a lot to me."

Then just as quickly as the warmth begins to pool in my stomach, it hardens, sinking to my feet.

"Wait," I start hesitantly. My mouth is dry, my mind racing. "So if you've been watching me since freshman year... I apologize if this comes off any sort of way, but... did you consider selecting me in the draft last summer?"

Alvie's voice comes through cool and calculated. "Of course," she answers nonchalantly. "But I was waiting."

"For what?"

I don't know what it is with this woman and dramatic pauses, but it needs to stop. Because yet again, there's silence on the other end of the phone. Only this time, when she speaks, I swear I can hear a smile in her voice. "For a little growth," she articulates, almost proudly. "And what I saw the LNHL finals the other week? That's *exactly* what we need."

I huff out an awkward laugh. "I didn't even score," I dismiss, tucking a strand of hair behind my ear.

Alvie makes a disgruntled noise, like she's unimpressed with my modesty.

"I'm not talking about scoring," she says plainly. "I'm talking about *team-work*. Think you can handle it?"

My heart starts racing, pounding so hard I feel the vibrations in my fingertips. "Yes," I answer, steadier this time. "I can handle it."

And in this moment, despite the storm of nerves swirling inside me, I mean it. Right now, I feel good. Maybe tomorrow I'll be filled with doubt and self-loathing, and nepotism spirals, but for now, in this heartbeat, I am enough.

She continues, tone turning blunt. "Listen, it's an immediate position. We'd want you to start conditioning and training as soon as possible. If you'd like, I can email you the details. It would start with a one-year contract, but we'd consider renewing provided everything goes *smoothly*."

She places extra weight on the word "smoothly", which doesn't at all heighten my anxiety. I swallow, trying to process the whirlwind of emotions swirling inside.

"So, what do you think?"

Another disbelieving laugh tumbles out of me, and I blink what has to be a hundred times, still trapped at the beginning. Still lost as to how this is happening. Considering, briefly, that Harlowe slipped me an edible and I simply forgot. "*Yeah!* I mean—" I shake my head excitedly, eyes flicking to my friends in the stands. Harlowe and Bailey are going to *lose it.*

"I—" I stop again, eyes catching on Darcy. Immediately, my grin drops, and my stomach plummets down three floors, shattering on the ground below.

This is the *Porcupines*. This was *her* team. The one she worked her whole life for. And here I am, swooping in, like it was mine all along. I didn't even know I *wanted* to be on the Porcupines until now.

My voice falters, guilt tugging at my chest. "Sorry, um—" I hesitate, fingers tightening around the phone so hard I swear I hear a crack. "Is there any way I could have some time to think about it?"

"I know it's a lot to take in," Alvie says, her voice softer now. "But we'll need to move quickly. Let's call it forty-eight hours. Deal?"

I draw in a slow, steadying breath, the excitement in my body tainting to something sour. I want this. I want it so badly I'm struggling to speak. But at what cost? I glance at Darcy again, thinking about everything she's been through. Everything she's lost. Everything she's done for me to even be seen by a coach like Alvie.

"Yeah," I manage, my voice tight. "Yeah, I'll definitely let you know before then."

"Alright then. I believe I have your email on file, so I'll send over the details. Do you have any questions for me?"

I blink, trying to find the words. I should have some. Anyone else would. And I probably do, but right now, all I can think about is her. Is what a twisted way this is for fate to intervene. "I'm sure I'll think of some," I say finally, my voice small. There's a hum of approval from the other end.

"I know this is a lot to take in at once," she says. "But I really think this could be an incredible opportunity for you. Please reach out if you think of anything. I look forward to hearing from you."

"Thank you," I gush. "So, so much for considering me. I'll let you know as soon as I have an answer."

"Of course," she replies. Then adds, "Take your time, but you know, not too much time."

A nervous laugh escapes me, and I trip over my own tongue. "Okay, I will! Or—*I won't!*"

I can hear the chuckle on the other end. Then, the line goes quiet.

I stare at the phone for a moment, my thoughts a tangled mess. The adrenaline of the call lingers, but now all I can hear is the beat of my own heart, pounding in my ears.

"What was all that about?" Darcy's voice sounds behind me.

Startled, I whip around, the lump in my throat making it hard to breathe.

"Uh—" My voice catches as I try to find my footing. I blink a few times, but it does nothing to help me process.

Her grin drops. "What's wrong?"

I swallow hard, letting out a steadying breath. "That was—" I hesitate. Even saying the *name* feels like a betrayal. "I'm not bullshitting you, Darcy, so don't think I am. But... that was Alvie Lippencott."

Darcy's brows furrow, confusion fluttering across her face before her eyes widen with recognition. "Wait. Not like—"

"Like the head coach for the Porcupines." I exhale sharply. *"Yeah."*

Her brows shoot to her hairline, gaze flicking between my eyes, just as disbelieved as I was.

"What did she want?" she asks.

I swallow again, my throat tight, trying to keep my composure. "She—" I breathe, steadying myself, and lock eyes with her. "She just offered me a spot on the roster. There was a major injury on the team, and the player isn't coming back next season."

My voice comes out lower than I intend, like I'm ashamed to admit it. Like I've done something wrong. Like *hey, I'm sorry I flew too close to the sun and now I'm being asked to play on the team that you had ripped right out from under you. My bad.*

"Wait, wait, wait," Darcy says, shaking her head like that will suddenly piece everythign together. "You're not saying that you were just offered a spot on the *Porcupines?"*

I nod.

"*Woah,*" she breathes, collapsing onto the bench beside us. I follow her down, sinking into the worn wood, which groans beneath our weight.

"Yeah," I breathe. "*Woah.*"

I open my mouth to apologize, to tell her I'll turn it down, that no contract is worth risking what we have. But I don't even get the words out before she lets out an electric shriek so high-pitched, I nearly tumble off the bench, startled.

Those ivy eyes are wild with excitement as she leans forward, knuckles going pale as she grips the edge of her seat.

"Well?" she asks breathlessly. "What did you say?!"

I clear my throat, a nasty infestation of nerves still crawling under my skin.

"I—I told her I'd think about it." I shrug. Like that's an everyday occurrence. Like it's normal to get the opportunity of a lifetime, something that could make your career, and say that you'll "think about it".

Her face falls, a crease etching between her strawberry brows. "You *what*?!"

"It's a *huge* decision, Darcy. I mean, if I take it, my NCAA status is gone. And if they don't sign me after the season, I'm pretty much screwed. Plus, there's Harlowe and Bailey and—"

Darcy cuts me off, her eyes narrowing suspiciously, like she can see right through me.

Which, you know, she can.

"Pine trees," she says calmly.

I blink. "What?"

"You said you didn't want to move to California because there weren't enough pine trees. And it was too far from your family. And you liked the rain." She crosses her arms. "But Portland's rainy. *And* piney. And it's not all that far. And you never worried about your NCAA status when you were trying to get drafted by the Sabertooths. So why is that suddenly such a problem?"

"Because I feel like an asshole!" I admit, tossing my hands up. "You had this job in your hands and had it ripped away from you. I don't want to—I *can't* do that to you. I feel terrible, Darcy. And I don't want you to pretend like you're okay with watching it happen if you aren't."

She stares at me, her arms tucked over her GU crewneck, red brows furrowed.

"I mean sure, it sucks. But it doesn't suck any less to watch you take it. It would suck a thousand times more if you *didn't* take it." She sighs, her handing finding mine, grip tightening. Her eyes begin to gloss over, and she sniffs.

"Look at me. The only reason it sucks is because I *lost the lottery*. And the truth is, if this call came from any other team in the Pacific Northwest, you'd have taken it without another thought. Don't make yourself smaller to make me feel better. It doesn't make me feel better. I want you to *move mountains*. Break records. You can't do that by giving up these opportunities."

I swipe a tear from her cheek, letting it dissolve into my hand. "You're crying," I say softly, heart breaking as the sight of her.

"They're happy tears." She sniffles, offering a weak smile. But it doesn't fool me.

"They're not *just* happy tears," I murmur, wiping another drop away. "And I'm not going to pretend they are."

"They are, Peyton," she insists, a watery laugh escaping her. "I'm so happy for you."

I wrap my arms around her, needing her close. I breathe in her perfume, the warmth of her body pressing into mine.

"You can be happy for me and sad for you," I say gently. "That's allowed."

Darcy's teary eyes lift to meet mine, and this time, a stronger smile breaks through.

"I'm not letting you make this about me," she says firmly, though more tears follow, tracing the soft lines of her heart-shaped face.

I kiss her forehead, then meet her gaze.

"It's not. It's about *us*. You and me. And yeah, I want to take it. But I'm not going to make that decision without factoring you in. You're always a factor, Darcy."

She leans in until her forehead rests against mine.

"You're always a factor too," she whispers. Her lips brush mine, then she pulls me into a kiss.

"You're going to take it," she whispers against my skin.

My hand finds her cheek, cupping it gently.

"Okay," I say. "I'm going to take it." I pause, then pull back just enough to flash her a teasing smile. "You know this means you're a WAG, right?"

She blinks. "Wait, what?"

I shrug. "Rules are rules. You're totally a WAG."

She rolls her eyes. "Does the PWHL even have WAGs?"

I raise a brow, grinning. "I'm pretty sure the PWHL *only* has WAGs."

She stares at me for a beat, then we both burst out laughing.

FORTY

Darcy

"WELL IF YOU'RE EVER desperate for cash, you could always turn your bedroom into a pawnshop," Peyton says, tugging her sleeve over her hand to polish off a layer of dust from one of my trophies. Not to toot my own horn, but there's a lot of them,

Thirty-seven to be exact.

They're scattered around my room like beer cans at a country music festival except instead of polluting the environment and funding bigotry, they pollute my bedroom and fund my ego.

"You know they're just gold-*plated*, right?" I respond, flicking a brow.

Peyton turns, gesturing to the collection of plaques and trophies. "Yeah, but you have enough to scrape them all into a ring or something."

I laugh, closing the space between us and cupping her face. "What can I say?" I tease, tilting my to the side. "I'm a winner."

Those full lips part into an amused grin, and she kisses me soft and slow. Tender. Like she's savoring it. And my heart still pounds like it did the very first time.

"So humble," she murmurs against my mouth.

I smile into her, slipping my tongue between the cut of her teeth. Her fingers knot in my hair, nails skimming my scalp, dragging a shuddered breath from my chest. My fingertips sneak beneath the hem of her shirt, slowly tracing the muscle-carved groove down the center of her abdomen, while my other hand rests at the small of her back, anchoring her to the edge of my desk.

We kiss like we've got nothing but time. Like our tongues are tectonic plates, slipping against one another, sending an earthquake down my legs. Already desperate, I grip her shirt and tug it over her head, revealing her pale supple chest beneath her black sports bra. It takes everything in me not to moan at the sight of her. Not to come just from the thought of pressing my face in between them. Instead, I slide my thigh between her legs, and press.

"You're getting cocky," she breathes.

"Gold'll do that to you," I respond.

A laugh tumbles from her perfect, wet mouth, and I kiss the sound right out of her, pressing her harder against the desk, feeling her perfect tits push against me. My head tips back as she yanks my hair more needily this time, a short whimper escaping me.

"I don't think you realize how badly I want to fuck you," she murmurs against my neck. "How badly I want to hear you scream my name. What I'd give to make that pretty fucking pussy of yours weep for me."

"*F—fuck,*" I moan. Her grip on my hair tightens, moving lower to the nape of my neck. The bite of the pull sends a wet rush between my thighs, and a hot pulse spreads through my body.

"Do you think you can handle that?" she asks lowly. "Me fucking you until you're nothing but a begging, pleading mess?"

It's been weeks since I got my chest tube out, and besides the scar, you'd never know it was there. My chest doesn't hurt when I laugh anymore, or breathe, or move, and even though I'm still set to get surgery next week, the new course of treatment has definitely helped the pain. I'm on something called certolizumab pegol, which is basically a biologic DMARD. The only downside is that it's an injection, and I'm *really* not a fan of needles. But if a couple needles a month gets me fucked by Peyton like she means it, I'd sign up for a thousand.

"*Yes,*" I beg. "I can handle it."

She grins devilishly. "Yeah?"

My pulse hammers into overdrive, and I nod like it's the only thing I can do, gasping for air. Still gripping my hair, her free hand travels to the waistband of my pants, finger dipping just barely along the seam, scrubbing goosebumps down my burning body.

"Then go over to my backpack and show me what's inside," she commands.

Letting go of her, rather reluctantly I might add, my breath and heart don't settle at all as I stroll over to the bed, where her backpack's sitting. I swallow when my fingers touch the zipper, then glance over my shoulder.

She's boasting that cocky grin again, and it makes my knees buckle. She grants me an encouraging nod.

I turn back and unzip the bag. Inside is a smaller black velvet pouch.

I don't need to open it to know what's inside.

"Take it out," she says, then strolls over to the pink upholstered bench along the wall. She sits, back arching slightly, perfect tits on display as she leans against it, patting her lap. "Then come here."

"Now who's cocky," I say, like her telling me what to do doesn't turn my spine to string. It's pathetic. I *hate* being told what to do. Always have. But when Peyton does it?

Yeah, it *wrecks* me.

My fingers tug at the dainty black strings, opening the bag. When they reach inside, they feel something silicone, and flexible. Heat pools in my cheeks as I pull it out, suddenly feeling a little shy.

"Remember that gift card Bailey and Harlowe got me?" she asks, still sprawled out like she's on display. God, if she was behind glass, I know I'd stare at her all day, just longing for a touch.

"This is it?"

She nods. I pull out the vibrator, revealing dusty pink silicone, curved like a lopsided "U." The shorter end has a soft, open mouth, while the longer one is thick and cylindrical. Picturing Peyton using it on herself is already enough to make the slick river between my thighs flood, but the thought of her using it on me forces my core to tighten, and my clit to throb.

"Undress."

My eyes snap up to meet hers. Those golden gems are glowing, hot and hungry. She pats her thighs again, raising her eyebrows like she won't be asking twice. I move fast. My shirt flies off first, and I toss it carelessly behind me. When I unclasp my bra and let it fall, I catch the way Peyton's throat bobs. By the time I'm completely naked, she's practically squirming. It's kind of funny. She's trying to act like she's in charge, but she's clearly just as desperate as I am.

I approach her, breath ragged, only prying my eyes from her bare, luscious chest to trail down to the button of her jeans. When I reach for it, she shakes her head, holding her hand out palm-up. My pussy tightens, slick and hot as I give her the vibrator. She nods in approval.

"Now turn around," she says.

"What are you—"

"Oh, sweetheart. You have no fucking clue what you're in for, do you?"

I swallow, my breath hitching in my chest.

"Turn around. Let me see that tight, pretty ass of yours," she repeats, softer this time.

I do as I'm told, feeling my pulse pound everywhere in my body, feeling the slick heat in my pussy drip for her. Suddenly, her hand strikes against me, a faint sting spreading on my skin. I suck in a sharp breath, and she does it again.

"God damn, Darcy," she groans, followed by a soft buzzing sound which I recognize as the vibrator. "I should just sit here for the rest of my life and stare at this pretty little ass of yours. Smack it." She smacks it again, and I wince in pleasure. "Bite it." I feel her teeth sink into me, and a soft yelp slips from my quivering breath. Then her hand clutches my waist, tugging me downward. I only get a few inches before the tip of the silicone presses against my entrance. Peyton holds the curve of the toy against her lap, using the leverage to slip the soft, round head between the slick folds of my pussy, lubricating it.

"So fucking wet," she murmurs, a growl as her voice trails away. "You like when I make you dripping wet, don't you? You like being desperate so I'll fuck you nice and hard?"

I nod, a whimper escaping my throat.

"Say it," she commands. "Tell me this whole time, you've wanted me to fuck you so hard you see stars."

"I have," I moan, tilting my head back as the vibrations travel though my skin, radiating in my clit. "I've wanted you to fuck me so…" I pant. "So fucking hard. I want you to make me scream your name while I come all over you."

Peyton seems to like that, on account of the deep, gravelly sound that slips from her lips. I feel her breath on the back of my neck as she glides the vibrator back down to my entrance, pushing me down on it slightly. My pussy tightens around it, the sensation buzzing through me in waves.

"You can take it," she whispers, using her pelvis to thrust it further into me. A pleasured cry slips out of me, and she buries it further inside. "Just like that. Let me fuck this tight, wet, pretty pussy."

"Shit," I cry, sinking my teeth into my lower lip until I feel my ass bounce against Peyton's lap.

"Good fucking girl," she praises. "You take me so well, don't you?"

I nod pathetically, eyes welling with desire.

Beneath me, I feel a shift, and when the mouth of that suction piece makes contact with my swollen, throbbing clit, I jolt. "F-f-f-"

"Cat got your tongue?" she teases, and though I can't see her, I'm willing to bet she's boasting that cocky fucking grin of hers.

"F-f-fuck you," I manage, though the stutter kills the bite.

Peyton just lets out an evil chuckle, one that sends a tingle down my spine. "Oh?" she challenges. Then she thrusts her hips, riding me up the shaft, my thighs crashing back down on her lap. I moan loudly, and she does it again, over and over, as the soft, rimmed suction laps at my needy clit.

"Someone's got to teach you not to run that smart mouth of yours," she coos as she pounds into me mercilessly. When I let out a guttural cry, my hands slip back, gripping the back of her head for balance. She covers my mouth with her free hand, thrusting harder. Faster. "I told you I was going to make this pussy weep, and now look at you. Look at what a fucking mess you are."

My stomach tightens, the shaft of the vibrator purring as she buries it deeper inside me. Goosebumps scrub my body as I grip her head harder, as I let out a desperate moan muffled only by the warm palm of her hand. As I roll and buck my hips, desperate for the coil inside me to unravel.

"Come on baby," she growls into the back of my neck, causing all the hairs to stand. Her hand tightens over my mouth. "Come for me. I want to see your cum dripping all over my cock."

"Oh fuck!"

And with those words, I come completely and utterly undone. My tired body spasms and rolls, a wave of pressure releasing as pleasure rolls through my body like waves crashing on the shore. Over and over until I am a tired, panting mess, still dripping all over Peyton's lap.

She lifts me up, only to pull the buzzing vibrator from me, turning it off and setting it aside.

"Jesus fuck," she groans. I slide off her lap, turning to face her.

All the blood in my body rushes to my face when I catch the sight. Her black denim is completely soaked, lap stained with my arousal. I open my mouth to apologize, to try to say anything but all that comes out is a strangled sound. Peyton, however, marvels at the sight.

"Damn," she breathes. "You are so fucking—"

She's cut off by a loud rapping at the door.

"Darcy? Are you in there?"

Shit.

Peyton's brows shoot to her hairline as she scrambles to her feet.

"Uh—" I clear my throat, but my voice still comes out panicked. "Just a minute!"

My eyes catch Peyton's, and after a beat of stillness, we move in tandem. Shirts fly across the room, exchanging with one another. I dig through my drawer for a clean pair of underwear. By the time Cleo opens the door, I'm mostly dressed, minus the bra still in hand, and Peyton is stretched out in my bed with the blanket pulled just high enough to cover her stained pants.

I make a mental note to wash my quilt.

"Okay!" I call.

Cleo bursts in with a grin the size of the sun, her gray eyes beaming in the spring light. She fishes something out of her pocket, a little cardboard tube, and before I can register that it's not a tampon, she pulls the string.

Confetti explodes into the air.

"I'm gonna be a veterinarian!" she shouts as the bits of colorful paper float down around us.

For the last eight months, Cleo's told me she's wanted to be about a hundred different things. But this is the first time she's ever celebrated it with confetti. I don't know if this is her final decision, but it only takes me a second to remember that whether or not she changes her mind again is none of my business. The only thing I need to do right now is support her.

So, without thinking any further, I throw my arms around her for the first time ever.

"Cleo, that's great!" I say, and she lets out a high-pitched squeal of excitement.

"Yeah, that's like, *perfect!*" Peyton adds.

"*I know!* I don't know why I didn't think of it before!" she gushes, bouncing on her feet. "I'm already majoring in bio-med, so when I graduate, I'll have all the creds to apply to vet school. It just makes sense, you know?"

I smile, squeezing her tight before collapsing back onto the bed. "It does."

Right on cue, Socks pads into the room, jumping up beside me. I'm so focused on Cleo rambling on about how excited she is that I barely notice when he settles in my lap.

I smile, my hand absentmindedly brushing along his fur as she keeps talking.

"And I already applied for a job at the shelter by the bodega, and—" She stops suddenly, eyes widening. Her gaze locks on me, and her jaw drops. She gasps.

"*Oh. My. God.*"

I frown, looking down at Socks in my lap, then back at Cleo. "What?"

Her eyes are still wide as she points at me, breaking into a grin. "You *love* him!"

I scoff, still petting the little demon. "I do not," I say, trying to sound firm. "He's just... *grounding.*"

Cleo shakes her head. "You love Socks! Say it."

I stare at her, deadpan. "I don't love Socks," I say, but the corner of my mouth twitches.

Peyton frowns. "It kinda looks like you do."

Cleo raises an eyebrow. "*Say. It.*"

I crack. "Okay, fine. I might like him a *little*. But he's still a menace."

Cleo beams, crouching down to scratch behind his ears. "Your Auntie D loves you," she sings, and I roll my eyes, a smile creeping up despite myself. She scoops him back into her arms, strolling back toward my door. Before she steps through, she turns to look at us. "Are y'all gonna come eat with me or did you do enough of that already?"

Peyton and I exchange a flushed glance, and a few minutes later, after she's changed into some of my clothes, we head toward the kitchen.

Peyton drops herself onto one of the barstools at the counter, spinning it a little. I grab a box of cereal from the cupboard and pour all three of us a bowl, the dry Cheerios clinking against the ceramic. Just as I place the bowls in front of us and sit down, a loud melody springs from my phone. Startled, I glance at it, frowning when a number I don't recognize flashes across the screen. With a quick swipe, I hit the decline button and set it back down on the counter. But before I can pick up my spoon, it starts ringing again.

"Who is that?" Cleo asks, thick dark brows drawing together.

I shrug, letting it ring out this time, Cleo bopping her head around to the xylophone melody until it finishes. Only, as I spoon another bite into my mouth, it just starts again.

Peyton's lips press into a flat line as she points at it. "Maybe you should get that."

I let out a reluctant sigh before answering, pressing the cool screen to the shell of my ear.

"Who is this?" I ask, voice clipped with frustration. There's a long pause on the other end. So long that I almost hang up, but just as I'm about to, a voice finally breaks through.

"Hello?"

The sound is deep, smooth, and unfamiliar, and it sends a confused shiver down my spine. I tilt my head, phone wedged between my ear and shoulder, balancing a spoonful of cereal halfway to my mouth.

"Is this Darcy?" the voice asks, and I freeze. The worst thing about the 21st century is that anyone can get your information if they really want it.

The frown on my face deepens as I shove my spoon into my mouth. "Yeah, who is this?" My tone is less than friendly. The man on the other end clears his throat before speaking again.

"Oh, good. This is Harrison Clarke," he says. "Peyton's dad."

Oh.

My.

Fucking.

God.

I try to swallow, but the cereal is lodged in my throat, refusing to budge. Milk trickles down my esophagus, and I start coughing violently, clutching at my neck like it will help. Cleo's and Peyton's gazes snaps to me, brows furrowed in concern as they watch me flounder, my hands moving from my neck to the counter, smacking it repeatedly.

Finally, a Cheerio rockets out of my throat and lands with a soft thud against the peeling contact paper. I cough one last time before I rasp into the phone.

"Sorry, can you hold for just a second?"

"Sure," he answers, and I immediately press the mute button, my eyes flying wide as I flash both Peyton and Cleo a frantic stare.

"What?" Peyton asks, eyes flicking from me to the phone, then back to me again. I swallow hard, trying to steady myself.

"I just sent your dad to voicemail. *Twice.*"

Cleo's jaw drops. She slaps her hand over her mouth, completely speechless, her eyes going as wide as saucers. Meanwhile, Peyton breaks into a cackle. My heart's still racing as I hop off the barstool, feet hitting the cold linoleum, the impact biting at my ankles. I shuffle across the kitchen, the stool still swiveling behind me, and shut myself into my room. I take the phone off mute.

"I'm so, so sorry about that, sir," I blurt breathlessly. "I had *no idea* who was calling me."

He chuckles softly, deep and warm, and the tension in my shoulders loosens just a little. "I wish Peyton shared that sentiment. The kid's never met a stranger."

I force a laugh that is way too loud. My hand slaps against my forehead in awkward frustration. "Yeah, that's... *true*. Um... so... what can I do for you, sir?"

"Harry is fine," he says, and I swear my whole body ignites. "And I wanted to talk to you a little bit about your plans after graduation. Peyton tells me you're a senior?"

My pulse stutters, hammering against the inside of my ribs. I take a sharp inhale trying to calm it. "Yeah," I say, tone deceptively steady. "I'm graduating with a BA in Kinesiology. Right now—" My throat tightens. I feel like there's a right answer and a wrong answer to this, but I have no idea which is which. "I'm not currently planning to attend any further education." I add quickly, and enthusiastically, "But that could change!"

The silence that follows is suffocating. It's like someone is holding a pillow over my face, and the only thing I can do is listen to my own pulse as I inevitably pass out. I'm only able to breathe when Harrison speaks again.

"Okay, cool. So, are you planning to take a full-time position on campus if it's offered, or do you have other employment ideas in mind?"

"Uh..." I falter. *Why is he asking me this?* "I don't have anything locked in yet," I say, my voice feeling smaller now. "I was considering physical therapy, but... I don't know. It doesn't feel quite right."

Harrison laughs, a smooth, knowing sound that makes the hair on the back of my neck stand up. "I get it," he says casually. "The reason I'm asking is that I passed your info over to my buddy, Duy Quyên, over at CAA. We've got a potential opportunity for you."

"*Duy Quyên?!*" I blurt the name out, almost laughing at the sheer absurdity of it. As if I weren't already on the phone with the Harrison Clarke himself. "The agent? *That* Duy Quyên?"

Duy Quyên is *the* agent in the NHL. If you're under his wing, you're practically guaranteed to be where you want to be. He represents all the big players, including GU alumini, Lachlan Hunt.

"Yes, ma'am," Harrison says.

Ma'am. Harrison Clarke just called me *ma'am.* I nearly pass out. My heart trips over itself, stomach fluttering with a dangerous cocktail of embarrassment, disbelief, and pure, giddy awe. I try not to fangirl but the words tumble from my mouth anyway.

"I can't believe this is happening," I squeak, swiping a bead of sweat from my brow.

"He happens to be a really close buddy of mine," Harrison continues, skipping over my spiraling in a move I'm grateful for. "I hope you don't mind, but I shared some of your ideas with him."

My ideas? Harrison Clarke shared my ideas with Duy Quyền? They talked? About me? Together?

"Turns out," he continues, his voice husky but bright. "Ehlers-Danlos runs in his family, which is why he stepped away from hockey after high school. He really liked your idea, Darcy. We both think it could go somewhere."

There's another beat of silence, but this time, I don't panic. Because I already know how things like this go. How complicated this is. How unrealistic.

"But?" I ask, aware of the intricacies.

A heavy sigh slips through the receiver. "But these things take time. A lot of time. Resources. Experience. Funding."

My throat hardens, and I force a nod, to myself more than anyone. It was a pipe dream. I knew that.

"Look, Darcy," he adds, voice softening. "We want to help. Until we can get this rolling, Duy's offering you a chance to get some experience. There's an internship for an assistant strength and conditioning coach with the Seattle Axolotyls starting this summer. It's yours if you want it."

"Sorry," I ask, trying to suck in a breath. But each time I do, my chest constricts. *"What?"*

"Since it's in the off-season, the pay isn't great. But it's a twelve-week contract with an opportunity to turn into a real role, if you stick with it."

My mind begins to spin, and I collapse onto my bed to steady myself.

The Seattle Axolotyls.

"Take some time to think about it," he continues. "But they'll want an answer by the end of May."

When I speak, my voice sounds like it doesn't belong to me. "You—why would you do that for me?"

Harrison chuckles warmly. "Because I believe in what you stand for." Through the receiver, I hear a muffled voice and the soft rustle of shifting papers. "Shit, I gotta go. Duy will be in touch soon, so don't decline his call!"

Heat crawls up my neck, expanding over my cheeks.

"And you save this number, Darcy," he adds. "Call me anytime, okay?"

I fumble for words, my brain scrambling to catch up. "Yes—uh, *yes.* Okay. Okay, *thank you so much!*"

"You too," he says, and then the line goes quiet. It's punctuated with the sound of three beautiful, monotonous beeps. I love those beeps. I needed those beeps.

Because that means what just happened was *real.*

For a minute, I can't move. I just stare at the screen, blinking. Like maybe if I do it long enough, another call will follow. One telling me that this was all a prank. But the call doesn't come.

I squeal so loudly that for a moment, I don't realize it came from my own mouth.

Cleo and Peyton both burst into my room, Peyton's amber eyes catching mine as she skids to a halt.

"Are you okay?" she asks, palms pressed to her knees, panting.

Harrison Clarke believes in what I stand for, I think.

I look up at her, blinking hard as tears start to prick at the corners of my eyes. "The NHL wants to offer me an internship."

EPILOGUE

Four Years Later

OCTOBER 1ST

WRITTEN BY LEXI NORWESTER

FORMER NCAA STAR FOUNDS WORLD'S FIRST "AUTOIM-MUNE" HOCKEY LEAGUE

As the weather cools, things are heating up at Portland's newly opened POWER Ice Arena, where founder Darcy Cole kicks off the inaugural season of the Autoimmune Ice Sports League. Cole, 26, founded the league after being forced to drop her draft for the Portland Porcu-pines due to an autoimmune illness that sidelined her at the end of her junior year. In the wake of that loss, she became determined to create a league that not only accommodated hockey players with autoimmune condi-

tions, but empowered them to become the best athletes they could be.

What she never anticipated, however, was that she would end up doing so much more.

You might think the first thing I noticed when I pulled up to the POWER Ice Arena would be the bold, glowing orange signage, but what truly caught my eye was the sheer number of accessible parking spaces. Under the ADA (Americans with Disabilities Act), arenas are required to provide a 1:25 ratio of accessible spots to total spaces. Most arenas meet that standard, but the POWER Ice Arena?

They've tripled it.

When asked about this particular accommodation, Cole's response was straightforward:

"Disabled people support other disabled people," she said. "Not only do some of our athletes and staff use these spots, but we wanted to make sure everyone who wants to enjoy our arena has the chance to do so without being held back by the lack of accessible parking."

And that ethos is carried through the entire arena. The POWER Ice Arena isn't just ADA compliant. It sets new standards for what true inclusivity looks like in public spaces.

Take their new heating system, for example. People with autoimmune illnesses often find their symptoms exacerbated by the cold, so Cole was determined to create a warmer environment without risking the integrity of the ice. Her solution? Heated seats.

What started in cars and massage chairs has now found its way into ice arenas, and fans are absolutely loving it.

"I've never had anyone consider how environments like this can impact people like me," said one new fan. "For the first time, I actually feel seen."

One of the players for one of the league's four teams echoed that sentiment. "In addition to our heated gloves, the player benches are heated too," she explained. "It makes managing my Raynaud's much easier.

But if you think the changes stop at heated gloves, you're in for a surprise. I asked Darcy for a deeper dive into everything that makes Autoimmune Hockey both inclusive and unique. Here's what she shared:

"Everything. All players wear vital monitors, which allows us to catch potential issues before they escalate. We also provide specialized orthopedic skates, gloves, and even undergarments designed with compression to improve blood flow. One common challenge with autoimmune illnesses is digestive issues, so we've built flexibility into the system. Players can use the bathroom whenever they need, even during a game. If they're up next, we have a teammate step in for them. Our periods are also shorter, and we offer longer intermissions to help players rejuvenate and get the medical care they need between shifts. I could keep going, but those are some of the biggest adjustments."

Curious about how shorter playing times and longer intermissions might affect ticket sales, I asked Cole if she was concerned that fans wouldn't be willing to pay for more downtime than ice time.

"If they want to watch sixty minutes of ice time with eighteen-minute intermissions, they can go to an NHL game," she said with a shrug. "This league is for everyone to enjoy, but it won't be everyone's thing, and I get that. But I'm not going to sacrifice the health of my players for a bigger paycheck. That's the whole point of this league. All the info is on our website, and if they choose to come anyway and complain, they can f*** off." She continued, "We have plenty of concessions and entertainment dur-

ing intermissions."

The POWER Ice Arena concession stand prides itself on being fully accessible to people with a variety of dietary needs. The staff undergoes comprehensive training on the dangers of cross-contamination, and there's a dedicated kitchen for preparing gluten-free, soy-free, nut-free, and dairy-free options.

As for intermission entertainment, I had the privilege of sitting in on a practice session for the league's ice skating team.

That's right—the AISL isn't just for hockey; it's for skating too! During our interview, Cole also hinted at plans to add curling to the roster, though they're still waiting on additional funding for that.

Which, of course, led me to ask the question we're all thinking:

How on earth did she afford all of this?

"It started out as a coping mechanism," Cole explained. "When I moved back to Seattle after dropping off the team, I honestly never thought I'd play again."

When I asked what changed, she gave a small smile and replied, "I met someone." She was referring to her now-wife, Peyton Clarke, the starting center for the Portland Porcupines.

"[Peyton] showed me how to get back up. How to adapt, how to persevere. And that's the reason this all exists." Her voice softened as she spoke about her wife. "When I told her about my idea, she shared it with her father, who's a well-known figure in the hockey community. From there, it snowballed. This league has been in the works for years with the help of hockey players, agents, coaches, and fans who believe in it. I've never been more proud of what this community has built."

The inaugural game for the AISL will take place at the POWER Ice Arena. Ticket sales are officially live, with limited availability. Don't miss out! Click <u>here</u> to secure your spot for the game years in the making!